3/17

NO-WHERE BUT HERE

KATIE McGARRY

HARLEQUIN®TEEN

Recycling programs
for this product may
not exist in your area.

ISBN-13: 978-0-373-21142-5

Nowhere But Here

This edition published by arrangement with Harlequin Books S.A.

For questions and comments about the quality of this book, please contact us
at CustomerService@Harlequin.com.

® and TM are trademarks of Harlequin Enterprises Limited or its corporate
affiliates. Trademarks indicated with ® are registered in the United States Patent and
Trademark Office, the Canadian Intellectual Property Office and in other countries.

Printed in U.S.A.

Emily

TOP THREE AWFUL MOMENTS OF MY LIFE:

Meeting my biological father at ten

Breaking my arm in three spots at nine

Falling into a hole and being trapped there overnight with a dead body at eight

Other than that, I love my life. While some of my friends are all, "Woe is me, no one understands my traumatized soul," I'm pretty happy. I like happy. I like simple. I like predictable and I hate surprises.

With that said, I'm not particularly thrilled when my father tries to hand me a piece of paper that causes my mother to choke up and excuse herself from the kitchen.

Dad and I continue to stare at one another as we listen to Mom race up the stairs then close the door to their bedroom. Life is out of whack and it's easy to tell. Dirty dishes are piled in the sink. A stack of unopened mail is tossed across the island. A pile of balled tissues creates a mountain on the wooden oval table. The yellow kitchen that seemed cheery this morning is darkened with emotional storm clouds.

The awkward silence between me and Dad has officially stretched into painful. I shift under the strain and my foot nudges my backpack on the floor.

"You should go after her," I say to break the stillness and to ignore the fact I haven't accepted what Dad is offering. Plus, Dad always knows how to pull Mom out of her drama pit. It's one of the million things I love about him.

"I will." His lips lift a little, a strong indication he's planning to mess with me. "How do you want to handle this? Straightforward, gradual introduction, or head in the sand?"

I brighten. "Head in the sand works well for me."

"Good try, but pick another option."

Fine. "Gradual."

"How does it feel to be a senior?"

Despite the impending knowledge that my life is about to suck, I smile. I'd walked into the kitchen after my last day of school expecting to gush to Mom about how Trisha and I were invited to Blake Harris's party tonight.

What I didn't expect? Dad home, Mom in tears and a note that possibly brings tidings from hell. "It feels awesome. It'll feel even better if you put that piece of paper in the garbage disposal."

"Please read it," Dad presses. "It was hard for your mom to make the decision to let you see this and we should respect her wishes."

My stomach aches as if I'd been elbowed. This debilitating reaction from my mother means one thing: contact from her childhood home in Kentucky.

Kentucky is a painful subject for her and there's nothing I wouldn't do to ease her suffering because, until Dad came into the picture and adopted me when I was five, Mom raised me on her own. That deserves some major respect.

Out of the corner of my eye I take in the collage of framed photos on the wall. The middle picture is my favorite. It's an eight by ten of the day Mom and Dad married. Mom's in a white wedding gown. Slender. Graceful. Her sleek blond hair falling around her shoulders as she beams down at me. Dad crouches beside me. His sun-kissed hair strikingly gold compared to his black tux.

He tucks a rose into my dark brown hair. I'm five and focused on him like he's Superman. That's because he is. My own personal superhero. He adopted me mere days before he married my mom.

Dad clears his throat and I snatch the paper from his hands with just the right amount of ticked off. I'll wander down this dark tunnel of insanity for a few minutes…for him and my mom.

It's an e-mail and it's short and to the point and it's from my biological father.

Jeff,
Please tell Emily.
Eli

Underneath the message are an obituary and a photo of a woman I've never met. Her name is Olivia McKinley and she's Eli's mother. A weighted sigh escapes my lips and I slouch into a seat at the table. *Please tell Emily.* Eli does his best to make an impression. It may not be a great impression, but he leaves one nonetheless.

I squish my lips to the side as I absorb Olivia's obituary. It's the first time I've seen an image of her. Eli's talked about her on our rare occasional visits, but he never drew enough of a mental picture for me to visualize what she looked like.

Eli's this biker my mom hooked up with once and he abandoned us the moment Mom said, "I missed my period." While he gave Mom the slip, he also gave me my dark brown hair and my matching dark brown eyes and the ton of freckles over the bridge of my nose. But other than that he hasn't given me much.

"So…" Total hesitation as I hunt for the correct words. "Eli's mom died."

"That's right. Your mom wants us to attend the funeral."

Um…I don't do funerals or cemeteries. Mom and Dad are aware of this situation. My fingers tap against the table. There's definitely a diplomatic way out of this. I need to find it and find it quick. "Why does she want to go? Not to be rude, but we don't know this lady. We barely know Eli and… well…I thought Mom hated Kentucky."

Dad rubs the back of his head. "I don't know why. I forwarded the e-mail to your mom this morning. A few minutes later, she called me at work in tears. I came home and she'd already purchased the plane tickets. Your guess is as good as mine here, but there's one thing I do know—I don't like seeing your mom cry."

Neither do I.

"What are your thoughts on this, Em?"

I shrug. There are no words for this. None. Zip. Zero. Nada. "I don't get it."

"I know."

That's it? He knows? "I was hoping for something a little more like 'I'll talk to your Mom and I'll convince her to shelve the crazy for a few days.' I mean, we are underestimating the value of sending a well-written note attached to a nice flower arrangement."

Dad does that thing where he's quiet while mulling over a response. It's reason one million and one why I love him. Dad hardly ever loses his temper or yells. He thinks everything through.

"I don't claim to understand most of this," he says. "But this is important to your mom, and you and she are the two most important things to me. If she needs to attend this funeral then we'll attend."

"What if I don't want to attend?"

Dad's patient blue eyes search me and I consider ducking under the table before he notices how much the prospect bothers me. Dead people. He's asking me to voluntarily enter a building where there are dead people. Inside, I'm screaming. Very loudly. Very manically.

"Your mom and I will be there and absolutely nothing will harm you. Besides, you and I have had this discussion. The best way to get over your fears is to face them."

Sure, his words sound pretty, but there's this serious anxiety suffocating me like a shroud. Hives form on my wrist and I scratch at the welts under the table while flashing a forced grin. "Are you suggesting a body isn't going to come back to life and try to eat me?"

"I'm going to go out on a limb and say you're safe from a *Walking Dead* episode."

I release an unladylike snort and Dad laughs. His chuckles fade and I loathe the heavy silence that follows.

"I'm not only talking about your fear of dead things," Dad continues. "I'm talking about the paperwork I found in the trash. I believe it mentioned visiting out-of-town universities with your school this summer."

Dang it, I should have used the paper shredder.

"There's more to life than Florida," he insists.

"I love Florida." I love it so much that I have plans that involve staying here in town after graduation. Specifically, Trisha and I have plans. We've spent the past two years dreaming of going to the local college and rooming together. We even have color-coordinated comforters picked out, because that's how Trisha rolls.

Dad waves his hand at the room. "There's more out there for you than these four walls."

"I love these four walls." I do. The kitchen, to the three of us, is the focal point of our existence. Mom's created a homey room with fresh flowers in several vases scattered on the table, island and counter. She painted the walls yellow because she read an article that said it's a welcoming color.

"Emily—"

"I love my life." I flutter my eyelashes in an attempt to appear cute. "I'm happy, so stop trying to mess with it."

Dad leans back in his chair and tosses a pen he's been fiddling with onto the table. "Aren't you even curious about what's out there?"

"No. But I'm curious about what the deal is with Mom

NOWHERE BUT HERE   13

and this funeral." I change the subject because I hate arguing with my father. I don't possess a burning desire to leave home and explore every part of the universe like he did when he was my age. He doesn't understand and I don't know how to explain it. Because of that, we fight and it's the only thing, besides Eli, we disagree about.

"I already told you I don't know," he answers, "but it's our job to support her. You know as well as I do that demons haunt your mother's past."

It's true. Mom avoids discussing her life before my birth. I assume it must be because it hurts to know she has family that threw her out because she chose to have me. "Do you think attending this funeral is her way of going home without going home?"

His eyes snap to mine and I know I hit the nail on the head. Nausea rolls through my intestines. This is one of those moments where doing the right thing makes me want to puke, but this is my mom. My mom. She's crazy and she's dramatic, but she has loved me since she saw two lines on the pregnancy test. I refuse to say no to a woman who raised me for the first four years completely by herself.

"Okay," I say. "I'm in."

"Thank you. And Emily..." A long, painful pause. "You need to view this as an opportunity. Maybe this will help you and your mother reconsider Eli's offer for you to visit him for two weeks this summer."

Oh, hell no. Three weeks ago, Eli contacted Dad with this massively awful idea. Seeing Eli when he wanders into town once a year is one thing, but visiting him—for two weeks straight—on his home turf? "Mom said no."

"I think it would be healthy for you to see where your mother once lived and to understand your father's history. I overheard you asking your mom questions the other day."

All right, sue me. Eli's offer made me curious. Actually, not true. My mother's sharp shout of "no" when Dad broached the subject of the visit is what did it. And I'm not concerned with Eli or his family, but more over my mother.

Were Mom's parents the superconservative people she's described them as? How did she meet Eli? Was it at school or did they meet the night they conceived me? Was Mom a crazy teenager or was she a good girl until she decided to hook up one night with a biker?

I've asked, but Mom redirects the conversation. I haven't found the courage yet to press for answers when she shuts me out.

"I see the curiosity in your eyes whenever Eli is mentioned," Dad tells me.

I push away from the table and as I go to walk past him, he gently snags my fingers. "It's okay to have questions. They're your biological family. In fact, it's extremely normal. I've seen it before with my patients."

A tremor of anger runs through me. I'm not one of his hundreds of pediatric rug rats. "I am not curious."

"Not at all?" he asks.

I swallow, attempting to sort through the thoughts. When I look at my father, I see the man that not only lowered himself onto one knee to ask my mother's hand in marriage, but dropped to both knees to ask for my permission to marry her. I see the smile on his face and remember the answering joy inside me the day my adoption went through. I see the man who has not abandoned me once since he entered my life.

Being curious would mean that I don't appreciate all Dad has done for me and I do appreciate him. I love him more than he could imagine.

"No," I repeat. "I'm not curious at all."

OZ

IT'S THREE IN THE MORNING AND MOM AND I
continue to wait. The two of us deal with the heaviness of
each passing second differently. She paces the tiny living room
at the front of our double-wide while I polish my combat
boots in my room. Regardless of what happens tonight, we
have a wake to attend in the morning.

The scratching of the old scrub brush against my black boot
is the lone sound that fills the darkened house. We each pretend that the other isn't awake. Neither of us has turned on a
lamp; instead we rely on the rays of the full moon to see. It's
easier this way. Neither of us want to discuss the meaning of
Dad's absence or his cell phone silence.

I sit on the edge of my twin mattress. If I stretched my leg
my toe would hit the faux-wood-paneled wall. I'm tall like
my dad and the room is compact and narrow. Large enough
to hold my bed and an old stack of milk crates that I use as
shelves.

Mom's phone pings and my hands freeze. Through the crack in my door, I spot her black form as she grabs her cell. The screen glows to life and a bluish light illuminates Mom's face. I quit breathing and strain to listen to her reaction or at least hear the roar of motorcycle engines.

Nothing. More silence. Adrenaline begins to pump into my veins. Dad should have been home by now. They all should have been home. Especially with Olivia's wake in the morning.

Unable to stomach the quiet any longer, I set the boot on the floor and open my door. The squeak of the hinges screeches through the trailer. In two steps, I'm in the living room.

Mom continues to scroll through her phone. She's a small thing, under five-four, and has long straight hair. It's black. Just like mine and just like Dad's. Mom and Dad are only thirty-seven. I'm seventeen. Needless to say, my mom was young when she had me. By the way she slumps her shoulders, she appears ten years older.

"Any word?" I ask.

"It's Nina." My best friend's mom. "Wondering if we had heard anything." Which implies neither Eli nor Cyrus have returned home.

From behind her, I place a hand on Mom's shoulder and she covers my fingers with hers.

"I'll be out there watching their backs soon." Now that I've graduated from high school, I'll finally be allowed to enter the family business.

A job with the security company and a patch-in to the club is all I've thought about since I was twelve. All I've craved since I turned sixteen and earned my motorcycle license. "They're fine. Like I'll be when I join them."

Mom pats my hand, walks into the space that serves as our kitchen, and busies herself with a stack of mail.

I rest my shoulder against the wall near the window. The backs of my legs bump the only piece of furniture in the room besides the flat-screen—a sectional bought last year before Olivia became ill. The couch and TV are extravagances we never would have bought if we'd known we would be covering medical bills.

Trying not to be obvious, I glance beyond the lace curtains and assess the road leading to our trailer. I'm also worried, but it's my job to alleviate Mom's concern.

I force a tease into my voice. "I bet you can't wait until Chevy graduates next year. Then there will be two more of us protecting the old men."

Mom coughs out a laugh and takes a drink to control the choking. "I can't begin to imagine the two of you riding in the pack when the image in my mind is of both of you as toddlers, covered in mud from head to toe."

"Not hard to remember. That was last week's front yard football game," I joke.

She smiles. Long enough to chase away the gravity of tonight's situation, but then reality catches up and her face falls. If humor won't work, I'll go for serious. "Chevy would like to GED out."

"Nina would skin him alive. You both promised Olivia you'd finish high school."

Because it once broke Olivia's heart when Eli, her son, dropped out of high school and instead took a test to get his

GED. I might not share blood with Eli's parents, Olivia and Cyrus, but they gave my mom and dad a safe place to lie low years ago when their own parents went self-destructive. That means Olivia became the closest person I knew to a grand-mother.

"No more talk of Chevy and GEDs." Mom tsks. "It's bad enough you won't consider college."

The muscles in my neck tighten and I ignore her jab. She's still ticked I won't engage in conversation about college. I know my future and it's not four more years of books and rules. I want the club. As it is, membership isn't a guarantee. I still have to prove myself before they'll let me join.

Mom rubs her hands up and down her arms. She's edgy when the club is out on a protection run, but this time, Mom's dangling from a cliff and she's not the only one. Lately the entire club has been acting like they're preparing to jump without parachutes.

My dad belongs to a motorcycle club that formed a secu-rity business when I was eleven. Most of the employees of the security company are members of the Reign of Terror. Not all, but most. It works vice versa, as well. Not everyone who's a member of the Terror here in Snowflake works for the business, but work is there for any member who needs it.

Their main business comes from escorting semi-loads of high-priced goods through highly pirated areas.

Imagine a couple thousand dollars of fine Kentucky bour-bon in the back of a Mack truck and, at some point, the driver has to take a piss or stop for a meal. My dad and the rest of club, they make sure the driver can eat his Big Mac in peace and return to the parking lot to find his rig intact and the merchandise still safely inside.

What they do can be dangerous, but I'll be proud to stand alongside my father and the only other people I consider family. Maybe Mom will sleep better at night when I'm out protecting Dad. "Try not to worry. You're acting as if they're the ones that could be caught doing something illegal."

Mom's eyes shoot straight to mine like my comment was serious. "You know better than that."

I do. It's what the club prides itself on. All that TV bull about how anyone who rides a bike is a felon—they don't understand what the club stands for. The club is a brotherhood, a family. It means belonging to something bigger than yourself.

Still, the medical bills from Olivia's illness aren't going away and between me, Chevy, my parents, Eli, Cyrus and other guys from the club giving all we have, we still don't have enough to make a dent in what we owe. "I hear that 1% club a couple of hours north of here makes bank."

"Oz."

As if keeping watch will help Dad return faster, I move the curtain to get a better view of the road that leads away from our house and into the woods. "Yeah?"

"This club is legit."

"Okay." Meaning that we aren't a 1% club—that we don't dabble in illegal.

"I'm serious. This club is legit."

I drop the curtain. "What, you don't want gangsta in the family?"

Mom slaps her hand on the counter. "I don't want to hear you talk like this!"

My head snaps in her direction. Mom's not a yeller. Even when she's stressed, she maintains her cool. "I was messing with you."

"This club is legit and it will stay legit. You are legit. Do you understand?"

"I got it. I'm clean. The club's clean. We're so jacked up on suds that we squeak when we walk. I know this, so would you care to explain why you're freaking out?"

A motorcycle growls in the distance and it cuts off our conversation. Mom releases a long breath, as if she's been given the news that a loved one survived surgery. "He's home."

She charges the front door and throws it open. The elation slips from her face and my stomach cramps. "What is it?"

"Someone's riding double."

More rumbles of engines join the lead one, multiple headlights flash onto the trailer, and not one of those bikes belong to Dad. Fuck. I rush past Mom and jump off the steps as she brightens the yard with a flip of the porch light. Eli swings off his bike. "Oz! Get over here!"

I'm there before he can finish his order and I shoulder my father's weight to help him off the bike. He's able to stand, but leans into me, and that scares me more than any monster that hid under my bed as a child.

"What happened?" Mom's voice shakes and Eli says nothing. He supports Dad's other side as Dad's knees buckle.

"What happened!" she demands, and the fear in her voice vibrates against my insides. I'm wondering the same damn thing, but I'm more concerned with the blood dripping from my father's head.

"Medical kit!" Eli bursts through the door and the two of

us deposit Dad on the couch. Mom's less than a step behind us and runs into the kitchen. Glass shatters when she tosses stuff aside in her search. Mom's a nurse and I can't remember a time she hasn't been prepared.

More guys appear in the living room, each man wearing a black leather biker cut, the vest that labels them as a member of the Reign of Terror. Not one man would be the type to leave a brother behind.

"I'm fine, Izzy." Dad scratches the skin above the three-inch-long cut on his forehead. "Just a scratch."

"Scratch, my ass." With kit in hand, Mom kneels in front of him and I crouch beside her, popping open her supply box as she pours antiseptic onto a rag. She glares at Eli. "Why didn't you take him to the ER?"

Dad wraps his fingers around Mom's wrist. Her gaze shifts to Dad's and when Dad has her attention for longer than a second, he slowly swipes his thumb against her skin. "I told him to bring me home. We didn't want it reported to the police."

Mom blinks away the tears pooling in her eyes. I fall back on my ass, realizing that Dad's not dying, but somehow cracked his head hard enough that Eli wouldn't allow him to ride home.

"You promised you'd wear your helmet," Mom whispers.

"I wasn't on my bike," he replies simply.

Mom pales out and I focus solely on Eli. He holds my stare as I state the obvious. "The run went bad."

Jacking trucks for the cargo inside is a money-maker for hustlers and the security company is good at keeping hustlers on their toes. But sometimes the company comes up against an asshole who thinks he can be badass with violence.

"Someone tried to hit us during a break at a truck stop, but we were smarter." Eli jerks his thumb in Dad's direction. "But some of us aren't as fast as others."

"Go to hell," Dad murmurs as Mom cleans the wound.

"You should have reported it," Mom says. "This is the fifth hit in three weeks. There's no way this is isolated bandits. The police need to look into this."

A weighty silence settles over the room and Mom's lips thin. The security company is as thick as the club. Business in both areas stays private. Everyone is on a need-to-know basis, me and Mom included...that is, until I patch in. I'll possibly learn more when I'm initiated as a prospect and I'm counting down the days until I'm officially part of the larger whole.

"He okay?" Eli asks.

"You of all people should know how hardheaded he is," Mom responds. Eli's a few years younger than my parents, but the three of them have been a trio of trouble since elementary school. "I believe everyone has a wake to attend in the morning, so I suggest sleep."

That's as subtle as Mom will get before she'll stick a pointed, steel-toed boot up their asses. Everyone says some sort of goodbye to Mom and Dad, but my parents are too lost in their own world to notice.

"Walk me out, Oz?" Eli inclines his head to the door and we head onto the front porch. The muggy night air is thick with moisture and a few bugs swarm the porch light.

Eli digs into the leather jacket that's under his cut and pulls out a pack of cigarettes and a lighter. He cups his hand to his mouth as he lights one. "We need you out on the road."

"They told me they'll send my official diploma next week."

I was supposed to walk in graduation tomorrow, but Olivia's wake is the priority. Not caps and gowns. "You tell me when to start and I'm ready to go."

"Good." He cracks a rare grin. "Heard that we might be adding a new prospect this weekend."

The answering smile spreads on my face. Becoming a prospect is the initiation period before the club votes on my membership. I've been waiting for this moment my entire life.

Eli sucks in a long drag and the sleeve of his jacket hitches up, showing the trail of stars tattooed on his arm. "Keep an eye on your dad. He cracked the hell out of his head when he hit the pavement. Blacked out for a bit, but then shot to his feet. When his bike began swerving, I made him pull over and double with me."

"He must have loved that," I say.

"Practically had to put a gun to his head." Eli breathes out smoke.

"Was it the Riot?" The Riot Motorcycle Club. They're an illegal club north of here. I've heard some of the guys talk when they think no one else is listening about how our peace treaty with them is fracturing.

Eli flicks ashes then focuses on the burning end of the cigarette. "As I said, we need you on the road."

Our club and the Riot have had an unsteady alliance from the start. We stay on our side of the state, they stay on theirs. The problem? A new client that the business has contracted with resides in the Riot's territory.

"This stays between us," says Eli. "This new client we signed is skittish and doesn't want the PR related with possible truck jackings. We need this business and I need people I can trust with those loads. I need you in."

"Got it."

"Two of those truck jackings were bandits, but the other three..."

...were the Riot. The shit has to be thick if Eli's talking to me so freely. "If you choose to start working with us, there won't be much room for a learning curve. You'll have to be vigilant at every turn. We haven't had trouble with the Riot in years, but when we did, they had no problem making it personal."

Meaning they don't have a problem hurting people—like my dad. Meaning I have to play it smart with them and be okay with the danger, which I am. I'd much rather be on the road protecting my family than sitting at home with Mom.

"The moment you give me a cut, I'm in." I throw out the question, not sure if Eli will answer. "You had his back, didn't you? You pushed Dad to the ground."

A hint of a smirk plays on his lips and he hides it with another draw. He blows out the smoke and flicks the cigarette onto the ground. "Be out here at six in the morning. I'll pick you up in the truck and we'll go get your Dad's bike before the wake. I want him to sleep in."

Hell, yeah. "You going to let me drive his bike home?"

"Fuck, no. I'm bringing you along to drive the truck back. No one touches a man's bike and in desperate situations only another brother can. You know better than that." Eli pats my shoulder and his expression grows serious. "See you tomorrow, and be dressed for the wake when I pick you up."

Eli starts his bike and rocks kick up as he drives off. I watch until the red taillight fades into the darkness. Through the screen door, I spot my mother still caring for my father. She uses special care as she tapes gauze to his head.

Mom smooths the last strip of medical tape to his skin and when she goes to close the kit, Dad tucks a lock of her hair behind her ear. They stare at each other, longer than most people can stand, then she lays her head on his lap. Dad bends over and kisses her temple.

They need a moment together and, having nothing but time, I sit on the top step and wonder if I'll find someone who will understand and accept this life like my mother. Mom loves Dad so much that she'll take on anything. His job, this life and even the club.

Emily

I'LL ADMIT IT. I'M FREAKED.

Freaked that the flight from Florida to Kentucky was nothing more than a turbulence-ridden nightmare. Freaked that the man beside me on the plane puked three times. Freaked that June in Kentucky means severe storms. Freaked because I'm sweating through my favorite black dress and it's dry-clean only. Freaked because I've been in this poor excuse for a cab for over an hour, with no air-conditioning and a driver who refuses to speak. Or maybe he's mute.

Or maybe he murdered the real cab driver, picked me and my parents up at the airport and is taking us to our final destination before he chops us into Kibbles 'n Bits. Maybe...but probably not. We entered the small town of Snowflake a few minutes ago and if this guy was a mass murderer bent on a little fun, he'd find somewhere more original than here.

"Did you say Richard's Funeral Home?" the cab driver asks. Wow, the man talked.

"Yes," Dad answers. We flew into Louisville in order to be relatively close to Snowflake. The rental-car company botched our reservation and paid for the taxi.

The cab driver eases into the left turn lane and stops at the red light. Blood pounds at my temples in the rhythm of the car's blinker when I spot the funeral home. It's no different than the ones at home in Florida, except this one is surrounded by oak trees instead of palms and is one stiff breeze away from being condemned.

"You'll be okay." Dad squeezes my hand and I wrap my fingers around his before he can withdraw. "Keep breathing and try not to overanalyze it."

Easy for him to say. "Did you get a hold of Eli?"

"No, I'm still going straight to voicemail." Dad probably has to force the patience into his voice. It's the fiftieth time I've asked since we disembarked the plane. Eli must have powered off his phone. Dad attempted to contact him, but I don't blame Eli for not answering. I'd be devastated if my mom died.

Dad offers me a reassuring smile. "Eli will be thrilled to see you."

I release a sigh... *Sure he will.* "What do I say when he asks about Mom?"

Dad's smile fades and he lets go of my hand to readjust the watch on his wrist. "Tell them that your mother is sorry for their loss, but that she isn't feeling well. She'll try to attend later if she's feeling better."

Mom morphed into an unnatural shade of blue when she spiraled into a panic attack the moment we left the airport. Dad decided, since the viewing ends at eight this evening, that he and I would pay our respects first. Then if, after a rest, Mom was able to walk and breathe at the same time, he would go with her again.

Mom protested, but Dad, with his smooth doctor way, won. So she's holed up at the sole motel in this dump of a town and I'm heading to a funeral home. I tried to throw myself into a panic attack in order to get out of this hellish event, but evidently holding my breath on purpose doesn't count.

The light changes, the driver makes the turn, and I press a hand to my stomach. Oh, God. Dad has way too much faith in me.

The cab driver pulls into the funeral home, but is stuck behind two cars. Neither car shows signs of moving as they chat to the people on the sidewalk. The driver taps his fingers on the steering wheel in a ticked-off thump. I totally understand the feeling.

"My daughter and I will get out here," Dad announces.

The cab driver assesses a group of men standing in a semicircle outside the entrance. "You sure?"

"It's not a long walk," Dad answers.

I open the door and the driver freaks. "Are you sure this is where you want to be?"

No. Dad maintains his superhero calm. "Yes."

"Snowflake's not exactly Disney World." The driver waves his hand toward the men. If Dad won't listen to me, maybe he'll listen to our now talking driver.

I lean so I have a better look at the men standing around. They all have Eli's style: redneck with a hint of grunge. Sort of like if Linkin Park fashioned their own clothing line inspired by L.L.Bean: jeans and T-shirts covered by flannel shirts.

Some wear blue University of Kentucky baseball hats—just like Eli. A couple even have his...well, my dark brown hair.

What probably messes with the driver is that almost every man here sports over their T-shirts or flannels a black leather biker vest with the words *Reign of Terror* in white lettering. On the back of each vest is a large white half skull with red flames raining down. Fire blazes out of the eye sockets. I bet the guys who designed the emblem pat themselves on the back for the play on words.

"This is not a place for a young girl," the driver exclaims.

He's off on the young part. I just turned seventeen. And despite my previous hopes, Dad doesn't share the cab driver's, or my, assessment of the situation. "We'll be fine. Right, Em?"

The driver rotates in his seat, reminding me of a possessed person in one of those horror movies. "Those are bikers."

In his dark suit, deep blue tie and clean-cut blond hair, my father could be a model on the cover of a business magazine. He screams competence and authority and all that's good in the world. So the next words cause the driver's mouth to slacken. "My daughter is a relative."

While the driver continues to gape in disbelief, I inwardly cringe. *I'm* related to *them*. More specifically, I'm most likely related to the men with the patch on the front of their vests stating *Mother Chapter*. Which, according to Eli, means the founding chapter of their club.

I'm a relative by blood and blood alone. We are not family in the ways that really matter. I may share genetic code with the people inside the building, but that's where our relationship ends.

Dad and I climb out and the cab backs up, leaving us alone.

Well, sort of alone. The side entrance of the funeral home opens and a woman with dark hair hurries out with a toddler on her hip. The baby's hacking the type of deep coughs that cause chills to run down my spine.

Without missing a beat, Dad starts toward them and I follow. The woman sets the blonde girl with pigtails on the ground and the little thing is a combination of red face, tears and coughs. The woman rummages through her oversized purse, tossing receipts and pens and other crap onto the ground.

"Excuse me," broaches Dad. "Can I help? I'm a pediatrician."

The woman's head jerks up and her eyes have a wild spark. "I can't find my phone. I need my phone. I can't get her to take the medicine. I can't get her to take this."

She shoves an inhaler into my father's hand and he reads the prescription. "Asthma?"

The woman nods profusely. "Yes. We have that machine at home with the mask and that works, but this was for emergencies, and she won't use it."

Dad gestures to the child, who is now hacking out more air than she's taking in. "May I?"

"Yes. Please. Help us."

Dad kneels next to the toddler. With a few calm words and an expression that makes every toddler relax, he has the inhaler in the child's mouth. It's not working exactly like it should. I mean, the child is young and doesn't suck in as much as she needs, but with Dad's help, she's inhaling some of the medicine and, more important, she's no longer crying, but breathing.

The woman strokes the child's hair as Dad continues to talk to both of them in his calm voice. He peers over his shoulder at me and my chest tightens. "Emily, I want to stay with them. Why don't you go in, find Eli and pay your respects, and I'll be in shortly to pay mine."

I fidget with the purse in my hand, clasping and unclasping the magnetic strip that keeps it closed. Um…no? "I can wait."

Dad inhales deeply and the disappointment is clear on his face. "Five minutes. That's it. Find Eli, say hi, tell him we're sorry for his loss and then we'll return to the hotel, get your mother and go out to lunch."

It's dawning on me that Dad doesn't want to be here any more than I do and that he's ready to return to Mom. His words from yesterday as he was trying to explain why he was allowing us to take this hellish trip float in my head: *it's our job to support Mom.*

Got it. This is the first time Mom has visited her childhood state in over seventeen years. If we check the "we attended" box then life can return to normal.

Dad excuses himself and walks over to me. "Sorry for snapping, Em. It's been a rough morning. Go in and pay our respects, and I'll be in shortly. And so you know, it's okay if you want to stay longer and talk to Eli."

Yeah, not going to happen. I pivot away from Dad, tug at the hem of my black dress to confirm nothing rides up and start for the entrance with my purse in hand. I whisper to myself, "No worries." Even though I have a ton.

As I step closer to the entrance, I hear several conversations at once and someone always seems to be laughing.

"…nothing larger than a 10-gauge…"

"…take a Ford over that foreign crap any day…"

"You lost?"

Everyone stops talking and stares at me. Great. I meet the eyes of the guy that called me out. He's part of the group, yet not. He doesn't wear a leather vest like everyone else, but somehow he appears just as dangerous.

The guy leans against the corner of the brick building as if he doesn't have a care in the world. He's around my age, has black hair, is definitely ripped and he has suck-me-in blue eyes that wander over my body like he's seeing me with my clothes off.

I cross an arm over myself and his lips edge up in response. My mom's warned me about bad boys and I trust that she understands the world here better than I do.

I appraise my black high heels. Nice, they're scuffed already. "I'm looking for Eli McKinley."

Smoke rushes out of the mouth of the older man standing beside the guy my age. I'd wager he's in his sixties and he scares the hell out of me. Well…everyone here frightens me, but him more. While the style here is stepped-out-of-a-trailer-park, he maintains the cliché of 100% pure biker thanks to his black bandanna, black leather vest and gray beard with matching ponytail. I attempt to ignore that his patch states *Mother Chapter* and *President*.

He keeps eye contact while taking a drag off his cigarette. "Eli's inside."

"Thanks."

They continue their conversation and I open the door then steal a glimpse over my shoulder. The older man angles his head and his mouth moves as he mumbles something to the guy my age. The guy nods and pushes off the wall. Not wanting to be caught spying, I slip inside and the moment the door shuts behind me, I freeze.

Let's get one thing straight. I hate funeral homes. Hate. I hate the smell of them. I hate the look of them. I hate the thought of them. Hate. And what I hate more than funeral homes are dead things. Dead bugs. Dead dried-up worms on the sidewalk. Roadkill. And since that ill-fated stroll in the woods at the age of eight when I fell into a hole and spent the night with a corpse, I hate dead people's bodies.

I force myself forward on the red velvet industrial carpeting of this outdated house of death and rethink this entire situation. Badly painted landscapes hang every few feet over the black-and-white peeling wallpaper. My muscles twitch as if a million spiders crawl over my skin. And the smell! I cup my hand over my nose to smell something other than tragically scented potpourri and wilting lilies.

Thankfully, there's only one viewing room, which means only one dead person to avoid. The fine hairs on my neck prickle as if eyes are trained on me. I glance back and my heart stutters when I spot black hair and a dangerous grin. The guy who called me out hangs near the door and he's watching me. His jeans ride a little low. Low enough that his boxers peek out and it's hard to tear my eyes away, but I do.

Not eager for anyone to touch me, I tuck myself in tight as I duck through the crowded hallway. If anyone runs into me, I'll recall being eight and enclosed and the feel of cold skin, and me spazzing out is not part of the plan.

"…playing at the bar tonight. Plan on taking the girl…"

"…hit that hard…"

"...and she said I don't want that trash on my property and I said I ain't trash, bitch..."

Trash bitch woman wears skintight jeans, a tank top that exposes her midriff and, holy mother of God, flip-flops. She steps back and nearly knocks into me. I sidestep her, but I collide with someone else.

Cold skin with black markings grazes my arm and my heart lodges in my throat. I flinch and suck in a sharp breath while twisting my feet. I stumble back, completely off-balance, and my arms flail in a poor attempt to stay upright.

A warm hand grips my elbow and halts me from ramming into anyone else. My head snaps up and I'm greeted by dark blue eyes. The guy who was watching me is now touching me. *Remember to breathe.* Yes, he's pretty, but bad things come in gorgeous packages—at least that's what Mom says.

"You okay?" he asks.

"Yeah," I whisper and immediately return my attention to the guy I crashed into. He's not dead. He's very much alive and he's taking a swig from a beer. Wait. A beer? My gaze switches from him to the bottle.

"Would you like one?" He motions to a cooler full of ice on the floor.

I shake my head. Major WTF.

Black hair guy releases me and motions with his chin to the left. "Eli's in the viewing room."

Viewing room. Right. I mumble a thank-you, but he doesn't notice as he's bumping fists and accepting a beer from the guy with the tattoos.

The viewing room is beyond crowded. Like the-fire-marshal-should-be-notified crowded, which means it will be difficult to find Eli. People laugh, shout and talk as if they're attending a pep rally instead of a funeral.

I rise to my tiptoes and clutch my purse. I haven't seen him in a couple of months, but Eli always looks the same: dark brown hair cut short, plugs in both ears, T-shirt, jeans and a smile that, for some insane reason, can make me smile.

My stomach sinks like the *Titanic* as I catch sight of him. Just no...why-does-it-have-to-be-so-difficult no. His back is to me, but I know it's Eli. A tattoo of stars runs the length of his arm. Like most of the other men here, he wears the black leather vest. And of course, he stands next to the one spot I want nothing to do with—the casket.

Reminding myself that I'm here for Mom, I squeeze through the mob. Eli stares at the body. The body I'm trying desperately to avoid, but it's kind of hard to so I focus on my biological father.

He doesn't seem to be upset. He's not crying or anything, but it's not really Eli, either. His hands rest in his jeans pockets and his typical grin doesn't grace his face. He appears... thoughtful.

Until he does something that makes me shiver. He touches her. The dead body. My grandmother. The one I've never met. Eli gently readjusts the blue scarf covering her hair, or where her hair would have been. Oh, God...cancer.

What's odd—other than that he's willingly touching a dead person—is that the casket is open. Completely open. Legs and all. Weird. Very weird. Now that I'm looking, I take a deep breath and permit myself to study the woman that brought me to the outskirts of nowhere.

My grandmother is dressed in blue jeans and a white silk

sleeveless top. A sad rush of air escapes my lips. She's young. A lot younger than I expected. Why this surprises me, I have no idea. Mom and Eli were young when they conceived me. Teenagers still in high school.

I hurt for Eli. I've never lost someone I was close to. He must have loved her and she's dead. Gone. I'd die if I lost Grandma or Gramps or Mom or Dad. "I'm so sorry."

His head whirls in my direction and my dark eyes stare back at me. "Emily?"

Yeah, I forgot. This visit is unexpected because he didn't answer his phone. "Hi."

He'll say "how are you," I'll say "fine," and we'll be done with conversation for the year.

Eli flicks out his arm, pulls me closer to the casket and him, lifts me off the floor and hugs the air out of me. "How did you know? What about school? Does Meg know you're here?"

Wow. A lot of questions in a short timespan. He kisses the side of my head and shakes me from side to side like a rag doll. My leg bumps into the side of the coffin and I swallow a dry heave. "Um. Dad, it's over and duh."

"What?" he asks, still hugging and shaking me.

I pat his shoulder and my nonverbal put-me-down works. The moment my feet hit the ground, his hands go to my shoulders as if the only way to confirm I'm here is by physical contact.

"You sent Dad the obituary, school's done and I wouldn't go anywhere without telling Mom."

"You have no idea how much this means to me," he says. His head jerks back and he squints. "Did you say obituary?"

"It means a lot to me, too," says a woman's voice to my side.

I scream. And scream again. And it doesn't stop. I can't make it stop. It's one long, agonizing scream, and I'm tripping over myself to get away. It's not just hysterics. It's my mind ripping in two. Into pieces. Multiple pieces. It's my worst nightmare.

The dead woman. She's sitting up and blinking and the scream stops for a moment as my body forces in air and the next sound is a sob. I must have hit a wall, because I can't go back any farther and I need to get back. I need to get away and run. Run as far as I can.

But I can't move to the side, either. I'm trapped! Now it's getting out of the coffin. One leg after another. It's climbing out and moving in my direction. Hands out. Head swaying from side to side and it's saying something, but I don't want to hear it. I don't want it to touch me.

"No!" It's the first word I can articulate, but it's hoarse and slurred through the sobs.

"It's okay." It's Eli. He's behind me and I realize I'm not against a wall. Eli's arms have locked me against him. "She's not dead, Emily. She's not dead. Stay back, Mom."

Two feet from me, it halts its advance. The arms slowly drop to its sides. "I'm sorry. I thought you knew."

I'm struggling, though I didn't know it until now. A monster wouldn't sound so nice and feminine. I press back against Eli, not trusting what I'm seeing. His arms hold me—a reassuring hug to confirm he's on my side. It glances behind me to Eli.

"Emily," says Eli, "this is your grandmother, Olivia. Mom, this is Emily."

I suck up the snot in my nose, but I can't end the tears.

They'll keep coming until I can understand that my mind is still intact. She smiles and it reminds me of Eli's smile, but hers is a little hesitant. "Let's take this somewhere a little more private."

I clutch Eli's hand and a blast of heat races along my body. She stares at me. I stare at her and as I attempt to respond, dizziness disorients me, and warmth rushes from my toes to my head. My mouth opens and the pathetic breakfast I ate on the plane lands squarely on Olivia's shoes.

OZ

"EMILY FREAKING OUT—THAT WAS SOME FUNNY shit." Chevy bites into the mammoth ham sandwich he created from the meat tray Mom prepared for the party. Except for me and Chevy, the kitchen area of the funeral home is empty. We sit at the table while everyone else attempts to decipher what the hell is going on.

Only a handful of us know why Eli's posted guards outside and inside every entrance and is allowing no access in or out. The funeral home is on disaster-area shutdown and if it wasn't for Cyrus telling me to follow the long-lost daughter, I wouldn't have had a clue that Emily has returned to Snowflake.

Eli's real secretive about Emily and this surprise visit must be his worst nightmare, especially with the shit going down with the Riot. The next few hours ought to be interesting.

"Ahhh!" Two young kids race through the kitchen with their hands raised in the air. "Dead person. Dead person."

Chevy laughs, then chokes on the sandwich, coughing into his elbow. Now that's some funny shit.

While I should be concerned he's choking to death, I'm more worried about the dark shadows under his eyes. The kid was up early running routes with his coach before the wake. Football and motorcycles are the boy's life. Chevy's an all-American boy with his dark brown hair, brown eyes and love of apple pie and football. That is, if Yankee Doodle went to town riding on a Harley.

I slap his back much harder than needed and he nearly spits out the sandwich. Chevy drinks from a longneck he swiped from a cooler. "Guess Emily thought Olivia was dead."

"You think?"

Sneakers scuffle against the linoleum floor and Chevy and I nod our heads in greeting to the fourteen-year-old standing red-faced flustered near the table. Brandon's a tall kid, fire-red hair like his older sister and as lanky as they come. More feet and height than he is muscle and he gets uncomfortable around people. We don't care how he acts because he's part of our non-blood family.

He blinks a lot then rubs his eyes.

"Contacts, Stone?" I ask. Good guess since those big, black, thick-rimmed glasses are MIA.

Chevy and I, along with another good friend of ours, Razor, nicknamed Brandon "Stone" when he turned fourteen last month. Some dickhead teenager who's my age jumped Brandon as a birthday gift. Even though he was beat to hell, Brandon never shed a tear. That kid, he's solid stone. The guy who gave Stone an ass-whipping—he cried after justice was served.

Stone shoves his hands into his pockets and blinks hard twice. "Eli bought them for me last week. What do you think?"

Chevy scans him as if he's honestly mulling over an answer. Chevy and I, we dedicate every second with this kid to building him up. "I think Oz and I are going to have to give you the birds and bees talk sooner rather than later. Here's the condensed version—cap it before you tap it."

The kid's neck flushes pink and he scratches his chin twice in that fucked up way of his when he's nervous, but grins. Stone's dad was a member of the club and worked for the business. He died in a motorcycle accident and since then the club takes care of Stone, his mother and his older sister, Violet, even though Violet is determined to extricate the club from her family's life.

"You look good," I confirm. Stone's smile grows as he focuses on the ground. The kid is awkward as hell, but he's one of ours. The club will always have his back. "You're going to hang with us this summer, right? We need you on our team."

His eyes widen. "You're going to let me play football? On your team?"

The way Chevy eyeballs me asks the same question. Football on Sundays is the way we like it—blood-and-guts rough.

"You're fourteen," I answer both of them. "You're a man now, and, yeah, I want you on my team."

Chevy nods his understanding. He gets that I have the urge to protect and help people younger than me.

"Cool." Stone goes to readjust the glasses that always slid down his nose and his hand twitches when he discovers them missing. "Who's the girl that freaked out?"

Chevy and I share a glance. Family rule: no one outside a select few can discuss Emily. We don't bring her up and no one else is allowed to know she exists. Because Olivia practically raised me for the first few years of my life, I'm part of the McKinley inner circle and know more than most when it comes to personal family business. But Stone is searching to feel like family and with Violet in his ear telling him we aren't, I make an executive decision. "She's someone who means something to Eli."

Stone trembles as he realizes I told him something serious. "That's Emily?"

"Never said that, but regardless of what you think, keep it to yourself."

"Olivia and Eli don't appreciate people discussing her," Chevy warns. "Even in meaningless conversation."

Chevy and Emily are cousins. The Emily situation is one of the sole reasons I'm glad I'm not blood-related to the McKinleys. Emily's mother is a traitor and because of how Emily constantly pushes Eli away, I consider her a traitor, too.

"Is she staying?" Stone asks.

Truth? Stone hit on a question that neither Chevy nor I will dare to answer. Stone's a part of us through the club, but only the McKinleys are allowed info on Emily. Though I'm not genetically a member, I'm an honorary McKinley so I'm more informed than most, but in the end, I'm still in the dark. Emily is this family's dirty little secret.

"Where's your sister?" Chevy asks like he doesn't care about the answer, but unfortunately, he does. The two of us got wasted last night and picked up two girls in an attempt to extract Violet from his brain. We both got laid and a hangover, but it didn't help his broken heart.

"She's…uh…well, Violet said…that she wants to go to Louisville today and she wants me to go with her and since it's such a long drive she had stuff she needed to do at the house—"

"Louisville's over an hour away," Chevy presses. "Why does she need to go there?"

Stone spirals into uncomfortable muscle spasms.

"Tell her to stay out of Louisville." Chevy's tone is demanding now. "There's something going down between the Riot and the Reign of Terror and we don't need trouble."

The Riot's based in Louisville and it's not where any of us should be. We aren't the type to run from a fight, but with the club's focus on Olivia, our resources are split. We don't need anyone associated with the Terror to take stupid chances.

"Tell her to go to Lexington," Chevy continues. "Or if she's so damned bent on going to Louisville, tell her to wait until I can go with her."

Because Violet can't remove her head from her ass, her younger brother is now dealing with the guilt of her selfish decisions. I tighten my fist, trying to squeeze away the sharp surge of let down and pissed off.

Growing up, Violet, Chevy, Razor and I were sibling-close and now…she treats us like dirt. Even on a day that's precious to Olivia. I passed up walking in graduation because the funeral home conceded and let us have a party. They said if we were going to do it, it was now or never.

Stone's still stuttering out whatever pathetic crap Violet

forced him to memorize and Chevy goes in for the deflection. "Hey, Stone."

Stone squints at Chevy. In a smooth motion, Chevy waves his open palms in the air, claps them together and in a twitch of his fingers produces a daisy. My eyes automatically flash to the now empty vase on the table.

Chevy's been doing sleight of hand shit since we were kids. "Give this to your sister and tell her we missed her."

Meaning Chevy misses her. Stone takes the flower and his eyes glow. "That's cool. Will you teach me?"

I wink at Stone. "Girls don't go for guys who do magic. If a guy relies on sad shit like that it means he's got no game."

Chevy snorts. "Tell that to the girl who let me in her pants last night. Stick with me, Stone, and the world will be ours to dominate and control."

"No, Mom." Eli busts into the kitchen with Olivia hot on his heels. His stride is wider than normal, indicating he's upset or pissed. I'm going with a combination of both. "I'm calling Jeff after she calms down to find out what's going on. Then and only then will I bring her over to see you and Dad. Not everyone in the damn place."

Chevy gets up, reaches around Eli and dumps his trash. "Where's Emily?"

"In the bathroom with the funeral director." Olivia has a hop to her step that makes me smile. The past week has been rough on her. So rough she wasn't sure she could last the whole party. But now there's color in her cheeks.

"You know Meg will make her leave. Meg thought I was dead. This was a pity offering. Let's take her up on it. Get Emily a drink, give her a second to collect herself then bring her out to meet her family." She motions to us. "Don't you want to meet Emily?"

The girl's my kind of gorgeous, no question: sexy, beautiful dark hair and eyes like a doe's. Gotta admit, her curves turned me on and that dress she wore sealed the deal. It clung to her in all the right ways, but what was smoking was the way she wore it. Mysterious. Classy. Never seen anyone from Emily's world walk up to the Reign of Terror as if they didn't have a single fear.

But Emily is bad news. She's been a nonstop thorn in this family's side and has continually caused the people I love to bleed. Her being here will rupture already vulnerable arteries.

"No." Chevy, as always, preaches the truth. "I don't want to meet her."

Olivia points at Chevy. "For that answer, you're tilling my garden and spreading compost to get ready for tomato planting."

"Hell," Chevy mutters.

"Hi, Olivia," Stone says quietly. "I'm really enjoying your wake."

Olivia touches her fingers to her lips. Twenty bucks she didn't notice him, otherwise she probably wouldn't have spoken so openly. She reaches out and pushes Stone's overgrown hair away from his eyes. "There's something different about you. What is it?"

Stone peeks at Eli, who stands behind Olivia beaming like a proud papa.

"Contacts, ma'am."

"Well, I love them, and don't ma'am me. You know better than that. Why don't you go find Cyrus for me? I need to talk to him after I get done grilling Eli. And Stone, remember, what's said in my house, stays in my house."

He beelines it out of the kitchen into the thick crowd in the hallway. Once Stone's gone on the hunt for Olivia's husband, she returns to hammering her son. There's no question of kicking us out—Olivia has always talked openly in front of me and Chevy because she considers us her flesh and blood, too. "She's my granddaughter. I want the chance to meet her. Talk with her. Get to know her. Meg will never allow that if she knows I'm alive."

"As I said, once she calms down, I'll bring her to the house. I don't like the idea of her being here." He drops his voice. "It's too wide-open. Too many eyes."

"A few minutes here won't hurt," pleads Olivia. "A half hour tops. If you leave, you'll have to tell her father. He'll tell Meg I'm alive and then I'll lose my chance."

"You're telling me what you want and I'm telling you what I can give you." Eli rummages through the two-liters, continually picking up the Sprites only to come up empty each time. "Damn leeches drank everything dry."

He goes to pull his wallet out of his back pocket and his face turns an unusual shade of crimson. "Chevy."

My best friend tosses Eli's wallet back.

"Do it again and I'll nail you to the wall, got it?" threatens Eli.

"It's compulsive." Never met a guy that can pick any pocket clean like Chevy. "Besides, I always give it back."

Eli checks his wallet and when he's certain everything's inside he yanks out a couple dollars. "Oz, there's a vending machine across the street. Go get Emily a Sprite. After that, help Cyrus keep this place contained. If they aren't associated with the Reign of Terror, throw their asses out. With Emily here and the shit going on with the Riot, I want this placed locked down."

"Dammit, Eli!" This gains everyone's attention. A lull falls over the once boisterous conversations in the hallway. Olivia hasn't raised her voice like that in months.

She continues in a whisper. "She's my granddaughter. My granddaughter."

Olivia thumps her fist against her chest each time she says *granddaughter*. Both Chevy and I shoot to our feet, but it's Eli that catches her before she sways too far.

My heart beats wildly and my throat constricts. I don't understand what the hell is happening inside me, but I know what's happening inside Olivia. She's dying and there's nothing any of us can do to stop it.

Eli hugs his mother. "We'll go in after we get you something to eat."

I move because it hurts too bad to stay still. "I'll get her the Sprite." Though I don't know why. It's Emily's fault that Olivia is upset. I wish Emily had remained the illegitimate daughter that disappeared and never returned.

Emily

THE OFFICE OF A FUNERAL DIRECTOR RESEMBLES those of normal people: file cabinets, a desk, a rolly chair, paperwork, a computer, pictures of kids and families. No jars of blood, no dead people or dead people parts. Small consolation.

I'm ticked. Extremely ticked. Like a-tick-interrupted-from-a-meal ticked.

She's alive. My freaking non-grandmother is still alive, and she scared the hell out of me.

Completely spent, I sit in the chair, hold my phone and wait impatiently for it to vibrate. I left Mom a message, and someone went to find Dad. I want to go home.

My legs have the strength of mashed potatoes. I'm cold and clammy, and my stomach churns like I vomited. That's because I did, in the viewing room, and I discovered that yellow bile does not blend well with red velvet industrial carpeting. My crowning achievement in overreaction.

Through the large window facing the hallway, I can see

the crowd hasn't dispersed. Instead, the mass of bodies has increased since my moment of glory. Almost everyone gawks at me—laughing. My mom said Eli's family was psychotic, but this...this is...

The door squeaks open and the guy who caught me and kept me from falling to the floor enters the room with a can of Sprite. He's rocked out in those loose jeans, a studded black belt and a black T-shirt. "Olivia says it's not officially a party until somebody pukes."

"Glad I added to the fun."

He perches on the edge of the folding chair across from me and offers the Sprite. "Eli told me to get you this."

I keep my hands planted in my lap. Nothing today has gone right and I'm not a hundred percent sure I'm done puking.

"It's Sprite, not crack," he says.

"Thank you." I accept the soda and set it on the desk. "Are you my cousin?"

He doesn't resemble me or Eli with his blue eyes and grown-out black hair. The type of hair that's not overly long, but long enough that girls would be drawn to him because it's the correct length for seductive rebellion. The ends lick the collar of his shirt and hide his ears. He has the type of hair Blake Harris was suspended from school over. But that's not where my eyes linger. What captivates me is the way the sleeves of his T-shirt cling to his muscles. He's ripped in a very awesome way.

"No blood relation," he answers.

Good, because he has that alternative-music-band hotness and thinking someone I'm related to is sexy could send me into another meltdown.

"Will you do all of us a favor?" he asks.

I shrug, not exactly in the mood for conversation.

"Play nice with Olivia, then leave."

"Excuse me? Play nice? With her? She freaked me out."

He leans back in the chair and sprawls his legs out in a way that makes him appear larger than life and leaves me feeling claustrophobic. "Look, I know you're going all prodigal daughter, but this ain't the time or place. This is Olivia's party and you're ruining it."

"Prodigal what?"

"Daughter. Bible. The long-lost son returning home."

I stare at him, not sure what to say.

He gives a short laugh. "I heard that about your mom. Gave up God and family."

No one speaks badly about my mom. "I heard you're all crazy. And guess what? It's true."

"Why? Because Olivia's enjoying her life?"

"Because she plays make-believe in a coffin and all of you are okay with it."

"Better than screaming like a two-year-old and puking our guts out."

I was wrong—he's not hot. He's evil. Very, very evil. "It's sick. This whole thing is sick. You people are absolutely insane!"

The guy stands. "You need to leave. You want to see Eli? Wait for him to spend all his money so he can visit you this summer. This party is for Olivia and the people who care for her. You don't belong here."

The door opens and Eli and Olivia walk in. Eli had been smiling, but one flickering glance between me and Sprite guy and Eli's mouth firms into a hard line. "Is there a problem, Oz?"

His crazy name suits this insane day. Oz flashes an easygoing grin and I'm overwhelmed with the urge to slap him. "Nope."

Eli surveys me and his jaw relaxes. "Are you okay?"

Embarrassed—yes. Mortified—definitely. Okay—not at all. "Yeah."

"I need to speak to my granddaughter." Olivia pats Oz's arm.

He envelops her in a bear of a hug, looks at me over her shoulder and mouths "leave." He walks out and I've never been so happy to see someone go in my life. Hot or otherwise.

Olivia eases into the chair across from me, pulls out a pack of cigarettes and a lighter from her jeans and lights one up. "I have cancer and the doctors aren't hopeful."

I steal a peek at Eli, who rests his back against the wall. He's watching me, and I suddenly feel like a fish in a glass bowl. "I'm sorry."

"Don't be," Olivia says. "I've fought a good fight and lived a great life. God calls us all home at some point." She blows out the smoke and I swallow the cough that tickles my throat.

"Funerals are expensive," she states. It's a pause and an uncomfortable one. She props her elbow on the desk, and I'm strangely fascinated by the way she holds her forearm up and dangles the cigarette from her bent hand.

"Okay," I prompt, hoping this will continue the conversation.

She nails Eli's smile and I notice her dark eyes—my eyes. Olivia is pretty and doesn't seem old enough to have a granddaughter my age. A part of me wonders if I'll resemble her when I grow older.

"And if I'm going to waste that much money on a party, I prefer to be part of the action."

"So you planned your own funeral and attended it." Weird. Very, very weird.

"Yes. Sorry about earlier. Bad timing. I thought I'd test-drive the bed in a box. See what these bones could be spending eternity in. It's either that or the furnace."

I shift in my chair. That's not weird. It's nuts.

"Eli fucked up the e-mail to your family. Put in the obituary instead of the party announcement. I wrote the two at the same time. Figured I'd be the best person to write what I want people to read after I bite." Olivia takes another drag off her cigarette and flicks the ashes into a coffee mug.

"Muck." I've heard people say fuck before. Guys say it at school constantly, but...

Her forehead wrinkles. "What?"

"You should use muck instead. You're a...grandmother..." and the words fall off because they sound stupid.

She cackles. Like a witch. Head thrown back and everything. I shrink farther into the chair and will my phone to ring or my dad to show. Why is it taking so long for him to find me?

"Muck. I'll remember it. Back to the conversation. I don't regret what Eli sent." She sucks in one more draw before dropping the cigarette into the mug. It sizzles in the liquid. "I'm meeting you."

Simultaneous buzzing. My phone vibrates against the palm of my hand. Eli yanks his phone out of his back pocket. Too bad he didn't answer it last night. He could have saved us from this terrible torment.

We both accept the calls. "Hi, Mom."

"Are you okay, baby?" She sounds close to hysterics. I regret leaving the message while sobbing like a lunatic.

"Yes. I'm fine. Just freaked." Nothing a lifetime of therapy won't fix.

Mom rattles on and I tune her out while listening for key words that indicate I should speak. I'm more interested in Eli's conversation.

"I know." Eli rubs his forehead. "Jeff…" It's my dad. "Hear me out."

From the silence on Eli's end, it's obvious Dad's in no mood to listen, and I wonder why he's not in here talking to Eli face-to-face. Mom pauses. "Em?"

Crap, caught not listening. "I'm here."

"I said you need to leave. Right now. Walk out the door, do you understand?"

A twinge of panic strangles my heart when I look out the office's window. Two men guard the door. These guys weren't present before. At least I don't think they were. They aren't laughing or carrying on like everyone else in the hallway. Their backs are to us and their spines are arrow-straight. But what causes the hair on the back of my neck to stand on end is how they turn their heads to observe the crowd as if they're expecting something…or someone.

"Where's Dad?" I ask Mom.

"Outside," she answers. "He's outside and he can't get in. Eli won't stop you, honey. He's capable of a lot of things, but he'll let you go. Do it now, Emily. Leave."

Eli runs a hand over his face as he continues his conversation with Dad. "That's not necessary. There's no reason to change those plans. Emily is fine. A little shaken up, but she doesn't need to go home."

He opens the door and snaps his fingers at the two huge men. Both wear the same black vest as Eli. "Emily's dad is at the front entrance. I told someone to get him in here. I won't ask nicely again."

Eli closes the door then returns to talking to Dad. "They're going to let you in. Give me your word that she can visit with my mother. Not here, though. Somewhere...quieter."

"No." Olivia's eyes widen and she touches Eli's arm. "You promised."

Eli gives his head a small shake. Olivia pivots in my direction. "Tell Meg to let you stay." Her voice rises with each syllable. "Tell her you want to meet your family. Tell her you want to spend time with me. With your father!"

"Tell her?" My forehead furrows. I don't tell my mom what to do. It's Mom.

"Tell me what?" Mom asks.

"Olivia wants me to tell you that I should stay."

"No." Mom grows suddenly firm. "Leave now."

"Thanks for the reminder!" Eli smacks his hand on the wall. A corkboard tacked up beside him crashes to the floor. I jump with the impact and draw myself in, wishing I could disappear.

I don't know these people and they don't know me and my dad's outside and not inside and these people could have tempers and they could hurt me and...

"I'm aware I have no rights to my daughter," Eli snaps. "I'm the one who signed the damn papers!"

"Baby," Mom says in my ear. "Say goodbye to Eli and leave. The cab is waiting."

"Okay." I focus on my shoes. I never want to wear them again. "I'll see you soon."

Even though Mom's still talking, I end the call and drop the phone to my lap. Eli, on the other hand…

"No, Jeff. Let her stay… No. No." He opens his mouth to speak again and then lowers the phone to look at the screen. "Fuck!"

I flinch with the anger shaking out of his body and Eli swears again under his breath when he notices. "Dammit, I mean…I'm sorry, Emily."

"It's okay." I comb my fingers through my hair and pretend to be interested in the strands. Mom said Dad's outside and I'm going to ignore any reason for why he can't make it in. It's not because I'm trapped here. It's not because these people are trying to force something I don't want.

This is okay and I'm going to be okay. Deep breaths in. Long breaths out.

"Call her back," Olivia says to me. "Call Meg back and tell her you're staying."

My hands tremble as I pick up my purse and slip my phone into the pocket. "She told me to leave."

"Do you always do what you're told?"

I cling tighter to the handles on my bag. My mom told me to come home. Home. A place that is safe and familiar and nothing like this insanity. This place is scary and confusing and… "She's my mom."

NOWHERE BUT HERE   57

"Don't, Mom," Eli mumbles under his breath.

"And you're seventeen," Olivia points out. "Old enough to make this decision."

"Barely seventeen," I whisper.

"Leave her alone," Eli says. "It's me you're upset with."

Olivia wheels around. "Not you. Your daughter is caving to that woman and I'm tired of Meg telling us what we can and cannot do with our flesh and blood!" She rounds on me. "McKinley blood runs in your veins. Take a stand and tell them you're staying."

My wrist begins to itch and I scratch, not caring that it will make the welts bigger. Hives, my Achilles' heel. The physical manifestation of the chaos inside me. I slowly stand, but not in the way she desires. "I need to go. I'm sorry."

"Eli!" It's a plea, and it causes guilt to ripple within me. I glance out the window and catch Oz watching me from the hall with his thumbs hitched in his pockets. He lowers his head and shakes it.

"She's a good kid," Eli says in defeat.

"What does that mean?" Olivia yells.

Eli pushes off the wall and settles his hands on Olivia's shoulders like he did with me earlier. "It means she's a good kid. She's a good kid with good friends and she makes good grades at a good school and lives in a good neighborhood in a good house in an even better community. She's a good kid with a great life and every now and then I get to be a part of it. Think about what Meg's given her. Think about what we really have the right to demand."

Olivia crosses her arms. "You mean she's locked up in a safe padded world and she does everything everyone tells her."

"Yes." Eli nods. "And she's happy."

My would-be grandmother studies me and for some reason, she appears to pity me. "And that is sad."

OZ

HOOK AND PIGPEN GUARD THE DOOR TO THE office, and it's a good thing, too. Otherwise I probably would have bolted in and shaken the hell out of Emily.

My teeth grind as I witness the drama unfolding through the window. Olivia, the strongest woman I know, is close to tears. She's been the focus of my life since I was a child, and I've never seen her this way. Not when she discusses the son she lost around the time of my birth. Not when she told me I wouldn't be living with her anymore when I was eight. Not when she hurts year after year as she marks another passing of Emily's birthday with no contact from her or Meg. Not when she found out she has greater odds of being hit by lightning than surviving the cancer.

Tears. Olivia's eyes are glassy and she lifts her chin like she doesn't give a damn, but there's only a fragile veil of pride hiding her devastation.

Emily stands in the middle of the room with her purse in

her hands, looking completely lost as Olivia cups her face. Fuck Emily for hurting Olivia. Fuck Emily for returning and ruining this day.

The door to the office opens and Eli walks out. Hook and Pigpen grant Eli their undivided attention and Eli points at me. "I need you in on this, Oz."

I slide closer and the four of us create a tight circle. Eli talks so only we can hear. "Pigpen, clear this hall. Hook, tell her father we're taking Emily out the back. I want a wall of leather cuts giving her shade, do you got me?"

They mumble their agreement and Pigpen rounds to face the crowd. Like a lot of the brothers in the club, he's ex-military. The voice of the six-two, massive former Army Ranger rumbles against the walls. "If you ain't a brother, clear out!"

The volume of conversation in the hall rises along with the sound of shuffling feet. Everyone associated with us comprehends that a demand is a demand, not a request. Hang-arounds, people not associated with the club, are permitted to party with us, but are only allowed on our terms. If they don't like it, they can get the hell out.

I shift to help Pigpen with the herding, but Eli catches my arm. "Walk with me."

Eli's on the move in the restricted hallway of the funeral home and I keep step by his side. We turn the corner and he imitates a Navy SEAL on a mission when his eyes roam the area. He's performing a run-through to confirm the area is clear. "What the fuck was Meg thinking letting Emily come here?"

His hand slams on a swinging door that's marked "No Entrance" and I keep my mouth shut. That question wasn't for me. We enter a barren hallway and I stay near the exit as Eli checks a room at the end. "Fifteen years since they've been in this town and now with the Riot breathing down our throats Meg allows Emily to show."

Eli kicks an empty cardboard box and it bounces against the wall. He breathes hard and I meld into the equivalent of paint. I've known Eli since I was eleven. He's the biggest badass I've met and he doesn't easily lose his shit. It's best to let him ride this out.

"I e-mailed Jeff." Eli stares at the wall. "I e-mailed him in the vain hope he'd let Emily come, but I didn't think he would. I knew Meg would say no, but I had hoped and then he did call and I didn't answer. I had turned off my cell, forgot I had and now…"

His hands go to his hips and his head falls back. "I have a huge favor to ask."

"Name it." This is the moment I've been waiting for since I was sixteen.

"I need you on Emily. Follow her until she gets on the plane. Stay close enough to make sure she's out of trouble, but far enough away that no one figures out that you're tailing them. If you do this for me, you'll have a cut on your back the moment you walk into the clubhouse and you'll be our newest prospect."

"Not a problem." I'll follow Emily through hell in order to make prospect. "Do you mind telling me what I'm watching for?"

Eli works his jaw. "The Riot."

Never thought of Eli as paranoid. My mind races for why

the Riot would give a rip about Emily. "The Riot would never step into Snowflake, so how would they know that she's here?" And why would they care?

"The Riot's pissed we're doing security business in Louisville. Even more pissed we won't give them a cut of our profits because we're running through their area. Remember what I said to you last night? The Riot can make a business issue personal fast."

"Yeah, but you think they'll go after Emily?"

"There's a scar forming on your father's head that tells me the Riot is ready for a war, and there are over two hundred people in this building. I can't risk the chance there's someone loyal to them here gathering info on us. I wasn't worried until I saw Emily. We're strong together as a club. We protect our own, but she's not one of us and I won't have them go personal with her. The Riot don't think straight when they're mad. They act first and never ask questions later. She's my daughter and I don't want her caught up in my shit."

I nod. This is the guy Eli is—loyal to those he loves. But it's lost on me why he has this sudden commitment to Emily. He visits her once a year. From what I understand, he never tried for custody, but I'm not going to question my path into the club. He wants me to watch Emily, so I'll watch Emily. She officially has a stalker.

"Meg will be able to spot a Terror member," he continues, "so you'll be driving my truck. If anyone can own the role of teenager out for a joyride who doesn't give a shit, it's you."

From Eli, that's a high compliment. "Emily will know me."

"Emily won't be looking for you, but Meg will be searching for the club." He digs into his pockets and tosses the keys to his truck to me. "Tail them until she boards the plane. I need to know that my problems with the Riot don't follow my daughter."

"Consider it done." I open the exit door and Eli stops me from walking out into the summer sun.

"Anyone who messes with Emily messes with me," he adds.

Which means anyone stupid enough to cross paths with her is suicidal. "I got her back."

Eli smiles like we've been chatting about the weather. "You're a good man, Oz." And he disappears back inside the funeral home.

In pleated khaki pants, Emily's adoptive father, Jeff, paces outside the sidewalk of his motel room talking on his cell. He sports a pair of Aviator sunglasses and holds himself like he's God. Heard he's a doctor so he probably thinks he is. I've been ordered to maintain my distance, otherwise I would have offered the three of them a ride into Louisville hours ago.

My cell buzzes. Eli's hourly check-in. What's going on?

Same thing as the past ten hours. Nothing.

I followed Emily and Jeff here after they left the funeral home. Three hours ago the rental-car company showed and dropped off an SUV. Emily and her parents piled into the rental and I rapped my head against the headrest of the truck when the engine of the SUV wouldn't turn over.

Since then, Jeff's bought takeout and talked on his phone. No sign of Emily or her mother. Both have stayed safely inside the motel room.

Buzzing.

I don't like them staying here overnight. We're hearing some chatter that the Riot are riding closer than normal, but we don't have visuals. Don't like the feel of the situation. Keep vigilant.

Like stalking a girl who hurt Olivia is my definition of a wet dream. Will do.

I toss my cell onto the bench seat and press the balls of my hands to my eyes. Last night's lack of sleep is catching up. First the private party at the lake with a twelve-pack, Chevy and two blondes more than willing to be on the back of a bike, then the hours waiting for Dad and then the adrenaline rush of all that followed.

I got an hour's worth of sleep, maybe less, before Eli picked me up to retrieve Dad's bike. I stretch my legs in the small space against the floorboard and roll my neck. Eli checked flights after it was clear their rental wasn't moving and confirmed that it would be impossible for them to reach Louisville and still board a flight out tonight.

It's killing Eli to do nothing, but they haven't asked for help and they aren't answering his "benign" texts asking if Emily's okay and if they arrived in Louisville without issue. Any further contact by him would tip them off that they're being tailed and Eli's adamant this remains on the down low.

Jeff ends a call and looks up at the sky. Night's falling. The lights on the motel overhang flicker on. He glances around the mostly abandoned parking lot, but dismisses me and the truck. I'm in the corner, near the Dumpster, and in the shadows.

Taking the key card out of his pocket, he enters the motel room. Another buzz and I wish Eli's cell would run out of power.

You gonna be able to stay awake on this?

Do I want Eli to think I can handle the club?

Yes.

Don't fail me.

Won't happen.

I wait for Eli's next text, but the silence confirms that he has faith. Should've asked for some coffee or a shot of adrenaline, but there's no asking for help here. I do this or I don't, and I won't let Eli down.

I rest my head on the seat and stare at Emily's motel room. If there's one thing that's been confirmed today, it's that she's more trouble than she's worth.

Emily

IT'S AS IF I'M LIVING THE OPENING SEGMENT OF
an apocalyptic thriller. Young family's rental car breaks down
in parking lot and they're forced to stay the night in dilapi-
dated motel. Soon, the local townspeople morph into skin-
eating demons and the family fights to survive until sunrise.

Maybe our situation isn't that dire, but it's close. The past
few hours have been the worst sleep of my life. With no rental
and no Louisville cab company willing to spare a driver to
take us back into the city, we're stuck here. To make matters worse, Snowflake is limited in overnight accommoda-
tions and, short of pitching a tent, this is where we ended up.

The stain on the sheets of the bed I lie in gives me the
bugs-walking-on-the-back-of-my-neck creeps and, speaking
of bugs, I'm sure there are a hundred million of them nest-
ing in the innards of the mattress. Something continuously
moves in the corner of the room, but disappears each time I
click on the light.

It doesn't help that Mom and Dad have been sharing a whispered intense conversation all night. Yes, they had a lot to discuss after the funeral home debacle, but a call from the room phone around eleven caused a new round of conversations. Most of it taking place in the bathroom.

For hours, I stared at the light streaming from the crack under the bathroom door. Occasionally their voices would rise, but they were still too muffled for me to understand. Even when I tiptoed to the door to listen.

I'm impatient for daylight yet the minutes drag into days. It's 3:03 a.m. and I've been parched since two. The thought of interrupting Mom and Dad in the bathroom for a drink of water doesn't thrill me, so I roll out of bed. In the darkness, I shimmy out of my pj pants and into a pair of shorts. There's a vending machine a few doors down and a bottle of cold water is calling my name.

OZ

THE SLAMMING OF A CAR DOOR JERKS ME AWAKE. My heart hammers with the realization—I fell asleep. I scrub a hand over my face to wake myself, then grab the phone. It's after three and there are two missed messages. Eli's going to kill me and I deserve his wrath. I messed this up big time.

Message one: What's going on?

Message two: You better be awake and taking a piss or you better be dead.

My fingers hover over the cell as my attention is drawn to movement from the right. On the opposite side of the parking lot are two guys who stand near the front of a blacked-out SUV. Cigarettes burn in their hands and I don't like how they're watching Emily's room.

I scan the rest of the area and my stomach drops. Dark chestnut hair. Tanned, toned legs. Damn me to hell, Emily's walking toward the vending machines. One of the guys drops his cigarette to the ground and smashes it with his foot.

His mouth moves as he talks to the guy next to him and in the barely dim light surrounding him, he slips off a cut. I don't catch the entire patch, but I see enough. With a surge of adrenaline, I start the truck and then my fingers fly over the letters.

The Riot are here.

Emily

GOOSE BUMPS RISE ON MY ARMS WHEN I OPEN THE door and the early-morning Kentucky air drifts over my skin. It's the first time I've stayed at this type of motel—the type with no interior corridors and only exterior doors.

I flip the security latch to prevent being locked out and follow the hum of vending machines. The lights of the overhang burn bright enough for me see where I'm heading, but are dull enough that I'm again reminded of walking into a horror flick.

The night surrounding the motel parking lot is dark. Very dark. My dad once told me that it gets darker before the dawn. I shiver. He must be right. I've never seen anything so black that it's completely void of light.

I turn the corner and pause. My back itches like I'm being watched. The sensation crawls along the fine hairs of my neck and my heart pumps hard. In a slow movement, I peer over my shoulder. Nothing but darkness. Nothing but small bugs swarming near the overhead light that leaves a green tint to the world. Nothing. Nothing but my overactive imagination.

One foot angles in favor of the room, but the rest of me pushes forward. Five seconds to get a drink and then back to the room. Maybe ten. With my stomach in my throat, I brave the enclave, slip the fifty cents into the coin slot and then attempt to shove the dollar into the machine. With a whine, it spits the money back out. With a second whine, the machine cranks the bill out again. "Come on!"

My skin shrinks against my bones. Saran Wrap tight, my flesh feels like it needs to be shed. There's something wrong out here. Something evil. With shaky hands I try one last time and the machine inhales the dollar.

A push of a button. A racket that could wake the dead. My hand swipes up the water. A flash of black to my right and I suck in a breath to scream.

Black hair. Blue eyes. Broad shoulders. Taller than me. And he blocks my way.

I stumble back, tripping over myself. The water thumps to the concrete and a hand whips out and grabs my wrist. Air leaves my lungs in a hiss when my body slams into the cinder-block wall.

My mouth opens again and a hot hand presses against my lips. A sob racks me and blue eyes lower to mine. "It's me, Emily. It's Oz. Right now I need you to be quiet. Do you hear me? Quiet."

He's whispering while he muffles my scream. Quiet is not what I need. My eyes dart around. We're wedged in a small space between the vending machine and the wall. His body is pressed tightly to mine, so much so that it's hard to draw in air. Cobwebs touch the top of Oz's head. A spider the size of my fist swings precariously above us, its legs twisting as it spins its web.

A sound leaves my throat as a tear cascades down my face.

"Quiet," Oz demands again. "Please, Emily. Be still."

I blink at the *please*. His blue eyes soften and my senses go on alert. Almost like my energy is reaching out to find the real threat—a threat my instincts inform me is worse than what's in front of me.

Oz slowly withdraws his hand from my mouth and the flood of cold air on my face causes me to tremble. He continues to lower his hand to his hip and wraps his fingers around the hilt of a blade stuck inside a leather sheath.

There's activity beyond us. A slow tapping of a boot against the sidewalk. A scrape comparable to sandpaper against the concrete wall. Then a shadow. Large. Looming. The head of the dark shadow hits near my feet.

"The water bottle." My lips move.

Oz tilts his head as if he sees the shift in my mood. "I know," he mouths. "Shh."

Chaos reigns inside my mind. Oz can kill me or Oz can save me or Oz can do one now and then another later.

The footsteps begin again, echoing closer to our hiding spot. Fear gains in strength, causing a wave of dizziness to wash over me. Oz weaves an arm around my back and circles us so that I'm wedged into the corner and he's positioned near the threat.

Heat builds between us and my pulse beats wildly at my pressure points. He continues to gently guide me into the extremely small crevice behind the machine. My foot tangles with a cord and I trip to the right. My hand snaps out and I grab on to Oz's belt loop as both of his hands land on my hips.

We're crushed against each other. Warmth rolls off his body and onto mine. He must feel it—my fear, the blood drumming throughout my veins. My eyesight nearly shakes with it.

Oz does a strange thing. He smiles. It's a crazy smile, but beautiful. My body tingles when he swipes his thumb under my shirt and across the sensitive skin of my waist.

He leans forward, his breath hot against my ear. Only one guy has been *this* near me before. Body against body. Thighs against thighs. Warm breath brushing the back of my ear. We didn't go far that night. We didn't go far at all—not emotionally, not physically...just not. And standing here pressed between a wall and Oz, my entire body becomes aware.

"If he finds us," he breathes into my ear, "you run, Emily. You run and keep running until you lock yourself in the room. Then you call Eli."

Oz pulls back and our noses almost touch. I strain to listen. No footsteps. No sound beyond my own frantic breaths. Then a thump to the concrete. Like a bottle dropping. My stomach sinks along with it. And there's a rolling of plastic... getting closer...closer. So close that it's next to us.

My eyes flash to Oz's. I'm about to explode out of my skin yet he's calm, steady, solid. He meets my gaze, never once looking elsewhere. The bottle continues to roll away...away... to the point I believe that the sound I hear is only in my mind. An echo of my fears.

No longer able to handle Oz's intense stare, I lower my head and my body sags. Oz eases a hand to the nape of my neck, encouraging me to rest my head on his shoulder. I do, then inhale the calming scent of burned wood. It conjures images of bonfires on the beach. S'mores on the back patio with my father. Nights by the fireplace as a child.

Oz's hand is hot on my skin and my muscles melt under his strong caress. An eternity passes. Stars are born then die. He relaxes his grip on me and my fingers curl into his belt loops when he tries to maneuver away.

"Did you hear that?" he asks.

The rolling? It's still in my head and so are the footsteps, but I shake my head no.

"It's my cell," he says under his breath, and sure enough I hear a vibration. "I need to answer."

I release him and he slips his phone out of his back pocket. "I nine-one-one'd Eli and he's on his way. I need to get you within walls. Stay here and don't move."

Oz steps back and I shiver with the cold infiltrating where he had been. My eyes widen. His knife is in his hand. I never saw him free the blade and I never felt him move to do so.

Oz peers around the corner. One way. Then the next. The fear is so encompassing that it almost shifts into hysterics.

"Stay put," he commands. I'm normally not a take-orders-from-a-guy type of girl, but I'm all for following directions since my feet are frozen to the ground.

Oz disappears and a small part of me internally cries. Alone has never felt so...alone.

An electric buzz of the vending machine. The gentle tap of water leaking from a pipe above. Not knowing if the footsteps drifting away are what I should be terrified of.

Because it's overwhelming, I count. Throwing in the Mississippi in between like Mom taught me. I count slower when

I hit fifty, then even slower when I hit two hundred. I start again at zero, pretending that his absence during the first three hundred seconds doesn't matter.

Oz appears in front of me again and my knees give out at the sight. He extends his hand. "Those two guys are still here, but they walked around the corner. I can slip you back in your room, but we need to be quiet."

"Who are they?" I ask.

Oz's shoulders stiffen and his eyes bore into mine. "People neither one of us want to mess with. Let's go."

OZ

EMILY'S CHEST RISES AND FALLS AT AN ALARMING rate and I pray she doesn't faint.

She's smaller than me and she's curvy as hell. She wears a pair of hip-hugging jean shorts and a tight blue tank that covers enough of her top, but rides short and highlights her flat stomach. I've never been so damned captivated by a belly button in my life. Hate to admit it, but with that long chestnut hair and those big dark eyes, Emily is hot.

She's also in a ton of trouble and if she doesn't trust me soon and take my hand, she's going to turn her problems into my problems and that will be dangerous for us both.

"If I was the enemy, Emily, I would have already slit your throat and thrown your body into the trunk of a car."

"You're not helping," she whispers.

"But it's the truth. Now, let's go."

She sucks in her bottom lip and I wiggle my fingers, signaling for her to follow. It's like convincing an injured animal to eat from my hand. I get why she doesn't trust me. If I were in her shoes, I'd be weighing my options. One of them being jacking the knife in my hand and slicing my way out of this situation.

Emily extends her hand—moment by moment. Centimeter by centimeter. At any point, I could have grabbed her and hauled her out, but something tells me that she's never faced any level of danger. To expect her to be braver than most is unfair, especially when she's impressed me with how well she's handled tonight.

The moment her smooth fingers touch mine, I link our hands together and we're on the move. As I tighten my grip on her, I secure my knife in my other hand. Eli and Dad have taught me stuff over the years. All of it without Mom's knowledge or permission. It involves the whereabouts of arteries, kidneys and liver, and each conversation and demonstration involved a blade.

We round the corner and I halt, hiding her from view. A burly guy with fists the size of concrete blocks stands outside the door to Emily's room. I push Emily back into the walkway and silently curse. "Tell me you locked the door behind you."

Her face pales out and I have my answer. She shoves at me, but she's such a tiny thing that it's nothing more than the beats of a butterfly's wings. "What's wrong?"

I don't bother replying. We go in the opposite direction of her room. Actually, I go and pull her behind me. She yanks at my hand and tries to dig her feet into the ground, but I'm bigger and I'm stronger and I'm getting her the hell out of here.

I peer around the other side of the building and when I spot nothing, I head for the truck, thanking God I had the forethought to drive it to this side before chasing after her. I drag Emily forward and open the passenger-side door. "Get in."

At the sight of the truck's interior, Emily tries to create space between us as she jerks at my hold on her wrist. "I'm not going with you."

Screw this. I lean into Emily and she stumbles until her back smacks the inside of the door.

"I don't know what's going on, but you have the biggest illegal motorcycle club in Kentucky literally on your doorstep. We don't have time to argue. Get in the truck now!"

Her frantic movements stop and I don't care for the deer-caught-in-headlights thing she's melded into. With a ragged breath, her eyes shoot to the small tunnel of a hallway we emerged from and I can read her mind.

My arm snaps out and I clutch the edge of the door, blocking her path. "Eli's on his way and he will protect your parents, but I can't protect you and them at the same time. You know as well as I do, you can't stop anything that's happening. By standing here fucking with me, *you* are placing them in danger. Not me. Get in the truck, Emily, and let me get help."

"They're my parents," she pleads.

"And you're stopping me from getting them help. Get in the truck so I can make some calls."

She swallows and in seconds she's in the passenger side of the truck. I shut her door, race around, slide in and start the engine. With my cell out and the number dialed, I place the phone to my ear and slowly ease out of the parking lot.

One ring and Cyrus answers, "Eli's coming in fast and dangerous, son. The text you sent better mean that death's on Emily's doorstep."

Close enough. "The Riot's at her motel. Emily's with me. Tell me where to go."

"You bring her home."

I check the rearview mirror as I floor the gas and pray I don't see headlights.

Emily

WE'VE DRIVEN IN SILENCE AND, MILE AFTER BLACK mile, I keep wondering if I'm in a dream. I've lost all sense of direction as we've ridden through a maze of back roads and a few minutes ago we ended up on blacktop so narrow I consider it more of a path than a road. There was a crudely made street sign at the turn and it read Thunder Road. Frightening how the name describes the storm I've been sucked into.

The truck gently jostles back and forth and dips with the occasional pothole. From the limited range of the headlights, I can tell that the sides of the road are thick with brush and trees. Every now and then a low-hanging limb smacks the cab of the truck. There's no moon. There's no light. There's only darkness.

My teeth chatter and Oz turns his head to look at me. "Are you cold?"

I don't know. Am I? Oz flicks a few switches, points the vents toward me and heat begins to dance along my skin.

Even with the added warmth, my teeth chatter again and I run my hands along my arms. The cold…it's not in a place that a heater can reach. It's past my skin, past my muscles and into my bones.

"Maybe we should go back for my parents."

"Maybe we shouldn't," he responds.

"Are they okay?"

His phone has rung a couple of times. Oz answers it, listens, then mumbles some sort of an "okay" and drops his cell back into the cup holder. Surely, he's heard something. We've been driving for too long. Forever. But according to the clock, forty minutes.

"We're almost there," Oz says as an answer.

"I asked about my parents," I snap.

His forever-roaming eyes check the rearview mirror again. "They're safe. At least they were the last time the club checked in."

I close my eyes as the tension escapes from my neck. "Why couldn't you say that?"

"Because I don't know how long that will remain true and I'm not about false hope." Before the shock of his words can set in, he continues, "The club's with them, but the next couple of hours are critical. Your job is to lay low and not contact anyone. Do you understand?"

No. I don't understand any of this. I draw my knees to my chest in an effort to fight the freezing temperatures in my veins. "Where are we going?"

Oz switches the hand on the wheel and leans against his door. "Olivia's."

Olivia's. My head hits the back of the seat. "Oh." Oh.

"I spend a lot of time there. Sometimes more than at my own home," he says, and before I can respond he continues, "And here we are."

My breath is stolen from my body as I take in the sight. It's an overgrown log cabin with every window lit up like a Thomas Kinkade painting. Running along the wraparound front porch are rosebushes tangled with vines of honeysuckle. It's beautiful, picture-perfect and surely not the place where bikers live.

"Shocked?" There's a bite in Oz's voice and it causes me to stare at him. He parks the truck off to the side of the house and shuts off the engine. "Considering what most people think of us, shocked is the most common reaction."

Because they are bikers and this...this place is gorgeous. Oz swings out of the truck and I'm surprised when he meets me at my side, opens the door and then offers me his hand. "It's a jump."

He's right. I didn't notice it on the way up, but now facing the prospect of down, I have a respect for the two feet. He has a strong hand. It's a bit rough, but not sandpaper. It's a hand that leads, not a hand that follows, and I really shouldn't be thinking too much about this anymore.

"Ready?" he asks.

I nod then jump. Once on the ground, Oz pulls on my fingers, encouraging me to move forward. I barely trust him so I slip out of his grasp and he doesn't fight the distance I crave. "The next time someone calls, can I talk to my parents?"

Oz's forehead wrinkles and suddenly the big, scary guy doesn't appear so big and scary as his eyes soften. "Let's go inside. We'll know more then."

"What if you're lying to me?" I ask, because I'd prefer that to my parents being in danger. "What if this was some sort of elaborate scheme to get me to talk to Olivia? I mean, you guys kept my father from me today." Well, yesterday.

"That was a misunderstanding."

"What if this is a—" air quotes "—misunderstanding?"

"Not that you'd know, but I don't jack off to shoving hot girls into spider-infested crevices between vending machines, so how about you cut me some slack?"

I blink. Several times. Did he just call me…? And did he just say…? Heat flushes my cheeks, a mixture of embarrassment and shock. The door on the porch squeaks open and a figure made of solid muscle stalks onto the porch. "Oz."

The porch light flips on and it's the man with the long gray beard and ponytail who stood beside Oz outside the funeral home. He's dressed in jeans, a white T-shirt and an open red flannel with the sleeves rolled up. Seeing him, I empathize with Jack swaddling the stolen goose in his arms as he faces down the very ticked-off giant.

His gaze lands on us and I don't miss how it lingers on me. I inch closer to Oz and my side brushes against his. I don't know why, but my instincts scream that Oz means safety. He presses a hand to the small of my back and it's as if an invisible force field forms around us.

Oz doesn't push me ahead. Instead, he skims one finger along my spine. I shiver and this time it isn't from the cold.

"That's Cyrus," Oz says so only I can hear. "He's Eli's dad. Your grandfather."

My heart aches. The pain comes sharp and fast and it hits so hard that I know it will leave a scar. "I didn't know I had one."

Eli mentioned Olivia before, but he never discussed his father and I never cared enough to ask or imagine one existed. Maybe Eli did mention him and I blocked it out.

Oz inclines his head to the house. I walk forward and Oz is kind enough to match his pace to my slow stride.

"You're being nice to me," I say. "Thank you for that."

"Did you think I was an asshole?"

Um…yeah. "Well…"

"Your first instinct was right."

"Why are you being nice to me then?" I ask as we reach the stairs.

Oz pauses on the bottom step and glances at the bear of a man towering by the front door. "Because nobody deserves to be thrown into the middle of a tornado."

The screen door opens again and the woman I had abandoned hours before shuffles onto the front porch. Her head is covered by a blue scarf and she wears a pair of jeans and a form-fitting black T-shirt. Olivia touches Cyrus's arm and smiles down at me. "Welcome home, Emily."

OZ

I ENTER THE LIVING ROOM AND RUB MY KNUCK-les against the stubble forming on my jaw. Every single baby picture of Emily has disappeared. That's left a lot of notice-able dust-outlined bare spots.

Olivia fusses over Emily in that demanding way of hers, telling her that she must be hungry and thirsty. Emily scratches a spot on her arm and my eyes narrow at the red welt devel-oping on her wrist. I don't like that. I don't like it at all.

Mom appears in the doorway from the kitchen and she rests a hand over her heart when she sees me. One of her men home. One more to go. From what I understood on the phone, Eli, Dad and a bunch of other members tore off on their bikes for the motel. Because of Olivia's cancer, Mom often stays with Olivia when Mom's off work.

"Don't stand there like a statue, child. Tell me what you need," says Olivia.

Emily rubs harder at her wrist and her eyes shoot to mine

as if she's asking me to answer for her. Guess I am an asshole because I don't swoop in for the rescue.

"Can I talk to my mom and dad?" she asks.

Olivia immediately glances to Cyrus and he clears his throat. "Soon."

"Are they okay?"

"Yes," Cyrus answers.

Emily's eyes dart around, trying to take in the people surrounding her and the bright, open room. Lincoln log walls. Wooden floors. Flat-screen television. Overstuffed couch. A recliner for Cyrus. Surround-sound system. Most of the furniture and electronics are gifts from Eli. His attempt to buy his way out of guilt.

"Why..." Emily's whole body shudders like an epileptic fit and she brushes her fingers over her arms as if to warm her skin. She's acting so damn cold that even I'm starting to believe it's winter. "What's going on?"

"There's been a misunderstanding," says Cyrus.

"Seems to be a lot of those." Emily throws a death glare in my direction. Damn, she's got fire. That's shocking considering I pegged her to be a mouse of a girl who did everything exactly as her mother told her.

"And we apologize for that," Cyrus continues. "We're having some business issues and our negotiations have hit a snag."

Emily tosses her arms out to her sides. "That doesn't make any sense."

"No," he agrees. "It doesn't."

That's the only explanation Cyrus will offer. Emily's inquiring about club business and Emily's not part of the club.

By the scowl on her face, she's pissed. Being shut out doesn't sit well with most girls. Women like Mom and Olivia are a rarity.

Olivia straightens her scarf as she starts to shake. Last week, Olivia was so sick she was in bed with an IV. While I love that Emily's brought a hop to her step, Olivia's wasting energy to put on a show for her long-lost granddaughter.

"Emily's in shock," I say. "She's cold and she mentioned she hasn't slept yet."

Dirty look number two. If Emily keeps this up, she might be elevated from good-girl status to bad.

"I'm fine," Emily mutters, but what she doesn't realize is that I didn't say it to humiliate her. I said it to force Olivia off her feet and my plan works.

Like she's herding a timid sheep, Olivia corners Emily until she practically falls back on the couch and Olivia relaxes beside her. Mom's in front of Emily with a mug of something steaming and uses a soft tone as she introduces herself.

Cyrus inclines his head to the porch and as I move to walk out, Emily's head snaps up. "Where are you going?"

All eyes land on me. Cyrus strokes the length of his beard as his eyes flicker between me and Emily.

"Front porch," I answer.

Emily scoots to the edge of the couch like she's going to stand and my mom and Olivia flutter their hands to keep her seated.

"Oz isn't going anywhere," Cyrus says. "I need to follow up with him on a few things and then he'll be back in."

"Oz?" asks Emily.

Cyrus motions with his head for me to confirm it and I do. "I won't be long."

Emily reclines back against the couch and cups the mug in her hands, but doesn't drink. Odds are she thinks it's poison.

Cyrus and I step onto the porch and, off in the east, dark blue creates a line against the black of night. Dawn's coming and I have no idea what this day is going to bring.

"You were supposed to become a prospect last night," says Cyrus.

I lean my shoulder against one of the log columns supporting the roof of the porch and cross my arms over my chest. Cyrus eases up beside me, resting a hip on the railing.

"I know." Today was supposed to be the first day of the rest of my life, but Emily's visit messed everything up.

"It'll happen," Cyrus says. "But Eli's priority is his daughter."

I nod, because there's nothing else to say.

"Eli called you, Oz. Multiple times. You texted as he was heading to hunt you down."

My gut twists. I fell asleep on my debut assignment. I didn't even get to wear a cut and I blew my chance. Anger and frustration tenses my muscles and I fight the urge to slam my fist against something. Anything. This is my life. My family. I may have lost it all because I fell asleep. "What do I do?"

Cyrus stares straight at me with those emotionless gray eyes. "Man up and accept the repercussions. Any other option isn't acceptable."

The club doesn't tolerate excuses. The brotherhood is built on family and trust. Lying my way out of a situation would be the same as showing myself the door.

"Tell 'em the truth. That's all you can do." Cyrus pats my

shoulder. "Besides, you saved his daughter and my granddaughter. That holds some weight."

His words sound good, but none of them erase the fear that I might have sabotaged the most important goal in my life. A sickening nausea envelops me and it's similar to the devastation of being told that Olivia has cancer.

Cyrus pushes off the railing. "You did good tonight."

"You never mentioned why the Riot would be going after Emily. Or how they'd even know who she is."

Frogs croak in the nearby pond. I wait for an answer and Cyrus smirks. "You're right. I didn't. When was the last time you had decent sleep?"

I shrug. I fell asleep for a half hour. A half hour that could cost me my future. "I'm good."

"Glad to hear it. The way Emily looks at you, moves in your direction—that girl trusts you."

"No, she doesn't."

"She trusts you more than anyone else on this property. I know you're tired, but I'd like you to stay. It'll make the next couple of hours easier on her and I know Eli will appreciate that."

While I feel sorry for the girl, she's a bomb on countdown. "She's bad news."

Cyrus's boots clomp against the porch as he heads for the door. "Then she'll fit in, won't she?"

The sky in the west continues to get lighter and the stars above dim like a candle flame down to the quick. Only a few more hours of Emily, then Eli will fix whatever the hell is going on with the Riot, she'll return to her spoon-fed life and I'll beg Eli for another shot. I shove a hand through my hair to shake away the need for sleep. Just a few more hours.

"You coming?" Cyrus asks.

"I'll be in in a sec. I need a minute to clear my head."

He leaves while I grip the railing and lean over. My life has become a waking nightmare.

Emily

IN THEORY, I'M WATCHING TELEVISION EVEN though I can't make sense of anything on the screen. Oz is on the front porch and everyone else stares at me. The everyone else would include:

Oz's mother, Izzy, the lone partially sane person in the state of Kentucky

Cyrus, a giant impersonating a human

Olivia, the once dead and now alive

They're probably wondering if I'm going to spaz at any second. So here's the thing: they may not be wrong.

Wrapped in a blue crocheted blanket, I sit in the middle of the couch. Olivia has staked a claim beside me. It's hard not to picture her popping out of the casket. Because of that, my spine is curtain-rod straight and I remain perfectly still. Sort of like those small woodland creatures when they realize the big, bad carnivorous beast has spotted them. Doesn't console me to know things don't typically work out for the woodland creature.

So long, woodchuck. I hope you had a great life, squirrel. You didn't really want that nut, did you, chipmunk?

Yes, I know, no one's going to eat me. My eyes drift over to Cyrus. He quickly turns his head and pretends to be immersed in the movie. He might sauté me up with some onions and throw me on a sesame-seed bun.

Stop it. This train of thought…it's because I'm exhausted and I'm scared and I'm desperate to talk to my parents and…

Moisture pools in my eyes and I wipe at it. I won't cry. Not in front of them. They are the enemy. They are the ones that created this situation. With each flutter of my eyelids, the urge is to keep them closed, but I force them open. I don't know these people. I don't know them and it's not safe to sleep.

"If you're tired," Olivia says as if she already knows the answer, "we have a spare bedroom. Two in fact."

"I'm not tired," I answer through the yawn. "But can I use the bathroom?"

"Of course," says Olivia.

Cyrus and Izzy hop up, but Olivia forces them to reclaim their seats with one slice of her hand. She's slow as she stands and a large helping of guilt plops into the bottom of my stomach.

"You can tell me where it is," I say. She repeats the gesture to me and I also withdraw into silence.

I follow her down the hallway. We pass two bedrooms and the hallway turns. In front of us is a larger bedroom and to the right is the bathroom.

Olivia prevents me from entering the bathroom by placing her cold hand on my arm. My heart stutters as if shocked by electricity. She's not dead. Nope, not dead. Very, very much alive.

"We're going to my bedroom," she says in a voice you don't argue with. She flips on a light and I'm surprised by the pink-and-blue pastels on her comforter and curtains.

"I like your room." I'm drawn to the door leading out of her room to the porch. I could bolt and possibly escape from this madness.

"Did you expect skulls and crossbones?" She opens a jewelry box on her dresser. "A gun arsenal and torture chamber?"

Well...yes. "No."

"You're a bad liar, Emily, and I'm going to need you to get better at it, but I have faith that will happen. You are, by blood, a McKinley."

A wave of defiance tightens my muscles. "I'm a Jennings."

"Thanks to a paper trail and a judge's signature, but you are one of us. You always have been." Olivia riffles through stacks of photos she took out of the jewelry box then offers one to me.

No. There's no freaking way that picture is real. Dizziness overtakes my mind as I lose myself in a haze. I'm asleep and this is a dream.

"Take it," she demands.

Can't make me. I shake my head and step back.

"Olivia?" Cyrus calls from the living room. "Are you okay?"

"Yes," Olivia raises her voice to answer while refusing to break eye contact with me. She lowers her tone again. "I promised Eli and your mother that I would take this to the grave. The way I see it, I already have one foot in, so what difference does it make."

My gaze drifts to the picture trembling in her hand and I wince. The pink elephant in the chubby hands of the baby in the photo is more than familiar. He's cherished and adored and has seen me through some of my scariest moments. His name is James and, at home, in Florida, he's propped on my dresser looking a lot more worn and a lot less pink and lot more loved.

The baby is old enough to rip through the mess of presents in front of her. She has long brown hair and she wears the same pink dress that my mother drags out on my birthdays to show how I've grown over the years. I hate that the baby sports a huge smile as she beams reverently at the person who's holding her—Olivia.

My lower lip quivers and tears burn my eyes. I'm too tired for this. I'm too tired and there's no way this is true. It's not. My mother would never lie to me. Never. "My mom left Snowflake when she found out she was pregnant with me."

"Your mother walked out of this house, your home, with you in the dead of night right after your second birthday."

This house? No way. "Your son turned us away. He left us. Both of us. Mom said not one of you wanted me."

"Your entire life is a lie and I'm the only person willing to give you the truth," she says. "And if you want the truth, you're going to have to stay here in Kentucky, because God knows that your parents won't tell you. Even if it'll cost you your life."

Olivia snatches my hand and shoves the picture into my palm, curling my fingers over it. I twist away from her grasp. "This picture doesn't mean anything. Maybe we came back for a visit but we obviously didn't stay."

"It was no visit. You lived here once and your mother stole you from us."

"Olivia?" Cyrus calls again.

She walks past me and this consuming anger causes me to lash out before she leaves me alone. "My mother told me that all of you are crazy. This photo is a fake and you're a liar."

Olivia smirks. "We both know that's wrong, don't we, Emily Star?"

The breath rushes from my body as if I've been socked in the stomach. "That's not my name."

"Yes," she says simply. "It is."

It is...rather it was.

Emily Star is the name on my birth certificate, but when my father adopted me, we changed it to Emily Catherine so that I shared my grandmother's, Dad's mom's, name. "So you know what used to be my middle name. It doesn't prove anything."

"It does, and so does that picture."

"Mom said that the people in Snowflake are the worst kind of evil." Cruel, I know, and there's a pang of hurt and guilt, but what she's doing to me right now is nothing short of agony.

Olivia pauses. Grandmothers are supposed to be maternal. They're supposed to bake cakes and pies and cookies and pat my hand and tell me not to worry. They aren't supposed to use curse words or speak in code or try to break me on one of the worst days of my life.

As she studies me, I one hundred percent understand that she's not the warm fuzzy type. But the way sadness weighs on her face, I discover she's not immune to caustic words.

"I'm not evil," she states.

My skin prickles. Well, she sure as hell isn't nice.

"I'm not," she repeats. Then she sighs. "Either guest bedroom is yours to use. The one on the left belonged to you. You used to lie in your crib and watch the sunrise with a smile on your face."

I shut my eyes. She's lying. Has to be. There's no other explanation for this. The picture is fake. Her words are lies. This entire scenario is me having a psychotic break after she popped out of the casket.

Without saying a word, I stalk past her into the bathroom and lock her out.

OZ

I ENTER THE LIVING ROOM AND THERE'S ONE major player missing: Emily. "Should I be concerned?"

Olivia rests her head against the couch and closes her eyes. "She's in the bathroom. The child has had enough to deal with and needs some time alone."

Because when I want time alone, I think toilets. "She's not a child."

Emily's far from it. That body she has—those curves, the way her hips move when she walks, the way I fantasized about worshipping that flat stomach if we had privacy and she wasn't Eli's daughter—that's no child.

Olivia cracks open an eye, but before she can respond, Cyrus jumps in. "Oz is right. She's not the two-year-old that used to follow you around in your tomato garden."

"If I wanted your opinion, I'd ask for it," Olivia answers. "Both of you."

Mom offers Olivia a hand. "You need to rest. I'll wake you when we hear from Eli."

The strain of the past few hours weighs Olivia down as she accepts. Together, they leave the room. Emily can't get out of here fast enough, in my opinion. Olivia will use the strength she needs to defeat the cancer in order to maintain appearances for Emily.

When the door to Olivia's bedroom shuts, I appraise Cyrus as I shift the chess pieces in my head. The board in front of me is complicated and I don't have many pieces to begin with. "What do you need me to do?"

"Entertain Emily." Cyrus reaches behind the recliner and brings out his double-gauge shotgun. "Didn't think I should keep it in sight with her ready to jump out of her skin."

I chuckle. "Good call. How long has she been in the bathroom?"

"Long enough that someone she trusts should check to see if she slit her wrists."

My head falls back. Screw me for asking. Cyrus focuses on the television, and keeps his gun in his lap. Suddenly the knife hanging on my hip develops an inferiority complex.

"Remember that she's scared," he says.

I flip Cyrus off as I head to check on Emily. Cyrus flips it back. The moment I have a cut on my back, I'm going to have to watch myself with the board members, especially being a prospect. But for now, Cyrus isn't the president of the club to me—he's the man who took care of me for the first few years of my life.

My mother's voice is muffled on the other side of Olivia's door. Not a good sign. Olivia has to be weaker than I thought to let my mother help her into bed. My neck tightens. Emily's going to kill Olivia if she stays much longer.

I tap on the bathroom door and when there's no response, I knock again. Still nothing. Damn, she probably has slit her wrists.

The voices from the other side of Olivia's door go quiet. The last thing I want is Olivia barging out of her bedroom and taking over again. She needs sleep, not to be babysitting Emily. I brought this trouble into her home and I can handle it for a few more hours.

I try the knob and it doesn't budge. Grabbing the skeleton key we store on top of the door frame in case Olivia passes out in the bathroom, I wiggle it around in the small hole until I hear the click of the lock giving. I'm slow opening the door, in case Emily is lost in her thoughts on the toilet.

Each push of the door is methodic and gradual. Empty floor. Closed toilet. Curtains blowing in the breeze and a wide-open window. My fingers curl until they form a fist. I'm going to wring Emily's tiny, delicate, hot little neck.

Emily

WITH MY KNEES PULLED TO MY CHEST, I SIT ON A
wooden bench that rests below a darkened window of the
house. According to Olivia, the room belonged to me, which
doesn't make sense on multiple levels. The impulse is to peer
into the room to see if the answers I'm searching for are in
there, but I don't. I keep my back to the house and my eyes
locked on the approaching sunrise.

I've been awake for over twenty-four hours and my brain
has disconnected from my emotions. I feel stretched and
numb. Cold and hot. Wired and exhausted. I sort of welcome it. I'm officially too tired for fear.

Oz was right earlier. I definitely was sucked into a storm
and I'm desperately trying to grab on to anything solid to prevent myself from plummeting into the vortex of the tornado.

There's a moan in the wooden window frame a few feet
down and out pops a jean-clad leg. It's the same black boot
that monopolized my space at the funeral home. Oz slides out

of the house with more elegance than me. I ended up on my butt. He lands on both feet. Even with all that muscle, he's graceful like a cat. Goody for him.

His eyes dart around and he does a double take when he spots me on the bench. He scans the yard and thick surrounding woods, then he strides over as if climbing out a bathroom window is normal. "And they say people from Kentucky are backward. We have a front door and one in the kitchen, or do you think you're too good for either one?"

"Would they have let me out?"

"Onto the porch."

"Sure they would have—with an armed guard."

"Not armed guard—escort," he corrects as he stands in front of me. "And if you had made a break for it, I would have had to tackle you and then we'd be in all sorts of trouble. Could you imagine me putting my hands on your body?"

He winks.

Winks.

Heat rushes up my neck and my earlobes burn.

"I…" Clear my throat so I can at least pretend that comment didn't slip under my skin. "I have no idea what you're suggesting."

"Yeah, you do. Since you arrived at the funeral home, I've been looking at you and you've been looking at me. Too bad you didn't go out the front door. Would have been fun, don't you think? Me tackling you. Us rolling around. Tell me, Emily, are you the type of girl that doesn't mind a good time?"

His strong body over mine. My hands messing through his hair. His hands touching my face. Holy hell, my nerve endings tingle.

The right side of his mouth tips up as if he can read my thoughts and his eyes wash over me like a lingering waterfall. That's when it hits me, he's playing a game with me. "You're full of yourself."

"Might be, but I'm not wrong, plus for thirty seconds you weren't having a pity party. So what happened with your escape plans? Did your momma tell you that you can't cross the street without holding her hand?"

I throw him a mock smirk, but oh how I wish there was a road to cross and that was my problem. Instead, there's woods. Lots of woods plus lots of darkness. Woods and darkness terrify me. Bad things live in the woods. Evil things exist in the dark. The inside of that cabin didn't feel any safer so I opted for the bench with the glow of the lights from the utility pole near the house.

For some, hell might be being buried alive in a coffin. For others, hell would be being covered to their heads in a tank full of spiders. For me, it's this. Encircled and enshrouded by claustrophobic darkness and foreboding woods. Dead things lie in wait in that black void.

In that house, a woman is battling death and also promising to tear apart the foundation on which I stand. Inside isn't an option. Neither is out. I'm here on this bench because I didn't know where else to go.

Oz assesses me. The same way my parents used to for weeks after they found me in that hole at eight. "You suck at running away. I found you in less than ten seconds."

"Are you going to continue to rub it in that I failed?"

"I was going to, but that question stole my thunder." Oz eases beside me and I curl into a ball toward the corner. Even with that move, the heat from his thighs wiggles past my jean shorts and caresses my skin. I rub my hand along my cold arms. I'd be lying if I didn't say I crave to crawl up next to him and live in that heat for rest of my life.

He sprawls the massive wingspan of his arms along the back of the bench then extends his long legs, kicking one booted foot on top of the other. His fingers "accidently" swipe across my bare shoulder and it causes a tickle in my bloodstream.

Oz commands awareness like no one I have ever met before. There's no denying his presence. No denying that his body is close to perfect. No denying that since I laid eyes on him I've wondered what he looks like with his shirt off.

Completely impervious to how his nearness affects me, he stares straight ahead and watches the sunrise. "Ever seen one of these before?"

According to Olivia, yes, but I shake my head no. I've been up before dawn, but I've never sat and admired how the stars are chased away by the sun rising on the horizon.

"Me neither," he says. "Mind if I watch it with you?"

"If I say no, will you leave?"

"No." At least he's honest. "But I'm trying to at least make you feel like you have a choice."

"But I don't."

"But you don't," he repeats. "Just a few more hours, Emily, and you can go back to your life and I can go back to mine. We can both pretend we never met."

That's all I want. "You don't like me, do you?"

"You make the people in my life sad and in the brief few hours I've known you, you keep racking up points in the heartache category. So, no, I'm not your biggest fan."

I bite the inside of my lip and focus on my knees. It shouldn't bother me what a punked-out moron thinks of me, but it does.

"Don't look like that," he pushes. "You could have killed me with some of the glares you've sent my way. Are you going to say you like me?"

He has been an ass, but he's also saved me so instead of answering immediately, I look at him. Oz wears a black T-shirt with the word *Conflict* scrawled in some fancy script. His jeans are loose and he sports the same black studded belt from yesterday. His arms are chiseled like he works out often and he keeps a hand near the knife at his side. Oz shifts as if he's uncomfortable.

"I don't know you," I finally answer.

Oz blinks like I said something profound, then returns his gaze to the east and appears to choose to ignore the past few exchanges. "You can go to sleep if you want. The window to that spare bedroom behind you is open. You can crawl in since you have an issue with doors."

"Why were those guys at my motel?"

"The bed, Emily. Do you want it or not?"

Like Cyrus earlier, he's not going to answer. The bed is tempting, but... "No, thank you. I'm going to wait for my parents and then I'll go to sleep."

"They're safe," Oz says, and I choose to believe him because the hollowness that happens inside me at the thought of any other option is too harsh to bear.

"You could be kidnapping me and trying to do that thing where I grow to love my captors. I've seen it on TV before."

"You caught us. We knew you were going to walk out of

the motel at three in the morning and we created this situation to freak you out into loving us. That's how fucked up we are."

"Why were you there?"

"Maybe I was using a room."

I flat-out frown at the thought and I don't understand why. My fingers tap my thigh and the picture in my hand moves. I seriously hate Oz and Olivia, and I shouldn't hate Olivia, because she's dying. "How far along is Olivia's cancer?"

"Too far." His voice is why-the-hell-did-you-bring-that-up clipped and I try to pretend I don't exist.

The chatter of bullfrogs, crickets and the wind. It's what's between us. That and the fact I asked about Olivia's health.

"I promise if you go to sleep, nothing bad will happen to you," Oz offers.

That's where he's wrong. If I go to sleep, I can't stop the worst from occurring. Staying awake is the only way I can chase the nightmares away. I am, like I was for twelve hours when I was eight, left to fend for myself. I shiver with the memory.

A light breeze dances across the yard and the picture Olivia gave me drops to the wooden porch. Oz leans forward faster than me, swipes it up, then pauses. After a second, he hands me the photo and I shove it into my pocket.

"Where'd you get that?" he asks.

"Olivia."

He's silent and he's watching me and I despise the expression that tells me he sees things and knows things he shouldn't. "Don't tell Eli Olivia gave you that."

"Why?"

"How far down this rabbit hole do you want to go?"

I don't want to even be in the same state as the hole. "Can we just watch the sunrise?"

"I mean it," he says. "You've already caused this family a world of hurt. If you tell Eli she gave you this, it'll end badly for Olivia."

Anger wells up inside me to the point I feel like a volcano. Olivia, Olivia, Olivia. I am so sick of him mentioning Olivia. "Well, I guess your precious Olivia is safe because besides having this picture I don't know anything!"

"Good," he snaps.

"Good," I shout back.

"Great!"

"Can we watch the freaking sunrise?" I seethe.

"That we can do."

A rumble of engines from the road and my heart kicks into high gear. Thank God, this is over. I jump to my feet and race to the front steps. Six motorcycles growl into the clearing. All the riders appear the same: big men wearing black leather Reign of Terror vests.

Four of them break from the pack and head to an overly large garage on the other side of the yard. The other two park along the edge of the driveway. With their backs to the light, their faces are blacked out by shadow.

My fingers twist and untwist together as I strain to hear another engine—a more familiar one, one belonging to a car, but as each bike shuts down, I experience a loneliness in the silence.

There's movement near me and sound…but not the sound I long to hear. The clink of men swinging off their bikes. Oz's boots thumping on the wood to be closer to me. The squeak of the door opening behind me. Even the coolness of the morning tries to steal my attention from the road, but I won't look away. They're coming for me. My parents are coming for me.

"I thought you'd be asleep," Eli says at the bottom of the stairs.

"I'm not." A cloud moves and a ray of dull early-morning light strikes the road. No car. No hum of a smooth engine. No crackle of rocks under a tire. "How far behind are my mom and dad?"

Eli walks up the stairs and puts a firm hand on my arm. "They're not coming, Emily."

My words haunt me: *You could be kidnapping me...* Eli's still talking. At least I believe he is, but all I hear is a low-pitched roar. *They're not coming. They're not coming...*

I spin, because if I do, then I'll see something else. Hear something else. But I only see Oz. He lowers his head so that his hair hides his eyes. The roar is replaced by a high-pitched ringing and it grows louder and louder, drowning everything out. Almost everything. I can clearly hear the scream inside my head.

I spin again, but then think oddly how my feet didn't move and how they are perfectly cemented to the ground and yet the world is twirling.

Twirling.

The last stars in the sky are twirling.

Heat creeps along my hairline while a cold clamminess claims my neck.

"Emily?" Eli's voice breaks through the chaos. "Emily, are you okay?"

For a second, I'm weightless. Like if I was to stand on my tiptoes I could lift into the air and fly, but then a sharp tilt causes the wooden floor to rush toward my face.

The world goes dark.

OZ

WIND BLOWS IN FROM THE NORTH AND A FEW pieces of Emily's dark hair sweep across her face. One minute Emily's a bright flame, then a gust snuffs out her light. Her body sways like a top at the tail end of a spin and I lunge forward.

Emily's knees give out and her eyes roll back into her head. I catch her inches before she crashes onto the porch. She's light as I swing her into my arms and her head circles onto my shoulder, reminding me of one of those rag dolls Violet used to play with when we were kids.

"Emily!" Eli's on top of me, attempting to yank her out of my arms. "Open your eyes."

Her eyelids flutter, but remain closed as her hand limply clutches my shirt. Eli rams his arms underneath mine and he makes Emily a rope in a tug-of-war. I should let her go. I should want to let her go, but then Emily goes and screws it up for me. "Oz."

It was a damn whisper, but I heard my name on her lips and so did Eli. His eyes flash to mine and Cyrus's words repeat in my mind. *That girl trusts you.* And screw us both for that.

"She's exhausted," I say. "Hasn't slept at all tonight."

Eli's expression hardens as he glares at me. I've seen Eli throw a coma-inducing punch for less defiance and I readjust the sleeping girl in my arms. A reminder if he decks me now, he'll be putting his daughter at risk.

Temporarily surrendering, Eli cups Emily's face in his hands and angles her toward him. "Emily, please open your eyes."

She does. It's barely a crack and they're completely glazed.

"Everything's going to be okay," Eli affirms.

"I want my mom and dad," she mumbles.

"You'll see them tomorrow." Eli pushes a strand of hair from her cheek. "You're safe here. I promise."

She rejects Eli by curling into me. Her head fits perfectly in the crook of my neck and I loathe the wave of protectiveness that rumbles through my body. Emily's fingers tighten their grip near my shoulders and the impulse is to shield her from the guys gawking at this intimate scene. Yeah, this is club business, but Emily never asked for any of this.

Cyrus opens the door and I move past Eli. He's hot on my heels. So close, his breath hits the back of my neck. Mom steps out of the kitchen and is down the hallway before me. She waves for me to enter the spare bedroom.

It's the bedroom no one ever uses. First it belonged to Eli's brother and then he died. Most can get over that, but people will crash on the couch and hardwood floor before sleeping in the bedroom that Emily and her mother once claimed. The purple room with white bedding is cursed. No one wants anything to do with a traitor.

I lay Emily on the bed. Her arms fall over her head and her dark hair fans out on the pillow. Her eyes are shut and her breaths come out in a deep rhythmic pattern. I ease back as Eli spreads a blanket over Emily and removes the shoes from her feet, dropping each one to the floor.

Emily's hand drifts to the edge of the bed and her fingers splay open. The picture Olivia gave her floats to the floor like a feather in the breeze. My heart pounds hard once. I go to retrieve it, but Mom snatches it with death written over her face. Her eyes meet mine and we stare at each other as if we're looking down the business end of a rifle.

If Eli found that picture in Emily's possession, he would have spiraled into dangerous quick.

"Where'd she get this?" Mom mouths.

I tilt my head toward Olivia's bedroom and her eyes slam shut. As Eli straightens, Mom shoves the picture in her jeans pocket then spins on her heel and touches Eli's arm to gain his attention. "Would you like me to stay with Emily?"

Eli draws a hand over his face and walks over to the window seat. He sags onto it and appears to age ten years.

Since Eli entered my life at eleven, he's always been badass. All the stories I had been told before he returned to Snowflake made him larger than life. In reality, Eli is larger than life. Over six feet tall. Broad-shouldered. The Reign of Terror's black leather cut strong on his back. I've seen him easily kick the shit out of any man stupid enough to stand in his way.

"Tell Cyrus I'll update him soon, but I need to be in here,"

Eli says. "Emily will need some things. Clothes, personal stuff. A burner phone. Can you handle that for me?"

"Of course," Mom answers, and I don't miss how she keeps a hand pressed over the pocket containing the picture. "Let's go, Oz."

I go to leave, but Eli stops me. "Tell me you didn't fall asleep on lookout."

I shove my hands in my pockets and point-blank meet his glare. Eli shakes his head in disgust. "We'll deal with this in Church later. Cyrus says that Emily trusts you."

If Eli believes it to be true and it works me back into his good graces then I'll take it. "She hasn't run away from me yet." At least not far enough that I couldn't catch her.

"We'll be leaving here around three. Get some sleep. If she trusts you then I want you riding with us when we meet with her parents. You better wow me if you want to make prospect."

I nod to him then glance at Emily as I leave. Amazing how someone so innocent and beautiful can wreak so much havoc.

Mom shuts the door behind us and leans into me like a rabid animal. "Did you know Emily had the picture? Did she bring it with her? Tell me that nod of your head did not mean that Olivia gave it to her."

From the living room, Cyrus pokes his head around the corner and we stay silent until he resumes whatever he was doing. I keep my tone down when I answer Mom. "Olivia did give it to her. I told Emily not to tell Eli."

Mom rams her fingers through her hair. "Eli will go ballistic if he finds out. You need to stay away from Emily."

I chuckle. "I'm not stupid enough to hook up with Eli's daughter."

"Ew." Her face crinkles. "Emily's practically family to us."

No, she's not. She's an outsider causing problems.

"But that's not what I mean," she says. "There's a lot of old unmapped land mines surrounding her and I don't want you to end up collateral damage."

"I can take care of myself."

Mom does that sad smile that she gave to me time and time again when I was younger after I came in bruised and bleeding from whatever trouble I had found. She touches my cheek. "That's what I'm scared of. You know your father and I are here if you need us."

"Yeah," I answer.

Mom presses, "I mean it. If you need anything—"

A ring of a bell cuts her off and both of us turn our heads to Olivia's room. We bought her that bell after her initial chemo treatment so she could call us in. She threw it at Cyrus and told him to shove the bell up his ass. She hates acting like a victim. "I hear the grumble of your voice, Oz. Get in here and give me answers."

"She needs sleep." Mom wavers on her feet and I despise the circles under her eyes. "But she won't settle down until she finds out what's going on with Emily."

"I'll take care of her." I hold my hand out. "And I'll get the picture back to her."

Mom digs the photo out and gives it to me. "This isn't the life I wanted for you. I had hoped you'd choose something different."

Something within me shifts and my forehead furrows.

What the hell? Mom collapses against the wall and scrubs her face with her hands. A pang of worry ricochets through me. There probably isn't a person in this house who has slept in days. Because of that, I let her comment go. College Mom mentions, but walking away from Snowflake and the club—never. Exhaustion is causing everyone to talk nonsense.

I wrap an arm around my mother and pull her into me. She hugs me back and I kiss the top of her head. "Get some sleep."

"Promise me you'll sleep, as well."

"Sure." Whenever I can.

"Izzy?" Dad stands at the end of the hallway in the living room. He surveys both of us and I hide the picture from view. If I had a patch on my back, I'd be required to tell Eli what Olivia divulged to Emily. For once, I'm happy I'm not currently under that obligation.

"You ready to go home?" he asks Mom.

Mom sends me that sad smile again before seeking the shelter of my father's body.

"You gonna man up tomorrow about falling asleep on the job?" my father asks as he hugs Mom.

"Yeah," I answer, then jack my thumb in the opposite direction of him. "I'm going to sit with Olivia."

He nods his approval and I leave my parents behind as I head into the room of the one person I can't imagine living without.

Emily

I SUCK IN A LARGE INTAKE OF AIR AND ROLL TO my side. On instinct, I reach for James, but then remember that he's not in my bed anymore. I banished the pink elephant that I slept with for years to my dresser back in middle school. It was my way of breaking a bad habit, but for some reason, I still wake up searching.

My entire body except for my brain is zoned out. My muscles are warm and heavy and I must have swum too much with Dad then had a long run with Trisha… My eyes snap open… I'm not home and I've been separated from my mom and dad.

A puff of air to my face and there are two large dark eyes. Adrenaline shakes through me, my mouth gapes and a scream ravages my throat, but no sound escapes. I scramble back as the eyes inch closer. I push away. Kick at covers, but I become ensnarled and entangled. The eyes lunge forward and then they…lick?

Hot, sticky wetness across my face, on my cheeks, in my

hair. Ugh. The smell of wet dog engulfs me. My hand grabs the muzzle of the beast in my bed and I nudge it away, but the drool monster keeps returning.

"Get down, Lars." Eli rakes a hand over his short hair as he sits up on the long window seat. A pillow crease streaks across his cheek and he has the groggy appearance that accompanies just being woken. Eli wears the same white T-shirt as last night, the same pair of jeans and his leather vest hangs on the post of the bed.

I shake my head and rub my eyes. Sleeping Beauty must have been seriously disoriented after she woke up, but then she slept for years and me—I've obviously only slept an hour or so. "What time is it?"

"Too early to be awake," Eli answers. "Go back to sleep, Emily. Your mom mentioned you don't like the dark, woods or the unfamiliar so she said Olivia's would make you uncomfortable. I'll stay up if it'll make you feel better."

A pang of hurt shoots through me that she'd tell Eli, or anyone, my fear.

Another huff of warm air on my arm and the basset hound blinks at me before easing onto its hind legs to sit—while still on the bed. Nice to see it listened to Eli's earlier command. Lars opens his mouth to allow his overly large pink tongue to spill out the side. He pants bad dog breath and looks at me like he's smirking.

I detest dogs.

I wipe the slobber off my face then choke down the dry heave. Thick drool clings from finger to finger. Bad form to now deposit the slime anywhere else. Eli stands, pulls a white handkerchief out of his pocket and offers it to me. "Here."

I accept the folded white square and take my time drying off my hand. According to the clock on the dresser it's six in the morning and it's too early to be attacked by drool. "When can I talk to Mom and Dad?"

"Soon," Eli says. "They've moved locations. Once you get some sleep, I'll take you to them."

"Take me to them now."

"You'll see them in a few hours. Chill and go back to sleep."

"Yay for your plans. Take me to them now." I stare straight at Eli and he stares straight back at me. My biological father should scare the hell out of me with his glowering, but I'm too tired to be smart enough to worry. People obviously don't talk back to him. My instincts must be right that he doesn't have any other children. Or at least not ones he interacts with.

There's a hard set to his jaw when he yanks his cell out of his back pocket and tosses it onto the bed. "They're worried. I told them you had a rough night and were asleep. You're so tired you passed out. You should be sleeping, not talking on the phone."

I take his cell and scroll through the list of text messages already appearing on the screen. A grin attempts to pull at my lips. My mother is going absolutely ballistic. Not that I enjoy her panic, but it's nice to see something familiar. The text conversations between my parents and Eli confirm it: I really wasn't kidnapped.

I swing his phone back and forth. "Can I?"

"Contact them? It'd calm your mom down." Eli relaxes back on the window seat and that stupid sloppy smile that I stupidly love crosses his face. "The past twenty-four hours have been so messed up that I haven't had a chance to tell you how happy I am to see you. Because of Mom's condition, I wasn't sure when I was going to make it to Florida for a visit."

My heart plummets and I focus on the texts even though I stopped reading. The expectant hope on Eli's face cuts right through me. God, I'm an awful person and I don't want to be an awful person. Eli's a good guy and he has no idea how much I dread his annual visit to Florida.

When I was ten, I made a horrible mistake. One I continually pay for. A mistake that has brought heartache to my mother and a ton of continual hurt for me. I asked if I could see a picture of Eli because...because...I was curious.

Until then, Eli was a figment of my imagination. He was this floating nonexistent guy who had spared a few minutes of his life to create me. Thanks to a school report on family trees that included pictures, the eyelid-flipping boy I had hated since kindergarten pointed out that I resembled no one in my family. Not Dad's parents, not my mother and definitely not my father.

I called the boy a jerk. He called me a brat. We were both called into the principal's office. My parents were also summoned and in the middle of the parent-principal powwow, I asked if I resembled Eli.

My one question snowballed into a slew of arguments between my parents, a whole lot of tears from Mom, and it avalanched into a day at McDonald's PlayPlace with this freaky-looking guy with tattoos and holes in his earlobes. He crouched in front of me with a sprig of daisies in his hand and introduced himself as my dad.

I've never been slapped before, but that's as close to the pain as I could imagine. I curled myself around my father and he had to repeatedly pry me off him like dried-on glue. Since then, Eli, my father and I have been playing this game of once-yearly awkward visits because I was curious.

Curiosity is highly overrated.

Pushing reply, I text my mother:

It's me. Just woke up with a dog next to me. Eli's here. Glad to know you're safe. I love you. Tell Dad I love him too. What's going on?

Mom's response is immediate. The cell buzzing every couple of seconds as she sends a flurry of texts:

We both love you very much. A dog? Please tell me they at least let you have a bed in the house. If you are in the clubhouse, tell Eli I'll castrate him. Did Eli explain?

Not one explanation. Will demand one now.

"Mom threatened you with castration. Besides that, would you mind filling me in on what's happening?"

Eli chuckles then pulls on his earlobe.

"She's serious," I say.

He chuckles more. "I know she is."

I can't stop gawking at his ears. I don't understand plugs. It's holes in your ears.

In your ears.

Holes.

Like stick-your-finger-through-them holes.

That will never close up.

I drag my eyes away and focus on the dog that currently has a sticky line of drool hanging from its mouth.

"You know the business I own?" Eli asks.

I should say yes because that would imply I know Eli, but the truth is I don't know much about him or his business. "No."

Eli's expression falls as if my answer disappointed him. Dad asked me once if I ever told anyone I was adopted or that my biological father was part of a motorcycle gang. I told him no. He asked if I was embarrassed by either and I gave him the truth: Dad was my dad, Eli was Eli and the most I ever felt about Eli was ambivalence.

I've never told any of my friends about Eli, not even Trisha, and she's the type of friend you can tell anything—the type that doesn't judge me for being scared of the dark or adopted.

"I'm part owner of a security company," Eli explains. "There's a ton of different aspects to the job, but the one that concerns you involves a company we do business with in northern Kentucky. We escort their most expensive semi-loads to make sure they aren't hijacked on the road."

He pauses. I make eye contact long enough to confirm I'm listening. Eli continues. "It's in a territory that another motorcycle club claims and they aren't happy that we've been running in their area without their permission."

"What do you mean 'claim'?" I ask.

"Think of it in terms of invisible boundary lines. Some clubs claim certain areas as theirs. We don't do that, but this other club, they do, and they expect other motorcycle clubs to ask for permission to ride their bikes through the area they consider theirs."

He gives me a second to digest and I'm not sure there's enough time in the world to comprehend this insanity. "They've been trying to sabotage us. Hitting us on the road with the business and our club, but we've taken whatever they dish out so they've changed tactics."

"Hitting? Like they've been attacking you?" Panic starts to crazily grow inside me.

Eli waves his hand like my questions are the type to be easily dismissed. "It's a part of our life but I promise none of this will touch you."

Not liking where this is headed, I tuck my legs underneath me. "What does this have to do with me?"

"You're my daughter."

"And?"

"They decided that since they couldn't get what they wanted through hurting the business or the club, they're going after my family."

"You have a ton of other family." Not that I'm wishing a mean motorcycle club would stalk Olivia or Izzy, but I'm in favor of them not chasing me.

"Yes, but I only have one child. One they didn't know existed until yesterday. They must have had someone at the wake willing to give them information on me and word spread rather quickly that I had a daughter and that she showed."

"Has someone explained to them that the only connection between us is genes? You know…that you didn't want me… and…you gave me up?"

Eli goes still—like a rock—and the dog beside me whines. As if this wasn't awkward enough, I also have a dog willing to do sound effects in Eli's favor. Wasn't this mutt supposed to hop off the bed? *He left me and Mom, Lars, not the other way around. You're rooting for the wrong team.*

"They know," he answers. "But it doesn't matter to them."

"If they just found out I exist, then how do they know all of this about me and you?"

Eli merely looks at me as if I never asked a question and I rub my temples as my head begins this slow pound. "Have you at least called the police?"

"And tell them what? That there were people outside your motel room? People who never made contact with you?"

Touché. "If that's the case, maybe you're overreacting. Maybe those guys were there to sleep because that's what normal people do at motels. And let's say that isn't true. Why not just ask these guys for permission to drive through their area?"

Eli looks me over. Not exactly in a disapproving way, but as if he's realizing that he has no idea who I am...which he doesn't. "Why should we have to ask anyone for permission to drive our bikes on a road? This is America. Constitution gives us the right to roam free. Over half of our members are veterans who've fought overseas. Do you think men who have been shot at for this country should be asking anyone's permission to walk down the street?"

Okay, stumbled into a live gun range there. "So we're back to maybe you guys were overreacting."

"Being part of a motorcycle club is a different life—whether you're a legit club like ours or an illegal club like theirs. You're going to have to trust me on this and if you can't, then know that your mom and Jeff agree with how I'm handling this."

"What do you mean by illegal club?"

Eli crosses his arms over his chest. "Complete outlaws with

no regard for society's rules. Yeah, we have our own code and our own rules, but we don't make money by working something illegal."

I concentrate on my nails and pretend I'm infatuated with the pink paint. The way Eli described the illegal club is exactly how Mom described Eli and his club, but I choose not to bring that up. As far as I'm concerned, they sound similar. "Are my parents safe?"

"Yes. Just like you are."

"Can you fix this?"

"I can fix this."

Nausea rolls through me. He's not exactly being forthcoming. "How?"

"That isn't your concern."

I straighten. "Yeah, it is."

"No, it's not." A wave of annoyance rumbles off Eli and I'm finally smart enough to shrink back. "I said I'll take care of it and I will."

Lars sighs again with a whine, but this time he moves closer so that his head is on my knee. My hand finds his body without thought and I pet him because *I* need the comfort.

"Listen," Eli continues. "I know you're scared, but I swear to you, you're safe. You have an army of men willing to lay down their lives for you. Fort Knox would be envious."

I don't want an army of men. I want my dad. Images pour into my mind of Oz grabbing me. The dark, serious set of his face as he hid me from view. My blood pumps faster as I remember the sound of the bottle rolling. Of how it had grown closer and closer… "What would have happened if Oz wasn't there?"

"What?"

"I went to get something to drink. Oz yanked me into a corner and guarded me. I mean—" my eyes dart in front of me as I watch the memory play in my mind "—he pulled out a knife and he told me to stay put while he made sure it was okay for us to leave. If Oz wasn't there, what would have happened? How dangerous are these people?" The reality of everything Eli is saying is sinking in. "Are you like those TV shows? Do people die around you? Oh my God, do you kill people?"

"No, Emily. Listen, you're safe…"

And he keeps talking, but I can't listen because the fear inside me is becoming a monster and I slide my feet off the bed until they hit the floor. The walls are closing in and so is the ceiling and it's hard to draw in air. "I need to go. Like now. Right now. Aren't there witness protection programs or something?"

Except I didn't witness anything to be protected from and they won't save me and this terrible pain happens when I breathe and… "I need to go home. Take me home."

"Emily!" Eli shouts.

I quake with my name and freeze in the middle of the room. He releases a long breath and crosses the room to me. Eli settles both of his hands on my shoulders and lowers himself to meet my eyes. "You watch too much TV."

"But you said—"

"I said you're safe. Your mom, Jeff and I—we are overreacting to this. Plain and simple. When it comes to your safety, none of us will mess around."

This little voice in my mind whispers that this is too simple. Too easy. But the rational part says that he's right. That stuff is only on TV. Gangsters and murderers and anything else are not real life. This is real life and in real life people don't behave like thugs.

I inhale then nod my head to my internal thoughts. Yes, this is business negotiations and Eli is being overprotective because my mom is being overdramatic.

Eli stands there looking mean and tough because that's what he is with those stars tattooed up his arm and a skull on his bicep. Anger and wrath and vengeance ooze off him just from existing, but his eyes soften to the point of pleading.

I shift my footing. "What happens now?"

"We're going to take things one step at a time. First you get some sleep and then we'll meet up with your parents this afternoon. Okay?"

It sounds like a question, but the way he speaks reminds me of my earlier conversation with Oz. Eli wants to create the illusion that I have a choice, but everything has already been decided. Even if I stomped my foot and demanded that we leave now it would be fruitless, so I give in. "Okay."

He smiles and it's a brilliant smile. It's that darn one that he flashes whenever he sees me and it's the one I hate because it causes me to smile in return. Like how I am now.

Eli draws me into a hug and repeats my answer. "Okay."

OZ

A SOFT LIGHT FILLS THE ROOM THANKS TO OLIVIA'S prized Tiffany lamp on her bedside table. As a child, I used to be mesmerized by the mosaic blue-and-green-colored glass and forget my nightmares. Too bad I can't lose myself in that lamp now and block out Olivia's cancer.

The only air-conditioning unit in the house is wedged in the window of her room, but it hasn't been turned on since last summer. Her treatments make her cold.

Olivia lies in the bed wrapped in a comforter even though it's warm. I grab the blanket at the end of the bed and spread it over her. She rolls her head against the pillow to study me. The black circles under her eyes resemble bruises. What she should be doing is resting, not worrying about the prodigal child.

"Tell me what's going on," she demands.

"Eli's with Emily. She'll be resting here this morning and

then she and Eli will be meeting with her parents later this afternoon."

"I want someone to wake me the moment she's up."

I'm already shaking my head. "You need to rest. Not to be worrying over some spoiled brat. Plus—"

"Don't remember asking for your opinion," she cuts me off. "Last I checked this is still my house and I'm still alive."

I plop into the chair beside the bed, stretch out my legs and toss the picture onto her stomach. "Lose something?"

"You don't wear smug well." Olivia picks up the picture, opens her Bible on her nightstand and slips it inside it. "It doesn't work well with cocky bastard."

"Nice to know you care, but on the serious side, Mom's bent over finding this picture near Emily. Mind telling me why?"

"Did Eli see it?" she presses.

"Nope. Mom saved your ass. I also covered for you when Emily asked about it. Now that I'm involved let's play a round of show-and-tell."

"As I said, smug doesn't become you." Olivia fixates on the blanket and the shadows in the room threaten to consume us. She stares blankly, like she's observing something that I can't. Another time. Another place. I hate it. Mom once mentioned that maybe she's seeing heaven. For me, that gaze sends me to hell.

Could be exhaustion. She could be lost in her own mind. According to the doctor, it's probably a mini-seizure. All part of the progression of her illness. The doctor said it as if this is some grand design by God. Olivia has had a few of these episodes lately. Too many for my taste. I fold my arms over my chest, trying not to let it bother me, but it does. It slays me.

A lump develops in my throat and I begin to count. On two, Olivia blinks back to life. "Don't tell Eli I gave Emily the picture."

She continues our conversation, pretending her mind didn't temporarily vacate the room, or maybe she isn't aware the episode happened. But it did happen and it's hard as hell to keep the anger simmering within me from seeping out in my tone. "What's my real name?"

"I'm not an invalid."

I overpronounce the words. "My name."

"Jonathan." No slurring and she's correct.

Guess to check for a stroke, the doctor said we should ask her several questions after we witness that vacant stare, but I value my life so I stick with the one. "You should be asleep."

"Sleep is a luxury I can no longer afford."

A pit forms in my stomach and I can't stand how my soul free-falls within it. She's too damn accepting of what doesn't have to be. "This round worked. I can feel it."

"That's one of the things I like about you. You're optimistic." Olivia removes the scarf from her head and I have to fight not to look away. Her bald head kicks me in the gut, but it's the horseshoe scar near her ear that rams me straight in the nuts.

I say nothing in response because I don't feel optimistic. I feel like my world is unraveling. We've received bad news before and Olivia always found a way to survive, but this round has a foreboding sensation. I lean forward and push the thoughts away. I loathe the emptiness they create. "Do you want something to eat? Drink?"

Her eyes are closed. Olivia does this now, can drift easily into sleep. When she's sick, we take turns watching over her. I'm a night owl by nature and prefer the later shifts. Cyrus, Eli and I are the only ones who can stay awake in the silent darkness for hours, waiting for the moment Olivia should need one of us.

My fingers weave together and my head automatically drops. *Please, God. Please let her live.* The drapes near the open windows move with a gentle breeze. If that's a response, I don't know what it means.

"I want to sit on the porch," she says.

I glance out the door to her room. Cyrus is on guard and he worries over Olivia enough. I could ask Eli or call my own dad for permission to take Olivia out of the house...

"When did you take to disobeying me?" she says with a hint of attitude.

My mouth twitches sarcastically. "When have you known me to listen?"

Her laughter is weak, but existent. "Do as I say."

Olivia hates being dependent and I hate having to say the following: "I'm going to have to carry you." Because with the toll this day has had on her body and mine, I don't trust her to walk or trust myself to catch her if she stumbles.

"Fine."

I lift her blanket-encased body from the bed. Olivia should weigh more, but the cancer has ravaged her. I ease out the screen door to her room, careful to keep it from slamming shut, and step onto the back portion of the wraparound porch.

I walk until I reach her favorite spot: the porch swing. That's where she prefers to sit, but there's no way she can support herself. Instead, I tuck her into the Adirondack chair Cyrus built for her last summer. Her head collapses back against the chair and she scans the yard. The dim light in the east casts a glow onto the drive that leads to town, the large garage that doubles as the clubhouse, and the woods surrounding the house. This porch is her favorite spot on earth.

I settle onto the swing beside her. She may not be able to sit in it, but the creaking sound of the swing brings her peace.

"Have you considered going to school in the fall?" Olivia asks.

It's her dream for someone in her family to go to college. Not one of her children made it. Hell, Eli dropped out of high school. Though I'm not blood-related, I'm one of Olivia's. "No."

"Why not? You're smart and have potential. You can still be a part of the club. Distance doesn't mean anything, not when it involves family."

"What's wrong with the family business?"

"Nothing," she says with a sigh. "But they do what they do because their options were limited, especially at the time. Your options are not limited."

"Next topic."

"You think you can push everyone away, but not me. You can't shut me out."

Then I'll change the subject. "Stone said Violet took on babysitting to make money."

The mention of the daughter of a club member who died

causes Olivia to grow reflective. Violet is a sore spot for Olivia and the club.

"Nice try," she says slowly. "Bringing up Violet thinking it'll blow me off course, but hear me—not working. Go to college. See what the world has to offer."

"I can throw a knife straight. Does that mean I should join the circus?" Ridiculous, yes, but so is this conversation.

"Yes, if that's what you want."

"Joining the business with Dad and Eli is what I want."

"How do you know?" Olivia raises her voice like she did with Eli when it came to Emily. "The only reason you want the business is because it's all you've known."

"Not true."

"Oz—"

"Not true," I say in a clipped manner that ends the conversation. Guilt twists my gut. Snapping at people is my norm, but I've minded my manners with Olivia since she got sick. "Can you drop it?" A beat. Then another. The crickets' chirping grows louder. "Please?"

She releases a deep, throaty chuckle. "Oz being polite. I must be dying." Olivia chuckles again. I don't. She then mutters as if in a dream, "You don't like her...you don't like Emily."

No, I don't. "Does it matter?"

"Yes, it does."

I extend one leg on the swing, prop my back against the armrest and ground the other foot so I can make the creaking sound Olivia loves. Her condition has declined sharply since the party and I blame Emily. "I don't see how. Emily's leaving and won't come back."

"I don't know what Eli was thinking at the party," says Olivia in defeat. "Shutting down the building and keeping Emily's adoptive father from entering. All it did was scare the child more. You should have seen her on the phone with her mom. Meg probably told her they were holding him at gunpoint. The poor thing was shaking."

Eli was probably thinking that the moment Jeff found Emily they'd be out the door, and we all wanted the same outcome: for Olivia to be happy. "She's not a child and she decided to leave. And as I said, don't get attached because she's not coming back."

"Then this mess with the Riot." Olivia rubs her temple. "Meg should have known better than to bring her into Kentucky unannounced and believe there wouldn't be repercussions, and Eli should have known better than to send that e-mail to them. As always, the two of them are a mess."

That sparks my attention. "Repercussions meaning what?"

Yeah, Meg's a traitor for leaving, but Eli signed away custody of Emily when she was two and he signed away his parental rights entirely when she was five. The supervised visitations that he's had over the years have been a pity offering.

"I wish Emily would stay." Olivia ignores my question. "I regret not knowing her."

"I don't think you're missing much." Gorgeous? Yes. A pain in the ass? Definitely.

Olivia's chest rises as she pulls in a breath. The sweet scent of the first blooms of honeysuckle hangs in the air and my chest hurts as she smiles. Olivia adores that smell. The happiness fades from her face. "Emily's my blood. How could you hate what is a part of me?"

"She's a rich girl from a big city who doesn't get a thing about Snowflake or the people in it." What Emily did— abandoning a dying woman who craved to spend time with her—was unforgivable. But what should any of us expect from the daughter of a traitor?

"Why should she understand us? Her mother ran when the child was barely two."

My fingers curl around the swing's chain. I have my theories, but I'd like confirmation. "Emily doesn't know that she lived here?"

"No. Eli said that Meg created a new version of her life. Meg told Emily her parents threw her out when they found out she was pregnant and that Eli didn't want either of them. Meg denies that Emily ever lived in Kentucky. When Eli could finally see Emily again, Meg was married and the child was ten. Part of the visitation agreement was for the past to stay buried."

I scratch my knuckles over my jaw. Interesting. Very interesting.

"Besides," Olivia continues with a hint of annoyance, "part of telling Meg's story would mean telling Eli's story and Eli doesn't want the child to know his past."

"You disagree with that?"

"I've never agreed with any of the choices Eli and Meg made. And don't act so high and mighty with your knowledge. There are things even you don't know."

"Like I keep saying, it doesn't matter. Emily's not coming back."

"Don't be too sure about that. Trouble has always followed

that child, whether she knows it or not. I have a feeling we'll be seeing her again."

"What does that mean?" A wave of tension ripples through me. So does an annoying twinge of protectiveness. The way Emily held on to me tonight...she was defenseless. That's the reason for this confusing reaction. "The Riot going after Emily has to do with club business. Not Emily being...Emily."

Olivia remains unusually quiet.

"I'm right on this," I add.

"I hope you are, Oz. You have no idea how much I hope you are."

The whine-creak of the porch swing creates a soothing effect that silences us both. There're secrets involving Eli and Meg. We are all aware of that. Secrets that have been buried deep and if something's been hidden that well, it's typically the type of news that can kill.

"I'd love a cigarette," she says.

I'm sure she would. "You were allowed one pack at the wake."

"Ingrate," she mutters. I maintain the constant rhythm of the swing. It's after six in the morning and the hypnotic creaking is starting to put me to sleep.

Olivia's breaths become consistent and when her eyes dart behind her lids, I pick her up, carry her inside and tuck her into bed. A huge shadow floats in from the hallway.

"The club is guarding the property," says Cyrus. "I need to sit with her."

I touch Olivia's hand in a goodbye then head for the door. Can't argue when a man wants to tend to his wife.

Emily

OLIVIA WAS ASLEEP WHEN WE LEFT AND I GUESS that's good, even though a heavy weight sloshes in my stomach. I had no idea what to say to her and I probably wouldn't have wanted to know what she had to say to me.

I gather my hair in a ponytail at the base of my neck, but, thanks to the wind ripping through the rolled-down window, wayward strands break loose. Eli's in the driver's side of what turns out is his truck. He props his arm on the open window and lightly grips the roof. His other hand steers.

Sweat forms along my hairline and I stick to the pleather seat. We've been riding along back roads, blowing past cornfields and forests, for an hour. There are two motorcycles in front of us and three behind. Passing cars reduce their speed so they can gawk at the procession.

"Did you go to junior prom?" Question number fifty-four from Eli's endless reserve.

"Yep." My eyes flicker to the passenger-side mirror. Oz

is on one of the bikes trailing us. As the group of men was getting ready to leave this afternoon, I caught Oz watching me a few times, but each time my gaze fell on him, he glanced away.

I'd be lying if I didn't admit a thrill would run through me when I noticed him staring, which is moronic because he doesn't like me. At all. And stupid me can't stop stupid thinking of stupid him. The latest Oz train of thought: Did he go to his junior prom?

"Who did you go with?" Eli asks.

"Some friends. The guys rented a limo so it was cool."

Eli switches his hands on the wheel. "Are you still in the advanced program at school?"

"Mmm-hmm." Oz weaves so that he reappears in the passenger mirror. He wears a folded black bandanna and his hair blows in the wind. He doesn't wear a helmet. Real smart. A car smashing into him would mean brain damage.

"Was one of those friends you mentioned your prom date?"

That question trips me up and I peer over at the walking, talking gene bank. Junior prom then advanced program and then back to junior prom. "Why the subject shift? Are you concerned a girl who's smart can't have a date to prom? Like all I do is stare at the walls in my room when I'm not scanning Wikipedia for mistakes? If so, you've been watching too many teen movies. Our generation believes in being well-rounded."

A smile plays on his lips while he shakes his head. "Just answer. Did you have a date?"

Yes, and I went to his senior prom. At the end of that night he tried to kiss me and it was comparable to kissing Lars the dog sans the handkerchief. "There was a large group of us. Guys were a part of the group. We had fun."

I didn't directly answer and the way his smile reverses into a frown lets on that he's aware. This is why I hate my annual visits with Eli. He's nice to me and he does what he's doing now: asks a million questions with this hopeful gleam in his eye that I'll answer.

Because I hate hurting people, I'll reply, but only so much because in the end there's this deep, dark voice that whispers, *Why does he care and what right does he have to ask?*

"You don't have your driver's license." Eli returns to one of his previous and safer topics. "How is that possible?"

"Where are we going?" I ask, not even bothering hiding the exasperation.

"Somewhere," he answers. "Why don't you have your license?"

"I don't know how to drive. That's how it's possible."

"Do you want to learn?" he asks.

"Yeah," I hedge, then nibble on my bottom lip. Dad attempted to teach me this past fall, but I accidently pushed the gas when I should have chosen the brake. I creamed a row of bushes in our front yard and totaled the front of Dad's Mercedes. Since then, neither Dad nor I have been eager to resume my lessons. "This past year has been busy. You know, school and stuff."

"Stuff," Eli says, as if he's trying the word for the first time.

"Stuff," I repeat.

His frown deepens and his fingers tap the steering wheel. The cords of muscles in his arms work with the motion and the tattooed stars move. Hmm. Never noticed before that not all the stars are shaded in.

"Do you have a boyfriend?" Eli doesn't look at me like he has with the two million other questions since we left Olivia's.

"Yes," I answer. "We've been together for a month. He's the captain of the football team and he expected sex on our first date. Initially, I said no, but then he was a little grabby and I figured everyone my age is doing it, so I thought why not? I went home and told Mom and she put me on birth control so she's cool when we do it in my bedroom now."

Eli slams on the brakes and my body whips forward against the seat belt then rams back into the seat. The two bikes in front of us U-turn and there's a loud grumble as the three behind us fly to catch up.

Completely red-faced, Eli glares at me with black, soulless eyes. "What did you say?"

"No," I tell him calmly. "I don't have a boyfriend."

Eli blinks and directs his attention to the steering wheel.

One of the bikes pulls up beside us. The name Hook is sewn on the front of his vest. "We okay?"

Eli nods then presses the gas. "Are you shitting me on the boyfriend or on the no boyfriend?"

"I don't have a boyfriend." I don't know why I ran my mouth, but it's annoying how Eli thinks he has the right to ask me absolutely anything he wants and how he expects a response. Year after year he visits Florida and year after year I try my best to play along, but why he craves an inside scoop on my life and why I owe it to him, I don't understand.

He deserted us—me and Mom. In the end, he abandoned me.

Eli flexes his fingers on the wheel. "Don't let any guy treat you like shit, do you hear me, Emily? No one. Any guy pushes you too far or hurts you, you tell me."

I sweep my bangs away from my forehead and when I readjust, my skin audibly peels off the seat. Eli watches me for a reaction and his eyes only glance away to confirm he's still on the road. "Did you hear me?"

I really, really wish Eli would drop this conversation.

"Emily?" he demands.

"Where was this gallantry when Mom cried to you that she was pregnant with me?"

A muscle in his jaw ticks and he visibly tenses. I have a friend whose parents divorced when she was younger. Her dad bowed out for a couple of years and now that he's back in her life, she keeps a tally of how many digs she can get in during their visits. I'm not like that. I don't want to be like that. I'm not proud of hurting Eli, but he doesn't get to act as if he's a good dad in this scenario.

The two motorcycles ahead of us veer right and Eli's posture straightens as we make the same turn. "We're here."

Here would be a warehouse. Literally. Gray metal walls. Brown roof. An entire row of motorcycles parked near the front. More men in black vests stand around except the bottom part of their patch states Lanesville instead of Snowflake. Each man studies the truck as Eli parks.

"There's no end to you guys, is there?" I ask.

"We're in forty states, ten countries and still growing."

"Hmm." Because what else do you say to that?

Eli shuts off the engine. "Your Mom and Jeff will be here soon. I have a few things I need to take care of in the meantime. Hang with Oz and don't stray from him."

In other words, Oz is my chosen "escort" for the afternoon. "Okay."

I crack open my door and Eli stops me. "Hey, Emily."

"Yeah?"

Eli focuses on the keys in his hand and he's completely still. "Follow me and then stick close to Oz." And he leaves the truck, closing the door behind him.

I sigh because, to be honest, a sorry for bailing when Mom and I needed him the most would have been nice.

OZ

I SWING OFF MY BIKE, SHOVE MY KEYS INTO MY pocket and head over to the only guy I'd be willing to call a best friend other than Chevy. The ultra-white three-piece Reign of Terror patch on Razor's cut is what makes him stick out among everyone else. The darker and dirtier the patch, the more honor there is. It means years of wear and tear within the club. Razor patched in a few weeks ago.

Razor's father, Hook, had no stupid rules about him graduating before entering the club. Razor's the same age as me, but because he was held back a grade in elementary school, he just finished his junior year. He's a senior in high school and was voted in before me. It's like salt on a bleeding wound.

Razor hangs back because that's the way the son of a bitch is. He's smart as hell, cunning and is one of those quiet guys that people warn you about.

"What's going on?" I greet him.

Most brothers I walk up to in the club, I'd pat on the arm

and avoid the cut, but I refrain from touching Razor. Done it before and I've been decked both times with his mean cross. He feels sorry as shit after it happens, but he's an unpinned grenade.

He's one of those guys that lives in his own damned head and will watch the internal demons that torment him more than he participates in the living world.

Razor glances over at me with those piercing blue eyes and his lips lift in that sadistic way of his. Girls flock to him with that golden hair and angelic look and now that he's wearing a three-piece patch, they constantly surround him, but underneath that angel facade is the devil lying in wait. "Heard you fell asleep on the job last night."

"Heard you were kicked out of school on the last day for shoving a guy's head into a locker," I retort.

He shrugs. It's not the first time he's been suspended from school. "I saw the guy harassing Stone at lunch. Decided to do some harassing back."

My spine straightens. "Who?"

"Chad Douglas. I don't think he'll mess with Stone again, but we should probably give him a good reminder before school starts that Stone's one of ours."

"Agreed." I roll my neck. I hate Chad Douglas and the rest of his circle. Fucking J.Crew-wearing assholes. They see anyone associated with the Reign of Terror and think thug. Yet they're the ones picking on the weaker links.

"With you graduating and me kicked out half the damned time, we're going to have to send a message over the summer for people to steer clear from Violet and Stone," he says. "Otherwise Chevy and I are going to have a load on our hands."

"Name the time and place and I'll be there. Pure balls to the wall, brother."

The doors to Eli's truck slam shut and Emily stands in the June heat holding her elbows like she's cold. She's statue still as she studies the mass of men swapping handshakes and hugs. Eli ignores everyone as he lops an arm around Emily's shoulder and ushers her inside. As he opens the door for her, he shoots me a glare that screams that I should have already asked how high to jump.

"Shit," I mumble.

Razor slaps his hand hard onto my back. "Have fun babysitting."

I flip him off as I move to follow Eli and what I don't expect is the barricade of black leather cuts slipping in front of me.

"Is there a problem?" I ask.

The sergeant-at-arms for the Lanesville chapter offers an apologetic tilt of his head. He knows me. I know him. His name is Dragon and he's been drunk at my house and Olivia's several times in my life. "Members only inside until this shit is cleared up."

It's like being offered a plate of food and being shoved into a high chair at the kids' table. I could run my mouth, but rules are rules regardless of who I am by blood. Blood doesn't mean shit. Being a member of the brotherhood is what matters and I'm not in. Thanks to Emily, I may never be a part of the greater whole.

Pigpen saunters up beside me. He's in his midtwenties and a wall of solid muscle. Most men wet themselves when he looks in their direction. "Eli wants him in."

Dragon nods and extends his hand to me, palm up. "I need

your weapons." I swear under my breath and Dragon continues, "Club rules. You're not a member so you don't carry."

Silence falls and the stare of the twenty-plus men beats down on me as I relinquish the knife secured to my back. I then lean down, lift the cuff of my jean and unstrap the knife from my leg. Regardless that I surrendered without a fight, they still pat me down. Anger pulses within me. I'm a second-class citizen and will remain one until I get myself into this club.

Pity rolls around in Dragon's eyes as he gestures for me to go in. That rips through me worse than any knife or fist that's been thrown at me over the years.

I step inside the dimly lit building and the entrance T's off into a hallway. I check right, then left and Eli rounds a corner in dangerous mode. "Did you stop and smell some roses while you were out there bullshitting?"

"I'm a hang-around to them."

"And you're going to remain one if you fuck this up. Emily's in the office and she's to remain there even if she hears her parents. I need to talk to them without her. Do you read me?"

Loud and clear. "Which door is the office?"

"Second one on the left. I don't need to mention that if Emily's unhappy, I'm unhappy."

Perfect. "I don't have a weapon."

"If you don't leave the office then that won't be a problem. If you want to be a part of this club, then I suggest spending the next few minutes keeping my daughter safe and happy." Eli turns his back to me and disappears around the bend.

Just a few more hours and I'll get my life back on track. Take care of Emily. Keep her in the office. Tell her a few

NOWHERE BUT HERE   145

jokes. I round the corner and stop dead. Every single time I see Emily she knocks the breath out of my body and that tank top of Violet's she's wearing sure as hell doesn't help. Spaghetti-strapped that cuts into a V-shape.

Whether Emily is aware of it or not, the trim of her white lace bra peeks out and so does a hint of her cleavage. I scrub a hand over my face to prevent myself from ogling, but the image is already burned in my mind.

God, she's beautiful. Tanned skin. Gorgeous legs. Everything about her perfectly shaped and the memory of how warm and soft her skin felt under my touch last night still haunts me.

She's Eli's daughter, Olivia and Cyrus's granddaughter and her continued presence is ruining my future, but damn if my body doesn't react to her being near. Emily stares up at me with those dark brown eyes and while they are as naive as a doe's there's absolutely no innocence in the smile that spreads across her lips.

"Your life," Emily whispers in this slow, seductive slide, "is about to suck."

She's a little late with that threat because it already does, but a sinking sensation suggests that she's going to make things even worse.

Emily

"GET BACK IN THE OFFICE." OZ TOWERS OVER ME as if his mere massive height and thick shoulders would freak me out into complying, but after hearing what Eli said, Oz sort of resembles a kitten with his hair spiked along his arched back.

"And if I don't, what are you going to do?" I probably shouldn't smirk while saying that, but I can't help it. This is too good to pass up. According to Eli, the big bad Oz has to listen to poor defenseless me.

Oz leans down and his powerful gaze hypnotizes me. "Are you begging me to put my hands on you to move you? Because I will. We already established last night that the two of us are three seconds away from tearing each other's clothes off."

My entire body runs hot. "We did not establish anything."

He smiles. It's not happy. It's not mean. It's a promise of a million things I've never experienced and it's the sexiest sight

I've seen in my life. "We established a lot last night and we're going to establish a few more things now. If you don't get back in that office, I will not only put my hands on your body, I will also lift you off the floor, toss you over my shoulder and carry you against me until we're in a room…alone…with a closed door behind us."

My mouth goes dry and yet I'm able to say the words, "You don't tell me what to do."

Oz reaches out and does exactly what he warned he would. His hands land on my hips and I suck in a sharp breath. Strong hands. Warm fingers. And they gently press past my jeans and into my flesh. A tug on my belt loops and in a swift motion, Oz drags me into him so that my body is flush with his. Heat curls along my skin and I have to fight from shutting my eyes with the sweet thrill.

The scent of burning embers overwhelms my senses. His thumb sneaks above the hem of my tank and I shiver with the swipe against my bare skin.

"Next step is to pick you up, Emily. Your body sliding against mine and when that happens I'm seriously going to want to kiss you. Is that what you want?"

Yes.

I blink.

No.

Definitely no.

With a half-numb brain, I shift back and Oz releases his grip. He inclines his head to the office and I half walk, half stumble into it. When I'm in, I slump into a chair.

"Glad we found a solution to the problem." Oz cocks his hip against the closed door and folds his arms over his chest.

I knead my eyes to wipe away the stupor. "We didn't find a solution to anything. I want to hear what Eli has to say to my parents."

"That's not going to happen."

"Yes, it is, or I'll tell Eli that you made me sad. I overheard what he said to you. You're not officially a part of this Boy Scout troop and if you want in then you have to make me happy."

His eyes narrow. "What are you going to do? Lie? You better think of a plausible way I made you unhappy because complaining that I kept you in here will add gold stars to my name."

This idea sounded fantastic at the time, but I'm evidently not diva enough to pull it off. Sarcasm I can do. Lying isn't my style. "I want to talk to Eli."

"You can't. He's in Church."

My eyebrows raise. "He's where?"

"Church," Oz repeats. "Our chapter's board and the Lanesville board are meeting. There's no disrupting them."

"What if I'm bleeding?"

"You aren't."

"What if I need to go to the bathroom?"

"Not falling for it."

"Please. I have a million unanswered questions and I want to hear what Eli has to say."

Oz lazily shrugs one shoulder up and then down. "Not my problem."

"Sneak me out. I'll never tell."

"You telling isn't the problem." There's a serious set to his face that captures my attention. "If Eli asks if I kept you in this room, I need to answer him point-blank yes. Part of being in this club is keeping my word and answering honestly when asked."

"I hate you," I mumble.

"Works for me," says Oz.

I grab a magazine off the desk and yank it open. Of course, it's full of motorcycles and I flinch. Inside I'm screaming. Naked girls. Very, very naked girls strewn across motorcycles. I toss it onto the desk like it was infested with bugs. Which it probably is. The type of bugs that give venereal diseases. "Classy."

"It's a good issue," Oz says. "And you didn't even get to the good part."

"The fascinating articles?"

"No." His mouth tilts in this teasing way. "The centerfold."

The centerfold. Gah. "And you didn't even get to the good part," I whisper in a high-pitched mock.

Oz actually gives a good-natured chuckle and I'll be damned if I don't smile in response.

"I don't understand it," I say without thinking.

"What?"

I pause, but decide to continue. I'll never see him again after today. "Why you make me feel comfortable."

Lines bunch together on Oz's forehead as he studies me. "Comfortable?"

I flex my toes in my sandals. "I don't normally push at guys like I do with you."

"I have a hard time believing that. Next you'll claim you're shy."

A sardonic twist of my lips. "I'm not shy."

"No shit."

I giggle, he grins, then I sigh. Heavily. The events of the past twenty-four hours catch up to me. Being ripped away from my parents, some illegal motorcycle club at the motel, Olivia telling me that my life is a lie, trying to please Eli, the guilt of not pleasing Eli, the anger at Eli... A choking sensation squeezes my throat and I scratch my neck as if I could tear away the invisible noose.

"You okay?" Oz asks.

No. I'm not okay. All of this chaos threatens to follow me home. I'm happy at home. Content. And this visit from hell is going to mess with that.

Olivia said my life is a lie and there's this dark suspicion that if I ask my mother for the truth, she won't give it to me. An ache courses through me and my shoulders curve in with it. I've never doubted my mother before. Never. The pain that a few hours can shake my faith in her is too much to bear.

A slight, distant feminine voice rises up from the vent below my feet. My skin prickles. She's here. My mother's here. I stand and Oz pushes off the door, his eyes narrowed. "Emily, are you okay?"

I swallow.

One moment—a few seconds—and my entire life can change. I can do this and looking at Oz convinces me that overhearing my parents and Eli's conversation is possible.

His black hair is an array of messy tufts sticking out in various directions. The bandanna is off and the urge is to knot my fingers in the strands. I step into his personal space. Close enough that heat instantly springs between us. Close enough that when we inhale to breathe, our bodies touch.

I lift my head and Oz's deep blue eyes dart around my face in confusion. There's a light stubble on his jaw and, being braver than I normally am, I reach up and gently brush my fingertips along the rough hairs. My heart beats faster with the soft scrape against my skin and Oz sucks in a breath of air.

"What are you doing?" His voice is deep and gruff. Each syllable caressing my soul.

What am I doing? I'm submitting to temptation. I'm taking control of my life. I lick my lips and Oz mirrors the motion. He's not lying. He's as attracted to me as I am to him and there's no part of me that will regret what's about to happen.

"I'm leaving soon," I whisper.

"You are."

"And I won't be coming back."

"You won't." His gaze wanders the length of my body. "But we can't do whatever it is you're thinking of doing."

Resistance—not what I need and, deep down, not what I want. "Why not?"

Oz pierces me with his eyes and I spot not only a shadow of lust there, but a seriousness I've never seen from anyone else before. "Because you aren't that type of girl."

Normally, I'm not, yet I bristle like a porcupine and try to ignore the sting of rejection. Maybe he doesn't want me like he claims. Maybe I'm making a fool of myself. "You have no idea who I am."

"And you don't know me and you don't understand my world."

His world. He's right. I don't, but I do know there's so much more going on than anyone will tell me and I'm bent on finding it out. Oz thinks he has all the power here, but

I'm not blind and I do listen. He wants to kiss me as much as I secretly crave to kiss him. This rawness going on between us is nothing I've ever felt before. It's primal, instinctual, and instead of fighting it, I'm bent on using it to my advantage.

The girl I normally am, she's begging me to return to my chair, but nothing about this moment is normal. Being here, the picture Olivia gave me, Eli's sudden interest in me…the way my blood pounds in an urgent rhythm whenever Oz is around. "Are you saying you don't want to kiss me?"

Oz rubs a hand over his face as if he's waging an internal battle. It's a battle against me and, in this, I will win. I step closer, my body pressing against his, and a slight twinge of a possible victory overtakes me when he closes his eyes as if he likes the feel of me.

"Are you all talk, Oz? In the short time I've known you, you keep saying you want to kiss me and I'm admitting I want to kiss you. This is a now or never. Once I leave here, I will never return."

I take a huge risk. I lay my fingers on his shoulders, my thumb tracing his collarbone through his shirt. His head snaps up as if I found his "On" switch. A wave of electricity crackles in the air when our eyes meet and I love the utter shock written all over his face. Yes, I am the person in control.

In a lightning-fast movement, Oz's hand snatches mine, the one that's touching him, and he holds it in his grasp. He shifts so that he towers over me, like he did in the hallway, in a way that suggests he's trying to take back control. "Is this what you really want, Emily? To kiss me? You don't think I see right through you? That you try to kiss me, I lower my defenses, and you push past me and out the door?"

His thumb moves over the top of my hand and I shiver with the contact. My mouth runs dry at the thought of how close we both are to going over this edge. "I can guarantee that bolting past you was never on my mind."

"Who are you, Emily?" he asks in a husky voice.

I don't know who I am here. At home, I'm definitely not this. But here? "I'm not shy, and for today, I'm bold."

"Are you sure about that?" In less than a second, Oz wraps his arms around me, erases the minute distance between us and presses me to him. One of his hands roams the small of my back while the other wanders to my hair. His fingers play with the ends and the gentle pull causes pleasing goose bumps to form along my skin. "Are you sure this is the position you want to be in with me?"

He's playing with me, he's testing me, he's insisting that I tuck my tail between my legs and admit that I can't go through with what I've started, but he doesn't get how badly I want to understand what's going on, to learn the truth.

My pulse picks up pace and adrenaline shoots through my veins. This is a means to an end, a means to an end alone, but what frightens me is how much I desire this.

I edge my hands up, brush them against the hot skin of his neck, let my fingernails dance near the tips of his longer hair. Oz's body tenses and melts into mine at the same time.

"Does that feel like I'm playing?" I whisper.

His hold in my hair tightens. "Whatever you think you've got planned isn't going to work. You're not walking out that door."

"Are you scared of me?" I taunt.

"I'm scared of no one. If you want to do this, we'll do this, but as I said, you're not going anywhere, so you might as well step back now."

I may not be going anywhere this very second, but I will be soon. Very, very soon. "Are you going to stop me from leaving?"

"Yes," he answers as his hands begin to wander and I move my head closer to his, placing my mouth undeniably near his.

"Unless you're scared, then stop me, Oz." Our lips briefly touch as I speak. "Kiss me and stop me from leaving right now."

His nose skims my cheek and he's still battling the chemistry between us. My own blood hums and frustration kicks in. "Kiss me. Just stop thinking and kiss me."

He accepts the challenge as he crushes his lips against mine. My knees immediately buckle and, searching for stability, I weave my arms around his neck. Oz uses his strength to support me in response. My fingers rake through his hair. His hands massage my back.

A warmth spreads in my stomach and it's a driving need that causes me to curl myself around him. Both of Oz's hands slip down my spine. A slight brush along my bottom and I suck in a surprised and excited breath as Oz grabs on to the back of my thighs.

My eyes open when Oz lifts me in the air and in a fast twist, I'm against the door right at his level. He stares at me. I stare at him. Our chests rise and fall at a rapid rate.

I have what I needed. The leverage to leave, but this…this type of kiss…I want more.

I tip toward him, letting my thighs carry some of my weight on his hips and Oz's mouth edges up as he briefly closes his eyes, as if he enjoys the friction between us. I like that I affect him. I like all of this way too much.

My fingers drift into his hair, fulfilling my fantasy from earlier, and I tilt my head closer. Oz does the same and heat builds. If we start this again, will we stop? Do I want to stop? The answer is no.

Mouths stir. A nibble on my lower lip. I take in his top one. A lick of his tongue. And the game continues to increase in intensity. Testing. Tasting. Teasing. Strengthening and growing and exploring and a silent rhythm is created. Soon not only our mouths are moving in time, but so are our bodies.

Oz redistributes my weight so that he's leaning into me and my back is flush against the door. I part my lips, and the entire world explodes. His tongue sweeps next to mine and we're both touching and moaning and so hungry for more. The delicious pressure of his mouth on my neck. More. The way his hips maneuver against mine. More. His muscles flexing under my caress. More...

I blink when Oz's fingers slip to my shoulder near my tank-top strap. My hands slide to his chest and I push. As if I flipped his switch again, Oz places my feet on the ground and jumps back.

A rush of guilt consumes me because none of that is me. None of it. I don't hook up, but that wasn't a hook-up. It was a kiss. Just a kiss. Just the best freaking kiss of my life with a guy who hates me.

Oh my God, we were mauling each other. Oz draws down his shirt and readjusts parts in his pants. I drag a hand through my hair and try to ignore how the strands are completely tangled.

I graze my hand across my swollen lips. Just a kiss. Just a kiss. *Just a kiss.*

I clear my throat and Oz glances at me as if he's startled.

"Um…" Think straight, Emily. "You need to sneak me out so I can hear what Eli has to say to my parents."

Oz laughs. "Did you think I'm going to ruin my chance with the club because you thought I'd get sentimental? You're wrong."

I shake my head because he misunderstands. "No, you're going to help me because if you don't, I'll tell Eli that you kissed me."

OZ

EMILY AND I ARE CROUCHED IN THE SMALL KITCHEN next to the general meeting area of the Lanesville chapter. Above us is the open serving window. In the room adjoining the kitchen, chairs shift and there's the occasional try at conversation between Emily's parents to fill time.

Anger is a pulse within my body. I'm risking my entire future in the club because Emily—little good-girl Emily— knows how to seduce. Her ultimatum: bring her here to eavesdrop or she'll inform Eli I kissed her. I have a better chance at surviving telling him we left the office than his daughter announcing we went at it and that I held her up against the door as I attempted to slip down her bra.

I silently rap my head against the wall behind me. What the hell was I thinking? I wasn't thinking. That was my problem. I blame it on the lack of sleep, Emily looking too damn gorgeous for her own good and how she acts all naive and seductive.

I'm fucked. I'm stupid and I'm fucked.

"I'm going to go use the restroom," says Emily's dad.

"All right," answers her mom.

Shoes against the concrete and the squeak of a chair being pulled out. From where we sit, we can see a reflection of Emily's parents from the glass of a cabinet. Along the shelves in front of us are unopened bottles of liquor, boxes and, across from Emily, a jumbo box of condoms and a pair of women's lace underwear.

Emily's face contorts and my lips turn up.

"Ew," she mouths.

My unrepentant smile grows and I shrug a so-what. Club life is club life and we don't apologize to anyone for it.

We sit beside each other and our thighs slightly touch. I knead my eyes and try to push away the memory of Emily's body moving against mine. That was the hottest damn kiss I've had and it's going to cost my life or my future. And I thought only guys did the seducing. I should feel cheap, but that kiss was too good to feel used.

Trouble.

Emily is trouble and she needs to leave before I end up with a bullet in my head.

The door to the general area opens then closes and Emily straightens. My eyes snap to the glass case and I stop breathing. Eli.

There's silence. A heavy silence as Emily's mom and Eli stare at each other.

"Where's Jeff?" Eli asks.

"Restroom," she replies.

Emily's fingers curl into her thigh and her knuckles grow white as we enter another long absence of conversation.

"It's been a long time since we've been alone, Meg," says Eli.

Meg stands. Her long blond hair is tied at the nape of her neck. Even in the mirror I can tell she's pretty, but Emily is gorgeous. It's obvious Emily inherited her height and soft features from her mom, but the rest of Emily is purely from Eli's side.

Eli shoves his hands into his pockets and shifts to one side while keeping his eyes locked on Meg. Meg, on the other hand, rubs her hand over her neck. Then she walks, quickly, killing the distance between her and Eli. He holds out his arms and Meg falls into them.

Emily jerks and I plant a hand over her knee in warning. Emily's eyes are wild as they beg me to explain what the hell is going on, but I've got nothing. This is new even to me. Eli gently enfolds Meg into him and kisses her temple. "I've missed you."

His hand clutches her hair as Meg rests her head on his shoulder. They stay that way. A second. Another. Too long for Emily and she begins to scratch at a spot on her wrist. An angry red welt forms and I snatch her hand, keeping her fingers firmly in my grasp.

Emily's chest is moving fast—too fast—and she focuses on the reflection with too much intensity. I glance over at the door we snuck in from off the back hallway. Emily needs to get out of here before she completely spirals.

A sniff from the other room and Emily's mom finally steps away from Eli. "Jeff says that you never married."

"No, I haven't found anyone worth being with." He pauses.

"You didn't need to work through Jeff all these years. It would have been nice to talk to you."

Mirroring Emily earlier, Meg grips her elbows. "It's better this way. Better for us to have distance… I should have never brought Emily here—"

"I'm glad you brought Emily," Eli cuts her off. "I'm glad you came. But this should have been done differently. To show up unannounced—"

"I know," Meg says harshly. "It's just that when I thought Olivia was dead…it brought everything back and I reacted without thinking and… Is Emily in danger?"

"Yes," Eli answers. "She is and I'm going to need time to fix it. You woke a sleeping giant and something that large takes time to put back to sleep."

Emily's hand goes limp and cold and I slip my fingers through hers. She studies me as she accepts the comfort I'm offering. Moisture lines the bottom of her eyes. The Riot. The Riot is after Emily and I don't understand why.

She's in danger and until now I honestly thought this was some stupid misunderstanding. The image of my father bleeding from his head enters my mind. That could be Emily.

The back door opens and my hand automatically shoots to my hip and my fingers clutch the air where my knife should be. Emily's father strolls in and his eyes land on the two of us.

Emily shakes her head and raises a finger to her lips. His eyes flicker between me and Emily and then settle on the reflection of Eli and Meg that Emily eventually points at.

I hold my breath. Waiting for him to blow our cover, waiting for him to nail me to the wall for holding his daughter's hand while sitting so close. Instead, he motions for us to go out in the hallway.

Quietly, we do, and once there he leans down and whispers to Emily, "I'll find you soon."

Emily

HOLDING MY HAND, MY FATHER GUIDES ME INTO the hot June sun and away from the men in black leather vests to a bench swing that hangs under a shade tree on the other side of the parking lot. Twenty minutes after Oz and I returned to the office and waited in silence, my parents walked in with Eli.

I hugged Dad and then Mom, but I have to admit to being numb. Eli told me this morning that I wasn't in danger and he told my mother I was. What does it mean? What does any of this mean? They hugged. Mom and Eli hugged like they meant it.

"Why don't you sit down, Em?" Dad says.

Parroting a puppet on a string, I do, and Dad claims the spot beside me. Mom exits the warehouse with Eli behind her. She veers right and observes me and Dad from an empty picnic table. Eli heads left toward a group of men, but I don't miss how his gaze roams to us. Oz also watches us as he talks to a guy about our age, except this guy has a vest on.

Dad takes a deep breath and I steel myself for his rip-the-Band-Aid-off method. "Eli wants you to stay in Snowflake for a while—for the summer, even."

"Oh, hell no." I go to jump up, but Dad places a hand on my knee.

"Will you agree to just hear me out?"

I want to scream "no," but the silent plea in Dad's eyes causes me to settle back on the swing. "Fine."

"Thank you."

He's totally not welcome.

"Eli feels that the Riot, the motorcycle club that they're rivals with, is a threat to you because of his current business issues, and that you'll be safer under his protection than you would be returning home. Eli believes that if the Riot thinks you're unprotected, they'll use you against him. Your mom agrees with him. No one has made this decision lightly. Not Eli. Not your mom. I want to know your thoughts."

Knots harden in my stomach as I lace and unlace my fingers several times. "You said *they* want me to stay. What do you want?"

Dad lays his hand over my fidgeting fingers. "The same thing."

My head falls back and I fight the way my lower lip trembles. "So I'm in danger?"

"No," Dad says with force. "You're not in danger."

"But I overheard Eli say—"

"You overheard what Eli believes. If you want my opinion, this is a game."

His leg moves, causing us to slowly swing, and I contemplate his words. "What do you mean?"

"Do you remember my cousin Josh?"

I can't help the lift of my mouth. Josh. He owns his own company, but odds are Dad's referring to the conventions he attends where he dresses up as his favorite characters. It's different from my world, but he's a huge teddy bear and I adore him. "Yeah."

"Sometimes people create a world that gives them power. Sometimes people create a world to find friends with similar interests. To me, motorcycle clubs are a rougher man's sci-fi convention."

A chill runs through me when I remember the men last night at the motel. "Are you saying that whatever is going on between the Reign of Terror and this Riot club isn't real?"

Dad merely inclines his head in answer.

An unsettling jolt of nerves compels me to glance around to confirm no one's overheard. A few hours with these people and even I'm aware that those are fighting words with men who are heavily armed. "I don't know. They seem serious to me."

"What danger have you truly met? You saw men in a parking lot in the middle of the night. If people from Eli's club weren't there, you would have bought your water and returned to the room. Eli's convinced himself this is a big deal. It's amazing what people can make themselves believe."

I tap my tongue to the roof of my mouth. "If that's the case, why have I been living in the seventh circle of hell for the past few hours?"

Dad chuckles. "I like that you chose violence."

Dante's *Inferno* and his nine levels of hell. It's one of Dad's favorite books. "It was a lucky guess."

"To answer your question, I thought you should come back to the motel immediately, but your mother felt differently."

My eyebrows rise past my bangs. "My mother? Mrs. Snowflake-is-the-devil's-playground is the cheerleader on this?"

"She hates you being here, but she went into hysterics when Eli showed at the motel. Crying and screaming like I've never seen. Your mother has secrets, Emily. Those demons we talked about, and they have a strong hold when they pop up. They don't terrorize her often, but when they do, she's unreasonable."

"What happened to Mom?" I ask. "And why is she scared of Snowflake—and Eli?"

He sighs. "I love your mom. I've belonged to her since she walked into that free clinic with you on her hip and told me I didn't know jack when I informed her that you had a cold."

I love this story. They've both told it to me a hundred times. Dad was volunteering at the clinic and my mother was a complete bitch to the know-it-all young doctor. She was right and I had strep. He was wrong and bought us dinner. The three of us have been together since.

"Your mom is persistent, headstrong, passionate and full of life and love. I traveled around the world after med school, not knowing what I was looking for, and I knew I had found it when I met her...and you."

Even though it's a million degrees outside and I'm minutes away from heatstroke, I edge closer to him. Sue me for this being my favorite part of the story.

"With that said, your mother has had this uncontrollable fear of motorcycle clubs. Terrified of their reach. Terrified of their violence. Terrified that at any moment they were going to barge into our house and rip you out of our hands. She told me stories and for the first few years I believed them, but then year after year we heard nothing. Saw nothing. My fear receded and yet your mother's stayed the same."

"Do you think she lied to you?" I broach. "About the club?"

"Not intentionally. Your mother believes the same lies they tell themselves. They act bigger and badder than they really are. They probably threatened her and she fell for it. The most dangerous part of ourselves can be an overactive imagination."

My cheeks burn and I lower my head. How many times has Dad reminded me of that when it pertains to my fears? "So I'm safe."

"You're safe. I guarantee they'll act overprotective, but things will remain silent and this part of the game will be over."

A group of women pull up to the warehouse in a minivan then hop out. Two of them have babies on their hips and a toddler in a T-shirt that proclaims him a "Reign of Terror supporter" follows. "If that's what you really believe then why do you want me to stay and feed into this game?"

Dad's blue eyes flicker over my face. He's done this since I was young—encouraged me to discover the answers without his help. *Sound out the word, Em. You can figure it out… Would a real friend treat you that way…? Don't you wonder what's out there in the world…? Aren't you curious about your heritage?*

"You want me to know my biological family."

He relaxes back onto the swing. "You're curious about them."

"I'm not. Trust me, I'm really, really not."

We swing slowly. His foot controlling the speed and how high or low we go. Dad's thinking and I'm used to this, but the longer he waits to speak the worse it will be for me. He's forming an argument, one I'll surely lose.

"There's more to life than our home and Florida. More to life than me, your mom and the friends you've made there. The world is a huge place. How will you know where you fit in unless you explore beyond your comfort zone?"

I wave my hand toward the warehouse in disgust, beyond caring that it's obvious to the gawkers that I'm hating. "And this is where I should start? I'll make you a deal, I'll go home and visit somewhere safer in Florida, like a prison. Maybe a toxic waste dump."

Dad laughs. I wasn't joking. "Anytime your mother even casually brings up the past, you pay complete attention. You've never been one to mince words so if you weren't slightly curious about Eli, you never would have agreed to the visitations. You're frightened of Snowflake because your mother raised you to be. If you stay, maybe you'll figure out that there's nothing to fear and maybe your mom will finally learn that she has no reason to be afraid of Eli or his club."

My stomach flips multiple times. Mom and Eli hugged. I'm not so sure that it's Eli she's scared of, but I choose to keep this tidbit to myself. There's no way I could ever tell my father that my mother, his wife, touched another man.

I listen to the creaking of the swing as I let the events of the past night and his words sink in. Dad informed me from the moment I walked off the plane that I wasn't in danger and that everything was fine, but like Mom I permitted my fear to lead me.

I release a long breath and bite the bullet. "Mom's lied to me, hasn't she? About Eli's family?"

The porch swing stills and my dad tenses beside me.

"Olivia showed me a picture of me and her together. I was a baby and James the Elephant was seriously pink and fluffy."

He's silent for a moment. "I promised your mother I would never discuss certain things with you. I agreed, not understanding the effect it would have on you both. I don't break my promises. Especially to your mother."

No, he'd never break a promise to either of us. "Which is why you fought for the visits with Eli and why you think I should stay here."

Dad wraps an arm around me and squeezes my shoulder. "There's a big world out there and you have blood family in it. I'm not suggesting that you forget us and fall in love with them, but—"

"It's okay to be curious," I whisper.

"It is," he agrees.

"I'm not saying I am," I mutter.

He ignores me. "Our fears are what stifle us and we're only scared of what we don't understand. Fear can be handed down generationally, kind of like eye color. I love your mom, but I also love you. I don't want to see your mother's fears turn into chains that drag you down."

I let my gaze roam. Men gather around their bikes. Another group of guys hang around the women and children. Mom still stares at us, as do Oz and Eli. It's the same picture from when we sat down, yet it's changed.

"These people scare the hell out of me," I say.

"They're flesh and blood like the rest of us. That, as a doctor, I can guarantee."

My mother was afraid. Very afraid. And she fled from here. Why, I don't know, but I run the risk of letting fear paralyze me if I don't overcome it and what better way to overcome it than to stay in the scariest town on earth?

"If I ask Mom what happened, she won't tell me, will she?"

"No," Dad says. "She won't, and neither will Eli. Just like me, he made a promise to your mother—and Eli might be a lot of things, but over the years I've known him, he's proven to be a man of his word."

Mom won't tell me. No one will tell me...except maybe the woman I accused of being a liar—Olivia.

Disorientation hits me as another shot has been taken at my relationship with my mother. Somehow this bleeding wound tastes like betrayal. My arm begins to itch. I scratch, not caring that it will make the hives bigger. "Hey, Dad?"

"Yes?"

I turn my head and look straight into his eyes. "Do you swear I'm safe?"

"I swear it, Em. If I thought you were in danger, you would have been on the first flight home to Florida this morning with police by your side. Eli's your biological father, but I'm your dad. I'm not asking you to stay here forever. A week. Maybe two. You decide the length, no matter what Eli thinks. I'll miss you every second you're away and we'll talk as often as you want. I want you to discover your biological family, but I'm your dad and you're my little girl. Always."

I rest my head on his shoulder. My dad. This is my dad. "I love you."

A kiss on my head. "I love you, too."

"For real, how long do I need to stay?" A sickening wave of homesickness hits me. I'm not just leaving behind my parents, but dreams for an entire summer.

I was supposed to go on vacation with Trisha next week to her grandmother's in New York. I had just discovered that I was selected to be the head volunteer at the food pantry. I had just gotten the attention of the cute guy in my math class. I was just on the verge of making some dreams a reality.

A lot of supposed-tos and just-abouts and now I'm stuck here—in Snowflake—in hell.

"Stay just long enough for you to get a taste of Eli and his family and for your mom to feel you're safe in returning home. When you're ready, I'll come and get you. What do you have to say?"

What do I have to say? From across the lot, my mother focuses on us with her hands locked together as if in prayer. Eli stands in the middle of a group of men, but his attention is fixed solely on me. My gaze reaches Oz and the moment our eyes meet, he glances away; then my heart picks up speed when he looks my way again. And I have my answer. "Mom is going to lose her mind when she leaves me behind."

OZ

NEVER BEEN THE GUY TO DEVELOP A NERVOUS habit, but I'm so damned twisted inside that I'm reconsidering. Violet taps her fingers when she's wound. Chevy rubs his hands together. Razor will take out that big blade of his and flip it around, making everyone around him jumpy and ready to call the police. Me? I go quiet. Still. And observe my surroundings.

I lean against the wall of the clubhouse and my muscles are stiff from staying frozen for so long. This building used to be a three-car garage, but as the club grew, the cars received an eviction notice and a bar now runs along the wall. When it rains, they'll lift the garage doors and park the bikes inside, but on dry days the place belongs to the pool table, mismatched couches, bar stools, tables, chairs and the bras tacked to the walls.

It's nine in the evening. Our caravan traveled home from Lanesville four hours ago. Olivia escorted Emily inside, Eli went into Church with the other board members and I returned home to get some sleep.

Eli texted me forty minutes ago to get my ass to the clubhouse. I rolled out of bed and hightailed it on my bike. Now I wait with my feet cemented to the concrete floor, hands shoved in my pocket and my eyes peeled on the clock on the wall over the bar.

Each passing second curls the coil inside me tighter and tighter and tighter.

Tick…tick…tick…

Razor and Chevy sit at the bar nursing the longnecks they bought twenty minutes ago. They could be here for the cheap beer since not a damn person at the bar cares they're underage. Hell, they could be here to watch the Reds game with the other members of the club. But the brief glances they send me and the fact that neither of them has said a word to each other or anyone else informs me they're here for support.

I messed up at the motel and tonight I'll learn my fate with the club.

The door to the back opens and Razor's dad, Hook, scans the room. He's the sergeant-at-arms and there's no doubt he's searching for me. His eyes fall on his son, but they don't linger. Hook would be the reason why his son had the longest prospect period in the history of the club. He refused to let Razor's membership go up for a vote with the club until bylaws demanded it had to be done. Not sure why he did what he did, but Hook's actions didn't help his already messed-up relationship with his son.

With one flick of a finger, Hook indicates for me to jump and, being in the position I'm in, I walk forward in a silent acceptance of how high. I barely catch the door before it shuts. Straight would lead me to the kitchen, but I hike up the stairs.

The second floor holds a dormitory-type room with cots for any club member to crash, whether he belongs to this chapter or another. Farther down the hall are a few individual rooms for our more important guests or for couples who prefer privacy instead of doing their thing in public. Where I'm headed is the door on the right: Church.

Church, for the club, is a reverent room. It doesn't contain pictures of dead saints or candles in red glasses, and there's no cross nailed to an altar. What is hammered into the wall is a huge black banner with a skull in the dead center, fire dripping from the sky and flames blazing out of the eyes. The white words *Reign of Terror* race across the top.

I follow Hook in and let the door close behind me. This isn't my debut visit in Church and hopefully it won't be the last, but to each man in here, this should be my first time. No one comes in here without permission. Chevy and I snuck in here a few times as kids. Cyrus caught us the last time at eight and he wore the skin of our asses out for it. I learned my lesson, though. Respect the rules. Respect the club.

Church is set up like any conference room with a long table and chairs, but the men in here are more serious than any CEO. Each member would die for their brothers or this club. That's what membership requires.

It's hard not to look in Dad's direction. He's the business manager and has been a member since he was eighteen. Dad taught me from an early age that I'm my own man when it pertains to the club. I'm his son, but these are his brothers. I must earn their and his respect.

I fasten my thumbs in the pockets of my jeans and hang next to the wall while everyone sits. Cyrus claims the seat at the head of the table. He's the motherfucking chief of the tribe. Eli and I are the only ones left standing.

Eli curls his fingers around the back of his chair and focuses on the mahogany wood in front of him. His knuckles are red and swollen. Two of them have been sliced open and are scabbed over with dried blood. He's been in a brawl recently. Not a bruise on his face so that means he was the one doing the hitting.

"You're not a member, Oz," he says. "You're a guest in this room and guest alone, and guest in this context does not mean welcomed or privileged."

I nod to Eli, because I haven't been granted permission to speak. Because of Eli's past and the club's bylaws, he can't be a board member. While I don't know the details, I do know that when Eli returned home after a long stint of being away, the club had a special meeting, a vote was taken and they allowed an exception to the rules in his case.

While Eli may never be an official board member, he is part owner of the security company, and, besides Cyrus, the most respected man in our club. As Cyrus explained once, while Eli will never vote, he's part of the board as a consultant and when he talks, people listen.

My eyes sweep the room. The five other men eyeball me like we've never met. Eli's words become a gathering storm in my mind and my gut twists. I'm a guest here. Not welcomed—no privileges.

In this club, a member can't hurt another member. You throw a punch on a brother then you're out. But I didn't make prospect last night, so there's nothing stopping any of them from nailing me. If Eli swung at me now, Dad wouldn't stop it. The patch is thicker than blood.

"Want to tell me what happened at my daughter's motel last night?"

Best way to handle this? Short and to the point. "I fell asleep."

Eli's nostrils flare. "Do you have any idea what would have happened to Emily if you hadn't woken up?"

The imagined possibilities cause a coldness to creep along my bloodstream. "No."

Eli lifts his gaze and meets my father's stare. "Walk me through this, Oz. I need to know exactly what happened."

I work hard to school my expression though everything's unraveling inside me as I explain—from waking, seeing the guys from the Riot, driving to the other side of the building and then pulling Emily into the crevice by the vending machine. All of it.

When I finish, Eli rocks the chair back on its legs and continues to glare at Dad—not at me. Never at me. In the seven years I've known him, Eli's never ignored me.

I risk speaking out of turn. "What's going on?"

"We drove north for a while last night and found a member of the Riot." Cyrus strokes the length of his beard. "We chatted and after some persuasion he told us that the Riot had heard a rumor that Eli had a daughter and they came to check it out."

"We have a rat," says Eli.

"Until last night, Emily's pictures were all over Olivia's

house," says Dad. "She's not the highly guarded secret you think she is."

"Baby pictures," Eli argues. "Nothing over the age of two. Hell, there were Reign of Terror members who've been patched in for over ten years who had no idea who Emily was yesterday."

"Why Emily?" I ask.

Eli assesses me. Boots to jeans to T-shirt until he reaches my eyes. "Why your dad the other night? Why does the Riot do anything? They're looking for a way to break us and they don't have a problem using my daughter to do it."

"You said that they were there to confirm the rumor," I say. "Olivia already wore herself out over the brief time Emily spent here. Wouldn't it be better if we send Emily home?"

Eli's head ticks to the side and before I can register the exact threat, he plows into me. My back slams into the wall and a frame falls to the floor and shatters. Glass flies across the tile. Large chunks and small shards hit our feet.

I raise my hands to push him back, but the click of a safety causes the entire room to fade. The only movement is my heart beating and the cold steel of a gun sliding against my forehead. "Do you think this is a game? That I can take pieces off the board and the Riot will believe they're no longer in play?"

A numbness eases into my brain and I keep my sights locked on him. If he's going to pull that trigger, he'll have to kill me while staring straight into my eyes. "No."

"The Riot is after Emily." Eli twists my shirt tighter in his grip. "They're pissed because we won't give them a cut of our profits since we're riding through their territory. They've been taking it out on us on the road and because someone told them about Emily, they decided to make this personal.

"My daughter's life is in danger. I've had to rip her from her home and I'm going to have to work like hell to keep the integrity of this club and my business intact while keeping Emily alive. I asked for one thing from you and you put my daughter's life in danger. On your fucking life, will that happen again?"

I overpronounce each word. "On my fucking life, I will never fail you or this club again."

"Do you know what I'll do to you if you put Emily's life in danger again?"

Eli swings the gun away, the bang reverberates through the room, then the muzzle of the gun is back in my face. A loud ringing in my head disorients me. My survival instincts scream to fight, but Eli's not through with me and I'm not done standing.

Not a guy in the room moves from their seat. The ringing gives way to silence and then Eli's voice comes out clear and calm. "You know what Cyrus told me?"

"What?"

"That Emily trusts you."

The safety clicks back on, Eli flips the gun away from my head and he offers me the grip. For the first time, I glance in Dad's direction and he subtly nods. I raise my palm up and Eli plants the gun in my hand. "It's yours. Keep it with you at all times. Do you understand?"

Not at all.

Eli reclaims his seat at the table, the tension from his body gone. "We have several runs over the next few weeks that are back-to-back and long-distance. The majority of the club will be working them, including me. I want you by Emily's side twenty-four-fucking-seven. If she has to pee, I want you outside the door listening to the toilet flush. If she's asleep, you better be stalking the outside of her window. You got it?"

Jesus Christ. I check the lock on the safety. I've shot guns multiple times in my life, but I sure as hell haven't carried one. Age of open carry in Kentucky is eighteen and with the job I'd be taking with the security business, I knew I'd be packing, but somehow, this gun feels heavier and hotter than anything I've handled in my life.

"What are you expecting to go down while you're gone?" I ask.

"Hopefully nothing, but I won't run the risk of them going for another grab at her."

My eyes snap to his. "Is that what it was? A grab?"

Eli flexes his jaw as if he's grinding his teeth. "Are you going to be able to do what I'm asking? Can you protect Emily?"

Every man fixes his eyes on me and the weight of their expectations smashes onto my shoulders. Eli's trusting me with his daughter, just like each man here will be trusting me with his life when I join the security business. I glance down at the gun. This is going to be my life.

"Listen to me," Eli says. "We're a legit club. We manage things aboveboard. You know this. No illegal shit is done within our community. With that said, you have the right to pull the trigger when someone is threatening bodily harm and I'm asking you, do you have the balls to do what needs to be done when the time comes?"

This is it. This is what should have happened last night. This is the start of them testing me. "Fuck yeah."

Eli tosses me the holster and I tuck in the gun.

"Congratulations," says Eli. "That gun is your graduation present from all of us. When we're in public you'll have to keep it on your hip as you're not old enough to conceal."

The guys start to clap and I can't help but smile. A couple of them call out their congratulations or a well-done. Eli lets the moment ride. When the room goes silent again, Eli looks me over. "You were supposed to become a prospect last night."

"I heard."

"If you join the club, I need to know you're going to be firm and do what needs to be done. I got a second chance once. Consider this yours. We're considering this your probationary period for a job with the security company. We'll vote on your position when this stuff with Emily calms down. Prospect is going to be a wait-and-see."

The muscles in my shoulders relax. I've bought myself time. It's not the best-case scenario, but it's not the worst. Keep Emily safe and alive and I'll have a job. As for prospect, at least I've been granted a fighting chance.

I head for the door and when I open it, Cyrus calls out, "For your information, I consider anyone hitting on my granddaughter bodily harm. Shoot any son of a bitch who's stupid enough to think of touching her."

My grip on the knob tightens. My entire future hangs in the balance and Emily and I couldn't keep our hands off each other for twenty-four hours.

Damn.

Emily

FRESH OUT OF THE SHOWER AND IN A PAIR OF black shorts that are way shorter than anything Mom would have ever allowed me to wear, I do a sweep of the room again. It has to be around here somewhere. Nothing else from the past twenty-four hours has been a dream so there's no way that picture Olivia gave me was a figment of my imagination.

I drop to my hands and knees and peer underneath the darkness of the bed. Guess I could have lost it outside. Two knocks and I jump to my feet. "Yes?"

"Hey." Eli opens the door and I lace my hands behind my back. Nope, I'm not keeping secrets.

"I know it's late," he says. "But Izzy put some sandwiches together for dinner. You should come out and hang with us. I promise nobody bites."

Ha. I bet they do, but they probably already ate the two orphan kids who left a path of bread crumbs. "I was hoping to use your phone again so I could video chat with Mom."

Eli refused to let me take my cell from my parents, insisting that I not have anything that was "traceable." Talk about being overly dramatic.

His eyebrows furrow together. "I thought you talked to her before your shower."

"I talked with Mom and Dad on the phone, but I'd like to see her." And I need to speak with my mom...without Dad, because maybe he's wrong. Maybe she *will* tell me the truth. "You said I could talk to them as much as I wanted."

"I did." He did.

He said it when Mom and I were locked in a hug outside of the warehouse with no signs of letting go. Mom's shoulders started to shake and my own eyes began to water and I sent a pleading glance to my dad because I was seriously backsliding on my decision to stay. Eli stepped in and said that I could call Mom and Dad whenever I wanted. Any time. Any day.

"Plus, I need to call Trisha. Her dad's a state trooper. If she informs him I've become a missing person then I'm not responsible for what happens after that."

I'm kidding, yet I'm not. Even though I did agree to stay here, I still feel rather kidnapped.

Eli pulls his phone out and hands it to me. "You need to eat and your mom would be pissed if I let you starve. Plus, it'd mean a lot to Olivia if you ate with us."

"Okay." I rub my thumb over the back of his cell.

"Izzy's going to buy you a burner phone tomorrow so I'd appreciate it if you'd wait until then to call your friend. Then we'll go shopping when I get back from this trip. Clothes. Everything. Just like our yearly visit in Florida, but bigger." He smiles and I force myself to return the gesture, but I spot in the mirror how fake it looks so I quit and, instead, nudge the floor with my toe.

"That sounds great."

"It will be." Eli stands there as if conversation between us should be easy. "Do the clothes Izzy got you fit?"

I twist, hoping he'll catch on that the clothes are tighter and shorter than what I own because it would be rude for me to point it out. "What do you think?"

"They'll work." So much for hoping. "On calling your friends, I'd appreciate it if you make a list of who you need to talk to and keep that list small. Also, be careful what you tell them. Don't say anything about the Riot. Maybe tell them you're visiting out-of-state colleges for a few weeks or something."

Shouldn't be hard. Only Trisha knows I'm adopted so no one will even begin to think I'm being sequestered by my crazy biological paternal family. "I'll only call Trisha and she'll tell everyone else I'm gone for a bit. I was supposed to go on vacation with her next week."

Eli stares at me. I stare at him.

"I'm costing you your summer," he says.

I shrug, but yeah, he is.

We continue to stare at each other and it's like Eli's searching for something else to say. We've already gone through the Spanish Inquisition in the truck earlier so we're good on conversation for at least a year.

"I'm sorry I won't be here the entire time. I'll check in, though, and make sure you're okay. These deliveries are important and after what's happened with you and the Riot, I don't feel right letting anyone else be point on it."

"It's okay." It is. This is his job. I'm not really a fixture in his life so he doesn't owe me an explanation.

"When I get back, I can teach you how to drive."

"Dad will teach me when I go home."

The lines deepen on Eli's face and I hate the guilt that rushes over me.

"But shopping will be fun," I add.

Eli does his own fake grin and then excuses himself, shutting the door behind him.

I ease onto the window seat, swipe my fingers over the phone and after a beep, my mother accepts the call. She's grainy on the small screen. Her image freezes twice before it clears. The internet reception in this area stinks, but I can't imagine it's much better in their hotel in Louisville. Mom and Dad will be flying home tomorrow.

"Hi, Mom," I say.

Mom's eyes are red and puffy. Leaving her was hard. Her leaving me might have been harder. "Hi, Emily. Everything okay?"

"Yeah. Is Dad around?"

"No, he's in the business center checking on some stuff for work, but I can go get him if you want." Her tablet shakes as she rises and I stop her from going forward.

"No. Don't. I was hoping we could talk…just me and you for a few minutes."

She settles back down. The bedframe behind her is mahogany. Twenty bucks they're staying at the best hotel in Louisville, which would be a switch from the hellhole we were in last night. Mom twirls her blond hair around her fingers. "What's wrong?"

Olivia told me that my life is a lie. That I lived here, in this house, with her, and that you stole me from her—which I don't even understand what that means. Plus, Dad sort of confirmed this by not confirming it and informed me that even if I asked, you'd lie.

"Eli's family seems nice." Or crazy, but nice might award me more answers. "I'm supposed to be eating dinner with them and I was wondering if you could tell me anything about them. I just feel…" Terrified. Confused. Alone. "Out of place."

Mom does that thing where her lips flinch up because she wants to pretend it's okay, but it's not. We left the land of okay without passports hours ago. "I'm sorry. I can't help you with much."

I lower my head and scratch above my eyebrow, searching for the courage to confront her. Unfortunately, arguing with my mother has never been my strong suit. "You were really upset when you thought Olivia was dead. Did you know her?"

Mom blinks as her expression falls. "Has Olivia said something to you?"

The door to the room opens and Olivia steps in with a plate of food. My stomach plummets. She does not need to be here for this.

"Emily," Mom presses. "What did Olivia tell you?"

I attempt to hide the wince, but it's hard to do while staying focused on my mother and ignoring Olivia. The intensity of Olivia's gaze creates red-hot heat on the back of my neck. I lock down my muscles to prohibit the fidget.

I've been caught with my hand in the cookie jar, but truth is, Olivia never instructed me not to ask…she merely explained that no one but her would tell me the truth.

Normal people would leave during a private conversation. Olivia's obviously not normal. She lays the plate on the nightstand, sits on the bed then turns her body toward me and cocks her head as if giving me permission to continue. She's evil and she's bold.

"Well…Olivia told me you two had met before." Not a lie and Olivia smirks as if she approves of how I handled that.

Mom's shoulders sag. "Yes, we had."

"You never mentioned that."

"I didn't see how it mattered. When I left Kentucky, I never thought either one of us would return. I was young and I was stupid and I made an impulsive decision with Eli that in the end gave me the greatest gift I have ever been given, but there was nothing but heartache in Kentucky for me so we left. Olivia was kind to me when a lot of people weren't. That's why it hit me so hard when I thought she was dead."

"Did she want me?" The words come out fast and sharp. "Was she willing to help us?"

Mom's face scrunches like she tasted something nasty. "Where's this coming from?"

The sheets on the bed rustle and my focus darts to Olivia. When my gaze switches back to Mom her eyes are narrowed on me. "Who's there with you?"

"Um…"

"It's me, Meg," Olivia raises her voice so Mom can hear her, then walks over to the window seat and settles beside me. The skin on my neck itches as she moves into my space so she can be caught by the camera. "I brought food for Emily. You look well."

Mom's lips thin into a line. "You look very alive."

Olivia does that cackle laugh. "That I am. You liked me better dead, didn't you?"

My eyesight flickers between the two of them. Mom must have been trying to be cordial when she said that Olivia was nice because the death glares between them now suggests absolute hate.

Maybe they did meet and that encounter didn't go well and Mom had a right to run as far from Snowflake as possible. Why bring up a conversation with me that would go like this: oh, and Emily, beyond the issue of your father not wanting either of us, I met your grandmother and she's psychotic, so good luck with those genetics.

"Emily's only there long enough for Eli to fix this mess," says Mom. "Then *her father* will be there to bring her home and we can put all of this behind us."

Mom smiles, but it's not sweet. It's possibly the nastiest look I've seen her give anyone. The smile fades as she turns her gaze back to me. "Besides the fact Eli's family turned us away, the other reason I kept you from them was because of the situation we're in now. I promise you, when you get home, you will never have to see Eli again."

Olivia straightens beside me. "You promised Eli a visit once a year."

"You *both* promised trouble would never end up at her doorstep. I was naive to believe you could make that happen. I was naive to believe that your group was a club and not a gang. That you played by the rules."

"The club is legit. You know that," snaps Olivia. "Don't blame this on our way of life."

That sets Mom into a tailspin and she's off the bed, her

tablet bouncing in her hand, and we get dizzying views of the hotel in Louisville. Olivia leans back so that her head is behind mine.

"Your mother always had a flare for the dramatic," she tells me.

I say nothing in response because she's correct.

"Eli promised your mom that if you stayed, the truth would stay buried," Olivia whispers to me. "You're calling her to see if she'll tell you what you're starting to realize is true, aren't you?"

"Maybe."

"Why would she do that when lying to you has worked so well?" Olivia pushes a stray hair of mine behind my ear. "You loved for me to brush your hair, but you don't remember that, do you? Your dinner is on the nightstand. Of course, you're more than welcome to join us in the kitchen if you'd like company."

She leaves as easily as she waltzed in. The scene before me is blurred and then my father appears on the screen. "Calm down, Meg. Let me handle this. What's going on, Emily?"

I draw my hair over my shoulder and twine my fingers into the strands. My father grew up in a gated community with parents who tried to shelter him. He craved to see the world. They demanded he stay home. He had courage, defied them and left. If he had never done that, he would have never met Mom, and he would have never adopted me.

How many times has he told me that story? A hundred times? A million? First as my own personalized fairy tale as he tucked me into bed at night. When I became scared of the dark at eight, it was the fable to show me what would be won if I found courage, then he recounted it several times over the past two years to inspire me to fly.

Well, I'm somewhere new and I'm flapping these new wings like crazy, and you're right, Mom's not going to spill. "Everything's fine, Dad, but I don't think Olivia and Mom like each other very much."

OZ

MY BIKE PURRS BENEATH ME AND THE WIND
blows through my hair. No helmet this morning and Mom
will be pissed, but I don't care. The open road calms me and
since Emily's popped into my life, I've been restless.

The first light of dawn peeks out in the east. Emily and I
never did see that sunrise. Truth be told, I don't know what
to think of her. She's hot, has an attitude, can kiss and she
sure as hell is handling this insane shit better than I expected,
meaning she hasn't gone psycho and shot any of us yet.

It's been three days since she said goodbye to her parents.
I've been around but mostly keeping my distance, and I'm not
the only one. Emily's silent as a church mouse and spends most
of her time in her room. At least she does when I'm at Olivia's.

I downshift and ease near the group of motorcycles parked
by the clubhouse. Standing beside the bikes are their owners.
Some smoke cigarettes. A few drink from steaming mugs.

With coffeepot and foam cups in hand, Mom flutters about

with a smile on her face. Her black hair is drawn back into a messy knot and she wears her Terror Gypsies cut. The Terror Gypsies support the Reign of Terror and their membership is made up of the Terror's old ladies. Can't be a member unless you're an old lady and you have to be an old lady who plans on sticking around for good.

Because Eli only does one-nighters and Olivia had to relinquish her duties, Mom is now the highest-ranking member of the Terror Gypsies. Most of the time, Mom doesn't mind the job. Dad loves the club and she loves Dad. As I said before, women like her are rare gems.

Eli nods his chin at me as I shut off the engine and swing off my bike. He leaves the circle of guys he was talking with and flicks his cigarette into the yard as he strides toward me. "Morning, Oz."

"What's up?"

Eli scans the yard to confirm no one else is listening then turns his back to the crowd. "Until I get back, you're Emily's last line of defense. I'm trusting you with her and I'll be real fucking pissed if she gets hurt, you read me?"

Like a book. Eli told me last night how he'll have other guys posted near the main road, but he doesn't want Emily to feel imprisoned. "Stick with her, but give her room and don't let her know you're carrying. That could scare her. You can let Emily wander the woods as long as you're with her, but she doesn't leave our property."

"That would require her to leave her room."

Eli freezes ice with the glare he gives me. "Cut her some slack. This isn't her world. I'm hoping when we leave she'll relax and at least open up with Olivia."

Doubt it. Emily's withdrawn already and she hasn't even seen what the club is really like in action. Cyrus and Eli ordered everyone to stay away to allow Emily room to adjust so the clubhouse has been empty when usually it's streaming with people.

"Are you getting me on how you need to handle things?" presses Eli.

"I got it." Just like I understood it last night. Keep Emily happy and in her helpless unrealistic bubble.

"One more thing," he says. "You keep my past a secret. If Emily wants to know about me then you dodge the question. If you hear anyone talk about me, Meg or anything involving the two of us you steer Emily clear."

"So Emily lived here for two years of her life. The end result's still the same. What's it matter if she knows?"

Eli tugs on his earlobe. "Because it's not the story Meg told Emily and it sure as hell isn't your place to ask."

I hold my hands up in surrender.

"She's my daughter. The only one I have and the only child I'll ever have. I see the fear in her eyes, I sense her hesitancy, but when I get her to smile it makes up for all those moments in between. I got this one chance. My last chance. I don't want to blow what little time I have left with her so no, I don't want anyone rocking her world."

I nod my understanding, but remain silent because there's nothing to say when he tells it like it is.

"Keep her in the dark," Eli says. "And consider that an order. Tell me you understand and tell me now."

"I got it."

He claps my arm. "You're a good man. It's why I'm trusting you with her."

"That mean I'm a prospect?"

Eli releases a crazy-ass grin as he walks away. "Don't push your luck."

It was worth a try. A pat on my back and I glance beside me to spot Dad. "You must have been discussing Emily."

"What makes you say that?"

"Eli only looks like someone split his rib cage wide-open and stole his heart when he talks about her..." Dad doesn't end the sentence as if a period belonged at the end. He said it as if there was more, but he'd decided to stop. "It's a place of high honor and esteem for him to trust Emily with you."

"You telling me not to screw it up?"

"Yeah. I am." Dad's tall like me. A year ago, I matched his height. A few gray strands mingle with his short black hair. He exhales as if he's weighted and that catches my attention. "That graduation gift was because we thought you'd be joining the business this week. It wasn't a gift for joining the club."

"I know." In order to work for the security company, I earned my gun permit a few weeks ago.

"This stuff with Emily and the Riot has complicated our world. It's a heavy thing, carrying. A certain responsibility. You can't bring back a life once it's taken. You know if you need to talk about anything...the club, this stuff with Emily... anything—I'm here."

Raised in this life for eighteen years, I know this, but if Dad needs to say it, I'll give him the respect he deserves. "I'm good."

"Then we're good. Watch your six," he says as a reminder to watch my back.

"Same to you."

Without a word to anyone, Eli and Cyrus straddle their bikes and strap on their helmets. That one act causes everyone else to mount up and start their motorcycles. Soon the yard shakes with the thunder of angry engines. Cyrus pulls out with Eli on his right. They head onto Thunder Road toward the main drag and the guys follow behind them in pairs.

On the porch, Mom watches the men ride off. She won't sleep much until Dad's back in town. Olivia appears beside Mom and wraps an arm around Mom's waist. Sitting inside on the window seat with sexy disheveled hair is my responsibility for the next week: Emily.

Reminder to self: hands off.

Emily

FOR SOME ODD REASON THERE'S A FULL-LENGTH mirror on the wall in the kitchen so with no one around, I suck in a lungful of air and pivot on my toes. Oh, sweet Caroline, my butt is a centimeter away from hanging out of this jean skirt. If I were to bend over, my underwear would show, and possibly other girly things. Who the heck wears stuff this short?

Lars waddles into the kitchen and deposits his butt on my toes. He glances up at me with those droopy eyes and blinks once. "I don't like you."

He whines. I wiggle my toes, but he remains on my feet. With a sigh, I return my focus to the material that is not doing its job.

"Nice ass," Oz says.

I spin, knocking Lars off, then realize I've given Oz a view of my rear so I spin again. Oz hooks his thumbs into his jean pockets and lazily cocks a hip against the door frame.

I've been avoiding him—on purpose. Because we kissed. Actually, I all but seduced him and then he kissed me and then there was lots of touching and then I sort of blackmailed him.

Warmth curls up my neck and I'm not sure if it's from the guilt of blackmailing him or from the dreams I've had since Sunday of us kissing again.

His hair is wet so he must have been the person in the shower earlier. My heart flutters at the damp sight and the way one charcoal strand hangs over those blue eyes. And those eyes are now trained on the mirror because he can still see my... My hands fly to my bottom and I try to yank the material down farther.

"Don't stop," he says in this low tone that vibrates against my insides. "It's sexy as hell you're checking yourself out."

Fire burns my cheeks. "I was not checking myself out."

"Yeah, you were, but as I said—don't stop. I've seen a lot of asses and yours is one of the best, though to make a proper evaluation, I'd have to see the whole thing."

He winks. And smiles. That smile. The wicked one. My mouth slackens and while part of me is absolutely frozen with embarrassment, another stupid part of me melts.

With a small wooden box in her hands, Olivia enters the kitchen. "What do you need to see?"

"Emily's ass," Oz answers as if this is normal conversation. "Emily was checking hers out in the mirror and I told her that I agreed that it looked nice."

"I never said that was what I was doing," I say as fast as I can. "I was looking at the skirt and I was wondering if it was too short and—"

"It's just right." Olivia studies me like I'm a runway model.

"Those clothes belong to Violet. Izzy ran by there to pick you up some stuff. Violet's taller than you, so it would be too short on her. Besides, you're a McKinley. We have fine asses. Be proud of your body, honey, it sags with time."

"I was not checking out my ass."

"Yes, you were." Oz pulls a mug out of the cupboard and fills it with coffee. "And it was fine for you to do it. As I said, nice ass."

Oz hands Olivia the steaming mug as she sits at the table. She accepts it with a nod of gratitude. "We might have to prohibit ass conversations. Emily's redder than a fire truck."

"I am not." I so am.

"I'm considering telling everyone we'll have to be conservative while she's here," she continues like I hadn't spoken. "I was even weighing whether or not to bake cookies."

Conservative? Olivia wears a pair of glued-on jeans and a white camisole that shows the outline of her bra. She has the blue silk scarf on her head again and today her gold dangly earrings reach her shoulders. From the obituary, I learned that she's in her fifties and she's one of those women who boasts fifty better than most people own their twenties.

"Don't let her bake cookies," Oz warns me. "She burns them and then gets pissed off when we use them as weapons."

"Ingrate," Olivia mutters as she blows on the coffee before taking a sip. I've never seen someone drink it black.

Their banter is easy and comfortable and it makes me hugely uncomfortable to be the third wheel in the scenario. Using my hands to shield my butt isn't helping.

Olivia tears the strip off a carton of doughnuts, lifts the lid, then slides the box to me. "Breakfast is served."

I choose the seat at the end of the table and gather the limited material of the skirt underneath me to prevent my privates from showing, then indulge in the white, powdery goodness.

The chair next to me squeaks and scrapes the floor as Oz yanks it out and sits. He kicks out his legs and crosses his arms over his chest. I automatically tuck my feet under my chair. This boy does not stay within his personal space.

Oz glances at me out of the corner of his eye and does an obvious double-take. The kind that causes me to look down to see if something is riding up or unbuttoned. Everything appears to be in order. "What?"

"Nothing." Yet his eyes flicker at me again.

"Not nothing. What?"

"You have powder near your mouth."

My tongue darts out and I quickly lick at the sweetness, but he stares as if he's drawn to my mouth so the sugar still has to be there. His eyes grow kind of dark and I flush with the memory of his lips pressing against my neck.

Napkinless, I raise my hand and rub the left side of my mouth and I wait for a sign of approval.

"It's to the right," he says in a deep voice.

I wipe and he sighs. "Lower."

By the annoyed set of his jaw, I must go too low. Oz rolls his eyes and leans forward. "It's here."

His thumb skims the corner of my mouth. My heart stops beating, and heat explodes through my body. A little gasp of air leaves my lips and Oz jolts back like electricity shocked us both.

Oz is up, out of his seat and across the kitchen before I can remember to inhale. The skin that he touched tingles and I twine my fingers together on my lap to restrain myself from brushing my fingertips over the sensitive area.

He flips the handle to the faucet and fixes a glass of water. His Adam's apple moves as he drinks and I have to work to tear my gaze away. When I do, I'm greeted by a very curious Olivia.

"I had powdered sugar on me," I say, because it feels like I should say something.

"I noticed," she answers. "Oz, would you go get me my reading glasses? I left them in the clubhouse. On the bar, I believe. If anyone is there, tell them Eli gave you permission to be in the clubhouse through me."

"My pleasure," he mumbles, and the front door creaks open faster than I thought it would.

Olivia opens the wooden box and rifles through it. "We can bake cookies later. You used to prefer sugar cookies and liked it when we iced them. You particularly loved the ones with chocolate sprinkles."

I sweep some of the powder sugar off the table onto my hand. Does she think I'm five? "Sure."

"I don't burn them."

"Okay." The garbage can must be the type that fits in a drawer because I'm not spotting one. "I didn't tell Mom about the picture."

"Figured you didn't. You're still here."

I rise and dump the sugar into the sink, then turn on the water to encourage the white specks to drain down the pipes. This is the first time I've been alone with Olivia since she gave me the picture and I have a sinking feeling that it won't be my last, but meeting her, talking with her, is the reason

I'm here. "Since I am, do you want to tell me this so-called truth of yours?"

Olivia slowly appraises me and she has this evil, heavy-lidded substitute-teacher expression. "It's not 'so-called.' It's the absolute truth. And no, I'm not going to tell you."

My head flinches back. "Why not?"

"Because you haven't agreed to stay."

Hello? "I'm here, aren't I?"

"I want you here for the entire summer. You're a smart girl. I see it in your eyes. Everyone thinks you're shy or freaked out, but I know better. You're observing us. Taking notes. Figuring out how we work so you'll know how to play us. If I tell you what you want to know now, I have no doubt you'll be on the next flight to Florida. If you want the truth, it'll be on my terms."

I blink to the point that little white lights emerge in my vision. "What do you mean?"

From the box Olivia pulls out a folded piece of paper with serrated edges as if it was torn out of a notebook. "You're half McKinley and the other part of you belongs to Meg. If that combination doesn't make you a master con artist, I don't know what would. Be careful how you try to play me. I've never been known for my patience."

She closes the box, places the notepaper on the table and shifts the newspaper closer to her as if we were done with conversation. I raise my chin. "Don't talk badly about my mother."

"You don't know what your mother did to this family." She doesn't even bother glancing up from the newspaper. "This is my roof so we abide by my rules."

"You're the one that wants me here so badly so if I do stay, you'll watch what you say. She raised me. You didn't. End of story."

Olivia lifts her eyes to me, her glare set to kill, but then her mouth slowly tips up. "Loyal to your blood. I can respect that. Remember that we're your blood, too."

The screen door opens and a second later, Oz's mother, Izzy, pops her head into the kitchen. "Are you ready, Olivia?"

"Doctor's appointment," she says and stands. "Go help Oz find my glasses. The clubhouse is the large building across the yard."

Olivia pats her hand over the notepaper on the table. Izzy leaves the room and I stop Olivia before she walks out of the kitchen. "What is that?"

"Incentive to stay."

From the living room, Izzy asks if Olivia needs her jacket and Olivia informs her that she's not a "fucking child" and Izzy reminds her that "fucking children" are easier to take care of. Something about the ticked-off, heartfelt fondness in Izzy's tone causes me to grin.

The two of them continue to bicker as the screen door opens then bangs hard against the wooden frame. In front of me, the folded paper appears absolutely harmless. Lots of things seem innocent, but in the end are deadly.

My fingers tap against the table. Curiosity is bad. Curiosity is dangerous.

I could visit for a week, tell Dad that I talked to my bio family and then return home, but evidently I'm more of a McKinley than I thought myself to be. With a slam of my hand against the table, I grab the paper and slowly unfold it.

OZ

I TOSS A BLACK BRA THAT'S MORE HOLES THAN fabric off the bar and still come up empty. Short of digging through the trash, Olivia's glasses aren't here. I take that back, they could be a million places within the clubhouse, but I'm not searching anymore. An itch in the back of my brain tells me that Olivia wanted one-on-one time with Emily and I just got played.

A car engine starts and I silently curse. Olivia left Emily alone. Not even a few hours into my first job for the club and I'm already failing. I stalk over to the door, grab the handle, yank it open—and my body rocks as someone runs into me.

My arm snaps out to catch the form and my other hand lands on the hilt of my knife. One breath in and my mind conjures up images of beaches and sand castles and seagulls eating my lunch. It's a great smell. It's a calming smell. And damn if that scent, along with the warm pressure of soft breasts against my chest, doesn't make me go hard.

I glance down at wide-eyed Emily. Every time I peer into

those dark brown eyes a part of me is lost. I better stop looking or I'll start losing pieces I'll miss.

"Sorry." Ah hell, Emily's voice is all soft and please-kiss-me breathless. "Olivia left and she told me to help you find her glasses."

A tickling sensation on my chest and that's when I notice her palms flat against me. She must have been trying to break her impending fall. One of her fingers moves and lightning licks up my veins. Her scent wraps around me and my fingers twitch with the desire to slide them through that thick silky hair.

Damn, I'm attracted to her, and by the way her body subtly shifts in my direction, she's feeling it, too. I imagine pushing her away. I need to push her away, but my body is not listening to my brain.

Emily blinks like she's waking up. I loosen my grip as she simultaneously steps back. Her hair brushes along my arm and I go up in flames as a fantasy overtakes my mind—Emily kissing her way down my chest and that hair drifting along my bare skin.

"I'm sorry." She twists her fingers. "For kissing you and then threatening to use it against you. That wasn't nice."

The red in her cheeks confuses the hell out of me. She radiates good girl—the ones I purposefully stay away from—but that kiss had bad written all over it. Fuck it, it doesn't matter. She's Eli's daughter and she's trouble.

"Don't worry about it." I pivot away and head to the bar. Emily and I—we require distance. Lots of distance. As in oceans between us. I pick up a stack of papers to check for Olivia's glasses though I've already canvassed the entire bar.

"You can look over there." I point to the couches on the other side of the room. The area that's the farthest from me. "Sometimes Olivia likes to sit in the recliner."

Emily stands there appearing as dazed and befuddled as I feel. Doesn't take her long to snap out of it and move toward the corner. Midway, she hesitates and her spine straightens.

I scan the room, hunting for the unseen threat. "You okay?"

"What is on the walls?" Hands to her hips.

"Bras," I answer, stating the obvious. A wide variety of them. From A cups to triple D's. Bright pink to black as night. Satin and lace. Conservative to see-through. Clasp in the front and hook in the back. Won't lie. At the age of thirteen, I found it quite educational.

Emily goes openmouthed with pissed-off round eyes. Shocked outrage. That would be the reason why I won't date or do good girls. There's a life I'm going to live and good girls want to break down, rebuild and reform. I'm not interested in being changed and I'm not interested in crushing the spirit of some girl so I can lead my life. I've seen both situations happen in the club and it usually ends in nuclear fallout.

"Why are there bras on the wall?"

"Where else would we put them?" I shoot back.

"Why would you even have them?"

"After a girl goes through the trouble of taking it off and giving it to us, it would be tacky to lay them on the floor." I'm screwing with her now, but my words are true.

Emily wraps her arms around her stomach as she assesses the clubhouse. Neon beer signs alongside posters of naked girls. Our skull with flames is painted floor to ceiling on the wall nearest her. Bordering the outside of the emblem are wooden plaques with pictures of deceased members. For Emily, it's possibly the most normal part of the building.

Behind me on the shelves, an endless supply of Mardi Gras beads hang from trophies earned from the annual get-together for the entire club, National Run. Mom received one of those first-place trophies a few years ago in the wet T-shirt contest. Dad's still damned proud.

Around the bar, it smells like spilled beer. Emily wrinkles her nose. Bet her area stinks worse.

"Suck it up and get used to it. From what I understand you're stuck here for the summer. Try the end table next to the recliner. Olivia will take her glasses off when she gets tired."

Emily picks up her foot and it makes a sickening sound as she has to peel it from the floor. Prospects are in charge of cleaning the clubhouse and the club's schedule has been shot to hell since Olivia's wake, which means not much work has been completed.

"Am I ever going to be left alone or are you and Eli going to take turns stalking me?"

"If you want we can pretend you're alone. Talking can be overrated and I'm fine with us ignoring each other."

"Sounds good to me." Yet she continues, "You guys take this Riot stuff too seriously."

Emily's not taking it seriously enough. I go behind the bar and search near the glass display case that holds the merchandise the club sells: T-shirts for members, supporter T-shirts that signify people are friends of the club, bandannas, knives, throwing stars, whatever shit you can think of.

"I found them," Emily says. "Half glasses that are red?"

"That'd be them." Rose-colored glasses. It's a joke Olivia likes to tell.

Emily tugs on the jean skirt as she crosses the room. Even though she's sexy as hell in it, it's hilarious to watch her mentally willing the material to cover more of her gorgeous legs. She slips the glasses to me from the other side of the bar. "Did she need them for her appointment?"

"She'll be fine without them."

Emily lightly lays her fingers on the bar like she's afraid to touch it and continues her examination of the clubhouse. There's a lot to see. Christmas lights are strung across the ceiling. Pictures of naked women engaging in very erotic things. Her head tilts as her eyes land on the trophies. When her face drains of color, I'm assuming she found the one with my mother's name. Hell, maybe she discovered several of Olivia's.

"Are you okay with all this?" she asks.

"Yeah," I answer without hesitation.

"I mean, you know this is not how normal people live, right?"

"Normal's overrated. You should try living on the wild side sometime."

Emily rolls her eyes, completely dismissing me.

"Our life isn't what you think," I say.

"I'm sure it's everything I think and more. Are you telling me you'd be okay with your mom's bra being up there?"

Guess she didn't find Mom's particular trophy or she didn't connect the dots. "Who says it isn't?"

Emily coughs through a choke.

"Don't judge," I say.

"I'm not," she whispers.

"You are, and the worst type of people are the ones who judge and don't think they do. If you want to judge us, do it, but at least own your opinion."

I expect her to digress into meek and keep her head down because I told her off. Sure as hell shocks me when she narrows her eyes and spits out, "Fine. This place is disgusting and it's a slap in the face to women everywhere. So which one are you going to do? Judge me in silence or own your opinion?"

A chuckle rumbles out of my throat and I'm drawn in by the mysterious smile forming on her face.

"You're crazy," I say.

She giggles and, screw me, I like the sound. Emily hops up on a stool and props her elbows on the bar. "You wear the crazy crown. For real, who carries a knife and, seriously? Who walks in with a bra on and is okay leaving without one? Those things are expensive."

"What do you know about money? Your dad's a doctor, right?"

"He is," she says in slow, methodical way. "But how do you know that?"

I shrug. "Eli talks about you."

She's silent. Too pensive for someone her age. I can practically hear her brain ticking, which causes me to be more curious about Emily. I like girls with brains and I like girls who don't mind using them.

"What else do you know about me?" she asks.

This is where Eli drew the line. "I know you live in Florida. I know Eli visits you once a year. I also know that Olivia almost canceled her doctor's appointment today so she could hang with you."

Her shoulders hunch over at the mention of Olivia. I should let it go, but I can't. "Spend time with her tonight and not in your room hiding or staying silent in the corner. Play cards. Can't have too much of a conversation when you're trying to hustle each other."

Emily's mouth moves to the side like she's considering what I said, which I admire. It means she listens and I've not met many girls who hear what anyone else has to say. They prefer to listen to themselves talk.

"I can do that," Emily eventually says, "but what about the other stuff? That photo of me and Olivia...she said that Mom and I lived here for a while. What do you know about that?"

More than her, but not as much as others. "You know we're the same age, right?"

Her eyebrows furrow together. "You're seventeen?"

"Eighteen. I'm a year older, but the whole point is, we were sharing a crib. I know as much as you do." It's a lie buried in the truth, but that true lie will make me a prospect.

"Were we really sharing a crib?"

Mom has a picture of me, Chevy, Violet, Razor and Emily in Reign of Terror shirts hanging out in a Pack 'n Play that was set up in this very bar. "I was proving a point."

"Do you know what Honeysuckle Ridge is?"

My eyes dart to hers. I do. But she shouldn't. It's family property ten miles up in the hills. Can be difficult as hell to reach and the reason it's a secret is because it's the hideout in case everything goes to shit. "No."

She digs into the skirt, produces a piece of paper and unfolds it. I blank my expression as I read Eli's handwriting: "Meet me at Honeysuckle Ridge at 8."

"Got a secret admirer?" I ask. "I wouldn't try going. Could be the Riot going after you again."

"Whatever. My dad told me the Riot isn't a big deal and that everyone is overreacting, so stop trying to scare me. Olivia gave this to me and I need you to tell me what Honeysuckle Ridge is."

As if her dad knows us. One more hater who thinks he gets to judge what he doesn't understand. "Ask Olivia."

"She won't tell me, and I think you know what and where this place is and I also think you know my past."

"You'd be wrong."

Emily taps her fingernail on the bar as she stares at me. I stare back. It's the same damn look Eli had right before he pulled the gun on me last night. If I didn't break with him, I sure as hell am not breaking for her. She slams her hand against the bar. "I don't believe you. I think you know everything Olivia knows."

Not everything. "Not my problem what you believe."

"Well, it should be."

This, I have to hear. I lean forward on the bar and gesture with my hand for her to continue. Hell, maybe I waved at her so she'd come nearer. She's already inclined in my direction and my heart skips a beat when she nudges closer. Her shirt dips and a hint of her beautiful cleavage is on display.

Won't lie. I peeked. "Why should I care what you believe?"

"It's an integrity issue. If you're lying now, then I won't believe anything you say in the future, even when it's the truth. Is that what you want?"

What I want is to be a prospect. What I want is to begin my job with the security company. What I want is for Olivia to come home and tell me that a miracle happened and she's cancer-free. What I want is for Emily to stop nibbling on her bottom lip so I can kill the fantasy of reaching across the bar and pressing my mouth to hers.

"You'll last a week before you call your mom crying to go home, so I can live with it."

"The longer I go without knowing, the longer I'll be here," Emily offers. "Are you excited to spend an entire summer following me around?"

Something flashes inside me. A warning. A thrill. A combination of both. I'm already imagining pushing her up against a wall again and kissing her until her knees go weak and my hands roam free. Not a good thing when touching her would be a death sentence. "Is that what you want? To stay in a place that disgusts you?"

My tone is lower, huskier than it should be and Emily's chest expands as she draws in a shaky breath. I will her to look away, but she doesn't and I'm secretly proud the girl won't back down. I hate this connection. I crave this connection. She's continually messing with my head.

"I need to know," Emily admits.

"Why? You've lived your whole life not knowing. Why now?"

"Because."

"Because why?"

"Because I need to know if my mother is lying to me," she shouts. "Because if my mother is lying to me then everything I know is wrong and that's not okay."

Emily's eyes moisten and I lower my head. Just shit. I walk around the bar and stand by Emily's side. My hands awkwardly move up then down because I don't know how this comforting crap works. Isn't this the part where the girl stumbles into me and I hug her?

But Emily doesn't collapse into me. In fact, she seems to have forgotten I exist as she twists her fingers into her hair. "What does it mean if she lied to me? Because this..."

Emily scrutinizes her surroundings. "This scares me and I've lived my whole life thinking that she wasn't a part of *this* so I need to know that she's telling the truth and that I don't belong here, so will you please tell me what you know?"

This. She refers to my life as *this.* As if we're poison. "You really are quick to condemn all of *this.*"

Emily breathes in deep then straightens. Gotta respect that she's refusing to cry in front of me. "In less than twenty-four hours I've been banned from my home and I'm hanging out in a place that uses bras as wall decorations. Find a way to justify all *this* to me and I'm game."

I take a step and tower over her. She's pissed. I'm pissed. Energy is building in the air. "If *this* is so disgusting to you, then leave."

"Maybe I will." She rises on her toes as if that will give her height.

"Then go," I say.

Emily and I are so close that I can feel when she inhales and exhales. Her dark doe eyes search mine and there's a spark of fear and lust. Dammit it all to hell. If she doesn't move away, I'm going to be the one to kiss *her.*

Emily

MY ENTIRE BODY IS WARM AND MY SKIN IS FLUSHED. Oz's head is close. So close. Close enough that my mouth waters with the idea of kissing him, tasting him, devouring him. This is crazy. This is insane. This is… "I don't understand what's going on."

"Neither do I," he responds. "But I'm not keeping you here."

He isn't and I don't move. Oz stays still, as well. My breaths come in and they go out and my heart beats in time with my thoughts: kiss him, kiss him. Kiss him? But… "I don't like you."

I hate him…I think.

"I don't like you, either." Yet Oz tucks the wayward strands of hair that had fallen between us behind my ear and little goose bumps form along my neck. "But no one said that this had to do with liking."

Oz slowly grazes his knuckles against my cheek. His skin

is the perfect combination of rough and soft and I lean into his touch like a cat begging to be loved.

I inhale and I'm greeted by his dark scent that reminds me of wood burning and open flames. It's an addictive aroma. One that calms me. One that encourages me to erase the gap between us. One that causes me to forget why I'm here and who he is.

Oz tilts his head and I mirror the motion. His breath heats my skin. My lips lightly part and a wave of desire runs through me. One kiss. Just one. Then it will be done. The craving satisfied.

Oz presses his forehead to mine, our mouths nearly touch, and…

The rumble of a motorcycle engine. My stomach jumps to my throat and I stumble back. The haze lifts and I drown in a rush of terror, excitement and this frustrated sense of loss.

"What was that?" I demand.

Oz drags both of his hands over his face. "A lack of control and thought—that's what it was. It's also nothing that will happen again. Stay here while I check this out."

"Stay here?" We were seconds from kissing again and now he thinks he can tell me what to do?

He moves away from the bar, toward the door and when I follow, he freezes me with a hard glare. "I said, stay there."

"You almost kissed me and so now you're going to behave like an ass?"

"I didn't hear you telling me to stop, and if you're going to call me a name, get it right. I'm an asshole."

I cross my arms over my chest. "My apologies. I forgot that you want me to own my opinions. You're right. You are an asshole."

OZ

FUCKIN' A, I'M AN ASSHOLE. I'M ALSO A MORON
for almost letting that spiral out of control.

The windows of the clubhouse are blacked out so I stand
by the door keeping an eye on the security monitor by the
bar. The gun feels heavy on my back, but if trouble's arrived
I won't necessarily have to pull it. There's so much tension
and anger built up in me, I'm practically shaking. A part of
me wishes for the Riot to show so I can throw a punch in
someone's face.

But it's not the Riot. It's Chevy and when he gets close
enough, I open the door.

I expect his easygoing grin and smart-ass greeting; instead
he stalks in like a tiger that lost his dinner in a bloody battle.
"We need to go."

I eyeball Emily then zero in on him. "Can't. I'm babysitting."

"Did you say babysitting?" Irritation leaks into her tone.

I ignore Emily and so does Chevy. "Olivia called. Violet and Stone are broke down on Applewood Pass. They have a flat and the spare is busted. I sent out a SOS to the club, but everyone is on that ride with Eli."

Not everyone. Eli held a few guys back to watch the perimeter of the property. I massage the knots out of the back of my neck. Violet's dad was a member of this club and he died not too long ago. Violet, Stone and their mother are our responsibility now.

"I have my own problems," I mutter.

Chevy glances over at Emily. She immediately looks away. "I see that, but I need the truck and I can't be alone with Violet. I'll be damned if we fail her on this and she has one more excuse to bitch about the club."

Technically, Applewood Pass is on Cyrus's property and Emily and I do need a chaperon and a distraction. I dig the keys Eli gave me last night out of my pocket. "Let's go fix some tires."

Emily

STOP ME IF YOU'VE HEARD IT BEFORE: ONE GIRL and two bikers ride together in the cab of a truck… Yeah, I know. I haven't heard the joke myself, but I sure feel like the punch line.

Oz opens the passenger-side door and does a sweeping motion indicating for me to enter. The guy who just showed hops into the passenger side and flings the door shut. The truck is old…like God created it on the eighth day then decided he made a mistake and went with us using horses for a few thousand years.

Rust lines the bottom edge of the frame. The pleather material of the bench seat is ripped and wires hang out in various spots in the dashboard. The scent of stale cigarettes drifts out of the interior. It's what I rode in the other day with Eli, but without him this has a more foreboding atmosphere.

I climb in and the guy near the passenger door rolls down the window. The second I'm across the seat, Oz is in and I attempt to make myself smaller. It's nearly impossible when I'm squished between two huge guys. Oz starts the truck and heads down the road.

"Hey," says the overly huge, brown-haired biker Ken doll. "I'm Chevy."

"Nice to meet you." Not really. "I'm Emily."

He rests his elbow on the open window and grasps the roof of the truck. "I know. I'm your cousin."

That draws my attention. "We're related?"

"By blood," he admits, sharing my enthusiasm for this family reunion. "Our fathers were brothers."

He doesn't even attempt to allow me space as he settles in his seat. I'm the equivalent of a thin slice of moldy unwanted cheese between these two massive guys.

Chevy spreads his knees and I scoot over only to end up with my thigh touching Oz's. I jerk back and crash into Chevy. He tosses me an are-you-impaired glare and the sigh that leaves my mouth is painful.

Oz peeks in my direction and my stupid body tingles. I've been kissed by three guys. Two of whom I at least liked and they liked me back. Both of those kisses were also comparable to licking live fish out of the ocean.

Never once did my heart race for them. Never once did my mouth dry out. Never once did my universe explode into fireworks like it did when Oz kissed me. I lower my head and rub my temples to keep from groaning in frustration. I don't even like Oz and for some stupid reason I dream of crawling onto his lap, wrapping myself around him and kissing him until our lips fall off.

The truck rocks on the worn-out road and when Oz accelerates, the potholes become unforgiving as my body is flung from one side to the other. First knocking into Chevy then back into Oz. This is freaking horrible.

My fingers fumble at the seam of the seat, but not a seat belt in sight. Neither guy wears one and I feel completely naked not strapped in. Oz hits sixty-five and with both windows rolled down, wind whips through the truck, causing my hair to sting my face. I gather the locks at the nape of my neck and my body flies into the air again as the truck pounds into a hole.

"Will you slow down?!" I slam back into the seat, reach for the console to steady myself and the result is a fistful of wires. With a turn, I slide to the left. My body completely flush with Oz's. This is worse than the Himalayan at the county fair.

"Can you try to sit still?" Oz asks.

"Can you try to drive like a normal person or at least tell me where the seat belts are at?"

Oz smiles and I notice my cousin sporting a smirk, as well. I hate both of them.

"There they are," says Chevy. "Stop the truck."

OZ

CHEVY'S OUT THE PASSENGER-SIDE DOOR BEFORE I stop the truck and jogs ahead. Around the curve of the road, practically hidden by the deep green of the trees, is a flash of red hair and the back end of a blue 1972 Chevelle.

Dammit. I'd love to smash Chevy's head into the side of the truck for leaving me alone with Emily, but I can't. Not when I understand why he's a mess. I cut the engine and angle to face her. "This is club stuff so stay here." We're deep on Cyrus's property and she'll always be in sight.

Emily focuses on the dashboard and I feel like a dick. I almost kissed her and now I'm treating her like shit. She deserves better, but I don't have time to make this right. "I mean it. I need you to stay in here."

Still nothing.

"Fuck it."

I exit the truck and Violet and Chevy are already going

at it like they had during the last few weeks of their doomed relationship.

"I said I got this!" Violet grabs hold of the jack in Chevy's hands. His knuckles fade into white as he clenches the tool.

Violet's seventeen, the same age as Chevy. She's all red hair, blue eyes, faded jeans, blue button-down, a few inches shorter than him and pissed off at the world. Specifically the club.

I nod my chin at the kid standing awkwardly off to the side. Odds are this is the first time Violet or Stone have seen the club since someone leaked to the Riot about Emily. He's the paranoid type that wonders in his jacked-up head if we would blame him when he didn't do anything wrong. Because I don't want him pissing his pants, I smile when I say, "What's going on, Stone?"

The kid lights up, but shoves his hands in his jeans when his older sister imitates a wall and slides in between us with her hand still on the jack.

"His name's not Stone." Pure venom spills out with the glare she throws me. "It's Brandon and, as I said, we don't need your help."

"I have to disagree with you on that," I say. "Seeing that it's me, Chevy and Razor who are your family and families help each other."

"Is she related to me, too?" asks a familiar voice.

I lower my head before I glance over my shoulder. Damn it to hell. "I told you to stay in the truck."

Emily flutters her eyelashes. "Since when did I volunteer to be your lapdog?"

Violet laughs and releases the jack. "I like you. What's your name and why are we not hanging out?"

Emily's eyes dart to mine and she shuffles back. *That's right, Emily. There's a reason I told you to stay in the truck and if I'm going to keep you from being abducted by the Riot, you need to start listening.*

"This is Emily," I say. Violet and Stone won't rat that she's with us. At least the old Violet wouldn't. "She's staying with Eli for a few weeks."

That shuts Violet up and it also causes her face to go white. "Oh, shit."

Oh, shit is right. Since the term "club stuff" didn't mean squat to Emily, I try another approach. "Do you mind giving us a few minutes? This is a family issue."

Emily pivots on her heel and returns to the truck. I should announce everything as a family issue and she'll run back to Florida on foot.

When Emily slams the door to the truck, Violet loses her crap. "Why on earth would you tell Brandon about Emily being in town? He can't handle secrets. I had a tough time getting him to go to sleep last night because he was scared he was going to spill about Emily being at the funeral home and now he has to be worried about spilling that she's staying with Eli. Call me crazy, but I'm assuming that's a secret, too."

Stone begins rocking back and forth. This day keeps getting better.

"Hey, man," offers Chevy to Stone. "Don't obsess over it. You just don't bring up Emily. It's nothing to worry over."

"That's it!" yells Violet and taps her finger repeatedly to her head. "He can't stop thinking about it. You boys with your stupid concept of making things better, and you only make things worse! He doesn't need you. I don't need you. You are nothing to us."

A muscle in my jaw ticks. "Once upon a time we were tighter than blood family."

"Once upon a time the two of you cared for me more than the club." Her eyes land on Chevy and he rolls his neck to keep his anger in check.

I've seen Violet like this a lot since her dad died. I don't pretend to fathom her grief, but I'm not dealing with irrational. "What's going on with the car?"

"Tire blew," Stone answers despite Violet's disgusted grunt. "And it was the spare. I was explaining to Violet that we need to get one of them fixed."

I lift the blown tire off the ground. "Stone, grab the other tire and throw it in the back of the truck."

"No! We're fine without them." Violet seizes her brother's arm. He pushes past her and does what he needs to do: accepts our help.

"Get in the truck, Violet," I say with forced patience. "We'll fix the flats at the clubhouse and then get them back on the car for you."

Violet leans into me. "I really hate you."

I offer the tire to Chevy and he stays solid, glowering at Violet before shouldering the tire and heading for the truck. When Stone and Chevy are out of hearing range, I step into her space, uncaring that she's praying for my death. "You might not want our help, but your mom and your brother do. And if you can't behave like a sane person around Chevy, then fake it with silence. The truck, Violet. Now."

"You're an asshole, Oz."

I shrug. "Not the first girl who's called me that today."

"It should upset you that you're being called that." Violet tenses like she's willing to take a swing. In response, I cross my arms over my chest and plant my feet. History has taught me that she owns a mean right hook. "It should make you wonder what it is about yourself that people can't stand."

"Truth doesn't bother me."

"Normal people would be bothered that everyone thinks they're crazy and an asshole and an outlaw, but you're more than happy to live in your sick world of whatever you say goes."

"It's a family, and it's your family."

"We are not related!" A wildness strikes her eyes as tears line the edges. "I don't want to be a part of your family because your family kills!"

To keep from reminding her that her father died when a pickup hit him while he was driving without a helmet, I breathe deeply. "Our family is the type that fixes tires and offers help. Come or don't come, but I'm taking your brother with me. He looks like he needs a damn meal."

"I'm not one of you anymore." Her voice cracks. "I'm no longer fourteen and I'm not a follower like all of you. I don't listen to you and ask how high when you say jump."

I turn my back to her and go for the truck. "Razor is the oldest of us. He's the leader."

"You're wrong," she calls out. "It was you we followed, but I stopped and Brandon's going to stop and soon it'll all stop."

"You don't make any sense."

"I do. You know I do."

She doesn't and I continue walking so I won't chew her

out for breaking the heart of my best friend and for making her mother and brother feel guilty for welcoming the club's help. I chased snakes out of the barn with her when we were seven. At eight, with Chevy's help and a baseball bat, we scared away the monsters under her bed.

Me, her, Chevy and Razor—we were tight.

Were is a son-of-a-bitch word.

Chevy watches us from the front of the truck and Stone stands in the bed with his hands resting on the roof of the cab.

A twig snaps behind me and footsteps pad against the dirt. I swing into the driver's side and Emily has the good sense to stay silent as Chevy opens the passenger side. He offers his hand to Violet to assist her up the two-foot lift.

Instead of accepting, she grasps the console and hauls herself up with a struggle. Chevy waits, but the stone set of his face tells me we'll be throwing a few beers back soon in the interest of forgetting Violet's name.

Once she's in, Chevy closes the door and joins Stone in the bed of the truck. Two taps on the roof and I rev the engine.

With a fourteen-year-old in the back, I move along at thirty and the truck gently jostles from side to side. This time, Emily's not crashing into me, but I'd prefer her soft body pressing against mine instead of the awkward, heavy silence.

The trees create a green canopy and we're surrounded by dark shade. In the rearview mirror, my best friend stares out into nothingness.

"You could be nicer to him." I typically would never toss around our business in front of a stranger, but Emily will be leaving in a few weeks and she won't follow the conversation. This might be the only time Violet and I will be alone together.

"I could," Violet says as she stares into the same void Chevy does. "But where would that get any of us?"

The club is a blessing and Violet treats it as a curse. This family, this brotherhood, it's not the enemy. The enemy is the outside forces attempting to shake us up or take us down.

Those forces are people like Violet or people like Emily who watch a few TV shows and think we're thugs. It's law enforcement who believe anyone with a biker cut runs guns, drugs or women. Or worse, what threaten us are diseases like the one that ravages the woman I consider a grandmother. Diseases like cancer.

A burning in my throat causes me to shove those thoughts away.

The overhead canopy gives way and sunlight streams into the truck when I ease onto the long driveway that leads to the clubhouse then farther down to my home. I'm not sure who nicknamed it Thunder Road or why, but the name stuck. Violet lifts her hands into a ray of light bouncing off the side mirror. Something her dad used to do.

Losing someone you love, it'd be similar to losing your home. I blink. My home is everything. I suck in a breath to apologize to Violet when she speaks again.

"Run as fast as you can, Emily." Violet eyes me in a way that suggests she knows more than she should. "From what I've heard, some members of your club are okay with homicide."

Emily stiffens beside me and my fingers flex on the steering wheel. I should have let Violet rot in the summer sun.

She's lying, but Emily isn't aware of that. "You know that's not true."

Violet's been hanging with those full-of-themselves snob kids at school who think the Terror is the devil's playground. Can't stop haters from hating, but it hurts like hell when one of our own begins to spew the lies.

She rolls her eyes and when she pops her mouth open again, I cut her off. "How secure are you in your new *friendships* at school? What happens when they turn on you? Do you think we'll protect you while keeping Stone safe? Are your new friends going to stick around forever or are they going to decide that once in the MC always in the MC?"

Emily's head snaps in my direction because there's no mistaking the warning in my tone. The truth is, I'll protect Violet until the end, no matter how she disrespects me or Chevy or the club, but I have to hold some leverage over her to prevent her from saying anything to Emily that will cost me the chance to be a prospect.

Violet closes her mouth and we turn into Olivia's. Today proved one thing: girls are nothing but trouble.

Emily

NOT SURE WHAT TO DO WITH MYSELF WHEN everyone else seems relaxed, I sit in the shade on the front porch swing while Oz, Chevy and Stone patch the tires. Lars lies on his side at my feet and does that fast, hot dog pant. His sticky breath hits my ankle. I'm beginning to think he's been paid in doggie treats to annoy me.

The afternoon sun is blistering enough that perspiration forms in every crevice imaginable, and there's a heaviness in the air that causes my lungs to have to work harder to draw in a breath. It's humidity. We have it in Florida, but here the air is strangling.

Violet slips out of the house with two frosty glasses of lemonade, wearing a stern expression. She and Oz obviously have some issues, but the fact that they hate each other doesn't mean anything to me in terms of a possible friendship.

Violet hands me a glass, sits next to me on the swing and tips her cup toward me. "To staying cool."

I clink her glass and appreciate the slices of lemon floating among the ice cubes. Wow, I didn't know that people drank lemonade like this. I let the cool liquid run down my throat.

Olivia's house doesn't have air-conditioning and the temperatures are easily climbing near the one hundred mark. Inside is dark, but the outside has a breeze. The clubhouse has central air, but I'm not too interested in hanging out in there again...ever.

"You're wearing my skirt," Violet says.

"It's short," I say. "But thank you. This was an unexpected visit and I didn't exactly come prepared."

"It is short, but I only wear it on special occasions." She waggles her eyebrows, giving me the impression that the kisses she receives from guys don't remind her of dead fish.

Oz is crouched in front of the jacked-up car and he looks up at me. His shirt is wet from the heat and stretched tight across his chest. A sheen of sweat glistens against his skin and the sight is way prettier than I really think it should be. The boy is definitely ripped.

"Don't let the pretty muscles fool you," she says, catching me ogling. "Oz is married to the club and we both know that once you're married anything else becomes the dirty mistress."

Well, to be honest, I never thought much of being married or of being a mistress, but what she says sounds logical.

"Plus, you'd be another number in a long line of girls with him." Violet studies me as if she can tell my virginity status like carnival roadies can guess weight and age. "I have a feeling you aren't the hook-up type."

I'm not and I also prefer for my sex life, or lack thereof, to remain private. "Doesn't matter. I'm only visiting."

"That's not a bad thing—not being the hook-up type," she says, ignoring me. "And neither is being the girl who likes the hook-up. What makes any of it wrong is when you pretend to be something you're not. That's when the heartache starts."

Violet drinks from her lemonade like she didn't just say something profound. None of my friends have ever said anything so blatant in regards to sex. Usually if they do, it's associated with gossip. Until now, hooking up has never been used as a proverb for how to live life.

I immediately love, hate and envy Violet. Bet the guys she's kissed didn't fumble around her body like they were putting together a Lego set without instructions. "You know Oz and Chevy?" Back to safe conversations.

"We were raised together. I used to think it was a conspiracy. That maybe the old ladies scheduled their ovulation dates to create the quintessential quintet. I have a feeling they were disappointed that I was a girl."

Okay, several things going on there. "Old ladies?"

Violet grins and the hardness fades. In its place is a very soft, very teenage girl. Her blue eyes laugh before she does and what I enjoy about the laugh is it's not so much at me as with me.

"Telling off Oz *and* you don't know what an old lady is? Please never leave Snowflake. Stay here and be the only sane person besides me. Even better idea, take me with you. Florida has more sane people, right?"

I laugh, loudly. So loud that all three guys glance over at us.

"Ignore them." She waves them off like they're flies. "Did you know that we were supposed to be best friends?"

I force a swallow so I don't choke.

"Our moms were close. Hung out a lot…and I can see from the look on your face that I might as well be speaking Chinese."

I clear my throat and try to figure out the exact expression that gave me away. Whatever it was, I need to master it if I'm going to decipher this puzzle. "My mom doesn't talk about Kentucky. It's a sore spot for her."

"Figures. I'm going to erase Snowflake from my memory after I leave this rat-infested doorway to hell."

"Do you know much about my mom?" And me?

The breeze lifts part of her red hair. "Nope. I hope you don't take offense at this, but no one talks about either of you. It's a taboo subject."

"Oh." We both drink from our lemonade and I search for something to ease the awkward silence. "You didn't say what old ladies were."

"Wives or serious girlfriends of club members. It's this special designation that means you belong to a guy and no one can mess with you without serious consequences."

"Belong?" I don't care for the sound of that.

"Some other clubs call the women their property."

"Property?" I've turned into a parrot.

"The Terror don't take it that far. Oz's mom, Izzy? If she ever heard Oz's dad calling her property, she'd tear his privates off and hand his balls to him. It's still a boys' club, though. Don't fool yourself into thinking anything different."

She slides her thumb against the condensation of the glass creating a path. My chest aches for her. Being the sole girl surrounded by a boys' club. It must be lonely. "Who's part of the quintet?"

"It was supposed to be you, me, Chevy, Oz and Razor. Razor was born first and the rest of us popped out within a year. Have you met Razor yet?"

I think the answer is yes, but I shake my head no.

"Good. If you see him, run in the other direction. The wires in that boy's head are messed up beyond repair." She pauses then angles herself toward me. "Look, I don't know how long you're here for and I know you don't know me very well, but I'm around if you want to talk or text or anything. This place is crazy and it's not for everyone. God knows it's not for me."

Her forehead furrows and, in that moment, I like Violet. She's real and she's honest and there aren't many people in life who are that way. I yank out the burner phone Eli bought me and hand it to her. After a quick sultry pout pic of herself, Violet types in her number.

"It's not easy to fit into Snowflake to begin with," she continues, adding another picture then another number. "It's harder when you have the title of Reign of Terror offspring to struggle out from underneath."

Her blue eyes meet mine and when she offers me the phone my heart folds in on itself. I can't imagine growing up around this house, next to a clubhouse full of bras, with a matriarch who's okay with jumping out of coffins. I've always been grateful for the life I've had, understanding that any choice at any time could have made my life completely different from what I know now, but the weight of that knowledge just got heavier.

I rest my hand over Violet's. "I puked when Olivia rose like a zombie out of a casket."

She flashes this brilliant smile. "Oh, Lord, lying in a casket. That sounds like something she would do. So do you know how long you're here?"

For as long as I want. "No."

"If you want out, let me know. There's some awesome field parties. Like real parties, not the crazy-ass things that go on around here."

"Okay." At home, I've attended a few parties. Nothing raging with heavy drugs or the ones that cops bust. The type where the parents stay upstairs while we watch a movie or play games. Then when it gets late, the lights will turn down and the couples will find dark corners to make out. That would be where I had my first kiss.

Oz lifts the hem of his shirt, exposing his cut abs, and swipes his brow with the material. Oh my with chocolate on top. That was just beautiful.

"A word of advice." Violet disturbs my gawking and embarrassment rages through me.

"Sure."

"Chevy, Oz and Razor...they're trouble. Pretty to look at, but trouble. Getting mixed up with them will hurt you in the end. They're club boys until their dying breath. Nothing good comes out of it for anyone else. Trust me."

Rocks crackle under a car tire and, from the passenger side, Olivia examines us as if surprised. I quickly ask, "Do you know what Honeysuckle Ridge is?"

Violet's head moves so quickly that her hair flies through the air. "Who told you about that?"

She's spitting daggers at me and I lose my voice. Izzy parks the car near the guys.

Violet leans into me and whispers rapidly, "Honeysuckle Ridge is club business. Very private club business. I'm not even supposed to know. Do not bring it up to anyone else. Do you understand? I like you, Emily, because you're the first glimpse I've had in my entire life that people can leave Snowflake, cut ties with the club and have a normal life. Don't let them suck you in. Get out of Snowflake as fast as you can."

When Olivia reaches the porch Violet stops talking. Olivia waves. The two of us act like marionettes as we wave back. Olivia then extends a plastic grocery bag in Violet's direction. "Nice to see you, Violet. Take this in for me."

"I'm not staying," says Violet. "As soon as the car is fixed, we're leaving."

"Doesn't mean you can't take this bag in for me." Olivia's glare chills me even though it's aimed at Violet. A few seconds pass before Violet snatches the bag and props the door open for Olivia.

"Are you coming?" Olivia asks me.

"In a few."

With Izzy right behind them, they walk in and I try to ingest the crazy pile of information. Dad told me I'm safe. That the reason that everyone overreacts is because they buy into what the club wants them to believe, but how can the concern and fear in Violet's eyes be part of a pretend game?

"You okay?" Oz's boots stomp against the porch stairs as he climbs them. He rests a shoulder against one of the huge logs supporting the roof and wipes his forearm across his brow.

Oz is dirty. Grease streaks across his cheek. Dust causes his arms to be browner than normal. He's in need of a shower— desperately.

Oz wet.

A warm sensation flutters through my chest. I am officially the most impaired person in the world because I melt into a puddle of goo around this guy.

"I'm fine," I answer. "Are you okay?"

"Why wouldn't I be?"

My lips squish to the side. *I dunno. Maybe because we almost kissed and then tore each other's heads off and you seem perfectly fine behaving as if none of it happened.* Which I guess is for the best, but it's unsettling how Oz can move on so easily from something so life-altering.

Violet's words about heartache and Oz replay in my mind. I sigh. I'm already a number on his still-growing list.

"You look freaked out," Oz says. "It's why I came over."

My legs flex and the swing creaks as it rocks. It's a soothing motion that's welcome in the chaos. "Have you ever seen this 'other' motorcycle club?"

Oz's eyebrow rises with the question and my hand gesture. "Did you air quote an illegal club?"

I shrug because I did.

Oz scans the yard and it's surprisingly empty. No Chevy. No Stone. To my shock, he defies unspoken personal space barriers and crouches in front of me. He's so freaking massive that even with me on the swing, he's only an inch or so below my eye level.

He grabs the swing by the seat and it grinds to a halt. Oz's fingers brush along the skin of my thigh. My heart stutters. Stupid heart. Stupid short skirt. Stupid deep blue eyes and wild charcoal hair. Stupid, stupid, stupid me for licking my suddenly dry lips.

Oz follows the action. The way my tongue snuck out and because he's staring so intently, I nervously suck in my bottom lip. He watches that too and those eyes grow dark. Breathing would be good and would possibly ease the burning in my lungs.

Oz drags his gaze to mine. "Our club doesn't kill people."

I blink. Kill people? "What?"

"You asked about the illegal club and I saw the look on your face in the truck and then when you were talking to Violet. We aren't what you think."

"Okay."

"Not okay. I need you to know that what Violet said in the truck was a lie. We're legit. What you see around you, what you will see once Eli returns and allows this place to go back to normal…it's a family. We take care of each other. Depend on each other. There isn't a situation we face alone, a need that isn't met."

His words sink past my skin, past my muscles and settles into a hollow area in my soul and I shift. I love my parents. More than most people would admit. And Dad's parents are amazing, but there's a part of me that wonders what it would be like to belong to something…more.

My lips twitch up, but the attempted grin feels empty. "Next you'll tell me you gather around a piano and sing Christmas carols."

Oz chuckles. "Won't lie, after a few shots, I've heard some of the guys sing a few tunes."

"Not lyrics to an old Guns N' Roses song. Christmas songs. 'Rudolph.' 'White Christmas.' 'We Three Kings.'"

"Hey, you haven't heard 'The Twelve Days of Christmas' until you've heard us, sweetheart."

"Liar."

"Cross my heart." And he does the accompanying motion.

"Tell me what Honeysuckle Ridge is."

Oz's entire face brightens with his smile. It's a gorgeous one. Dazzling even. "Good try, but not good enough. Already told you, I have no idea."

"Now you're a liar."

One slow, sexy-as-hell shoulder shrug. "What are you going to do about it?"

Is he flirting with me?

The screen door screeches open and Oz casually stands as if it's normal to be crouched in front of someone he barely knows. Violet and Oz eyeball each other as she walks out and he walks in.

When the door shuts again she clicks her tongue at me. "You are destined to be the type that learns the hard way, aren't you?"

My body rolls forward and I lower my head into my hands. Evidently I am.

OZ

IT'S CHAOS.

Yelling.

Screaming.

And it's only the second quarter of the game.

I'm blowing my damn ears off with the whistle, but the little punk kid from the home team is still chasing the skinny kid with the ball. "You're not on the field anymore!"

Both kids turn their heads to look at me and realize they've raced past the end zone and onto a farmer's private property. There's a chuckle from the parents on the sidelines as the two run their asses back.

"Ball," I call out because they never remember to hand the football back before they huddle with their coach. It's summer so it's flag football instead of tackle. Half the time, the kids forget the flag part and hammer the hell out of each other.

"Time out!" Two hundred and fifty pounds of once-upon-a-time linebacker and now dad to the little punk in question waves at me.

There's only seconds left until the half, but it's eight-year-old flag football so why the hell not? "You got it."

The kid with red hair being chased attempts to throw the ball to me and misses by twelve feet. There's a reason why he's not the quarterback. The ball lands behind Emily. She sits on a blanket beside Mom and Olivia and the three of them are grinning at me, but Emily more. Fuck me for liking it. She has the type of smile that can light up a black hole.

The two of us have been around each other for over two weeks. Hanging. Not hanging. Just sort of existing while she and Olivia hustle each other in cards. So far, it's been low-key, but being around Emily makes mundane easy.

"Hey!" Chevy sidles beside me wearing the same black-and-white ref shirt that I am. "Eli's coming back today, right?"

"Yeah."

"Think he'll give you the night off from Emily?" Chevy inclines his head to two girls from school. "If so, we have plans."

I graduated with them. Hell, I played on the monkey bars with them in kindergarten. One is blond and all legs. The other has brown hair and is all big breasts. Neither has anything on Emily.

"They're good girls," I say. "You know where I stand on that."

They're honor roll, panic about curfew and are on time for church every Sunday morning. I don't have a problem with good girls. To be honest, I'm hoping I can find a good girl with a bad side to marry me one day, but this isn't one day and right now the only thing that happens with a good girl is they get hurt because they're hunting for what I won't give.

Chevy flashes a sly smile. "They came to me, man. Not the other way around. Both of them are leaving town next week to travel Europe before they head out of state for college. They said they've watched the Terror their entire lives and want to experience one night with us before they leave town."

Because there's an invisible force field surrounding Snowflake. Once people leave, they never come back.

"Sometimes a good girl needs to be bad," Chevy continues.

Right as he says it, the blonde smiles in a way that promises a night that has my type of bad written all over it. "Gotta check with Eli."

"It's all I'm asking." Chevy blows the whistle to indicate the time-out is over.

Emily

OZ JOGS ALONGSIDE A YOUNG BOY WHO DOESN'T run right. He doesn't walk right, either. At least he didn't when he moved onto the field. His legs are in braces and he spent most of the game on the sidelines in a wheelchair.

That is until the game ended and Oz immediately lowered himself to the boy's eye level and tossed him the football. Oz talked with the boy and then to his parents. Minutes later, both teams met at the line of scrimmage with Oz and Chevy shouting instructions.

The ball was handed off to this boy and now the crowd is yelling and cheering and my pulse pounds. Oz is jogging backward now, encouraging him to continue forward. Both teams sprint alongside Oz and the boy. All of them calling the boy's name. The kid is pumping his little arms, pushing legs that seem to weigh against him, but he has this utter look of joy that brings tears to my eyes.

I'm on my knees on the blanket, clapping and praying and begging for him not to fall. To finish and to finish strong.

He crosses the line and the sideline explodes into a deafening sound of happiness. My arms are in the air and I'm laughing. Laughing because the kid is laughing. Laughing because Oz is laughing.

Oz picks the boy up and all the kids applaud. Chevy comes up on the other side so that they both carry his weight. Chevy, Oz and the massive crowd of kids begin a victory lap.

"He's good with kids." Eli crouches next to me.

"What?" It's like he started in the middle of the conversation instead of the beginning.

"Oz is good with kids. Always has been." He gestures to the wheelchair a little farther down. "Especially the ones with disabilities. He has a patience and gentleness most men don't. That's why Brian's parents are here. Oz includes him in the game."

Brian must be the child with the braces.

"What's wrong with Brian?" I ask.

"Cerebral palsy."

"Oh." Oh.

"How's it been?" Eli asks.

"Good." I watch the party on the field, wishing that I was part of the celebration. "How was your business stuff?"

"Good," he answers.

Eli's been gone for two weeks and it's odd seeing him, but it shouldn't be. This is his hometown, not mine. I've settled into a weird but comfortable routine with Oz and Olivia and have even gotten used to Eli texting me to confirm I haven't dashed back to Florida yet.

In the parking lot a herd of guys in black leather vests hang out near a gaggle of motorcycles. "Do you ever travel alone?"

"Yeah," he says. "But you and I have a shopping date and I'll feel better doing it with some backup. What do you think of heading to Nashville and letting me buy you some clothes that don't encourage me to tear the eyes out of every man here?"

I laugh and it surprises me. By the way Eli's grin grows it must have surprised him, as well. I pick at the grass in front of me. "Isn't Louisville closer?"

"Nashville's a hell of a town. There's a bar on the strip that serves a great pulled pork sandwich."

I detest pork, but Eli means well so I keep my food preferences to myself. "You don't have to do that, you know. I get that when you visit Florida shopping is a way to fill the time together, but I'm here so you don't have to spend money on me."

Eli pulls at his earlobe. "I haven't been much of a man in your life and taking you shopping doesn't make up for not being there, but I want to do this for you."

As I sort through the grass, I spot some clover and pretend I'm interested in it. I don't know what to say or do. Eli entered my life seven years ago and never has he said anything so real and raw. It freaks me out and creates an ache I don't understand.

Why couldn't he have said that seven years ago? Or maybe seventeen years ago or whenever my mom was on the verge of leaving?

"Hate to admit it, but I've spent a good portion of your life wondering what to buy you for Christmas or your birthday, but I never get you anything because I don't know you well enough to purchase anything that would mean shit. So this, taking you shopping, it's all I have to give and I'd appreciate it if you'd let me do it."

I peek at him out of the corner of my eye and the expectation on his face absolutely hurts. "Okay."

His good mood seems to return. "Okay."

"Hey, Eli." Oz approaches us and both Eli and I stand. They share a fist bump and Oz and I share a loaded glance that causes my skin to tingle.

"I'm going to take some of the crew I left behind and go to Nashville with Emily for the night," says Eli. "We'll be back tomorrow."

I pop my mouth open to protest an overnight trip, but Eli's already shaking his head. "You agreed."

I shut my mouth. I did, but not to him spending money on a hotel room.

Oz spins the football in his hands as his eyes flicker between us. "Do you want me in on this?"

"No. You can take a few days off."

Chevy calls Oz's name and Oz tosses the football to me. "Stay here, will you, Emily? I need to ask you something."

Oz walks off without waiting for my response and I expect the two of them to head over to the two girls circling near us like the little vultures they are. He talked to them during halftime and I'm going to pretend that every single second of those five minutes didn't bother me.

I roll the football, trying to figure out why he gave it to me and why he asked me to stay. Eli raises an eyebrow and it's freaky because I did, too. I force mine down, wondering if Eli noticed. Eli excuses himself to discuss plans with someone in the parking lot.

"Hey!" Violet's red hair is pulled up and little wisps frame her face.

"What are you doing here?" I ask.

"You see that?" She points to a guy on the football field across from ours. He's tall, has blond hair, is broad-shouldered and, after hanging out with the Terror for the past week, appears very, very normal.

"Yeah?"

"That's Jared and he's going to be my ride tonight." The way she emphasized *ride* makes my cheeks blush. "Have you considered my offer? Jared has a friend."

She waggles her eyebrows at *friend* and I have to clear my throat so I can breathe.

Violet and I talk on the phone. She digs for info on my life in Florida and fills me in on her adventures in Snowflake, which includes a lot of parties with a lot of people who sound a million times more dangerous than anything I've experienced while being at Olivia's.

"I'm telling you, if you go to bed early, I bet you could slip out through the kitchen and hang with me for the night and then I'll have you back before anyone notices."

She wants me to go to a party with her and, well…lying isn't my style. I texted Eli for permission to go and I was greeted with a firm: hell, no.

"Why don't you come to Olivia's and hang out?" I ask.

"They're getting to you, aren't they?"

A *pshaw* sound leaves my mouth because they so aren't, but then my eyes automatically trail over to Oz and he's speaking to them. Oh my freaking God, he's speaking to those girls again.

"Emily!" Violet slips into my line of vision. "What did I tell you? They are pretty looking, but they're full of hurt."

I sweep my hair away from my forehead and try not to let it bother me that the girl with the overly large chest touched Oz's arm. "What happened between you and Chevy?"

A shadow crosses her face. "The club is what happened to Chevy and the club is what's happening to Oz. They can act nice and sweet, but they're dogs. Mark my words on this."

My stomach bottoms out. "Did he cheat on you?"

"Yeah," she says. "But not in the way that you think. He said he loved me and then...when it counted he didn't love me."

Violet presses a hand to her stomach in a way that causes me to take her other hand. She's in pain and I wish I could remove the part that aches.

"Violet?" The soft way Chevy said her name startles me more than his sudden appearance. "Are you okay?"

Her blue eyes snap to his and there's no mistaking the absolute sadness there. They stare at each other. One second. Two. As we wander into three I feel like an intruder in a very intimate yet electrically charged moment.

"Violet!" Jared cups his hands to his mouth to get her attention. "Let's go."

Chevy's eyes briefly close and when he reopens him, the breath is knocked out of me by the hurt haunting him. "Don't do it. I am begging you to not do this."

Violet's spine straightens as she lifts her chin. "Just like I asked you not to do what you did."

She walks away, slamming her shoulder into his arm, and

Chevy remains still, focusing on the ground as if nothing else around him exists.

Oz swipes the football I had forgotten I held and presses it to Chevy's chest. "Everything's in order. Why don't you go and get the kids together."

It takes a few seconds, but Chevy accepts the ball and heads onto the field.

"*That* was comfortable," I say.

"You get to leave Snowflake." Oz watches his best friend, my cousin, round up some kids. "I get to live with it for the rest of my life."

"Super." Because what else do you say? "I stayed, so what do you need?"

"Well." He studies me in a way that makes me feel like he's seen me with my clothes off. "I have a boy in a wheelchair who asked if he gets a kiss on the cheek from the prettiest girl here since he scored a touchdown."

I cross my arms over my chest. "Did the two girls drooling over you refuse?"

Oz cracks this smile that makes me love and hate him. "I said pretty, Emily. You're the only girl around here who fits that description. Are you in or what?"

"Yeah," I say, as I secretly dance within. "I'm in."

OZ

I LEAN DOWN AND I'M EYE TO EYE WITH ONE OF the craziest sons-of-bitches on the planet. Sweat drenches my T-shirt thanks to the muggy night. Razor's jaw swells from the last play and my hand throbs from a hit I took from him a few series back. Blood drips from each scrape on my body and I chuckle when he wipes at the small trickle of red at the corner of his mouth.

A sharp gust rushes through the trees of the forest surrounding the property, bringing with it the smell of honeysuckle. The branches bend and the leaves flip back to show their white underbelly. A few stars twinkle overhead through the racing clouds, but the wind warns of an impending storm.

Razor's golden-blond hair falls over his eyes and being on the opposite side of the line from him would cause most men to shiver. A slow sadistic grin promising pain slides across his face. "You think you can handle me, Oz?"

"I think you're all talk." I think Razor could easily slit my throat with that knife strapped to his leg, and he wouldn't shed a single tear as he witnessed me bleed out. Because we've been close since we were kids, I gamble that he'll keep his knife and his impulsive tendencies to himself.

"I'm man enough to take you down," he taunts.

"Nah," I answer. "I don't think you are."

His insane smile widens. "Know what happened when I used to walk into the shower in the locker room at school?"

Knowing he's a crazy bastard, guys tripped over themselves to get the hell out of his way. "What?"

He winks. "They took one look at me and applauded."

I snort and when Chevy calls the snap, I have to switch gears and throw myself at Razor to stop him from tackling my best friend before Chevy throws the ball.

"Touchdown!" Chevy calls, but Razor rages forward. I dig my feet into the ground, determined not to allow him an inch. With muscles locked tight, I break through his arms and push off his chest, causing him to stumble.

Razor's eyes glaze over and he's a bull seeing red. His arm swings back with a ready-made fist. Not noticing how Razor just lost his shit, Chevy slips between us. I grab Chevy and toss him to the side and yell, "Chevy said touchdown, bitch."

Razor blinks, and the horror mirrored there as he realizes he was two seconds from pile driving me and Chevy causes me to ache for my longtime friend.

Chevy offers Razor his fist and with a deep breath Razor shakes off Mr. Hyde for Dr. Jekyll.

Regret deepens the already constant pain in Razor's eyes and instead of bumping Chevy's fist, he holds out his hand for a shake. Chevy accepts and the two end up in a brief half hug.

Razor's haunted by a hurt too deep to understand. His mother messed him up in ways that none of us can begin to know how to heal, and because of that, we'll always have his back.

When they let go, Razor nods at me. I nod back. The all clear that we're good.

Razor picks up the football, taps Stone on the back and pitches the ball in the air. "Let's work on your catching."

Stone reaches out his hands and the ball soars straight through. Chevy turns his head to hide the wince. I school my expression but internally feel the pain. Olivia used to read a book to me when I was a kid about a lion that was a late bloomer. I sure as hell hope that fifteen will be Stone's bloom year because, for him, fourteen ain't doing shit.

Not missing a beat, Razor swipes the ball and leads Stone away from the guys shooting the breeze. A few light cigarettes and laugh loudly. Everyone's roughed up and bleeding. The game's more tackle than two-hand touch and that's the way we like it.

We're in the large grassy area between Olivia's house and the clubhouse. Thanks to the utility poles, we can play football all night and typically we do, but this summer, my ass has been on Emily patrol.

I lift my shirt and remove the blood from my lip and when I glance over to the porch to check on Emily, she quickly looks away and slides that long dark hair forward like a shield. She's playing cards with Olivia on the porch and even though she's dealing, I will her to peek at me one more time.

Eli's gone again and so is most of the club as they've been traveling for the business. He was here for a few days and was stuck to Emily's side and now he's on the road and I'm back on duty.

Everyone was banned from here when Eli was away the first time. Now, with him gone again, anyone who is a brother is allowed to come and go, but there's no partying, no old ladies, no friends of the club, no hang-arounds and above all, no strangers.

All of it is to protect Emily. The slow introduction, according to Eli, is to desensitize her to the way things really work around here.

Chevy kicks at the back of my knee and I sock him in the shoulder. "What was that for?"

"For staring at Emily like you're three seconds away from showing her the back of the clubhouse and sharing dirty secrets. You do that with Eli around and you can forget making prospect. He'll put a bullet in your brain." He mimics his finger as the gun, pulls the mock trigger, then stumbles with the imagined impact.

I shrug even though I know he's right. "She's hot."

"That's sick. She's my cousin."

I don't mention how Violet was like a sister to me and how Chevy buying condoms six months ago when he was solid with her made me want to vomit. If he didn't love her, I would have torn out his jugular.

Chevy flicks his chin to where Razor's showing Stone how to hold his hands together for a catch. "Ever wonder if we'll get a text from him telling us that we need to help hide a body?"

"Yeah." Not if. At this rate, with his temper, it'll be a when. "I kissed her."

Chevy drops his head. "When?"

Out of the corner of my eye, I look over at the porch again. Emily lays down her cards and smiles at Olivia. Fucking smiles. The type that brightens her face. The one that she doesn't do often. The one that she's given me more than a few times. The one I crave for her to give me again and again. The one I see in my dreams as she's crawling up the bed half-naked to kiss me.

God, there's something wrong with me.

"We kissed at the clubhouse in Lanesville." I withhold the part where she blackmailed me. I've gotta own some pride. "I thought she was leaving."

"Why are you telling me?" he asks.

I meet his eyes and he shakes his head in pissed-off understanding. I'm telling him because someone knowing I made a mistake will prevent me from doing it again.

"You're messed up," Chevy says. "You know that, right?"

"Yeah. I do."

"You want me to snag some girls again? Maybe that will help."

It helps him with Violet. He gets buzzed and loses himself in someone else. He did it two weeks ago with the girl we met up with after the peewee football game. But me? The girl I was with wanted sex. Pretty much asked me to fuck her in several languages, but I ended up taking her home. I couldn't stop comparing her to Emily.

Pigpen strides up to us. "Are we going another round?"

Over on the porch, Olivia laughs and rolls her head against the Adirondack chair to appraise her granddaughter. Emily watches her for a second, then gathers the cards and picks up two glasses as she stands. Good girl for reading the signs of Olivia's exhaustion.

The games are over for tonight.

"Tell everyone to pack it in. Olivia's heading to bed." Which means Emily will be following soon and my next phase of protecting her begins.

Emily

TRISHA: ELI STILL GONE?

Me: Yep. His job requires him to travel a lot. You should have seen Oz and his friends play football tonight. It was full-on tackle. No pads. Definition of insanity.

After I brought Olivia inside, almost everyone tore off on their bikes, and it's left the house very quiet and very lonely. It's moments like this that I appreciate that Trisha never sleeps. She's one of those people who thrive off four hours of sleep and copious amounts of coffee in the morning.

Trisha: You talk about this Oz guy a lot. Are you sure nothing is going on with you two?

Me: Nothing. There is nothing going on between us.

Going against what Eli had asked, I told Trisha that I was visiting my biological father's family. That was a bomb she didn't expect me to drop. Because that was big enough, I was able to easily avoid telling her anything about motorcycle clubs or gangs or the Riot or the Terror or any of this nonsense that has hijacked my life. I also didn't tell her that I kissed Oz.

But she does know about Olivia and Eli and Oz always being around and how I want to come home, but then again how I find myself...curious. She's promised not to tell and if I believe anyone about anything, it would be Trisha.

Trisha: Daddy says fervent denial is a sign of hiding something. :)

But I don't believe her on this, even though her dad does question people for a living. Me: And I'm going to bed now.

Trisha: lol Night

Me: Night

I toss my phone onto the bed beside me, ease onto the floor and open the door to my room. A glance down the hallway toward Olivia's room and my heart jumps. Razor leans with his back against the wall and he peers into Olivia's darkened room.

Violet's warnings go off in my head. That I should stay away, that I should run, but there's something very broken in his expression and it's not the type of broken that causes fear, but the type I've spotted in my mother whenever she talks about her old home—about Kentucky.

"She fell asleep a while ago," I say. I know because I checked on her twice. She seemed more exhausted than normal this evening.

"I know," he replies.

Razor doesn't say much to me, and from what I observed when he accompanied me and Eli to Nashville, he doesn't say much to anyone so I don't feel slighted by his lack of conversation.

"I was going to get something to drink. Do you want anything?"

He looks wearily into Olivia's room again and then follows me down the hallway. Once in the kitchen, I get some water out of the faucet and set a full glass for him on the counter then work on fixing a glass for myself.

"Nashville was fun," I say to fill the void. Reality is, it was fun in a weird way. Each of the guys went out of their way to talk to me or tease me in a good-natured way, and Eli...Eli and I shared some awkward conversation and a few times we shared some easy conversation. It's surprising how much even I enjoyed those moments. "So your dad is Hook?"

Lars pads into the kitchen. When I turn off the faucet and open my mouth to speak again, Razor's crouched on the floor scratching Lars behind the ears and Lars's leg kicks as if he's in heaven. What's amazing? Razor is smiling.

Smiling.

I've been here for weeks and I've never seen him smile.

He has a gorgeous smile and it makes me realize just how beautiful the boy is. Blond hair, blue eyes, built a lot like Oz, but when I look at him, there's no flutter in my stomach. No sense of urgency to be near him and I scowl. There goes my theory that the only reason I have tingles in my blood when Oz is around is because he's attractive.

Lars plants a large wet kiss on Razor and instead of pushing him away like I expect the big bad biker to do, Razor only plants a kiss back on the dog's head. He then stands like none of that happened. "Thank you for what you're doing for Olivia."

My stomach sinks. "I'm not doing anything."

He shrugs again. "She's like a mom to a lot of us and it's hard to lose your mom."

Pain flashes in his eyes and because this moment is nearing uncomfortable I ask, "Is she like a mom to Oz?"

Razor's gaze darts toward the living room. "Ask him."

OZ

RAZOR'S TALKING AND THAT'S A BIG DEAL. YEAH, he shoots the shit with me and Chevy and, once upon a time, he and Violet were the best of friends, but the kid doesn't talk. His past with his mother messed him up so much that he feels safer inside himself than he does with the rest of the world.

He may stay bottled up within himself, but he's loyal and has heart. I couldn't think of anyone else besides Chevy I'd want by my side if the world went to hell, and it moves me to see that he's talking with Emily. That he said thank you to Emily.

I'm not the only one who's noticed how her presence has brightened Olivia's world.

"I'm out," Razor says then walks out the back door.

Emily stands stunned near the sink. Yeah, a lot of girls look at Razor like that. He's like an angel with a demented side and girls either flock to him or run away. Emily seems to be leaning toward the running away, which means she has some semblance of a survival instinct.

What I'm not liking is my sense of relief that she's not attracted to him.

"You okay?" I ask.

Emily drinks from the glass of water in her hand. "Yeah. Why are you still here?"

Because it's my job to watch over you. To protect you. "A few guys stayed behind to talk and I saw the kitchen light flip on. Just thought I'd check everything out."

She shifts her lips to the side as if she doesn't buy my answer, but moves along. "Is Razor okay?"

No. "He misses his mom sometimes and Olivia is one of the few people he feels he has left."

Emily frowns. "What happened to his mom?"

"Razor's right to thank you. Olivia's happier with you here."

Emily's eyes immediately flash to mine with the non-answer. What happened to Razor's mom is his business and it bothers him when people talk about it behind his back.

"Is Olivia also like a mom to you?"

Even though I overhead Emily ask the question of Razor first, it still creates a ripple of pain. I love Olivia and she's dying. "Olivia is a lot of things to a lot of people. Me included. The world will be a dark place if she dies."

If, because the next round of chemo will work. Because the doctors will figure out something new. They have before. There's no reason to think they won't present us with a miracle again.

Emily sets the glass on the counter and hugs her body. "I'm sorry she's sick."

Me, too. "Not living here—you missed growing up with a hell of a woman."

Emily laugh-snorts and it's cute on her. "I mean this in a better way than a few weeks ago—but she's still crazy. All of you are."

"And we wear that title proud." I like a little too much that Emily smiles with my words. "I'm dying of curiosity. What do your fancy rich-doctor's-kid friends say about you being a child of a motorcycle club?"

Her smile fades. "They don't know."

I didn't realize how much I had been enjoying Emily's company until the weight of her statement crashed into me. A few weeks ago, I would have been angry at her for obviously looking down on us, but tonight, after watching her with Olivia, after seeing how she's made people I love happy, I offer her a chance. "How come?"

Emily worries her bottom lip and her finger taps against her arm. She's nervous about my reaction and given how I've treated her, she has good reason to be concerned. I walk across the kitchen and then lift myself until I'm sitting on the counter beside her.

The scent of the beach hits me as I nudge her with my knee. "I promise I won't tear into for your answer. No judgment."

"Be careful, Oz. You're acting like we're friends or something and that will totally ruin the whole 'the only reason we're in the same room is because we're being forced to by tragic circumstances' thing."

I chuckle and I get a ghost of that beautiful smile she

showed before. "Isn't this what people do? Ask random questions to find out if they want to be friends?"

"Then try favorite color, do you have a pet, what's your favorite food."

Fine. "Give me the answers to all that."

She rolls her eyes. "Blue, a goldfish and meatballs."

Say what? "Meatballs? Who the hell likes meatballs as their favorite food?"

"Wow, that sounded judgey." But there's a tease in her voice.

"You got me. I judged, but meatballs?"

"Spaghetti is boring without them, plus they make a great sandwich. You are totally underestimating the power of a meatball."

I am and I'm smiling and she's smiling and I should leave well enough alone, but it's bothering me that she didn't answer about why she hasn't told anyone about Eli. "Why haven't you told anyone?"

It's like I blew out a flickering flame and I somewhat hate myself for it.

Emily readjusts her footing, sucks in a deep breath and says, "I don't like reminding my father I'm adopted."

Out of all the answers Emily could have given, that isn't the one I expected. I had prepared myself for her to be ashamed, but when I search her face, I see she's telling me the honest-to-God truth. "Why?"

Emily looks over at the pictures taped to the refrigerator. Most of them are group photos and there isn't a snapshot that doesn't show our crazy side. My favorite is of me, Oz, Chevy, Razor and Violet from last year, covered in mud after we created a homemade waterslide on a steep hill on the other side of Cyrus's property. You can't tell much about us beyond our open eyes and smiles.

"I may not understand a lot about all of this craziness, but I understand that Olivia loves you like you're related to her. Like she never had a choice in loving you, but my dad did. He could have taken one look at me and decided he wanted nothing to do with a woman who had a child. He had a choice and there isn't a day I don't thank God that he chose not only Mom, but me."

My gut twists for her. "I've seen your dad around you. The man is nuts about you."

"He is, but wouldn't it hurt him if I was curious about any of you? If I talked about Eli with all my friends?"

Emily turns her head so she can meet my eyes and there's a striking honesty that almost brings me to my knees. Olivia didn't have to love me. Neither did Cyrus or Eli or anyone else in the club, but they do. Somewhere deep down inside, I understand what she's saying because what does it say about me if I do think about something more than the security company? But I shut that thought down. This club, this family...it's all I want.

Hating that I took her to a place that bothers her, I hop off the counter and draw Emily into a hug. She keeps her arms wrapped tight around herself. She doesn't fall into me, but she doesn't pull away.

"Thank you for not judging me," she whispers.

I lower my head and whisper back, "Thank you for being here...for spending time with Olivia." With me.

"Does this mean we're friends?" she asks.

I chuckle and at the same time she giggles. "How about it means whatever it needs to mean."

"All right. I can live with that."

Emily

I OPEN THE DOOR TO MY ROOM AND PAUSE WHEN pipes squeal, then water hits the base of the shower. I stepped out a few minutes ago and like every morning when Eli's gone, Oz gets in after me. There's something intimate in sharing a shower. I was naked in there. Now he's naked in there. Sweet baby Jesus, Oz naked.

With a shake of my head, I follow the scent of freshly brewed coffee into the kitchen and twist my hair off the back of my neck, secure it in a messy bun then sweep my bangs away from my forehead. I'm barely out of the shower and sweat's already dotting my brow.

I crack the window over the sink. The loud clicking of the cicadas drifts in. Ugh. Nine in the morning and they're already making that racket. That means today is going to be blistering.

"There's no reason you can't get my coffee." Olivia enters with a home manicure set basket and is her usual ball-of-sunshine self.

"Normal people say 'good morning' and follow up requests with strange words like 'please' and 'thank you.'" Mimicking what Oz has done every morning, I pull a mug out of the cupboard, pour Olivia some coffee and deposit it in front of her.

She picks it up and blows over the top of the mug. "Your father will be back tomorrow."

My head snaps in her direction and then I open the fridge. She meant her son, not my dad. "Oz mentioned Eli should be returning soon."

I dip my head into the cold air of the fridge. If I tuck myself into a ball maybe I could squeeze in there and hang for the day.

"Electricity costs money," Olivia mumbles. "Have you figured out what Honeysuckle Ridge is yet?"

I roll my eyes, grab the orange juice and we fall into our normal routine. She asks the same question every morning and every morning I have the same answer. "Nothing yet that pertains to me."

I fill my cup and, instead of abandoning the subject, I sink into my chair three spots from hers. "Why don't you tell me what it is that you want me to know?"

"You've only been here a month." Olivia hunts through the basket. "You're just now starting to act like a normal human instead of a wild rabbit terrified of being shot. You and I have a lot more to learn about each other."

I sigh and the slant of her mouth tells me she caught it. I've played the game with her. Literally. Every card game imaginable, and I've even sat with her as we flipped through endless photos of people I care nothing about. "What more can you want from me? I've answered every question you've asked."

"This isn't a job interview," she says. "You already have the position of my granddaughter. I want you to stick around until you actually believe you're part of this family."

I am never going to discover what transpired between my mom and Eli.

Olivia produces a fingernail file and that's when I notice the split nail on the pointer finger of her right hand. I tap the tip of my tongue to the roof of my mouth. Olivia's left side isn't strong.

"Can I do it?" I ask.

Olivia shoots me a glare that makes me want to shrink into a corner. "I'm not a fucking invalid."

Won't lie. She scares the hell out of me. "I never said you were, but this is the kind of thing Mom and I would do for each other—for fun. *Fun.*" I overemphasize the word. "Excuse me for trying to act like *family.*"

I kick away from the table, put the orange juice back in the fridge with more racket than needed, and right as I leave the kitchen, Olivia calls out, "Do you always resort to behaving like a two-year-old when someone yells at you?"

The muscles in my back tense. Who interacts this way? "Have you ever tried being nice, or is that what will cause you to melt? It must have been a bummer for you with what happened when water was poured on your sister."

Olivia laughs. The deep one, and my lips twitch with it. I don't understand her, but for some reason when she does laugh, I like it because it's a confirmation I won at least one round.

She waves her hand in the air. "Get back in here."

Reluctantly, I sit next to her. Relationships shouldn't be

this way—continual fights for dominance. I take the nail file and her hand then pause at the cold temperature of her skin. She's freaking ice cubes. Crazy since the house is the desert at high noon.

I start filing and Olivia breaks the silence. "You don't feel sorry for me because I'm dying, do you?"

An overwhelming chill causes my stomach to roil. "I do, but you make it easy to forget that you're sick." It's the truth and I'm a horrible person. "Sorry for the witch comment."

"Don't apologize for that. Never for that. I like that you don't treat me differently. You've done more good for my soul than you can know." She breathes in deeply then releases the air at a slow pace. "Oz treats me differently."

I nibble on my bottom lip. "How so?"

"The second tree on the left," Olivia says. I should've known better than to expect a straight answer.

My hand freezes midfile. "What?"

"Where you'll go today, there will be a large oak tree. The second tree from the left. Look there."

"But I'm not going anywhere—"

She shushes me and Oz's heavy boots clump against the hardwood floor of the hallway and then enter the kitchen. The skin on the back of my neck prickles with anticipation. I lift my eyes to the mirror on the wall and sure enough his are locked on me and Olivia.

His hair is damp and sticks up in various ways. It's sexy as hell and my fingers flinch with the desire to run my hands through it again. Oz's gaze switches to the mirror and the breath catches in my chest when his blue eyes meet mine. We hold it that way. One second. Two.

Olivia clears her throat and I focus crazily on her nail again.

The cupboard squeaks behind me and then closes. A few seconds later Oz drops into the seat on Olivia's other side. "I would have gotten your coffee for you."

"I'm perfectly fine getting it myself."

I work hard to not look at either Oz or Olivia. She lied. Blatantly. She must have a reason for it, but I can't fathom what. Lying doesn't have a place for me. As I've mentioned to Oz, it creates integrity issues.

"I want you to take Emily swimming today," Olivia says. "I have the doctor's appointment in Louisville and it's too hot for the two of you to stay around here."

Um... "I don't have a bathing suit." I didn't buy one in Nashville.

Olivia slips her hand from mine and appreciates my filing job. "Izzy told me there's one in the bag of clothes she brought from Violet's house. She hasn't taken the bag back yet. I believe she left it in the hallway closet."

My cheeks warm rapidly. That's not a bathing suit. That's tiny strips of cloth barely held together by dental floss.

Oz shifts back and folds his arms over his chest. The narrowed expression in Olivia's direction tells me he's as excited about this as I am. "Eli doesn't want her off the property." His eyes flicker to me. "Sorry."

"I sort of figured something like that accompanied the whole escort thing."

He smiles. I smile. I should eat breakfast so I can stop appearing and acting so stupid.

"I'm aware," says Olivia. "I was referring to the pond.

That's on our property. It's a half mile if you cut through the woods."

A pond in the woods? Little tremors course through my bloodstream. "I don't hike." I don't do woods.

Both Olivia and Oz stare at me as if I'm crazy then return to each other and pretend I'm not in the same room.

"Take her on your bike," Olivia continues.

On his bike? Do either of them detect my internal scream, because I hear it. "Why can't we use the truck?"

"Chevy needs it," answers Oz. "His bike broke down last night and he has football conditioning."

Oh. My biker cousin plays football. Like the real kind. Not the kind without pads in the yard that resembles sixteenth-century warfare.

"You'll have fun," says Olivia. "The pond has trees."

Trees. Second tree on the left.

"What does that mean?" Oz double-takes Olivia and if it weren't for our previous conversation I'd think she was crazy, too. Well, more crazy than usual.

"That we should go swimming," I suggest.

A muscle in Oz's jaw twitches and I'm curious why he's unhappy. I thought after our bonding moment last night, we were friends. "Wear jeans over your swimsuit and some real fucking shoes."

He gets up and stomps out of the room.

"What else?" Mom's drinking tea in our kitchen during this morning's video chat and she's pumping me for information.

"Oz and I are going swimming today. For real, who doesn't

have central air in this century? I swear to God I'm going to melt."

Mom lightly traces her throat. "Where are you going swimming?"

"A pond, I guess."

Her eyebrows rise past her blond bangs. "But you hate the woods."

"I didn't say it was in the woods." Olivia did. And so did Oz. But me? Never mentioned it.

She sets down her cup of tea. "I was assuming that. There're lots of woods in Kentucky and…here comes your father! Jeff, come here and say hi to Emily. I have to go. I have a meeting…"

Mom flees from her chair faster than a traumatized hummingbird.

Dad settles into Mom's seat and he watches the direction in which Mom left then eventually turns his attention to me. He's in a white shirt and tie, which means he has hospital visits today. "Hey, Em."

There's a part of me that always relaxes when I see him. "Hi, Dad."

"What did you say to freak your mom out?" Dad's eyes contain a spark of amusement. He's finding this whole digging into Mom's past thing enjoyable for some reason.

"I told her I was going swimming at a pond."

He nods as if he knows why this pond is a big deal. "That would make her unhappy."

"I'm tired of being the only one in the dark," I say.

"I imagine you are." He leans forward so that his head is closer to the camera. "Are you ready to come home yet?"

Surprisingly... "No. It's weird here, but I'm handling it."

"Good," Dad says, and he looks as though he means it. "That's good."

A part of me feels better that he's supporting me in this, but the other half sinks in guilt. "Hey, Dad?"

"Yes, Em?"

"I love you."

Dad grins in a way that causes me to soar. "I love you, too."

Good.

That's good.

OZ

I WAIT ON THE FRONT PORCH WHILE EMILY'S locked in her room getting ready. A whine of hinges and Olivia joins me. She wears a top that's more corset than shirt and a pair of painted-on jeans. She must be scheduled for another MRI. "If you don't watch it that hospital in Louisville is going to be down an MRI tech. Cyrus will be pissed that you're dressing up for your smart boy toy."

"A little flirting doesn't hurt anyone. It's something people do when they feel alive."

All the happiness drains out of me and I scan the yard. She's dying. Inside her is something that is spreading and she's dying.

"You're going to have to deal with this," she says. "With me. I'm short on time and miracles. I thought having the wake while I was alive would help, but I don't think it has with you."

"Are you having a stroke? Because you're talking nonsense."

She chuckles at my response, but then the lightheartedness fades. "Why aren't you living?"

"Speak English."

"While I love that Emily is here, and that she is because you're doing what Eli asked of you, I'm wondering when you're going to start living your life."

"If it wasn't for Emily, I'd be on that run making money for the company instead of sitting here with my thumb up my ass." I don't want to have this conversation. It's one I avoid because I'll be damned if I'll let my anger get the best of me, so I switch gears. "You need to stop dropping clues to Emily about her past."

She flutters her eyelashes as if she could pass for a Southern belle. "Why, Oz, I have no idea what you're talking about."

"Sure you don't. Eli flat-out told me he doesn't want Emily to know anything and you go and tell her to hunt for Honeysuckle Ridge. She's asking people about it, and if she asks the wrong person she's going to end up in deep shit that I can't pull her out of."

Olivia admires her nails like we aren't discussing topics that could harm Emily. "She really did do a good job. You're tasked with protecting Emily, correct?"

"Yes," I say with exasperation. "And you're making it harder."

"If you want to keep Emily out of trouble, then help her discover the truth."

My muscles lock up. "You mean tell her what I know."

"No, I mean help her find out. Even you don't know what it is that Eli and Meg are hiding and, you're right, Emily asking about Honeysuckle Ridge will get her in trouble. If you want to protect her, then help Emily discover the truth. Become her ally."

"If you want Emily to know so badly, then you tell her, but stop messing with my future. If I help her then I lose my shot at the security company and the club."

"I can't tell her. I promised Eli I wouldn't."

I swear to God fire is shooting out of my eyes. "And I gave Eli my word she wouldn't find out. You can't betray Eli or the club, but you don't mind if I do."

"You aren't part of the Terror yet. You have a grace period. The three-piece patch is not on your back, otherwise you would have already told Eli I gave Emily the picture." Olivia lays a fist over her heart and drops her voice. "I'm asking you to save my granddaughter and yourself."

I narrow my eyes. "What the hell are you talking about?"

Olivia rests her freezing hand on my arm. "The club has never been a herd."

My mind mulls over her words, searching for her meaning, but I come up blank.

"At its heart, it's about the individual's search for freedom." She squeezes my arm.

"I know."

"I don't think you do, and Emily doesn't know this, either. If you help her, you'll save her. If you help her, then maybe you'll find yourself."

Dammit. "I already know who I am! You're the one who can't accept it."

Olivia doesn't flinch from my words. She smiles instead and puts her hand on my face. "You know what I find amazing? How much alike you and Emily are."

Her words are a fist to my gut. "What does that mean?"

"You're both afraid to find out who you might be." She lightly pats my cheek then lowers her hand. "That's the type of fear that can damage your life. Help Emily and I promise you'll be helping yourself, as well."

Emily walks onto the porch wearing an old pair of Olivia's boots, a skintight pair of jeans, thanks to Violet, and a T-shirt. A thin piece of blue ties at the back of her neck.

"I'm ready to go." Emily warily takes in Olivia and then me. "Is everything okay?"

No, it's not, but there's not a damn thing I can do to fix it. I look Emily over and begin to imagine her in a bikini. Parts south of my brain start spinning fantasies that will never happen. I run a hand over my face. I'm looking forward to this too much. "I need your helmet, Olivia."

"Don't have it." She turns her back to us as she returns to the living room. "It's a short drive. Some wind in her hair won't kill her."

Eli might if he finds out I permitted Emily to ride without one, but it'd take longer to head to my house for Mom's helmet than it would to go straight to the pond. "Let's roll."

I'm down the stairs and pulling my keys to my bike out of my pocket. Emily's behind me. I straddle the bike then gesture for her to hop on. She sweeps her long bangs away from her face and massages her neck. "Seriously, are you and Olivia okay?"

Seriously, we are not. "How much did you hear?"

"Enough." Emily nudges at the gravel with her toe. "She wants you to help me find the monsters haunting my past."

Yeah, she does. "I can't help you."

"Can't or won't?"

"That is a fucked-up question because it means the same thing."

"No, it doesn't. One means you can help but you're refusing to. The other means you would love to help, but you don't have the ability to."

I insert my key into the ignition. "Emily, when it comes to you, can't and won't share the same definition. Now get on the bike."

Emily tangles her fingers near the end of her hair and hesitates.

"Are you scared?" I ask.

Furious dark eyes stab right through me. "No."

"Have you ridden before?"

She shrugs a maybe then her shoulders roll forward. "No, but how hard can it be?"

Driving one? Harder than she thinks. "Direct blood of Eli McKinley has never been on a bike. It feels sacrilegious."

"I'm a Jennings," she corrects.

"So you've mentioned and you just told me you're a virgin so let's go over the basics."

Her mouth slacks. "I never said I was a virgin."

"Never been on a bike before, right?"

She nods.

"As I said, virgin. I'm in a hurry, otherwise I'd be willing to swap sex stories, but you can dominate that conversation because I'm more interested in yours. When you do tell me, talk slow since I'm a details type of guy."

Emily morphs a shade of red that's too damn gorgeous and I force my eyes away. She's too easy to get lost in...lost in conversation, lost in those damn eyes, lost in her beauty and gentle sexiness, but getting lost in Emily is not an option.

"When it comes to the bike, I'll take it slow. You'll only be on it for a few minutes. Hop on and I'll walk you through this."

With another tuck of her hair behind her ear, Emily exhales and climbs on behind me. My bike rides double, but it doesn't have a bitch strap or a back rest so if she's holding on, it'll be me she's clutching.

Emily sits as far back as possible and even with that distance her inner thighs still rub against my body. An image flashes in my mind of Emily lying next to me with her legs wrapped around mine and her warm breath tickling my neck. I inhale to gain some control.

"Okay, jackass." Emily chases the vision away. "What now?"

"You can hike through the woods and I'll meet you there."

"Could," she says. "But I don't know where it is and I thought an escort was required. Take back what you said about the sex stories and I'll take back the jackass."

"You're the one that brought up sex," I respond.

"No, I didn't. You did. So I'm standing by what I said, you're a jackass."

"I like how you do foreplay." I twist to face her. "Hold on to my belt loops."

She blinks, twice. "Your what?"

"Belt loops. The ones on the sides. Hold tight and if you're feeling frisky I'll let you wrap your arms around my waist. Cop a feel if you'd like—and so you know, I'd prefer if you head south instead of north."

"Belt loops will be fine," she says.

Her choice. "This is serious, so listen up. When I lean to the side, you go with me, never against me. Don't go throwing yourself over, move naturally with the bike. If I stop and you have to readjust, get my attention before moving, you got it?"

Because riding is a balancing act and with her doubling up with me, I have to manage both of our weight. Last thing I need is to go down and for Emily to become embedded with gravel. "All joking aside, if you get scared, rest your head on my back, close your eyes and wrap your arms around me. I promise I won't let anything happen to you."

"I'll be fine." Emily twines her fingers around the loops in my jeans while still trying to keep space between us. I turn the key and soon my bike's purring underneath us—a gentle vibration that immediately smooths out every frayed nerve in my body.

A quick look down shows Emily still has her feet on the ground. I point to the notches closest to her. "Place your feet on the floorboard."

Emily's hold on me tightens as she lifts her feet and balances on the bike. I peek at her over my shoulder. "You ready?"

She gives me a weak grin. "Yes?"

I chuckle then twist the throttle. "Hold on."

Emily

THE MOTORCYCLE ACCELERATES AND THE FEW inches I had established between me and Oz: gone. My body slides forward, colliding into his, and we click together like two puzzle pieces. Heat rushes up my neck and onto my cheeks. My thighs are too close to his, too tight against his body and this is way more intimate than I have been before with a guy.

Even when the two of us kissed.

Oz veers left, away from Olivia's, away from the main road, and the entire motorcycle pitches to the side. My heart thunders and my fingers clutch not only at Oz's belt loop, but at the material of his jeans, and his hips.

Oz glances at me over his shoulder as the bike straightens out. "Lean with it, Emily."

Right. Lean with Oz and the bike. Got it. The narrow road curves ahead and this time when Oz and the bike tilt, I move along with it. Oz releases one of the amazingly high handlebars and massages my knee before returning his hand to the grip. Whether in reassurance or to affirm I mastered the curve I don't know, but either way, I sit higher.

The wind whips through my hair and onto my face and I shut my eyes for a brief second and pretend that I'm flying. There's something energizing, something hypnotic, something inside me that begs to burst out of a cage in search of freedom.

The motorcycle kicks forward and our speed increases. Beams of sunlight filter through the towering trees and green foliage blurs together as we fly over the road. From head to toe, my body vibrates with the loud growling of the powerful machine.

My knee still tingles from where Oz laid his fingers on me and I've never been more aware of my hands in my life. I should let go of Oz's body, but I can't. Belt loops weren't enough and my fingers have somehow edged up and onto his sides. Oz is solid. Yes, definitely solid. Every inch of him that I touch is tight muscle.

Oz is a year older than me, but somehow he seems older, wiser and hotter than any other guy I've known. Just the way he rides his bike creates this overabundance of confidence.

Warm sensations I've never experienced before blossom through me. We enter another curve and I lean with him. I like how in sync I've become with Oz and the motorcycle. Like we've merged into one.

The purr of the engine deepens and Oz eases the bike to a stop. His feet hit the ground and he turns the machine off. It's as if all sound in the world ceased, or maybe I've gone deaf because there's no way anything can be this still or silent.

The wind picks up and the silence is frightened away with

the roar of the trees bending. Both Oz and I shift with the flow of air and Oz doesn't move the bike until the breeze gentles.

Oz kicks down the stand and the bike tilts, but not too much. He sets a hand over the fingers that I laced together across his stomach. Oh, hell, I'm plastic wrapped to him. I drop my head onto his shoulder and it places me closer, and closer is not what I need.

I go to unglue myself, but Oz squeezes my fingers, sending a jolt of electricity up my arms. "You okay?"

I have to clear my throat to speak and that just sucks. "Yes."

Oz slides his fingers against mine and a fluttering occurs in my stomach. It's a light fluttering. Ticklish even, and my survival instincts scream at me to get off this motorcycle.

Placing distance between us, I remove my hands and when I swing my leg over, I accidently tap it against the bike. The material of my jeans rides up and a burning pain flashes against my skin.

I yelp and jerk to get away and, because I possess no grace, end up with my hands flailing in circles in an attempt to find balance while I stay precariously upright on my heels.

Oz snatches my wrist before I begin the descent to the ground. In a heartbeat, he's off his bike and he yanks me until my body collides with his. I melt with the pressure of his hand on my lower back.

"Are you okay?" he asks again. Concern softens his face and damn, he's handsome.

Because any and all words are trapped in my windpipe, I nod. His black hair is a mess. Spiked up into multiple tufts and I'd give anything to touch it right now. To brush it away from his forehead. To caress the shadow forming on his jaw.

Oh, holy hell, he's warm and solid and I enjoy being pressed up against him too much.

"Did you burn yourself?"

Does he think he's that warm? "What?"

"You cried out. Did you burn yourself on the exhaust pipe?"

"No." Probably. I step back and Oz lowers his arms. "I'm fine."

I suck in a surprised breath at the view. "Wow. This is what you call a pond?"

OZ

THE PURE JOY ON EMILY'S FACE BRIGHTENS MY mood and creates a surge of pride. I've put a ton of hours into this place. I helped Dad hang the rope from the old oak tree, nailed in over half of the shingles on the small cabin and stood waist deep in the water as we sank in the posts for the dock. The property belongs to Cyrus, but it's a part of me.

Emily walks onto the dock and shields her eyes from the glare of the sun hitting the water. "It's really pretty."

"I like it," I respond. With her back to me, I unfasten the holster holding the gun Eli gave me and hide it in the saddle-bag, then join her on the dock.

"What you did for Olivia today…her nails. Thanks for that. She has diminished strength in that side and it's hard for her…" To accept the repercussions of the stroke that started this nightmare. The ache in my chest steals my breath.

Emily's gaze flickers in my direction then it jumps to the water. "It was no problem."

"Did you fix her coffee for her?" Because Olivia is left-handed and doing things with her right side has been challenging.

"Ponds are large holes," she says. "This is a small lake."

That'd be a yes, but as Emily suggested before, she won't lie. My respect for her grows.

Now would be the traditional moment when we strip. Emily does slip off her boots, but remains clothed as she settles on the end of the dock. Fuck it. I peel off my shirt and toss it behind Emily. "You know it's a million degrees, right?"

Emily looks up at me and her focus wanders down. Crimson races across her cheeks and she immediately redirects her attention to the water. "Um...yeah."

"Are you coming in?"

I flick the button of my jeans and undo the zipper. My lips twitch when Emily's head lifts with the sound. Is she also remembering that kiss a few weeks back? Because I am. Standing behind Emily as she sits painfully straight, I reposition a part of myself and then slide off my jeans.

Three steps and I cannonball it in. The rush of cold water is exactly what's called for and when I kick up from the bottom, I tie my swim trunks. Emerging naked in front of Emily isn't what either of us need. I surface and shake the water out of my hair.

Emily throws her arm up as the droplets land on her. "Oh my God, you're half dog."

I chuckle. "If you only knew the truth. Jump in."

A bead of sweat rolls down her neck from her hairline. Wearing jeans is required when riding with me and she's suffering for it. Jeans won't protect her from everything, but they can help keep her legs safe from burns, road debris or if I screw up and we take a fall.

"What does that mean?" she asks. "About the truth?"

It means she's not the first girl I've kissed. "Nothing. Come in or I'm coming out to throw you in. You're not going to die of heatstroke on my watch."

Emily's legs nervously swing. "This isn't my swimsuit."

"So?"

"So…it's not mine…and…this…shows a lot more…than I'm used to."

I cough to cover the laugh. Even with the Nashville shopping trip, she's been rocking Violet's clothes and there's a part of me that's considered writing Violet a thank-you note. Especially for those cut-offs from yesterday. Jesus, Emily's sweet ass was practically hanging out.

"It's just us and if you're scared I'm going to cop a second-base feel, don't worry. What happened at the Lanesville club-house was a onetime deal."

With a dramatic sigh, Emily sheds her shirt then shimmies out of the jeans to expose the blue bikini. She frees her hair from its bun and it spills like water around her shoulders. My lungs constrict so damn tight I have to force in air.

Emily's beautiful. Gorgeous. She's got curves a guy could spend hours worshipping. Swimming was a bad idea. An evil one and I'm wondering what the hell Olivia was thinking. Emily wraps her arms around her bare stomach. She's uncomfortable and I'm horny as hell.

"I'll race you," I suggest quickly.

"Where to?" she asks.

Chevy, Razor and I have swum across the pond easily

enough, but it wore our asses out and that's what I need—to be so damn tired that I tumble into a coma tonight and keep my hands off her body. "If you're a good enough swimmer then let's race to the other side."

Emily's lips slant up. "I swim in the ocean with my dad. This could be very bad for you."

Competitive. Gotta say I like it. "I don't listen to talk. Only action. Jump in and quit running your mouth."

With her arms stretched over her head, Emily dives in.

Emily

MY MUSCLES MELT INTO THE WOOD OF THE WARM dock. With my eyes closed, I flip over onto my stomach. Even with the sunscreen and the afternoon shade of the oak tree, odds are I'll burn. Oz and I have spent too much time here, but swimming and being lazy has been fun.

Won't lie—I also enjoy having won the race.

A huge breeze slams across the water and little waves lap against the dock. I pop up onto my elbows when the dock gently drifts with the current. Lying a foot from me, Oz opens his eyes. "We should get going. A severe storm is supposed to come through this evening."

Not a fan of storms, I snag my shirt. "Then let's go. It's gotta be, what? Five o'clock?"

"Seven-thirty," Oz answers.

My head whips toward him. "Seven-thirty?"

He slowly sits up and rests his arms on his bent knees. "You dozed for a few hours."

I blink. Rapidly. Yeah, I fell asleep, but I didn't think it was for that long. "You should have woken me."

"Why? You were under shade and we don't have anywhere to be."

My pulse pounds rapidly as I take in the fading light. The thick woods surrounding us have lost their friendly glow and now possess a foreboding shadow.

It's toward the end of June. The sun will set late. Between eight and nine and it's already seven-thirty. It only took a few minutes to get here, but I still need to hunt down the tree. Dang it, how could I forget this? It's the whole reason I'm here.

I fumble with the shirt, drop it, and when I try to pick it up again, my hands shake. We'll make it. We'll definitely reach Olivia's before the sunset and I won't be left behind, smothered by darkness and woods. But Oz said a storm is coming. Sure enough, massive clouds race across the sky. A storm will mean losing daylight faster and I scramble to my feet.

"We have time before the storm hits," he says.

"I know." And while nervous adrenaline engulfs me, I can't help but notice how the muscles in Oz's abdomen ripple as he stands. "The time surprised me."

"So are you ready for the rope swing?" Oz asks.

My head inclines to the side. "I'm sorry?"

"The rope swing. It's tradition. Everyone who swims in the lake has to jump into the water using the swing. Then you carve your name on one of the trees."

"Well..." I assess the rope. It dangles over the water and it's attached to the aging tree. The one I'm assuming Olivia wanted me to find. Off to the side of the swing, in the water, are several large rocks and in the middle is a deep pool. It appears safe enough, but I don't have time.

I can't be caught out here. Not in the woods. Not with the darkness. "I'm okay with being the exception."

Oz crosses his arms over his chest. "Classic Emily."

"What?"

"Backing out of things. You engage just enough and then you skulk back into your shell."

Uh… "It was *me* that kissed *you*."

"Yeah, and you stopped before it got good. Think about it. You've been here for a month, and tell me what you've learned about any of us."

"Plenty."

"What type of cancer does Olivia have?"

Oz swears when I don't answer.

"No one's mentioned what type," I whisper.

"And you've never asked. Day after day your body is here, you play nice, talk to your parents and then you go to bed. Like today, you spend the day with me and then I give you an opportunity to be a part of the bigger picture, part of a family tradition, and you rein yourself back in where it's nice and safe."

His words sting. Very much so, but how dare he throw anything in my face. "I have shared. I told you about how I'm scared of upsetting my dad by being curious about Eli."

"And then you crawled back into your hole—proving my point."

"Like you've tried so hard to get to know me?"

Oz tosses his arms out. "Why should I try? Olivia's been busting her ass asking you question after question and you sit around giving her half-truths. Eli's been doing this dance with you for the past seven years. Why the hell would I want to play monkey for someone who doesn't respect anyone else?"

"Oh my God!" I shriek. "I don't ask about you because there's nothing to know. You graduated from high school and your job is to follow me around. I have ears. I listen. Especially when everyone thinks I'm not. Following me around is your job for some stupid reason and you are perfectly okay with that. What type of life is this? Olivia says do something, you do it. Eli calls or texts and you're immediately on your feet. Nope, you don't play monkey for me because you're already doing it for everyone else!"

Oz towers over me. "You have no idea what the club means!"

A voice tells me to stop, but I can't. A raging flood has taken over my thoughts and my emotions are being carried away by the rapid current. "And when you aren't busy doing what everyone wants you obsess over Olivia."

"She's dying!"

"But at least she's living. Can you say the same?"

"Like you know anything about living. You never take a risk!"

"I'm here, aren't I?"

"But not fully engaged. When the hell are you going to step outside of yourself and experience what's going on around you? You have a huge family I would kill to be blood-related to and you can't appreciate it to save your life!"

"Take me back to Olivia's."

Oz lowers his tone and those blue eyes freeze into ice. "Not until you jump off that rope."

He wants me to cower. He wants me to boohoo and do

what he demands, but that's not going to happen. I step into his personal space. "Can't make me."

His eyebrows shoot behind his hair. "I can't?"

"You. Can't."

Oz stoops and before I can ask what he's doing, his shoulder connects with my stomach and then I'm off the ground. A squeal leaves my mouth and my hair dangles over my face. I kick and Oz wraps both of his arms over my legs and locks them to him.

"Put me down!" I yell.

Oz's response is to walk off the dock onto the grass, and he stalks around the edge of the lake toward the rope.

"I mean it! Put me down!"

He moves swiftly. Stealthily. As if my weight was nothing more than a helium balloon.

"You'll have to put me down in order for me to grab on to the rope and I won't do it! This is stupid."

"You won't have to," Oz says. Some of the pressure releases from my legs and I wiggle for escape, but he still has a firm grip on me. "Because I'll hold it for you."

In less than a second, I slip down. My chest sliding against his until I'm face-to-face, nose-to-nose, lips near lips with Oz. His arm snakes around my waist and his strong hold squeezes us closer together until there's no space left. I become aware. Very aware, and this awareness creates a warm tingle in my lower belly.

"Let me go," I whisper, but there's absolutely no conviction in my voice.

"I wish I could," he mumbles. "But for some reason I can't."

Both of our chests rise and fall and my fingers curl into

the hair near the base of his neck. My mouth dries out and I swear my blood vibrates with the beat of my heart.

The thick twined rope is by my head and Oz fists the cord in his hand. "If you don't want to do this, tell me and I'll let you go. I'm an asshole, but I'm not that bad of a person."

"Will we leave after?" My eyes frantically search his face. "As soon as we jump into the water can we leave?"

Oz's forehead wrinkles. "You're not scared of the rope, are you?"

I shake my head and try to swallow the large lump forming in my throat.

"What are you scared of?" Oz glides his thumb across the bare skin of my back. The same type of caress he gave me weeks ago when he was trying to comfort me at the motel. Goose bumps spread rapidly along my arms and it's a pleasurable sensation.

You. "Tell me what to do."

"Emily—"

"Tell me what to do!"

"Hold on to me and when I tell you, you let go."

I nod while wrapping my arms around his neck. I've accomplished this feat before—jumping from a rope swing—but I've never done it with another person. I could inform Oz of this. I could tell him I'm brave enough to do this on my own, but I like how my body presses to his. I like too much how his arm holds me tight.

Oz nuzzles my hair and his warm breath tickles the skin behind my ear. My knees weaken and I lean completely into him.

With a push off the ground, wind blows through my hair as the two of us defy gravity. My stomach performs summersaults as we coast up into the air, dip down and then swing high over the grass. We repeat the loop, three times. Each swing causing us to go higher in the air.

"On this one," Oz says. "When we're over the water—jump."

The trees blur into green as we race past, then there is sparkling blue.

"Jump!" Oz shouts.

I do. Releasing Oz. Falling backward. Letting my arms and legs stretch. The sun blinds me, the air warm on my back and then cold. A splash and the muffling sound of my ears filling with water. Pain slams into my leg and a cry leaves my throat.

My body convulses with the intake of water into my mouth, my nose. My hair spreads around me, strangling me, and my lungs burn for oxygen. My feet immediately kick for the surface. Fast. But not fast enough. I need air. Need air. I break through the water and my gasp is audible. The coughs rack my body.

"Emily!"

My head snaps to the right and with perfect form, Oz swims to me. I wipe the water from my eyes as I choke. Oz sweeps an arm around my waist and draws me into him. "Are you okay?"

I cough repeatedly, the spasms rocking my body. My arms go for Oz's neck, but he ducks and turns me, supporting my back with his chest. His fingers splay over my stomach and he tips me so that my body is floating and my head rests on his shoulder.

The coughs keep coming and Oz is talking. Low. Softly. Words that I cling to like a life preserver about how everything is okay. I suck in my first real breath and the clean intake of air feels good. A few more breaths and I flinch with the throb on my shin. I lift my leg out of the water and a stream of blood flows like an oil slick.

Oz shifts so that he's facing me. His eyes are wide. Wild even. "Shit. How bad is it?"

I blink, several times. "I don't know."

"Can you swim?"

"Yes." But I don't move. Instead, I sort of lock up as Oz treads water for both of us.

He smooths some strands of hair stuck to my face away and cradles my jaw. It's an intimate gesture. One that I like, but am too dazed to fully appreciate. "I got you. Okay?"

Oz kicks hard for dry land, dragging me with him. "You jumped toward the rocks. You scared the shit out of me."

The rocks. A quick snap of my gaze over my shoulder and chills run through me so quickly that I shake. Razor-sharp rocks less than a foot from me. I must have hit the real deadly ones. The quiet danger that you can't see below the surface.

"Isn't it always the things that you can't see that hurt you?" I mumble.

Oz says nothing as he pulls both of us out of the water. He immediately eases down to my leg and blood steadily flows from the long wound.

"That's a nice gash."

"Thanks."

"You're welcome. It's not deep, but the son of a bitch is going to bleed. Don't move. I need to make sure your leg's not broken before you try to walk, but first we need to stop the bleeding."

Oz strides over to the small shack of a cabin and undoes a combination lock. He disappears inside then returns with a first-aid kit. A curse leaves his mouth when he opens the kit and only finds an ACE bandage. He works it over my leg and I watch as a wet dark line soaks through the material.

Oz pokes and prods my leg, asking if this or that hurts, and after a few minutes declares that he doesn't believe the bone is broken.

"How do you know how to do this?" I ask.

Oz closes the now empty kit. "My mom's a nurse and she taught me first aid because of my jobs. I used to lifeguard at the local pool and you know I referee peewee football. She'll be pissed when she hears that no one has refreshed the supplies. There's been talk of bad bacteria in the lakes. When we get back to Olivia's pour some antiseptic over it."

A part of me sinks with so many revelations. Several weeks here and I've never asked what Izzy does or if Oz has had any other part-time jobs. I've made assumptions. Lots of assumptions and I need to stop. "I'm sorry."

"I should have told you which way to jump. This is on me."

"Not for that...for never asking about you."

Oz's eyes meet mine and the surprise in them causes the guilt to fester. "I am sorry."

He shrugs off my apology and focuses on my shin. His hand still rests on my leg and I wonder if he notices, because I notice. The warmth of his palm seeps through my skin and into my blood.

"I've mostly been a dick to you and I'm sure that hasn't helped," he says. "Being thrown into this mess has to be hard.

No one here is the type to bend easily. Not even for you. Considering the circumstances, you've done good."

Pride tingles through me with his compliment and I smile. Oz's mouth edges up and it's the most endearing gesture he's given me yet. Oz is the epitome of sexy wickedness, but this is the first smile that doesn't make me empathize with a mouse the cat's been toying with. It's one that makes me feel included.

"Hey, Oz," I say.

"Yeah?"

"Do you remember the conversation we had that night on the porch?"

"You mean the one where you sucked at running away?"

I scowl, he chuckles and I pick up my other foot and shove his shoulder with my toe.

"Yeah, that night," I answer.

"What about it?" he asks.

"Do you remember how I said I didn't know if I liked you?"

"Yeah?"

I glance down because shyness overwhelms me. "I like you."

"Hey, Emily."

I force my gaze to his and when I do, he performs another heart-stopping brush of his fingers across my leg and the world fades away except for the two of us. "I like you, too."

A strong wind bends the trees. My hair blows across my face and Oz scans the sky. "We need to go. I'll get everything together. You stay here and then I'll carry you to the bike."

Without waiting for a response, Oz grabs the medical kit and heads back into the cabin.

He likes me. Oz likes me.

As a friend. Just how I like him because I totally meant it as a friend and not as anything else because anything else would be stupid because he's trouble and I'm leaving soon and he lives hundreds of miles away and I have a plan and a life and he has a plan and a life and we don't belong in each other's plan or life and I sort of want to squee because Oz likes me.

I lift my head as the happy feeling fades. The tree. Olivia said I needed to look for a tree. Placing more pressure on my good leg than my bad, I stand and then redistribute my weight.

Nope, not broken, but it throbs. I count over two spots from the oak tree and I hobble past the first tree then pause. Wow. That's a lot of names for a trunk of a tree. One rotation of a dizzying circle and my world becomes distorted. Oh my God, it's not just one tree. It's several and stacked one upon another is name after name.

"Two spots over," I whisper. This tree isn't as towering as the others. Its bark is white and peels off in sections. The leaves aren't as big. My eyes shoot to the top of the list then frantically search down. Some are first names. Some are initials. Most of the names don't make sense. The world grinds to a halt as a cold clamminess overtakes my body. MZN... Megan Zoe Nader.

It's not possible. It's not. I stumble back from the tree and into Oz.

His glare pins me to my spot. "I told you to stay put."

He did, I didn't and now I've plummeted down the rabbit hole Oz warned me about.

"If I asked you a question would you tell me the truth?" I ask. "Because we're friends now and that's what friends do."

Oz hardens. "It's my job to watch over you."

"Yeah, I kinda assumed that, but we're friends now, right?" He didn't outright say it last night, but he suggested it and I have a hard time believing there isn't some sort of connection between us—even if it's just friendship.

He reaches down to his hip and extracts his knife from the sheath. "The tree we're using is over there. Let's get going before the storm blows in."

He walks away and I have my answer.

OZ

WIND SHAKES OLIVIA'S CABIN. IT'S BEEN STAND-ing for over a hundred years and I can't imagine any storm blowing this house down. We've heard a few rumbles of thunder. Heat lightning flashes in the dark overcast sky, but the front that we were promised never arrived.

The air is thick with humidity, with expectation. Each night we go without a storm only builds the electricity. The air is practically crackling with the shit.

I sit on the steps of the porch and nurse a beer. Emily's muffled voice drifts out of her window. It's ten at night, which means she's either on the phone with her parents or her friends. Chevy said that Stone told him that she and Violet talk on the phone. According to him, they discuss girl crap: clothes, hair, colleges in Florida. Violet better be keeping her mouth shut about the club to Emily.

Lights glow from the open bay doors of the clubhouse

across the yard. A group of five guys hang around in a circle talking and smoking cigarettes.

The summer crickets are quiet. So are the frogs. Even the voices from the garage don't carry right. The clubhouse should be exploding with people and noise and the silence gives the place an eerie mood.

My instincts scream that something's wrong. That we're teetering on the brink of a moment so huge that if we topple it'll lead to a downward spiral straight to hell.

My phone buzzes. Ten fifteen on the dot. Eli hasn't missed a check-in yet.

Eli: Give me an update

I take a long draw from the beer then set the empty bottle on the porch.

Me: Emily's in her room talking on the phone

Eli: We'll be back tonight.

They've been gone for over two weeks. Longer than expected. It's eaten Eli up to be gone this long from Emily. From what I understand, Cyrus is also close to losing his mind with the distance from Olivia, but business is booming with the security firm and we need the money to pay for Olivia's treatments.

I pop the cap off another beer. This will be my last one for the evening. After two, I get my buzz on and I can't buzz since I have a girl to protect.

Eli: Anything happen I need to know about?

I should tell Eli that Olivia gave Emily the picture, that Emily's asking about Honeysuckle Ridge and that today she saw visual proof on a tree that her mother has been around the family more than Eli claims.

Emily saw her mother's initials. She begged me for the truth and I walked away. An unseen wall divided us after so many layers had appeared to be peeled back. For a few minutes, I had connected with Emily and with three letters carved into a tree, that connection was shattered.

Fuck it. It was destroyed because I'm doing what needs to be done: keeping Emily in the dark. I take another deep swallow of beer. Why it bothers me that Emily withdrew, I don't know. Attraction. That's what's between us. Just attraction.

Me: Emily scraped and bruised her leg today, but she's fine

She's fine. Fine enough to barely look at me when she went in to take a shower. Fine enough to eat dinner with Olivia and make conversation with her and not acknowledge me. She's fucking fine without me.

Eli: We've run into trouble with the Riot over the past two weeks. Bad tonight. Keep vigilant. We've heard reports of the Riot 30 miles out. Too far south for them. I don't like it.

This latest trouble with the Riot is news to me and the entire text causes me to pause.

A roar of motorcycles and the gun on my back radiates heat. The guys near the clubhouse spread out and it hits me that they aren't visiting for shits and giggles. They're here because we're on the verge of nuclear warfare.

They're here because Emily—the girl who has lit up my life like a fireworks show—is in danger.

And I've gotten lazy. Been so focused on getting to know her and on my problems with Olivia that I've lost sight of what could lay in wait for Emily in the shadows.

Me: No one will get past me to Emily

Emily's light flips off. I pour out the rest of my beer on the ground, rise to my feet and then settle down on what's been my bed night after night for the past few weeks: the bench outside of Emily's window. Except tonight, I won't be sleeping.

Eli: I'm counting on that

Emily

I JERK AWAKE AND MY HEART POUNDS HARD. AT the end of the bed, Lars picks up his head and groggily assesses me as if I'm the one out of place. Stupid dog. "I didn't invite you on the bed."

He huffs and lays his snout on my ankles.

"There was a noise," I say as if the dog could explain what ripped me out of a deep sleep.

The curtains near the window billow out in the strong wind and the fine hairs on my neck stand on end. I sit up and listen. The wind through the trees makes a noise similar to waves crashing along the beach and it's an ominous sound.

It's three in the morning. The witching hour. At least that's what a friend of mine called it at a fifth grade slumber party. This is the time that the evil spirits of the world frolic and play. Should have thought of that weeks ago. Then maybe I would have stayed in the motel room and I'd be home in Florida.

Another powerful gust and a heavy vase on the dresser

pitches over and rolls. Almost every window in this house is open and stuff is probably falling everywhere and banging to the floor.

I yank my feet out from underneath Lars's head and slip onto the floor. The breeze is a blessing because of the heat, but a curse if I want to sleep. I ease across the floor to the window seat and set my fingers on the window to push it down.

Large clouds fly across the dark sky at unnatural speeds. As I go to close the window, a black form demands my attention and a rush of panic instantly paralyzes me. The shadow sitting on the bench outside the window inclines its head in my direction and I exhale in relief. It's Oz. He looks me over and I wonder how much he can see.

My hair's in a messy knot. Because I was hot, I stripped to my tank top and my boy shorts. Oz turns away from me, leaning forward to rest his elbows on his knees. My eyes are drawn to the way the muscles in his arm flex with the movement and my mouth goes dry.

My lips part because I feel like I should say something. Maybe ask why he's there or if he's slept. To start some sort of conversation to return us to the easiness the two of us had shared before he caught me at the tree with my mother's initials.

A bulge on his back along the edge of his jeans stops me from speaking. It's shaped like a holster and a holster usually contains a… Oz glances over his shoulder at me again. I shut the window and the curtains collapse over the glass.

Adrenaline shoots through my veins. He has a gun. Oz has a gun. No, I was mistaken. It's something else. Or maybe it's not. I don't know. I…just don't know. Dad said I'm not in danger. I'm not. He wouldn't lie to me. Everyone else might, but he wouldn't.

It's like ants are crawling on my skin and I can't remain still. I pull on a pair of shorts and head for the bathroom. A cold washcloth should help with the heat and to clear my head.

Not a fan of the dark, I'm slow tiptoeing down the hallway. I move around the corner and a clink from Olivia's room causes me to pause at the bathroom. A dull light floods her room, she lifts her head off the pillow, and our eyes meet.

A sudden drop of my stomach disorients me. The typical scarf that covers her head is missing. Exposed is the dark hair shaved close to her scalp and a crescent-shaped scar near her ear.

"Are you okay, Emily?" she asks, and the question sounds sincere. Reminding me of how my mom spoke when I used to drag James the Elephant with me into her room when I was younger and had a nightmare.

"Yeah," I answer. "Just hot. I was going to get a washcloth. Do you need anything?"

"Come here." Olivia waves me in. Not what I was hoping for, but I go in regardless. I stand at the foot of the bed and twist my fingers behind my back, feeling like a pauper in front of royalty—which is strange, but maybe not. Everyone treats her as if she's the queen.

Olivia pats the empty space next to her. "Turn on the window unit and sleep in here."

"I'm fine. Really. I'll go get—"

"Emily," she cuts me off. "Unit on, get in the bed, I won't eat you, but I will tear you a new ass if you don't do what I say."

I have never met anyone so rude or demanding in my life. Wait, I've hung out with Oz. I press a button on the window unit. Air blasts from the machine, and then I sit on the empty side of the bed. One leg on. One leg off. "You're not used to people telling you no, are you?"

"No. If you're going to be here for any length of time, you better get used to it."

While her room is hot, what's weird is that Olivia wears a long-sleeve shirt and is buried under a quilt. My other foot hits the floor and I reach for the air conditioner. "You're cold."

I push the off button and search the room for another blanket. How the freak can she be cold? It has to be in the high eighties in the house.

"Emily Star, turn that back on!"

"You're cold," I say.

"And you're hot. There isn't much I've been able to do for you for fifteen years and, because of the cancer, there isn't a ton I can do for you now so please let me do this."

There's a fierceness in her eyes. A warrior's soul in a body that appears frail tonight.

I press the unit back on and cold air once again roars into the room. I return to the empty side of the bed, but this time I draw both of my legs up and lock them to my chest. Olivia snuggles deeper into the blankets.

I peek at her from the corner of my eye and she adjusts onto her side to face me. "Eli will be home soon. You should spend the next couple of days getting to know your father."

A twinge of resentment snakes its way up my spine. "I know my father."

"Jeff's a good man," she says. "And so is Eli."

That's up for debate. I visit Eli once on his home turf and I may or may not have been almost abducted by a rival motorcycle club. "Eli seems nice. He visits me once a year."

I say it as if she's out of the loop because, well...there's the possibility that conversation between us could get thin.

"I'm aware," she says in a short way that makes me wish I could claim I was mute. Very long pause and she speaks again. "Everyone keeps reminding me that you aren't the child I knew and as much as I hate it, you're not."

I'm not and for some reason this honesty causes me to be uncomfortable. I point then relax my toes. "I found Mom's initials on the tree, which, according to Oz, means that she jumped from the rope swing. So now that I figured it out, will you fill me in on my mom's past?"

"Tell me the significance of Honeysuckle Ridge and then we'll have a different conversation. How did you get Oz to tell you about the rope?"

"He had me jump."

Pure surprise softens Olivia's features. "You jumped?"

I gesture to my bandaged leg. "I jumped wrong and hit the rocks."

Olivia traces the outline of her lips and stares off into space. "Oz had you jump."

"He explained it's a tradition and how everyone who comes to the pond has to do it."

"No. It's what we have the people we care for do. Most of the names there are club members, but not many of those names belong to women. That's a rarity."

"I'm sure Oz had me do it because I'm related to you."

She shakes her head halfway through my response. "That's

not how our world works. The only females on those trees are old ladies."

My mind stretches in two different directions and the resulting aftermath is a brain freeze.

"There may be a few exceptions," she admits, "like Violet, but overall, it's a privilege granted to few."

"Which one was my mom?" Which one am I? "Why was her name on there?" If asking me to jump, if carving my name into the tree meant something special, then why did Oz share it with me? Or is it because I'm an exception, like Violet, or was Mom an exception?

"Why do you think your mother's name was on there?" Olivia asks.

All the possible answers spin so fast in my head that the world tilts. "If Mom was an..."

Old lady. It feels wrong to refer to her that way. "...Attached to Eli then why not tell me? If they knew each other before she got pregnant it still doesn't change that Eli didn't want us."

"He wants you," Olivia whispers.

I snort. "Because that's how people feel when they give up their custodial rights."

"There's more to the story," Olivia counters. "More you need to know."

"More what? No one will tell me and my patience is running out. What I don't understand is why everyone is so damn secretive."

"Speaking of secrets," she says, "I'd appreciate it if you'd keep it from Eli that I'm supplying you with information.

Keeping your past from you is important to him and I stand to lose a lot if he finds out I'm denying his wishes."

"I'm not a liar," I say.

"I'm not asking you to lie. I'm asking you to not mention it."

Great. I'm officially a secret keeper. "What do you have to lose? Isn't everyone in this town your minion?"

"What you see is respect, but the power you believe I have, I don't. The club is what rules. The rest of us figure out our positions around it and make the best of it. You know, the club would give you the same respect they give me if you let them."

That resembled a guilt trip. "You didn't answer my question. What do you have to lose?"

"I risk losing my son's respect. If I lose it, I'm not sure how much time I have to regain it."

I focus on my toes because I'm lost on what else to say or do. That's wrong. She's divulging something personal with me, I can reveal something personal back. Something that I've been dying to purge since it happened. "I saw my mom and Eli hug at that warehouse."

I hug my legs and rest my chin on my knees. It doesn't sound like much, but witnessing that wounded me. More than the picture of me and Olivia. More than seeing Mom's name on the tree. Maybe more than when I thought I was being kidnapped.

"It wasn't a hey-let's-hug-because-we-made-a-kid-together hug. It was a real hug. Intimate. The type that she should only share with my dad."

A cold hand on my arm and I glance over at Olivia. "Whatever you find out, it doesn't mean that she doesn't love you or your adoptive father."

My frown deepens because that's exactly what I'm afraid it means. "If this is as big as you make it out to be, then isn't it possible that she's lied about everything?" Integrity issues, as I explained to Oz.

An ache slices through me at the thought of her not loving my father and Olivia must sense it as she squeezes my arm. "I swear I'm not doing this to hurt you. I just want you to understand your past."

Moisture stings my eyes and I rock slightly in a poor attempt to prevent tears from escaping. "All of this feels an awful lot like hurt."

"Unfortunately, that's something your mom and Eli were good at. Hurt. I'm trying to stop them from passing that hurt down to you." Her hand slides along my arm until she reaches the fingers that are still clasped around my legs.

"Then maybe they were right to hide this from me. If what you're saying is true, then maybe keeping the past a secret is the best way to stop me from hurting because this sucks."

"The pain the two of them created was built on secrets and lies and regardless of what they think, the past would have caught up to you. Hiding and denying does nothing but cultivate the fear."

"You sound a lot like my dad."

Olivia smiles. "I told you already, he's a good man."

"He is," I say. "He's the best."

I loosen my grip on my knees and let Olivia take my hand. She lowers our joint fingers to the comforter. While Olivia still scares the crap out of me, this moment feels right. Like how it should be between a grandmother and her grand-daughter.

"I'm assuming Eli and your mom didn't know you saw them hug?"

"No." My face becomes a space heater. "I blackmailed Oz into letting me eavesdrop."

She laughs so loudly that I'm both startled and amused.

"You are your mother's daughter," she says between breaths.

My eyes narrow on her and she holds up a hand. "I mean that in a good way. Meg and I were close once, which is why I'm assuming she sent you to the wake."

Mom and Olivia were close once. I test the words in my head, but the entire sentence tastes sour. How could they go from being cozy to the bitterness they now share?

"We sat on this bed once—holding hands. In fact, she was the same age as you."

I peer at Olivia out of the corner of my eye. "That sounded an awful lot like sharing. Are you sure you don't want to go ahead and spill?"

She chuckles. "It's late, I'm tired, and if I'm going to say anything else that will get me into trouble I might as well say this. Your father, Eli, he wanted you."

A wave of agony devastates my soul. "My mother's a great mom."

It needed to be said. Even if she's lied to me. Even if my worst fears are confirmed and my mother caused these peo-ple pain.

Weary and defeated, I collapse back onto the pillow. It's soft and comfortable and Olivia pats my hand. The air conditioner blows on the bed and I'm suddenly envious of Olivia and her blanket.

"I won't say there isn't bad blood between us and your mother," says Olivia, "but it would be tough to argue that she didn't do a good job raising you."

Was that a white flag? "See, it wasn't so hard to say something nice, now, was it?"

She smirks. "Don't get used to it."

What's shocking is that I'm not swamped with animosity for her, nor is there any pulverizing terror that I'm next to the lady who voluntarily lay in a casket. And what's kick-in-the-head surprising? I'm genuinely grinning. I notice the bruises dotting the inside of Olivia's arm and my happy moment fades. "How sick are you?"

Olivia produces the sad smile. The type where the corners of the mouth tilt up, but the lower lip is yanking down. The one my mom does when she pretends everything is okay and it isn't. My stomach cramps seeing it on Olivia.

"Sick enough that I threw my own wake."

A shiver runs through me and I push the conversation forward, away from coffins. "What type of cancer?"

"You've been hanging out too much with Oz. He focuses on details he can't change, never on what he can." Olivia's eyelids flutter and my time with bio-grandma is coming to an end. I extend my legs to slide off her bed and Olivia stops me. "Stay."

"But you're tired."

"Stay," she demands in the kind of voice that causes me to immediately comply. "I'll give you another clue tomorrow.

This one should be easy to figure out, especially if you can convince Oz to help you."

"You realize that this is a messed-up scavenger hunt, right? You have to admit it's a little deranged. What do you do for birthday parties around here? Load up piñatas with snakes? You are, by far, the strangest group of people I have ever met."

I expect Olivia's witty comeback, but nothing. Odds are she's heard the same distant rumble of motorcycles that has caught my attention. "Maybe that's Eli."

And what's weird is the happy anticipation of seeing him again. Does it make me a bad daughter if I'm looking forward to the next few days?

The sheets shift and then my hand begins to tremble. A deadly cold overtakes my body. It's not me that's shaking. It's Olivia. Her body flinches uncontrollably. Quaking in a way that's unnatural. Her eyes roll back in her head and her arm drops off the bed.

I hover over her as I hold on to her hand. "Olivia!" She continues to shake and panic bursts inside me. "Olivia!"

Terrified to leave her, unsure what to do, I turn my head and scream, "Oz! I need you!"

Her body still twitches under my touch and she needs help and I don't know what to do. Her body moves closer to the edge and I lean over her to prevent her from slipping off. My eyes search frantically for a phone and when I come up empty my head whips over my shoulder again. "Oz! Plea—"

My cry is ripped short as a large man in black leather barrels into the room. Fear spikes into my chest and as I shield Olivia with my body, he speaks. "How long has she been seizing?"

I blink at the familiarity of the voice. It's Cyrus. My grand-

NOWHERE BUT HERE   313

father. Her husband. He rushes to Olivia's side of the bed and his eyes dart to mine. "How long, Emily?"

"A few seconds," I answer. A dip on the bed and Eli's by my side. He attempts to tear me away from Olivia, but I dig my fingers in. If I let go she'll fall. If I let go she could die. My throat burns and wetness fills my eyes. "I turned the air conditioner on and I shouldn't have and we talked and this happened."

"Holy fuck," another guy mutters as he enters the room then yells down the hallway, "Someone call Izzy."

The convulsing stops. Cyrus crouches next to Olivia and brushes a finger slowly along her cheek. "Olivia?"

She opens her eyes, but there's no awareness there and what frightens me more is how her hand remains lifeless in mine. "Is she okay?"

Cyrus looks up at me and then behind me. Nausea rages in my stomach. This man is huge. Death-defying. He should be answering yes. He should be able to fix her. That's how strong he is, but he's not fixing her. His eyes are glassed over and he's a mirror of Olivia—broken.

"You were real strong staying with her," says Cyrus in this gentle voice. Too gentle. So gentle that I check to make sure that Olivia's chest rises with air. It does. Her eyes are still open, but this feels final. "Why don't you let me take over?"

"She asked me to stay." My voice sounds hollow. Echoed. As if I'm floating. Detached from the entire situation.

Fingers in a black glove slide along the hand I've linked with Olivia's and then slowly extract my hand from hers. In a heartbeat, my body moves and I'm in the arms of someone as they carry me out of Olivia's room.

OZ

EVEN IN ELI'S ARMS AS HE CARRIES HER AWAY,
Emily's hand stays outstretched toward Olivia. Tears pool
in her eyes and a pulse of protectiveness races through me. I
step forward and Dad pounds a hand on my chest with such
power that it nearly knocks the wind out of me. "Let Eli take
care of his daughter."

"Emily screamed for me. She wants me." She needs me.
Her panicked voice still rings in my head. She called for me
right as Dad, Eli and Cyrus walked up the porch after returning from their run. It was almost a fight as the four of us
raced to get to Emily and Olivia.

Dad's towering over me like he's willing to take a swing
and he motions to my fisted hands. "Get it together."

I ram a hand through my hair, trying to silence the noise
in my mind. Running in here, seeing Emily losing her shit,
watching as Olivia's body twitched like she was some washed-

up fish on the shore. I bend over, slamming my hands on my thighs. Jesus. This isn't it. This can't be it.

"How far out is the ambulance?" I ask.

Cyrus is still crouched on the floor next to Olivia. His forehead rests on the mattress and Olivia weakly raises her hand and touches his gray hair. "You have to be strong for me."

He doesn't lift his head, only shakes it. I rock with the sight. Olivia makes a shushing sound that pierces my heart.

"How far out is the ambulance?" I demand.

No one says a thing and, except for Cyrus, they all stare at me. My father, Hook and Olivia. Each one shares a haunted expression. The type where they know you're the only one who hasn't received news of a death.

"Pigpen called your mom," says Dad. "She'll be here in a few minutes."

The world sways. "I didn't ask that. I asked about the ambulance."

"There's no ambulance," Dad responds in a low tone.

"Why the hell not?"

"The tumor's grown," Olivia whispers. "And the cancer's spread to my blood."

I turn away as my eyes burn and I prop both hands on the wall to keep myself up. What the hell?

"We found out not long after Emily came, but decided to keep it quiet." Dad's footsteps tap against the wooden floor and a heavy hand gently presses on my shoulder. "Olivia wants to die here, son."

Shit. Just shit. "They said they'd do another round of chemo."

"It's over, Oz," Olivia says.

I smack my hand against the wall and my palm stings. "It's not."

"Jonathan," she whispers.

Fuck this. "No!"

Dad squeezes my shoulder and I recoil with my hands in the air as a visual stop. "This is bullshit!"

My gaze immediately hits Olivia. She presses a hand to her heart, like she did when she lowered herself to my height and explained that it was time for me to go live with Mom and Dad. Just like she did when she wiped my tears away and explained that this would always be my home. That I would always be her family.

Ten years later and when I tell someone I'm coming home, it's not to the trailer down the way, it's to here. Olivia is my home.

"Why are you giving up?" I beg. "You swore to me you'd never give up."

Olivia closes her eyes. A single tear escapes and slowly slides down her cheek.

She's giving up. The person I love more than anyone else is giving up on living. She's giving up on me.

My insides twist and all of the building hurt bursts through into anger as I punch open the door in her room that leads to the porch. The cooler air of the night crashes around me as I clutch the railing and lean over.

She's dying. The person I love the most in my life is going to die.

Emily

MY BODY IS SET ON SOMETHING SOFT AND THEN there's the click of a lamp. The smell of leather overwhelms me when black gloves frame my face.

"Is she dead?" My voice isn't my own. It's too high-pitched. It's too hysterical.

Eli fills my vision and my body starts to tremble. His hold on my chin is firm and gentle and it prevents me from jumping off the bed and returning to Olivia.

"No, Emily, she's alive. This happens. Not a lot, but it happens."

"So this is normal?"

Eli maintains eye contact, but he doesn't respond, which is the worst type of answer. She's dying. This is his mother and he should be with her and not me. "You should go to her."

"No, I'm staying here."

She's dying. Olivia is dying. Her body is breaking down, no one can fix her, and I don't want her to die—I want her to live. My lower lip quivers. "She's your mom."

"And you're my daughter."

I detest dead things. Dead things are cold and unmoving and terrifying, but Olivia is very much alive and I need her to stay alive. She may not be the cookie-baking type. She might scare me and act crass and rude, but I like her. I briefly close my eyes as pain rips through me. I more than like her, and I haven't spent enough time with her. Not enough time...

"Dad's with her," Eli says and I spot the ache in his eyes. "He needs time with her. He just needs...time."

Eli rarely refers to his parents as Mom and Dad. Instead, he uses their names, except when he's hurting. I don't know much about Eli, but I can tell an awful lot about him when he's in pain and that's not right. There's something fundamentally wrong that I understand him better hurting than I do when he's happy.

"Don't you need time with her?" I ask.

He barely nods. "Mom understands I'm running out of time with you, as well."

All of the emotions of Olivia and Mom and Dad and Eli and even Oz crash into me and I lower my head into my hands, but I bite my lip to keep from crying. Somehow it doesn't feel like I have the right to cry. I'm not the one on the verge of losing my mom.

"Hey." Eli lets go of my chin, settles on the bed next to me and wraps an arm around my shoulders, gently pressing so that I'll lean into him. Because I'm a mess, I do, and feel worse that I'm letting him comfort me. "It's okay, Emily. For tonight, she's okay."

I push down my hurt and rapidly blink to keep the tears away. Eli's strong. Olivia's strong. I can be strong, too, but as I go to pull away, Eli only readjusts us so that we're sitting back against the wall with me still tucked close to him.

"It scared me," I admit, and hope it's a plausible explanation for why I'm so messed up because I'm not sure he'd believe that I like her and I'm not sure how I feel about it myself.

"Scared me, too. Each and every time it happens, it scares the shit out of me." Honesty is etched over his face.

"I have a hard time believing you're scared of anything. I mean...you're you."

He's a lot like his father, Cyrus. He's big and he's strong and basically has an entire army of scary men in black leather who ride motorcycles and carry guns at his disposal.

"I'm scared of a ton of things and all of them have to do with losing the people I love." He pauses. "I learned a long time ago that I can't control everything and now I'm learning I can't control death. Sometimes I feel cursed. Like I get to watch everyone I love slip through my fingers."

He wanted me. Olivia said he wanted me. I open my mouth to ask if I'm one of the people he's referring to, if Mom is, but I snap it shut. I don't know how to ask without divulging that Olivia is sharing secrets with me and I can't take the respect Eli has for her away over my need to understand my past.

"What?" Eli asks.

"Nothing."

"No, you were going to say something, what?"

My mind is completely blank. What can I say? What should I say? "I don't like pulled pork. I don't like any pork actually. It's tough and it's stringy and it's a pig and...well...pigs gross me out. Which means I don't like bacon either, so... yeah...that's it."

Eli blinks as he tries to understand any of the hot mess that just fell out of my mouth. He pulls on his earlobe and his face contorts as if he's trying not to laugh. "You ate an entire pulled pork sandwich in Nashville."

I did. "You were superexcited about me trying it and I didn't want to hurt your feelings. I feel like that's all I do—hurt you. I don't want to, but I do. Even when I'm not trying to, it still happens."

"Emily." He lowers his head so that we're eye to eye. "You don't hurt me."

"Yeah, I do. Every time I look at you, I see that you're in pain."

He shakes his head. "You don't cause that. It's something I did to myself. But thank you."

My forehead furrows. "For what?"

"For telling me something about you." And he leaves off how he didn't have to ask a million questions to learn it or how he appreciates how honest I was. Hating pork, it's simple really, but to Eli, it seems like a lot.

Crap, now I really feel bad. I've been here over a month, I've known him for seven years and pulled pork is the first real truth he knows about me. Eli and I...maybe we also need time.

A knock on my open door and Oz enters the room. "Cyrus is asking for you, Eli."

Eli glances over at me as if he's weighing telling Oz no, but then Oz adds, "I'll stay with her." He rests a hip against the door frame of my room with his hands shoved in his pockets and eyes me in a way that suggests he'd like my help.

"I'll be okay with Oz."

Eli's eyebrows pull together in worry, but he quickly stands and kisses the top of my head. He then goes to Oz, cradles one hand around the base of his neck and says, "I owe you."

Oz nods, Eli leaves, and we study each other. Men in black vests float like ghosts along the hallway. For as many people as there are in the house, there's only a low mumble of conversation. An occasional distinct voice here and there. No panic. No hustle. No phone call to 911 or distant wail of an ambulance.

Oz watches me as if my gaze on him is the sole thing keeping him upright. Through my window, the clubhouse is lit up and beams of motorcycle lights flash into my room as more people arrive. The roar of engines the lone sound that resembles the actual chaos inside me.

"Why aren't they taking her to the hospital?" I whisper.

Oz's head falls back until it hits the door. "Because Olivia has made it clear that she wants to stay here."

"What? But she needs help. She needs a hospital. She—"

Oz cuts me off. "She wants to die here."

My mouth drops open, but no sound comes out. Dad's mentioned this before. Hospice, I think? It's care for people who are dying. For people who have exhausted all medical options. "But she seems so…alive."

"Get some jeans on," he says. "Then meet me outside."

"Don't you want to stay? If she's dying, don't you want to be here?"

"Do you?" he asks.

No, I don't and from the way Oz's blue eyes are begging me to move, I guess he doesn't, either.

"Where are we going?" I inquire.

Oz glances down the hallway toward Olivia's room. "Away from here."

OZ

MY MOTORCYCLE RUMBLES BENEATH ME AS EMILY and I race along the road away from Olivia's. Just like we raced out of the cabin as the guys from the club asked if we were okay. Just like we raced past my mother as she tried to talk to both of us. Emily opened the door to her bedroom, I offered her my hand and we ran.

Wind whips through my hair as we head deeper into the woods. The road narrows and we pass the clearing of land where I should be living now.

This was supposed to be our last year in the trailer. We were supposed to build a new house. Just like Olivia was supposed to be better with this new treatment. Just like how the treatment before was supposed to defeat the cancer.

My life has been full of supposed-to-bes and I'm tired of nothing working out.

From behind me, Emily edges closer. Her arms tighten around my waist as her fingers clasp over my stomach. Her body is wedged into mine with her head burrowed into my back.

Emily's frightened and that causes me to fly faster into the night. It could be the bike, but I don't think it is. She loved it when we first rode. She was flying in the seat, but this time she's trembling.

I let go of a handlebar and lay my hand over hers. A silent gesture to reassure her that she's not alone.

Emily

THE VAGUE MOONLIGHT DISAPPEARS AND A cooler patch of air drifts along my arms. The night grows darker and clouds drown the light from the moon. The fierce wind that had woken me up earlier tonight returns and batters me, slapping my cheeks.

A chill within me forms ice in my bloodstream. I was so cold in that hole as a child that I shook uncontrollably and I couldn't stop. My teeth chattered and my fingers became numb. I thought I'd never be warm again. That I'd be frozen forever.

Heat rolls off Oz and I press into him as if there was space left between us. I'm not trapped in a hole. I'm here. It's okay. Everything is okay.

The motorcycle slows then Oz eases it backward with his feet as he parks. He slips off the bike and offers me his hand. I accept it and this time I swing my leg out so I don't touch any burning part of the engine.

"Good girl," Oz says.

"For what?"

He inclines his head to the bike. "For not hitting the exhaust. It'd be a shame for you to burn your leg again. Too many burns and you'll get a Harley scar to match mine."

"I'm a fast learner."

"Yeah," he says as he squeezes my fingers. "You are."

Attempting to ignore the darkness and the claustrophobia it creates, I strangle Oz's hand. "Are you okay? With what happened with Olivia?"

A shadow darkens Oz's face and I immediately ache with his pain. "I brought you here so we could escape. Is that okay?"

Meaning he doesn't want to talk about her. "That's okay."

Oz flips off the headlight and a small dim light emerges to the left. It barely highlights a door to a trailer. My expression falls and I try desperately to hide it, but the annoyed set of Oz's jaw informs me he caught it. "Let's go."

Oz drops my hand. He walks forward and I sprint to catch up. It's too dark out here. Too many unknowns. Too many ways to get lost and never be found. We climb up a small wooden deck of a porch and the graying wood beneath my shoes appears to be fraying on the top layer.

Oz sorts through his keys and with each second we remain in the open my senses heighten. Hair stands on my skin as if the bony fingers of the night are reaching out to snatch me, as if they're begging to suck me in and imprison me. I twist my fingers together, silently willing Oz to move faster. He's already unlocked the dead bolt, now he's undoing the actual handle.

Please hurry up, please hurry up, please— The lock gives,

Oz places his hand on the knob and I push open the door, practically jumping over Oz to enter.

Inside, a clock flashes on a microwave. Little red-and-green lights twinkle, indicating electronics, but it's not enough. Not nearly enough. "Turn on a light."

With a flick, he does and I find myself in the middle of a tiny living-room-slash-kitchen combo. Keeping those curious blue eyes on me, Oz shoves his keys in his front pocket. "You're weird."

A bitter smile creeps along my face. "Seriously? You carry a gun and a knife and I'm the weird one?"

"Yeah. That sums it up." He shuts the door behind him. "Who said I carried a gun?"

"I saw it when I went to shut my window earlier. Tucked near the small of your back. Sound familiar?"

"It was dark and you didn't see a thing," he says. "You have an overactive imagination going on in that pretty little head."

"I don't have an overactive imagination."

"Funeral home. You. Olivia. Zombie attack. Sound familiar?" he mocks.

"So if I looked under your shirt what would I find?"

Oz steps toward me and lifts the front of his shirt. Sweet home Alabama, those are some serious and glorious abs. "Is this what you were looking for?"

My mouth dries out so responding immediately is a problem. A quick swallow helps, but Oz drops his shirt as he strides into the kitchen.

"Lift up the back of your shirt."

"Not a good idea." Oz rifles through the fridge. "If I take

off my shirt, you'll want to take off your shirt, and then the two of us will be distracted and end up in a bed."

My heart beats, falters, then picks up again at a rapid pace. "You're avoiding the question, which is the same as lying."

"There's no gun on me."

"Don't take a lie detector test. You'd fail. It exposes those integrity issues we've been discussing. Have you found a lawyer yet? It's probably nice to have those things taken care of before you go to jail."

He barks a short laugh. "I don't do illegal shit and if I did, the club has a lawyer."

"Of course you don't and of course they do."

"Don't complain about things you don't understand. You're safe, aren't you?" His eyes meet mine and I shiver with the unspoken threat that Dad claims doesn't exist.

"Am I really in danger?" I ask.

Oz pops open a bottle of beer and takes a drink. "You want one?"

I shake my head. "I don't appreciate you drinking and driving."

"We're staying here tonight," he says. "I had already cleared it with Eli before everything went to shit with Olivia."

My eyebrows furrow together. "Why would you have done that? And you haven't answered my question."

"I am answering it." Oz pulls a long draw off the beer and then sets it on the small bar separating the living room from the kitchen. "The Riot was spotted thirty miles north of Snowflake. That isn't their territory and Eli liked my idea of moving you in case they decided to stop by for a visit."

I shrink into the sectional couch that encompasses most of

the space in the room. No wonder my mother is a train wreck. It's almost easy to believe everything Oz is saying. Almost easy to believe that it's true. "Do you get tired of living this way?"

"Which way is that?"

Delusionally? But it's not my intention to argue with Oz. Especially when he's hurting.

"Which way, Emily?" There's accusation in his voice. I may not be looking for a fight, but Oz is.

"Have you ever thought of a life outside of the club? You know, get an office job, settle down in a nice neighborhood, have two point five kids and a dog named George. Maybe a goldfish or two?"

"If I get a rope and tie it around my neck, will you help push me off a cliff?"

"I'm serious," I say. "I don't understand why you want to live like this. You're supersmart and superawesome when you want to be. I'm just saying that the rest of the world isn't cloak-and-dagger. It's easy and peaceful."

Oz scratches the sexy stubble along his jaw. "Know what I don't have to deal with in my world?"

"Sanity?"

He grins. "I could say the same about your world, but listen up."

Oz drags a chair from the small table in the kitchen area into the living room and straddles it. His biceps flex as he crosses his arms over the wood of the chair and when I tear my gaze away I find amusement flickering in his eyes.

I've been busted. "I never said you weren't pretty."

"You lied, Ms. Integrity. You are bold. And if we're swapping compliments, you're fucking gorgeous."

Heat flashes on my cheeks and I immediately look down. "Don't do that," says Oz.

"Do what?"

Strong fingers underneath my chin and I swear it's harder to breathe. Oz lifts my head so that we're staring at each other again. "Don't deny a true compliment by looking away. You're braver than that."

I bite my bottom lip and Oz swipes his thumb over my mouth, causing me to let it go. His thumb stays at the corner of my mouth and I swear he must feel my pulse pounding in my veins.

He lowers his hand and I clear my throat. "I believe we were talking."

"Yeah," answers Oz.

I search frantically for what we were discussing. "You were going to give me some great insight into your world."

"Yeah. That. In my world, we don't have to worry about half the shit that you do."

This I have to hear. "Like?"

"Backstabbing. Trust issues. The Terror is about family and loyalty. When someone says they're going to do something they do it. When one of us has a problem, every man in the club will drop whatever they're doing to help. I've seen how the rest of the world works and I don't care for it. Everyone out for themselves. Shoving knives into each other in order to reach another rung on the ladder. Lying to save face. Once you're in the club, you have a family you know won't abandon you."

My mind wanders to the countless relationships I've had over the years with girls who swore to be my friend one minute and then wouldn't speak to me the next. The hours of gossip that fill my school day. The lying, the manipulation, the constant power struggle between social groups.

And then I go home and listen to my parents talk about the same issues, but in adult terms. How someone cost Mom her spot on the PTA board. How another doctor lied to my father and took credit for research he had accomplished.

Me, Mom and Dad—we have each other, but how many times have I felt hollow because the three of us were outnumbered?

Oz's words sound seriously pretty, but it's easy to disregard the ugly when it doesn't fit your argument. "Eli left me and you're currently lying to me. The club can't be as perfect as you think."

Oz reaches behind him and my eyes widen when he produces a very real, very terrifying handgun. I draw my feet onto the couch and scramble back, but only end up a few inches farther from the weapon.

"Calm down, I'm not going to shoot you."

"That's a gun. It could go off and kill me. Those things happen. I've seen it on the news."

"The safety is on. Look." He tilts the gun and slides his thumb over something, shifting it toward him. "Safety off." Click. "Safety on, but if it will make you feel better…"

A louder noise and out pops a part that I assume contains the bullets. He holds up both parts in the air for me to see then rests them on the end table at two different corners. "I'm carrying a gun. See—I told the truth."

I slowly edge my feet to the floor as if I'm testing the temperature of the water surrounding us. "Why tell the truth now?"

"Because when it comes to the club, I won't be the one to put a bad taste in your mouth. Yeah, I haven't been completely honest with you, but it's either because I've been ordered to keep my mouth shut or I've been doing it to protect you. I didn't tell you I carried a gun because I knew it would scare the shit out you. It's nice to see I wasn't wrong."

"So if someone from the club orders you not to tell me something, you won't? Isn't that the same as lying?"

Oz's jaw ticks. "You're not a brother and as a woman you will never be, but you are important to this club. We will protect you. There isn't a need of yours that won't be met if you allow us in, but my obligation is to the club before anyone else."

"If that's the way it is," I hedge, "then why don't you wear one of those vests that everyone else is wearing?"

"I was supposed to start my initiation period, become a prospect and get my cut the night of Olivia's party, but you showed and messed everything up."

"How?"

"My job was to watch you until you stepped on the plane, but then I fell asleep in the parking lot at the motel. I woke up as you walked out of your room."

"I'm not the one who fell asleep," I say. "So I'm not seeing how this is my fault."

"You're right." Oz cracks his head the side. "You coming to Snowflake changed everything, but I'm the one that fucked up and I can't tell you how sorry I am. Scares me more than you know that they could have taken you—that my mistake could have hurt you."

I pause at that. A few minutes later and how different would my life have been? Would Dad have been right? Would I have bought my water and returned to the room, and I would now be home getting ready to attend Blake Harris's next party? Or would my mother and Eli's fears have come to life and I'd be a pawn between two groups of men who detest each other?

"Am I in danger?" I ask again as a whisper.

Oz is quiet. Maybe thinking or fighting internally, I don't know, but either way his answer could change everything. "Eli says you are."

"Why?"

"I don't know, but I trust Eli and if I didn't, I like you too much to take the chance."

I rest a hand over my heart as if that could calm the frantic beating. "Dad said I'm safe."

"You are," Oz says. "I swear nothing will happen while you're with me."

"No." My lungs constrict. "Dad said that this whole thing isn't real. That you guys are playing games and that you take things too seriously and that I shouldn't be afraid. That's one of the reasons why I stayed—because I wanted to prove to myself that there was no reason to be scared."

Oz slips out of the chair and is immediately on his knees in front of me. His hands cradle my face and his warmth sinks through and combats the fear chilling my body. "Do you trust me?"

"You've lied to me."

His eyes search mine and the silence surrounding us sucks the air out of the room.

"Honeysuckle Ridge is a safe house ten miles north of here. You can only get to it by bike and then you have to hike the rest of the way. It's a cabin smaller than the one at the pond, but it doesn't have shit within it. Sometimes guys from the club use it for hunting, but no one else goes there without club permission. No one beyond brothers and immediate people with the club are supposed to know it exists."

"What does Honeysuckle Ridge have to do with Mom and Eli?"

"I don't know."

My head attempts to tip back, but Oz's strong grip prevents me from completing the motion.

"I don't know," he repeats. "Whatever it is, it couldn't have been good, but the truth is your mom would have known about it because she was Eli's old lady."

His words pierce through me like a sword.

"They were teenagers," I say. "In high school. She couldn't have been."

"Yeah, they were still in high school when they met, but she'd graduated by the time she had you. According to my mom, they were very much in love. So much that after your mom had you, she had an engagement ring on her finger and she moved into Olivia's."

I lift my arms to push Oz away, but he releases me before I have the chance. I sway as if I'm being tossed around in waves. "She was in *love* with him?"

"I'm not telling you anything you don't already know. You saw how Eli and your mom hugged. You saw your mom's initials on the tree. You held a picture of you and Olivia. You're smart. You know the truth. You haven't been looking for someone to prove it. You've been searching to disprove it."

"Then why lie to me?" I snap. "Why does everyone want to keep it a secret?"

Oz lowers his head and my gut twists. He knows and he won't tell me.

"Oh my God." I stand and Oz simultaneously bolts to his feet. "You know why this is a huge secret and you've seen me beat myself up over it and you won't tell me because you want to belong to a boys' club?"

"Because I'm a part of a family and I've been entrusted with a secret that I swore I wouldn't tell. You accuse me of having no integrity, but integrity doesn't mean breaking a promise. It means keeping it."

"It sounds like pretty words to cover up the truth. Take me back to Olivia's."

"Emily—" Oz starts.

"Take me back to Olivia's!" I yell and start for the door. I yank it open and Oz stalks up behind me and slams it shut.

"This is your family, too. If you want the truth, then you have to keep doing what you're doing. Stick with us. Become one of us and I promise that you'll find out. If you run away, you'll be like your mom and you'll remain an outsider."

I pivot on my toes in a flash and I'm in Oz's face. "I'm already an outsider. My mom may have run away, but Eli left me, too. He was the one that abandoned us. He signed the custody papers. He's the one that gave me up for adoption!"

I can't take in air fast enough and a lump forms in my throat. I shove a hand through my hair, trying to understand the heartache because it shouldn't matter that Eli abandoned me. I have my dad and I love my dad and that's what matters. It's all that should matter.

But there's this pain ripping through me. This agony tearing at my soul and a sound leaves my mouth that only begins to describe the misery inside me. "Don't tell me that he wanted me because if he did, he would have never signed those papers."

Oz swears under his breath then engulfs me into his body. I press back, pushing for release, but Oz wraps his arms tighter around me. The stronger his embrace, the more the tears threaten to escape from my eyes.

This is too much. It's all too much. Eli. Olivia. My mom.

"Will you stop fighting?" Oz whispers. "For once, lean on one of us."

Exhausted, tired, emotionally drained, I bury my face in his chest and large, warm drops slide down my cheeks. I'm not crying. Not at all. Because I wouldn't do something like that over a man who has never shed a tear over me.

OZ

EMILY SITS ON MY BED WITH HER BACK AGAINST the wall and her knees drawn to her chest. It's almost four in the morning and I led her here after she stopped crying. I'm paralyzed by crying girls. Not sure what to do with one in complete meltdown mode, I relied on what helps me. When I'm upset, a change of location can create a change in perspective.

Eli texted a few minutes ago to check on Emily and told me that Mom and Dad are staying the night there so Mom can watch Olivia and so Dad can discuss the Riot situation at a late night session of Church. He also informed me that Olivia is alert and fine.

Fine.

Dying of cancer is not fine.

I rest at the end of the bed and pluck an old guitar I bought when I was thirteen and dreamed of being a rock star. Emily rolls her head and glances at me with barely cracked eyes.

"Can you play anything else besides the opening to 'Smoke on the Water'?"

I cock an eyebrow as I switch up and strum the first few chords of the "Mexican Hand-Clapping Song." Emily laughs and the sound dances along my skin.

"How's Olivia?" she asks.

"Fine." I spit Eli's answer.

"I asked her what type of cancer she has and she didn't answer."

I say nothing. The pain of discovering that we're out of options and running short on time is still too fresh. There's a beat, then another, and Emily talks again. "Are you okay?"

Am I okay? The woman I'm closest to in the world is on the countdown clock. No, I'm not okay. "I don't want to talk about Olivia."

"Maybe you should."

"Day in and day out for the past year I've watched Olivia deteriorate. I don't need to talk about it when it constantly stares me in the face. I'd give everything if I could forget that Olivia is dying for at least thirty seconds, so excuse the fuck out of me if I don't want to talk about it with you."

Emily tugs her hair over her shoulder so I can't see her face. *Good job, Oz. Make Emily feel like shit. She'll forever remember you as a grade-A asshole.* It's better that way. At least she'll go home with the truth.

I grab the beer I had placed on the window ledge and Emily yanks it out of my hand. I open my mouth to tell her to give it back, but she shocks me speechless when she tilts the bottle up. Emily lowers it and her face puckers as if she tasted a lemon.

I chuckle and Emily glares at me like she wishes she had a knife.

"Never had alcohol before?"

"I'm not that naive." She hands the beer to me. "We have parties in Florida."

I'm sure they do, but my idea of party and her idea of party live in different zip codes. "The type where bras come off and end up on the wall?"

Emily spits out a strange sound that involves sticking out her tongue. "No one should be at that type of party."

"Don't knock it until you try it." I drink, thinking of how her lips had touched the rim. "Do you go crazy with pouring vodka in your slushies?"

Emily giggles and my spirits lift. "No. I've had a wine cooler before."

"One?"

"Yeah." Emily slides her mouth to the side as she morphs into shy. "I totally got light-headed and laughed at my toes for an hour." She raises her feet for effect.

I bet Emily is a cute drunk. Not the damn sloppy ones I have a habit of ending up with. The ones that cry when they get wasted and drop every damn problem they have or think they have on me. Emily would be the dancing-in-the-sand type and I regret that I'll never know.

"Beer sucks," she says.

I shrug. "It's an acquired taste."

"So's caviar, but I'm not eating fish eggs." She yawns and I check my phone for the time. It's too late or too early. Either way, Emily should be tucked safely in bed.

"I'm sorry," she says out of the blue. "I'm sorry that I pushed you about Olivia and…I'm just sorry."

I press the beer to my lips again and keep drinking until it's gone. If Emily doesn't believe I'm bad news, she will now. "It's not your fault. I'm sorry for biting your head off."

"It's okay. I…" She inhales deeply and wraps her arms around her knees. "I don't know what it's like to lose someone, but I understand being messed up and confused and not wanting to discuss things."

One month. Emily's survived over one month in my world and she's hardly batted an eye. Granted, she's lived in the tamer version Eli and Cyrus created, but the girl's been away from home while she's being stalked by some jacked-up people. I know girls who cry when they chip a damn nail. Not Emily. She's a strong one that rolls with the punches.

"I lied to you," I admit.

She levels her shocked eyes on me. "What?"

"At the pond, when I said that I liked you…" I rub my thumb over my eyebrow as my brain tingles with the slight beer buzz. "I more than like you. Being with you over the past month…"

I could blame my declaration on the beer, but what I'm experiencing is nothing more than a head rush and I didn't drink nearly enough to claim stupidity. All the emotions within me collide and I choose a safer path. "You've been good to Olivia. And how you were with during her seiz—"

I choke up and my teeth click together in an effort to erase the image of Olivia helpless and shaking on her bed. Soft fingers cover mine and a part of me hates when I grab on to Emily's hand and hold tight.

"I like her," says Emily, so softly that her voice is like a caress on my skin. "Olivia is definitely crazy, but I like her. And I also like you—maybe more than like, too."

Emily craves the truth and I've admitted to keeping some of it from her. I won't betray the club, but I can give Emily more. I tip my chin, indicating the top drawer of my nightstand.

"There're some pictures in there. They used to be on the fridge, but Mom took them down when you arrived at Olivia's. The one with the two babies?" I turn my head to look straight in her eyes. She won't be calling me out on integrity issues with this. "It's me and you."

Emily

THERE'S A FLASH IN HIS BLUE EYES—AN UNSPOKEN challenge to call him a liar, but I don't have to push for the truth. It's written all over his face. Nervous adrenaline floods my system as I wipe my palms against my jeans.

I open the drawer, grab for the stack of pictures and my entire world freezes. A small toddler. Chubby cheeks and fingers. Black hair. Big blue eyes. An infectious grin. He's settled into a patch of tall green grass and he's extending a dandelion to a baby girl old enough to sit. Long brown hair. My eyes. Pink Elephant James is by my side. I'm smiling as I accept the gift.

I twine my fingers in my hair and pull tightly enough to cause pain at the roots. Another picture from another time with another person who should not be a part of my past.

My back hits the wall and I lightly rap my head. "I don't understand."

Oz extends his leg so that it touches me, then he gently bumps his knee to mine as if offering comfort. "As I said before, I'm not telling you anything you don't already know. You lived here. Farther down the road, that's your family. Me and you, Emily? This isn't the first time we've met."

My body goes numb and I sort of enjoy the feeling. Numb's better than confusion and hurt and anger. All of which I should be experiencing, but I'm embracing numb. Numb chases away the terrifying, nausea-inducing memories of Olivia's twitching body.

Even though I'm welcoming numb, even though I'm trying desperately to dive headfirst into it and lose myself in the blackness, an overwhelming wave of sadness hammers into me like a tanker truck and I flinch with the impact.

Olivia's dying and if she was supposed to be in my life, but wasn't because my mom ran... "What did I miss? With Olivia? What did I miss not being around her?"

OZ

EMILY'S KILLING ME. TEARS POOL AT THE BOTTOM of those dark eyes and I watch helplessly as she bleeds. What did Emily miss by not living here? What will she miss if Olivia dies? Everything worth living for.

"Olivia took care of me," I say and my own voice tastes foreign. My heart rate increases because this sharing shit, it sure as hell isn't me. "When I was younger, my parents weren't ready for..." Me. "A kid, so Olivia took care of me until they could. Don't get me wrong. They love me and I love them, but Mom was working her way through nursing school and Dad had a job with jacked-up night hours. A kid made things complicated."

Emily's waiting for me to continue and I don't want to continue. I'd prefer to return to the kitchen and suck down a few more bottles of beer.

Olivia had a seizure tonight.

A seizure.

She's had them before. It's not new, but the cancer has spread to her blood. It's over. It's all fucking over.

"Olivia…" My voice breaks and I clear my throat. "She raised me. The room across from the one you've been sleeping in? That was mine. Slept in it every night until my mom switched shifts when I was eight."

Emily's too damn pale and those eyes are too damn wide. Who the hell can process so much shit in such a short period of time, but because Emily's quick on the draw, she does. "So Olivia is like your mom?"

My throat goes raw and I can only nod. Screw this. "I don't want to play this fucked-up history game anymore. You can go to sleep if you want. I'll take the couch."

"Oz," she says.

I strum the guitar again. "Can we let this go?"

She sighs and I accept the sound as her moving on from the conversation.

"Want me to head to the living room?" I ask.

Emily yawns while she shakes her head no. She's fighting sleep and I don't understand why. "Tell me why you're scared of the dark."

"If you could do anything other than work for the security company, what would you do?" she counters.

"Nothing. The security company is what I want to do."

"Yeah, but what do you like to do? You know, in your down time, and please don't tell me play guitar."

"Don't think I'm rock-star material? I took two months of lessons for this." I play one more chorus of "Smoke on the Water." "Why are you scared of the dark?"

"I'll tell you if you tell me what you would do if the security company didn't exist."

In the soft lamplight, Emily looks like a dream. White cotton shirt that hugs her perfectly, those skintight jeans and her silky chestnut hair tumbling around her shoulders. Normally, I wouldn't answer this type of question, but Emily's breaking down her walls and I'll be damned if I give her an opportunity to build them back up.

"Deal."

"First off," she says. "I'm not scared of the dark."

I raise both of my eyebrows in disbelief and she has enough of a sense of humor to smirk. "Technically, I'm scared of the combination of the dark and woods."

"Thanks for clearing that up." I pick at the strings as if I'm on the verge of playing something brilliant, but I've already run through my entire music catalog. Those two months of lessons were all I cared to take. "Mind telling me the story now?"

"You know how on the six o'clock news they report when a dead body was found?"

Not liking where this is headed, I lay my hand over the strings and they vibrate beneath my skin. "Yeah."

"Have you ever considered how the body's found?"

"Can't say I have." Until now.

Emily shrugs her shoulders like what she's about to divulge isn't a big deal. "Neither did I until I was eight, got separated from my Girl Scout troop in the woods, got turned around, fell into a hole covered with sticks and leaves, and spent the night with the next headlining story on the six o'clock news."

I can't breathe. "You're shitting me."

"Wish I was. By the way, I will totally accept your apology for making fun of me for freaking out at Olivia's wake whenever you're ready to give it. Your turn."

I prop the guitar against the wall. "Fuck, no. You don't drop that type of news then switch subjects."

"Well." Emily lifts the ends of her hair and twists her fingers into it. "There's not much to tell and, to be honest with you, I enjoy talking about hanging with a dead guy as much as you enjoy talking about Olivia dying."

Touché.

"As I said, your turn."

Guess it is, but it feels wrong to switch the conversation to me after Emily declared something so huge. "Does Eli know?"

"No. Only a few people do. The media and the police never released how the body was found, just that it was. You don't have to look at me like that."

"Like what?"

"As if I'm going to go spastic like I did at the funeral home. That was a special circumstance. I hate the dark and the woods so the worst that will happen is that I'll stay up until the sun rises."

My world narrows in on Emily. "How many nights have you slept through since you've been here?"

She rubs eyes that are plagued by dark circles and exhaustion. "Probably as many as you have sleeping outside my window."

Fuck this. I stretch past her and pull down the blanket. "Lie down and get some sleep."

"It's been a crazy night." She draws her knees in closer to keep from touching me, but it's a twin bed and I fill the entire mattress on my own. "I thought I was watching Olivia die and the woods are practically covering us and it's after four so the sun will rise soon. I'll be okay. If you're tired, it won't bother me if you go to sleep."

"I'll stay with you while you sleep." I prop myself onto my elbow on my side to watch her reaction. "Will that help?"

She fixates on her thumbnail. "It doesn't work that way. It's as if there's a monster under my bed and as long as I keep my eyes open, then it won't escape and attack me."

"I'll take on your monsters," I tease, but I'm dead serious.

Paint that was on her nails before is stripped away as she mulls over my offer. "When I was trapped, I screamed for hours and nobody came. Eventually, I curled myself into a ball next to the feet and stared at the body. If I watched it then it couldn't hurt me so I stayed up and stared. Even when it was pitch black."

Emily goes silent and I feel like an asshole for every bad comment I made.

"Do you know why I joined the Girl Scouts?" she asks.

"Because you like cookies?"

That earns me a short-lived smile. "Because I wanted to see the world. Experience new and different things."

"Think you got more than you bargained for." It's a joke. A bad one, but it's my attempt to lighten her mood.

She laughs, but it has a bitter edge. "You could say that."

Emily absently scratches at her arms. I immediately snag her fingers and gently tug until her body drops next to mine. Keeping her fingers, I brush my other hand along the angry welt forming on the inside of her arm. "Do you notice when this happens?"

"Usually not until the hives are huge. I started getting them after, well…after that night."

Emily blinks several times as she rests her head on my pillow. It'll absorb her scent and the thought pleases me more than it should. It's time to let Emily go and roll out of bed.

Because I promised, I'll stay with her, but it needs to be at a distance of five feet. But I don't move. Instead, I keep massaging the smooth skin of her inner arm.

"I hate new," she confesses. "I despise different. I like calm and mundane and routine. Snowflake is none of those things. It's been chaos and change and unpredictable. This town frightens me, which probably is a huge joke to you. I can't imagine one thing scaring you."

You scare me. "I liked both of my jobs."

"What?" Emily readjusts her head on the pillow and I enjoy the sight of her in my bed so much that space in my jeans becomes an issue.

"You asked what I liked to do. I liked both my jobs. This is my first summer in years not lifeguarding. Even when I start working for the security company, I'll continue to ref football. Chevy and I are considering coaching a fall team. I know it sounds stupid, but I'd like to do something with disabled kids. It's a big county, but not large enough for there to be resources for them like there are in Louisville or Nashville. So they sit on the sidelines a lot. Doesn't seem fair."

"That doesn't sound stupid," she says.

I say nothing and I'm not sure how I feel that I spilled so easily to Emily.

"So you enjoy being around kids?" she presses.

Never thought too much about it. We're still holding hands

and I wonder if Emily notices. Her skin is soft. Warm. I bet she feels this way everywhere and not just the areas I've explored: her mouth, her neck, her arms. I also bet she's a vision with her shirt off.

A shot of lust heats my blood. I focus on answering her question and not acquainting myself with the color of her bra. "Yeah. Kids don't bother me. Most of the time I like them a hell of a lot more than I like their parents."

There's an inch between us. Maybe less. When she moves slightly her legs brush mine. Images of weaving my hand around her back and sliding her body underneath mine torture me.

As if by instinct, I release her fingers and claim the curve of her stomach. Emily's eyes flash to mine and there's a hooded look to them that screams she's sharing the same thoughts. Her hand hovers off the bed. With a deep breath she slowly reaches over and rests it on my bicep. Electricity shoots up my arm with her touch and I blink with the dizzying caress.

"Why's that?" Emily asks in a hoarse voice. When it's obvious I lost the conversation, she prompts, "Why do you like the kids better than the parents?"

"Some people around here think the Terror are the shit, but there're others that treat us like garbage. People see the cut, see the tattoos and earrings on some of the guys, and they assume that we're a bunch of felons. Both Mom and Dad have lost jobs because they were told to choose between the club and where they worked."

"Did the club interfere with their jobs?"

"No. It's a small town and people know that Dad rides with the club and that Mom is a part of the support group, the Terror Gypsies. Guess their bosses thought it was bad for business to have a club member working for them. That's a huge reason why Cyrus started the security company—to give jobs to brothers who the community shut out."

Emily bites her bottom lip and over the past few weeks I've learned that means she's analyzing and worrying. "Do people treat you differently?"

"Most years at school I was labeled a disciplinary case before I walked into the classroom. What school never understood is that I didn't just have to answer to my parents about my grades and behavior at school—I answered to the whole club. The club pushes the 'it takes a village' concept to the extreme."

"I'm sorry," says Emily.

"Don't be. It's what people do. Judge before they bother getting to know someone. Judge before they understand what the club's about. Their loss as far as I'm concerned."

"No." Emily stares into my eyes. "I'm sorry for being the person who judged you."

Her words are like two slugs to the chest and I sway. Emily's hand on my arm tightens as if she could carry my burdens. It takes a big person to admit when they're wrong and it takes an even bigger person to admit that they're wrong to the party that wounded them.

If she can be honest, then so can I. "I'm sorry the club hasn't done right by you. All this secret stuff—I don't get it. You're Eli's daughter, Cyrus's granddaughter. If you grew up around here you would have been the princess. Still could be if you wanted. There's not a man in the club who wouldn't do what you asked."

Ingesting the concept that she's royalty, Emily fiddles with a loose string on the sleeve of my T-shirt. "As long as whatever I asked for didn't interfere with what Cyrus or Eli wanted, right?"

She's learning fast. "That'd be right."

"Is that the reason why we're friends? Because Eli told you to be?"

The sadness in her voice creates an ache in me. My fingers ease to the small of her back and I edge closer as I pull her to me. She doesn't protest. Just places her other hand on my chest as those dark doe eyes search me for an answer.

"I'm done bullshitting you. At first, I was nice to you because Eli told me to stay near you and protect you. I…"

Emotion locks the words in my windpipe. I almost failed her and knowing what I could have lost if I had fucked up that night at the motel causes hurt and anger to weave together in my gut.

"I fell asleep the night I was supposed to be watching you at the motel. That mistake almost harmed you and almost cost me my chance at membership in the club. Following you around was my penance. But then being around you…"

There's a reason why people shouldn't talk at four in the morning. Exhaustion eliminates the ability to lie. It demolishes the ability to tiptoe around the truth. Emotions are too exposed and real. Heightened to the point of explosion.

My hand roams up her back until I can tunnel my fingers through her hair. I slide a chestnut lock between my thumb and forefinger and enjoy the silkiness as it falls back to her shoulder. Her breath catches and the sound causes my cells to spark to life.

"But being around me...what?" Emily whispers.

"You're beautiful," I say, and the honesty of my words stings. "You're beautiful inside and out. I like how you challenge me. I like how I can never figure out what you're going to do or say. I like how we've thrown weird shit in your direction and you take it like a pro."

I cup her face with one hand and caress her soft skin. "I like how you smile and how you laugh. I like how you love and defend your family and I like how you're trying to love mine. I love how you trust. But mostly, Emily, I like how I feel when I'm around you."

Shit. My heart bursts as the words tumble out. "I'm falling for you."

Emily

OZ'S FINGERS BECOME INDIVIDUAL FLAMES LAP-ping against my skin and my whole body is on fire. Mom has warned me about boys like him. Boys who are dangerous. Boys who say pretty things. A voice in my head screams to run, but instead I lean into his touch.

"What's going on between us?" I ask.

Oz shakes his head slowly. "I don't know."

"I like you," I admit. More than like. Whenever I look at Oz it's butterflies and tingles and it's not just the fantasy of him kissing me that sends me into a tailspin. It's the idea of him in general. I do like him. Enough that it feels an awful lot like I'm falling, too.

"I like you so much that I'm..." Terrified. Falling means scary things. Unknown things. And I don't like scary or the unknown. "I'm not supposed to be falling for you."

"Since the moment you walked into my life, I've wanted to crawl into your head and know what you're thinking, what you're feeling. You scare the hell out of me, and if your father knew how you constantly cross my mind, how badly I want to kiss you, he'd put a bullet in my brain."

I shiver as Oz traces my lips. "Who are you referring to? Eli or my dad?"

Oz's face lights up with his grin. "Both of them. I've seen Jeff around you and he looks capable of pulling the trigger. I've learned to never discount the ones wearing a tie. They're the ones that scare the shit out of me."

I laugh and Oz laughs with me. The bed shakes and the vibration shifts our bodies closer together. So much so that my breasts are flush against his chest, my toes nudge his and his thighs lie over mine. When the sound fades our eyes meet and the smiles vanish.

Our chests move in unison. My pulse thunders in my ears as it silently begs over and over again for Oz to kiss me, kiss me, kiss me.

Oz drops his hand from my face. I grab it, hating the cold left behind. "Don't."

"You're tired," he says. "And we're playing a dangerous game."

But it's a game I don't want to stop playing. A gust of wind hits the trailer and the walls surrounding us creak. I weave my fingers through his. "Please stay."

There's a quaver to my voice. Being this near Oz makes me nervous. The thought of his lips on mine, his hands on my body, a return to the rhythm we had so quickly found when we kissed weeks ago is enough to cause me to tremble.

That day, we had grown into an inferno with a good reason to dampen the flames. But here, we're alone and there would be nothing to prevent us from going further, searching for the more my body desires. I care for Oz. Oz cares for me, but is that enough to cushion the fall I'll take if we succumb to the heightening attraction?

"You're tired, Emily, and I want to kiss you until you breathe out my name, but there's nothing good that will come out of this."

Oz is right. I'm so tired I'm fuzzy; so filled with a need to kiss him I'm light-headed. But that isn't the only reason I want him to stay.

The wind hits the trailer again and the roar of the trees sends a chill down my spine. At least at Olivia's there was a huge open space between the cabin and the forest. But here, we're in the thick of it. The dark enclosing us like a casket. "Just stay."

"Emily," Oz warns, but he doesn't leave. Instead, he releases my hand and rewraps his arm around my waist. "Eli will kill me and I'll lose any chance at prospect."

As if we've been extremely intimate before, as if we've been together forever, Oz extends an arm under my head. He then wastes no time inching up the material of my shirt until he can rest his palm against my skin. I melt under the heat from his hand.

He's right, I'm being selfish, but I don't push him away. Instead, I lick my lips. Oz settles his head on the pillow and our faces are close. Extremely close. So close that his exhalations move random pieces of my hair.

"You're right. You should go," I say.

"I will," he responds.

"Okay."

"All right."

"Good night, Oz," I whisper.

His fingers begin this slow brush along my stomach. Each goose bump–inducing glide edges farther up a centimeter and then down with each cycle. My breathing hitches when Oz skims the bottom seam of my bra.

"Good night," he says against my mouth.

"Good night," I repeat, and as I say it, my lips touch his. Energy builds between us and my legs become restless with this pent-up urge for more.

Oz takes in my lower lip and I'm overwhelmed with this sensation of awareness, this realization of each and every nerve ending I possess. Oz's hand, which had trailed south, tightens on my hip.

His lips pause on mine. He's waiting on me. I want this. No, I crave this. I brush my mouth against his and the movement is so slight he could miss it. So delicate because I'm afraid if I do too much then the two of us will explode.

My hand slides up his arm to his neck. A whisper of a touch as I let my fingers tease the ends of his hair. Oz sucks in a breath and my mouth turns up at the idea that I have this effect on him.

I've dreamed of this. Night after night. Woke up morning after morning to Oz sitting across the table from me acting as if he's in total control. But as Oz curls me into him, his body informs me that he's seconds away from shattering. And so am I.

Excitement unfurls within me with the expectation of what's on the verge of happening. I allow the tip of my tongue to lick Oz's lips and there's an almost audible crack of electricity. Our mouths part and…fireworks. The beautiful kind. The loud kind. The type you lose yourself completely in. Reds and blues and an array of bright colors burst behind my closed lids.

My hands wander Oz's back, pulling the material of his shirt up along the way. Oz rolls us and he uses his arms to balance his weight, creating the sweetest pressure of his body over mine. My legs hook around his and it's easy to pick up Oz's rhythm.

He leans up, yanks his shirt off and my heart goes completely still. Oz is gorgeous. His body hard and ripped. I stroke my fingers along the cut lines. In return, Oz circles my belly button and the caress sends pleasing waves throughout my body.

"Are you a virgin?" There's no judgment in his voice. No tease. He says it in a way that indicates he already knows and is perfectly fine with the answer.

"Yes," I tell him, unashamed.

There's no doubt Oz is more experienced than me. Not just because of what people have said, but by how expertly he maneuvers. It doesn't bother me to be more naive. My body is a gift, not something to be carelessly given away.

Violet was right. What's important is accepting what type of girl I am and I'm the girl happy to share this with Oz, but I'm not willing to share too much. "I'd prefer to stay that way…for a while, but I'd also like to keep kissing you."

"We can definitely do that." His eyes grow dark as he watches his hand inch the material of my shirt up and over my bra, and I slightly tilt up to allow him to ease the shirt off my body.

Oz lowers his head and blows air across my stomach. My

toes curl and I wiggle under the luscious sensation. He kisses a path along my stomach and my muscles dissolve to liquid.

Fingertips along my bra straps. One down and then another as Oz continues this divine assault. Wherever his hands touch, his lips soon follow and what started out as slow has increased in speed.

My fingers entwine in his hair and thanks to the clasp in the front, cold air nips across my breasts quickly followed by the warmth of Oz's mouth. We blend into this seductive rhythm. A synchronized dance that makes me dizzy, that makes me ache in a very good way.

He reclaims my lips and we continue to escape from unnecessary clothes. We roll, we explore and we move. Move in a way that I don't want to stop. Move in a way that causes me to hold on tighter to Oz. Move in a way that causes soft sounds to leave my throat and makes Oz moan as he nuzzles his head into the crook of my neck.

A rush of energy. A rush of power. A pure rush of adrenaline that causes us to fly faster and faster until the entire buildup deliciously shatters. My body arches at the same exact moment that Oz's arms constrict around me and then we're gasping for air.

Oz kisses my lips again and this time it's lazy and sweet and the most beautiful kiss I've ever been given. His warm palms caress my face as if I'm glass and then he sweeps the stray strands of hair away from my face. "Thank you," he whispers.

"For what?"

Oz shakes his head as if I should already know. "For this. For allowing me this. I don't deserve it. You're so damned beautiful."

I'm a puddle and Oz adjusts so that he's flat on the bed and I'm tucked into his side. He gathers me close and encourages me to mold my exhausted and sated body around his. My arm rests over his bare chest. My leg lies over his. I should care that the only piece of clothing I have on is my underwear. I should care that all he has on is his boxers, but I don't.

Oz is into me and I'm into him. He cares and so do I and we shared this. *This.* I never knew I could be so intimate with someone and still be a virgin. He never pushed for more than I was willing to give and for that I kiss his chest before resting my head back on him. His fingers play with my hair again and the gentle massage causes me to drift near sleep, but as the wind rocks the trailer, my eyes flutter open.

Oz kisses the top of my head. "Go to sleep. I'll stay up and chase your monsters away."

I slowly inhale and contemplate his words. Even with Oz surrounding me, I can still sense the dark and the woods pressing in on me from outside. "I know it's silly. Logically, there's nothing to be scared of, but…"

"Trust me to protect you."

Trust him. "It's only until dawn. Then I'm not as scared of the woods."

"I got you," he says. "I promise, I got you."

I cuddle into him, close my eyes and trust.

OZ

MY PHONE BUZZES AND I STRETCH. THE SCENT OF sand at the beach fills my senses as I inhale: Emily. I open my eyes and what we did this morning collides into me with the impact of a Mack truck.

Shit. I hooked up with Eli's daughter.

Fuck. I poured out my soul to her.

Damn, I'm falling in love.

Emily's pressed tight into my body with her back to me. My arm is slung over her, my fingers splayed over her flat stomach. A man of my word, I kept her monsters away and Emily slept deep. When daylight hit the window, I drifted off…cradling her in my arms…and I don't do that. I've never slept with a girl.

I close my eyes and breathe deeply again. She smells so damn good and feels like heaven. There's a shifting inside me. Emotions everywhere. Emily's going to leave. She's going to return home to Florida and leave me.

Emily sucks in air then peeks at me from over her shoulder. Big dark eyes. The type a guy can easily get lost in and I did. I got lost and now I'm screwed.

"Hi." Emily's eyes flicker between the bed and me. She's awkward. Unsure. Possibly regretting what we did.

"Hey," I respond.

"What time is it?"

I reach over Emily and grab my cell off the windowsill. With a swipe of my finger, it springs to life. "Four."

The late-afternoon sunlight streams in from the cracks of the shade in my room and highlights the dust hanging in the air. We've slept the day away. Emily discreetly yanks at the blanket, covering one of my new favorite parts of her body I love to worship.

There's one text from Olivia:

I want to see you and my granddaughter. Come back now. You can't keep running from this. Life and death happen regardless of what you want.

A ripple of anger through my system. I didn't run and I don't care for reminders of the death sentence I can't control.

Me: She's waking up now. We'll be there soon.

"Olivia wants to see you. I told her I'll bring you back."

"Okay."

"Want to take a shower?"

Emily fingers the hem of the blanket that's now tucked close to her neck. "I can wait."

I caress her face. Fuck me. Just fuck me. I can't do it. I can't treat her as a hook-up, but where the hell do we go from here?

I knew this. I knew the aftermath, but I couldn't resist her last night. Kissing her, holding her, it was like being called home.

A squeak of hinges and my eyes snap to the living room through the cracked door of my bedroom. Adrenaline pushes into my veins as I grab for my knife on the floor.

"Oz?" Mom calls out. "Emily?"

"Shit." I'm in motion, tossing another blanket over Emily as concerns for her modesty fly into my head. I roll to spring off the bed, but I'm not fast enough. Right as I plant a foot on the floor I glance up and meet the horrified expression of my mother.

"Tell me you didn't have sex with some girl with Emily down the hall," she whispers furiously as if Emily couldn't hear. "Tell me I raised you with some decency. Eli will gut you open if he finds out about this."

I sit up, aware of my movements so that I keep Emily's face blocked. There's no way out of this, but I can buy Emily a few minutes to compose herself. "Shut the door, Mom."

Fire rages out of her eyes. "Oz—"

"Shut the door and I'll be out in a second."

Mom's nostrils flare and, with pissed-off zeal, she slams the door to my room and the entire trailer vibrates. Great. Fucking great.

Emily eases up behind me while pinching the blankets to her body. Her mouth trembles and my heart is ripping into multiple pieces.

"I am so sorry," she says.

I weigh my words carefully. "Mom's not mad because a girl stayed overnight. She's mad because she thinks I did it with you around. So if you feel bad about me being caught, don't, but odds are she's not going to be too happy when she finds out that you're the one in my bed."

Considering there's only one way out of this trailer and Mom's bent on talking to me, she's going to discover that I was in here with Emily very soon.

Emily won't look at me. "What's going on between us?"

We should have thought of that before we made out. "I don't know."

She stares at the blanket as if maybe concentrating hard enough could help her disappear. "You care about me, right? I didn't imagine that, because I know I told you that I care about you."

"Hey." I slide my arms underneath her legs to bring her onto my lap, blankets and all. "I care about you. You got that? This wasn't a hook-up. I swear it. But what's happening between us...you have to admit it's complicated."

"Like how I live in Florida and you live in Kentucky and how my mom used to be in love with Eli and for some reason she left, pissing off everyone you love?"

Evidently, I'm not the only one who has thought about this. "Yeah."

"It doesn't mean we can't be together." But the defeat's clear in her tone.

"Are you going to call your parents and inform them you're living here next year? You're seventeen and have one more year of school and even if you didn't, would you call Kentucky your home? Because, this—Snowflake—this is my home."

Emily draws in a quavering breath. Jesus, she's killing me. I position my fingers under her chin, forcing her to face me.

"Forget what I just said, all right? We'll figure it out. I promise."

"No one will be happy about this. I mean, Eli and Cyrus won't let you into the club if they find out we did this, will they?"

I shake my head no. I'll be lucky if I walk out of this alive. If I do emerge still breathing, I can't guarantee I'll be mobile. "I'm going to talk to Mom. Ask her to keep this quiet. Take your time. Get dressed. And then come out when you're comfortable."

She lowers her face into her hands when I release her chin. "Then I don't think I'll ever be able to leave this room."

I can't help but chuckle as I pull her into my body. "You're not the first person to be busted half-naked."

"Well, it's my first time." My world rights itself when she lays her head on my shoulder.

I kiss the top of Emily's head before easing her onto the bed. I stand then shrug on my jeans. "Welcome to Snowflake."

Emily

IZZY'S PENSIVE AS SHE SHUTS THE DOOR TO HER car. After hearing Oz explain it was me in his bed and after she faded into ghost white when I walked out of his room, Izzy grabbed her car keys and declared she was driving me home. I'm still attempting to figure out if she meant Florida or Olivia's. She found me half-naked with her son in his bed. I'm betting she's sending me to Florida.

"I'm sorry," I say, because I can't stand the silence any longer.

Izzy's dressed in blue scrubs. She's worked third shift this week and when she left the hospital last night she went to Olivia's, so I'm officially the worst person ever for piling stress on the sleep-deprived. She starts the Ford Focus and the wheel whines as she turns it. The motor doesn't sound much better. A single crystal hangs from the rearview mirror and it creates small beams of rainbows on my lap.

Izzy flips her long black hair over her shoulder and peeks

at me out of the corner of her eye. "Are you in love with my son?"

Yes. My entire body convulses with the truth. I was falling for Oz before and after what happened last night...it changed me. It changed him. It changed us.

"Shit," Izzy whispers. "Just shit."

We hit a pothole and the car dips. Izzy peers in the rear-view mirror and I glance at the passenger-side mirror when a motorcycle rumbles behind us. Oz has a folded black-and-white Reign of Terror bandanna across his forehead and his black hair blows wildly in the wind. I tear my eyes away and focus on the rainbows.

"Did you know that if Eli or Cyrus or my husband or any man from the club walked in on the two of you, Oz would be ostracized?"

I sink lower in my seat. God, I'm in love with him. I've fallen in love with Oz and I'm costing him his dream.

"Did you know that you're my goddaughter?" Izzy asks without waiting for my answer.

Like so many other times during the past month, the sensation of running face-first into a wall stuns me. "No."

"You are." She concentrates on the road and through the limbs arching over the road, the sunlight bounces on and off her face. "I wasn't the best godmother at the time, but I loved you. Oz told me about the picture you found and your talk with Olivia, otherwise I wouldn't bring it up. I need you to hear what I'm saying because I love you and my son."

She commands my attention like a dropped nuclear bomb. "Okay."

"Your mother ran from Snowflake for a good reason. She

ran to keep you safe and she did an excellent job. Thinking that Olivia died must have completely floored your mom for her to make the mistake of allowing you to return, but it happened and I'm praying that neither you nor my son pay the price."

Izzy slows the car as we near Olivia's cabin. "You're in danger here and I see how my son looks at you, even before I caught the two of you today. He's falling for you and Oz doesn't fall. Even if Eli told him that his assignment was over, I doubt Oz would leave your side."

There's a buzz filling my ears as I try to comprehend what she's saying. Stuff about my mom, about how I'm still in danger and about how she *sees* how Oz looks at me. "My dad says I'm safe."

She places the car in Park and Oz flies past us for the clubhouse. Izzy regards him in the same way my mother used to watch me when I would climb to the highest diving board at the swimming pool. "I wish you weren't in danger, but you are. And as long as you stay in Kentucky you're putting a target on my son."

With a sigh, she faces me. "There has been a gaping hole in this family since you left and I've prayed for years for your return, but now that you're here, I fully understand why your mother had to go. When you go home, tell her that for me and also tell her to never make the mistake of bringing you to Snowflake again. For all of our sakes. You need to go home, Emily. I love you, but I love my son more and I am begging you to not drag him into this mess."

Oz swings off his bike and he's immediately on the move toward us, but his dad steps in front of him. A slow dull throb pulses in my head. I rub my temples, and the anger that's been simmering at my mother for lying to me over this entire fiasco begins to evaporate.

Everyone's so paranoid, so terrified, that I'm starting to get swept up in the mania. I've been here for over a month and the most dangerous thing I've experienced is me jumping in water the wrong way.

A loud growl of engines and I suck in a breath when bike after bike, too many to count, race past the car. I press into the seat as a sea of black vests leave the clubhouse and swarm Oz and his father. The newcomers park their bikes and create another layer around them. I can't spot Oz anymore. Instead, what glares at me are half skulls with fire blazing out of the eye sockets.

"They're patching Oz in tonight," Izzy says quietly.

I jolt as if electrocuted. "But he's not a prospect yet. Oz said that he has to go through that period before he can officially join the club."

"If it weren't for me and Olivia insisting that Oz not be allowed to be a prospect until he graduated, Oz would already be through his prospect period and patched in. They took a special vote because of Olivia's declining health and everyone agreed that she should see him as a member before she passes. They also felt that thanks to the past month Oz has spent watching you, he's served his time."

Served his time...with me. I sound like a prison sentence.

"Against anything I've wanted," she says, "Oz has been a prospect of this club for eighteen years. Some things are so inevitable that they don't need to be made formal."

Izzy departs the car and I follow her as she goes up the steps of the porch. I blink as Olivia exits the house. The screen door shuts and the yard plummets into silence. Every man honors Olivia as they turn to acknowledge her.

She nods to me as if the last time I saw her she wasn't in the midst of a seizure and I wasn't screaming for Oz to help. Her blue scarf covers her head. Her jeans as tight as normal. She has gold dangling earrings that almost touch her shoulder. She wears that black top again that resembles a corset. As always, she's striking and radiates kick-ass.

But as I step closer to her, there's a slow deliberateness to her movements. A tiny quiver of her hand and that tremor slowly progresses up her arm. I slide up beside her and ease my fingers underneath hers and she grasps on to me. The slight shake of her body would only have been noticed by someone standing near. She knows this and so do I.

Olivia inclines her head and we walk together on the porch, past my window and the seat Oz has used as a bed for too many weeks. The lone sound in the yard is our footsteps against the wood. Hand in hand we reach the corner of the porch and there's a part of me that feels self-conscious that everyone stares.

A breeze rushes through the trees. The leaves clap against each other and a few maple helicopters drift to the ground. There are so many men in the yard. Seventy. Eighty. A hundred. So many. Too many. And Olivia and I have their undivided attention.

The wind dies and this moment is too intense with silent expectation. I search the crowd for Oz and when my eyes meet his, he imperceptibly nods at me. The world fades away and, suddenly, I can breathe again.

I wait for Olivia to do whatever it is everyone is expecting her to do, but nothing happens.

"Are you supposed to wave or something?" I whisper. When Olivia raises an eyebrow, I curl my hand and tilt it side to side. "Like the queen does on TV?"

She laughs. The loud one. The one from when we first met that scared the hell out of me and, this time, I can't help but giggle along with her. She squeezes my fingers, releases them, then cups my face as she leans over and kisses one cheek and then another.

"If I'm the queen, then you're the princess, and this is your kingdom."

When she lets go of me, Cyrus calls out, "Reign of Terror!"

"Hoo-ra!" is the answering rumble.

"Reign of Terror!"

"Hoo-ra!"

"Reign of Terror!"

"Hoo-ra, Reign of Terror!"

Someone applauds and the entire yard bursts into noise. Both Eli and Oz are grinning at me. I can't help the silly and shy smile forming back.

"This is your family," Olivia says to me. "If you learn to love us then you will forever have our love in return."

I think I am falling in love and that love would belong to Oz. I search for Oz again and I spot him just as Eli slings an arm around his neck and leads him away from me and into the clubhouse.

"Come on," Olivia adds. "We have a ton of work to do and not enough time to do it."

OZ

I TOOK A QUICK SHOWER IN THE CLUBHOUSE'S bathroom, changed clothes and now I'm bounding up the stairs to Church. Hook's at the door and opens it the moment he sees me. This is nothing like the last time I was invited in here. Each man at the table peers at me as I walk in and it's not with the look they had last time, as if I were a man strapped in the electric chair.

I don't know what the hell just happened outside with me in the middle of it, but whatever it is, it's good and I'm walking on air. There's no doubt I'm becoming a prospect today and odds are I'll be working for the business, as well.

Cyrus owns the seat at the head of the table and my eyes flicker to Eli, who sits on his right, and then Dad, who sits on his left. Neither of them gives anything away with their blank expressions. I've never seen a guy receive his cut before. It's a private ceremony during Church.

"We're having a party tonight," announces Cyrus.

My muscles go stiff. "Where do you want me to take Emily?"

"She's going to be here for it," says Eli. "At least until we send the families home."

It's club rules: no kid at the clubhouse after eight at night. This brotherhood is family-oriented, but it's still a motorcycle club and the partying can get fucked up and crazy.

I pop my neck to the side to release some of the tension. I'll overstep my welcome by speaking out of turn, but this involves Emily and it's already hard not to lash out like a pissed-off bear. "What about her safety? You said that the Riot was thirty miles north of here last night. And if that's not an issue anymore, then remember how pissed you were at the funeral home at the idea of people knowing she was around? We bring in strangers and news will spread that your daughter is here."

That the girl I love is staying here.

The girl I love.

My heart beats hard as the realization plows into me. Last night, I said I was falling, but I was dead wrong. The falling did happen, but it happened over time. Happened without my knowledge. I love Emily. I am in love.

And the girl I love is in danger.

The gun in the holster at the middle of my back grows heavier. Cyrus asked me weeks ago if I had the balls to do what needed to be done. When it comes to protecting Emily, hell yeah, I own a pair.

Cyrus eyes the board and after a few nods from several guys he casts his gaze to Eli.

"The Riot either knows she's here or they don't." Eli shrugs as if he doesn't care, but there's something off about his movements. A rigidness that tells me he's hiding something. "They haven't made a grab for her since the motel and because of that I think she's safe. While I love Emily being here, her dad called this week and he wants her back in Florida."

His words slam into me. "She's heading home?"

"It's been over a month. She has a life and it's time for her to return to it."

Jeff wants her home. They're throwing a very public party. I pinch the bridge of my nose as the puzzle pieces click together. "You're using tonight to see if anyone will make a grab for Emily."

"We'll have people on her," Eli says. "We're considering this a trial run of what will happen when she returns home."

When she returns home... It's the second time he's said it and each time my heart clenches with the words. "Does the Riot know Emily's here? The truth this time."

There's silence and when no one answers I search my father's face. When he won't look away, I have my answer of yes. I suppress the urge to scream. Even when I'm patched in, unless I'm on the board, there will be things that will never be my business.

"If they know she's here, if you think it's possible the Riot will make a grab for her, why send Emily home? Isn't she safer where we can protect her?"

"Not your place to question my decisions," Eli says in a low warning. "Especially when it involves my daughter."

I nod and Eli nods back that he's cool with me even though I spoke out of turn. Eli loves Emily. He would never intentionally put her in harm's way.

My arms flex as I straighten. "I got her back. She trusts

me." She cares for me. "We're friends." I'm in love with her. "She won't question me being stuck to her side." As long as she doesn't mind me stripping her naked in my mind the entire time. "No one will touch her." And if they do I will snap their fucking necks.

The man who's been my surrogate grandfather sizes me up. "You screwed up a few weeks ago when Eli asked you to watch over Emily."

"I did." When I stood in the same spot I am now, the gravity of what I had to lose almost crushed me. But now that I'm in love with Emily the reminder causes a lethal combination of fear and anger to swirl into a storm. "I swear I'll never let her or Eli down again."

"We know, son. All of us have watched you over the past few weeks and you've done everything we've asked you to do and more. You've stayed by Emily's side, kept her safe and somehow gained her trust. Through that she's spent time with Olivia and—"

"With me," interrupts Eli. The sincerity of his words hits me hard. Fuck, this meeting is gaining momentum.

"She's spent time with most of us and that's because you've made her comfortable," says Cyrus. "You've sacrificed weeks of your life to protect someone we care about and we want you to know we've noticed."

I scan the room, hunting for the blank cut. This moment is so huge that I redistribute my weight. This is Christmas morning times a million. But then the blood rushes out of my head and I all but sway on my feet. I'm lying to them. They're about to make me a prospect and they have no idea that I spent the night in bed with their daughter…their granddaughter.

Cyrus stands, then lays both of his hands on my shoulders. "We're patching you in tonight."

The world zones out. "What?"

"We took a special vote and the club agreed to consider the past month your prospect period. Tonight, you're becoming a brother of the club."

A raw emotion builds inside me and I hook my thumbs into my pockets as I try desperately to keep my shit together.

"Jonathan," Cyrus says in a low tone and it's not the president of the club talking to me, but the man who taught me to fish at four. The man who drilled it into my brain to hold the door open for a girl. The man who helped care for me when my own parents couldn't.

Cyrus's arms close in around me and mine do the same to him, careful not to touch his patch. The hug is strong, tough and intense on both ends and when we let go the entire room is on their feet. Each man waiting for his turn to embrace me and one by one I embrace them back.

Emily

NO ONE IN THE CROWDED KITCHEN MENTIONS Olivia's seizure, not even Olivia. There's a ton of women in here. All shapes. All sizes. Most of them wear a black vest similar to the Reign of Terror, except there's no skull with flames bursting out of the eye sockets, but a simple patch that reads Terror Gypsies.

Olivia sits at the table next to me and her job appears to be carrying me through most of the conversation and introducing me to so many people that there is no way I'll remember their names.

"...as it turns out Emily is a bit of a hustler in a game of poker," says Olivia, and as always multiple women insert their multiple comments. It's not bad, it's that there's a lot of women, with a lot of opinions, and I've never been in a room with so much chatter or so many people at one time for so long.

There's a consistent pounding in my head and I'm attempting to smile through it. I crack another hard-boiled egg and pick the shell off. "For real, who eats this much potato salad?"

The women laugh and maybe they missed I wasn't joking. After a shower and a fast change into clothes and a touch-up of cosmetics, I was whisked by Olivia into kitchen duty.

Some lady with extremely long bleached-blond hair sweeps the pile of egg shells in front of me into a garbage can. "Honey, those boys can eat more than you can imagine. I'm Peach, by the way."

Like I have with the other women who have introduced themselves to me since I arrived, I accept her quick and, for me, awkward hug. "Nice to meet you. I'm Emily."

And like everyone else, she responds, "I know, and welcome home."

The living room has been rearranged and in it, next to the window, is a hospital bed. I hate that it's there and, like the seizure Olivia had, everyone appears to ignore it. What I can't ignore? "How is it that everyone knows me?" I quietly ask Olivia.

"Everyone knows Eli had a daughter," she responds in kind. "And they know that this is their one opportunity to meet you."

A fortysomething redhead named Pony makes a fuss over a photo on her phone and most everyone heads her way to look. I lean over to Olivia. "Does anyone have a normal name?"

Sure, I caught on early that the guys in the club have nicknames. Even Cyrus and Eli have nicknames sewn on their vests and most of the people call them those names.

"The women have road names," she answers. "Just like the club has them."

I'm more methodical as I peel off the shell from the current egg and weigh asking if Oz's name really is Oz, but I keep the question to myself. I glance over at Olivia and she's studying me. Her dark eyes are soft. So soft that I can see a hint of sadness in them.

"Are you okay?" I ask.

"This is how it was supposed to be. You here with me. Being a part of this. This should have been your normal and I should always have been your grandmother."

There's this pain and it cuts right through me. Past my heart, past my soul. I place the egg on the table and slide my hand over hers. "I don't want you to die."

That's the moment when the entire room had fallen silent. The moment when everyone had been shifting away from their current conversation and had yet to begin another. There's wetness in my eyes and Olivia moves her hand so that she's now offering me comfort with the slightest squeeze.

"I have always loved you," she says.

I clutch her hand back because I think I love her, too. What causes this wound in my chest to bleed is how I learned to care for someone and now I have to let them go. It feels too cruel, too mean. My gut twists and my face contorts with the agony.

She holds my hand tighter. "It's okay, Emily. I know."

"It doesn't seem fair...to have just now met you when you've always been here. It's just..." No other words. "Not fair."

"Death never is, and most of the time neither is life." She pauses. "Emily, it's not enough for you to care about me. I want you to care for your father, my son."

I'm shaking my head because I don't want to hear anything

else, but because it's Olivia and she does whatever she desires she continues, "Do you know why Eli has all those stars tattooed on his arm?"

My muscles lock up as I become paralyzed by the silent stares of the room. I'm crippled by this moment.

"There's one star for each year of your life. The shaded-in ones are the years that he saw you. The ones that have no color represent the years that his life was empty without you. You want to make a dying woman happy? Don't let him go another year tattooing an empty star on his arm."

My windpipe constricts and even if I could talk I wouldn't know what to say. The back screen door in the kitchen opens and the creak fills the deafening void of silence.

A clearing of a throat and I force myself to forget the other women and the occasional hand that lifts to wipe at tears as I meet the eyes of my cousin Chevy.

He and I, we haven't interacted much. Haven't said more than a "hi" or a "bye." He's around Oz a lot and he also comes over daily to check on Olivia. I never showed an interest in him because he never showed an interest in me, but Oz is right. I never fully engaged.

"Hi, Chevy." My voice is raspy and rough, but I need to try.

His eyes flicker between me and Olivia and he nods at me as if he senses all the chaotic words in my mind that I don't have the ability to speak. "Hey, Emily."

"How are you?" I say, and I hear how awkward it sounds, but how else do I start?

Reminding me of Eli, he pulls on his earlobe, but there are no plugs in Chevy's ears. "Good. You?"

I'm a freaking basket case. "I'm doing well."

He clears his throat again. "Some of us are going to be hanging out together once dinner begins." Chevy tosses his hand in the air to indicate a direction that I don't quite comprehend. "We'll be on the other side of the yard." A yank at the neckline of his shirt. "People our age. Me, Oz, Razor, Stone, a few others. Maybe Violet."

Oz, maybe Violet…a moment where I could get to know my cousin… "Sounds good."

"Eli said I have her for an hour." Olivia saves us both from dying of trying too hard. "My eggs aren't done being shelled and I have five more minutes."

The women part as Chevy strides through the kitchen. He's tall and broad-shouldered and most of them have to press against the wall or fridge to let him pass. There's a kind spark in his dark eyes as he inclines his head toward the yard. "I'll finish cracking the eggs while you go get some fresh air. Make sure you find Eli, though."

Pressure on my hand from Olivia confirms she approves. I could hug Chevy for rescuing me from this uncomfortable moment, but instead I smile.

He flicks his chin in understanding and the entire room groans and starts harassing him the moment he pops one of the hard-boiled eggs into his mouth.

I walk out the door and lift my face to the sky. Who would have guessed that I could learn to like so many people— especially people who are so different from me?

OZ

EMILY SLIPS OUT THE BACK DOOR TO THE KITCHEN and I glance around. The men are either hanging in the clubhouse, setting up tables and chairs in the yard or manning the grills full of hot dogs and hamburgers. Behind the house, there's no one.

Emily pauses when she sees me then flashes this soft smile. I like that look on her. I'd die a happy man if I saw that expression every day.

I stride over to her and link our hands together. "Do you trust me?"

"Yes," she says, not missing a beat.

I walk backward, gently pulling her with me. She follows, but her smile fades as her eyes drift over my shoulder to the woods that I'm leading her to. "Oz."

"Not far in," I say as if I'm coaxing a wounded animal to abandon its hiding spot. "Just far enough to where I can kiss you."

She brightens at *kiss*, but then she assesses the sky. It's evening and with it being the middle of summer, the sun still shines from the west. Blue sky above. A scattered white cloud here or there.

An edge of panic tightens her features, but Emily still walks with me, her hand grasping mine as if she's floundering off a ledge. As I guide her past the tree line her chest begins to flutter at a faster rate and sweat breaks out on her palm.

I rub my thumb over the top of her hand and keep my eyes locked on hers. "Have you ever jumped into a pile of leaves?"

Emily shakes her head no as we ease through the trees. Her face loses color and I stop us when she visibly quakes.

I inch into her personal space and then gently back her up until she's supported against the trunk of a tree. Because I can't help myself, I rest a hand on her hip then step near enough so that our bodies are touching. This is how it's meant to be— me this close to her.

"Don't be scared," I say. "I won't let anything happen to you."

"I know. It's just hard." She raises my hand to her chest and lust surges through me as she presses my palm to her heart. Damn, her skin is soft and the tissue beneath my hand is even softer. "I need to calm down or my heart is going to explode."

Because I'm not intent on taking Emily's virginity on the floor of the forest, I lower our hands. "In the fall, there's a million red, orange and yellow leaves. In the winter, it's real quiet and when it snows you can see animal tracks. Chevy, Violet, Razor and I used to play back here all the time. The tree house we built as kids sits farther back."

"Were you close with Violet once?"

"Yeah. She created these elaborate hand signals for us to use while we were playing hide-and-seek or capture the flag. She's the one that convinced us to hang that." I tip my chin to the right and Emily tracks my gaze to a rope hanging off a huge oak.

"You guys are obsessed with ropes," she says.

I chuckle. "Every fall we make the biggest pile of leaves you can imagine. So huge that it's a mountain. We use the rope to jump into the pile. I've never invited anyone to do it with us before and I decided that when we do it this year, I'd like my girl to be there."

I skim my knuckles along her cheek and she leans into me. Good God, she's the most amazing creature I've come across. "What do you say, Emily? Will you come back to Snowflake this fall and jump with me into some leaves?"

She sucks in her bottom lip. "I'm your girlfriend?"

I tuck her silky hair over her shoulder and drop my head so that my lips brush hers. "If you'll have me."

"Yes."

Because Emily is a mixture of bold and innocent, her lips meet mine in a rush then slow as they continue to move. Her hands delicately glide along my shoulders and into my hair. A hypnotic action that draws me in. Each of her fingertips are hot on my skin, her lips sweet to taste, her scent engulfing my senses. My hands drift to her thighs and the memories of the rhythm Emily and I shared last night in my bed circle in my brain.

Heat races in my blood and Emily slides her leg against mine. The urge is to lift her and kiss her until I'm dizzy. Kiss her until our clothes are off. Kiss her until the only thing left in the universe is us.

A booming laugh echoes into the woods and Emily immediately turns her head away from me. We're both panting and it takes every ounce of self-control not to kiss the patches of red skin forming along her neck.

She flattens her palms on my chest and I step back while lacing her fingers with mine. "They're patching me in tonight."

"I heard. That's amazing."

It is. "Will you do me a favor?"

"What?"

A part of me sinks. Odds are she'll hate this. "I'm going to be distracted tonight and I won't be by your side when you head into the house later. The clubhouse is going to get crazy and I want to know you're safe. Promise that once you go in, you'll stay in."

"You are the millionth person to tell me I'm not allowed out of the house after eight." There's an annoyed set to her lips that causes me to stroke my thumb against her mouth and I chuckle when she jerks her head away. She's not searching to be pacified.

"I'm starting to get insulted," she bites out.

"Prepare yourself," I say. "Eli will probably tell you, too."

"Super. Is there anything else you need to discuss before a giant hole appears at my feet and swallows me up?" She's kidding, but I don't miss how her fingers tighten in mine.

"I know you prefer not to lie, but me and you...it's going to be a lot for people to digest. Eli entrusted me with you and if he had known that this—" I rock our joined hands

"—would happen, he never would have picked me. He trusted me to protect you and not to break his trust by getting emotionally involved. I've been thinking nonstop about this, and I'm going to tell Eli and Cyrus you're my girl, but I'd like to wait until after I'm patched in."

Emily pales out. "If they know now, you think they'll keep you from being a part of the club?"

"I don't know." Guilt festers within me. I don't want to lie to Eli, Cyrus or the club, and I don't want to make Emily a secret. On the ride back here I'd thought about talking to Eli this evening, but I wasn't expecting to be patched in and I sure as hell wasn't expecting that Olivia wouldn't live long enough to see the ceremony. If we push this off—if I tell Eli tonight and he decides to wait until he can digest that I'm in love with his daughter—Olivia might miss this moment and I'll miss knowing that she was there.

"If you're uncomfortable with waiting, I'll tell Eli now. I'll tell him I have feelings for you that I want to pursue, but otherwise I'm asking for you to give me tonight and then tomorrow, I'll tell him everything."

"Is that what's happened?" A spark of humor lights up her eyes. "You have feelings you want to pursue?"

I frame her face with both hands, letting my fingers tunnel to the roots of her hair. She's so beautiful it hurts. "I've already fallen for you, Emily, but Eli and Cyrus are real protective of you. This is going to shock the hell out of them. Besides..."

I trail off and Emily's forehead wrinkles. "What?"

I swallow down the hurt. "Eli said your dad called him. You're going home soon."

The bright cheer that had been on her face is replaced by

a shadow. "What? But I told Dad on Monday I wasn't ready to go back yet. I told him I wanted to spend more time with Olivia and Eli said something about going on another weekend trip and—"

"Your mom and dad miss you," I cut her off. "That's not a bad thing."

She throws herself into me, wrapping her arms around my stomach and burying her face in my chest. I rest my chin on her head and squeeze her into me. I'm going to miss this. Having her in my life day in and day out. "I want to make this work, but we have to play our cards right. Are you with me?"

She pulls back and looks up at me. "I don't want to be a secret."

"You won't be. I promise. Let me get patched in tonight and then I'll have some footing in the club. Trust me, I'll need it. Eli won't be happy with me."

"But he can't take back your patch because we're together, can he?"

It's what I'm banking on. That and I hope Eli will get his shit together sooner rather than later in understanding that I would die for his daughter. I have no doubt Eli will come to his senses on this, but I can't risk him taking longer than Olivia has to live. "I'm not asking you to lie. I'm asking if we can move slowly."

"Okay."

I kiss her forehead and then lead her out of the woods. A foot from the edge of the tree line Emily hesitates. "Is your name really Oz?"

The majority of people in my life think it is. Only a handful of people know my real name. "It's Jonathan, but Olivia started calling me Oz when I was little and it stuck."

"Why Oz?"

I watch as a group of guys raise the American flag next to the Terror's flag on the pole. "Because she said that growing up here, around all this, must be the equivalent of Dorothy being born in Oz."

Emily smiles and she doesn't lose the expression when I release her hand, but she does stroll close enough to me that sometimes our hands brush against each other as we walk. We round the cabin and Eli leans against his old pickup and grins when he spots the two of us.

"Eli wants to see you," I say. "Find me when you're done and we'll get some food."

I wink at Emily and force myself to turn and walk away. By this time tomorrow, I'll be a full member of the Reign of Terror and one step closer to having her by my side in public.

Emily

DON'T MENTION THAT I KNOW WHAT THE STARS on his arm mean. Don't mention that every time I sneak a peek at him, I'm counting again and again, or how I'm freaking frustrated that it always adds up to seventeen.

Eight stars are empty. Nine stars are colored in. Seventeen stars. One for each year of my life. Why the hell would a man who never wanted me mark himself this way?

Don't go there, Emily. Just don't. Focus.

Don't mention to Eli that I've fallen in love. Don't mention to him I spent the night half-naked wrapped up in Oz's arms. Don't mention that I've never felt this way and that it's a wonderful feeling and a terrifying feeling and it's similar to being on the back of a motorcycle.

Don't mention to Eli that while he's sitting there all expectant in the passenger side of his truck, I'm thirty seconds away from puking on his steering wheel. "I can't do this."

"Yes, you can," Eli encourages me. "Foot on the brake,

turn the key in the ignition, shift the truck into Drive, then gently tap the gas."

Nausea bubbles up my throat. The windows are down, but the day was hot enough that any exposed skin left by my shorts and tank top sticks to the plastic seating. I flex my fingers and inhale the scent of cigarette smoke and pleather.

I can do this. I can freaking drive a truck. No. No I can't. "There are a ton of people around here. Maybe we should wait until everyone's gone."

"We're not NASCAR driving. You're going to gently tap the gas and if you think we're moving too fast, you're going to press the brake."

The front porch is full of gawkers. Olivia watches us from her Adirondack chair. Cyrus holds her hand as he stands next to her. Razor sits on the porch swing and rocks it in a slow motion. Chevy and Oz each rest a shoulder against opposing beams near the stairs and Violet and her brother, Stone, are planted on the bottom step.

"I want you back in the house by eight tonight," says Eli. "After that, no one under eighteen can be around the club-house."

I have to focus very hard so I don't roll my eyes. "I can't watch Oz patch in?"

Eli gives me this dark expression that tells me the answer is no. Rules are rules I guess, and it's not my club. It's a boys' club. With that thought I'm drawn to Violet. The moment she walked up to the front porch she announced that she was only here to visit me.

This club has hurt her somehow and while we've chatted

on the phone about clothes and some guys she's been dating this summer, we never discuss anything important.

Olivia glances in Violet's direction and Chevy looks like someone shot him in the chest multiple times. Sadness settles in my gut. When I arrived, I was almost as bad as she is now and for that, "I'm sorry."

I seem to be saying that a lot. Eli peers over at me as if I told him I was pregnant. "What?"

For those years you asked me a million questions and I gave you half-truths. For that—I'm sorry. "I'm sorry I'm being a spaz. It's just..." I wipe my sweaty palms on my jean shorts. "The first time I drove, I pressed on the gas too hard and then freaked out and accidently pressed on the gas more thinking it was the brake and it obviously wasn't the brake and well... I wrecked Dad's car. No one was hurt or anything, but the car was..."

I use my hands to measure a foot then squish it to an inch. "Smooshed."

"No one was hurt?" he repeats.

"Not even a bruise."

Eli scratches his jaw, but I spot a smile. "The reason you haven't learned to drive is..."

"Did you miss where I said I smooshed his car? Like an accordion. Dad's a fantastic guy, but come on. I wrecked his car, which proves I am a freaking menace behind the wheel."

"It's okay to be afraid," he says. "But it doesn't mean you shouldn't try it again."

"I'm not afraid," I counter, but I am. I always seem to be afraid and my stomach dips. Everyone here in Snowflake is continually brave. Olivia, Oz, Eli...all of them.

"When your mom told me she was pregnant with you, I was afraid."

The truck rocks with how fast my body moves in his direction. Eli's never spoken so openly about our past before. "What?"

Eli stares out the front windshield. "Besides what's happening with Mom, I'm not sure I've ever been so scared in my life as when Meg told me she was pregnant. We were young and still in school and I didn't feel old enough to take care of myself, much less a baby."

My mouth dries out and a million questions form in my mind, but I don't know how to ask any of them. I crave for him to tell me more, but at the same time, I'm terrified of what I might learn.

"The point is, I was scared and so was your mom, but she figured out how to work past the fear. When I look at you, I see Meg. Your mom—she was fearless."

I've heard a lot of people say a lot of negative things about my mother in the past few weeks, but I don't see hatred in Eli's eyes. I spot the same pain that always seems to live within him, but I also spot admiration and possibly love. For me, for Mom, maybe for both of us...but regardless, there is love.

Maybe there's room to love him—that is if he really does have room in his life to love me.

Eli reaches over and the air rushes out of my lungs when he turns the keys. The engine rumbles to life and he straightens back in his seat. "This truck is a piece of shit. There's not much more you can do to it and my life insurance policy is paid up, so we're good."

"Eli..." I protest.

"Put your foot on the brake, shift into Drive, then *gently* tap the gas. I also suggest holding on to the steering wheel."

"Eli..." I try again.

"You can do this," he pushes. Okay. I can do this. A surge of adrenaline grabs me and I do exactly what Eli asks.

OZ

I'VE NEVER BEEN SO BUZZED IN MY LIFE AND I haven't had a drop to drink. Cyrus grins at me as he holds out my cut and beyond him, Olivia smiles. My road name is sewn on the front right underneath the words *Mother Chapter*. I slip my arms in and, I swear to God, I'm a fucking king.

I inhale and the scent of leather hits me. Cyrus pulls me into a hug and when he claps my back, it's a high hit to keep from touching the three-piece patch. It's a sign of respect. No one touches the patch and now I'm a brother who deserves the respect Cyrus is offering.

He releases me and a round of cheers fills the yard packed with hundreds of people. A ton of brothers, some Terror Gypsies and other people ready to party. It's after nine in the evening. The sky is black and because of clouds that rolled in there's not a star in the sky. Off to the side, a bonfire roars and embers float in the dark night.

Music pumps from the clubhouse. Loud guitars. A drum

line that rattles the bones. All of it the foundation for a night I'll remember forever.

There's a flurry of embraces and congratulations. A sea of faces and smiles. There's Eli, my father and Razor. Each of them with a bottled beer in hand. Dad offers one and a hug. I accept both.

"Tonight's about you." Razor raises his beer and the four of us clink glasses. I'm a brother now. My dream come true. The only one missing is Chevy, but in a year he'll be beside me. He'll complete this circle.

Following tradition, the three of them shake their un-opened beers and I pop off the cap of mine.

"Let's go, boy," my dad says.

I chug as the rest of them open theirs and spray me with the contents. There's beer up my nose, dripping down my hair as I swallow the last gulp. When I finish, the four of us throw our beers into the fire. Glass shatters and little bursts of flames appear from the alcohol.

More whistles and shouts. Another beer in my hand. An arm around my neck and I'm led into the clubhouse. The music is deafening. Topless girls dance on the bar. The building is wall-to-wall people. A commotion of sights, colors and sounds. The stench of beer, body odor and sex hangs in the air.

I hesitate before walking all the way inside. A glance over my shoulder and the light turns off in Emily's room. Two prospects stand guard near the front door of the cabin. To-night's a test. A test to confirm that Emily's safe.

Eli's chatting with a brother from another chapter and I reach past two people and grab his arm. "Are you sure Emily's good?"

Eli shoves past the people and wraps his hand around my neck, leaning me into him. "Your job is done. You enjoy tonight and you let me worry about Emily. Welcome to the brotherhood, Oz."

He kisses my cheek and I quickly lose sight of him in the crowd. I look back at the house again. Arms around my waist and Pigpen has me in the air. The entire world moves and I take a deep breath, trusting Eli and the club with protecting what I love.

Emily

I SIT ON THE WINDOW SEAT IN MY ROOM AND read the text sent from my father:

I'm flying to Kentucky tomorrow. We miss you and it's time to come home.

Home. I miss home. I won't say that I don't. I miss air-conditioning and my mother's laugh. I miss the easiness of conversation with my father and how Mom checks on me at night before she turns in herself. I miss uncomplicated and I miss Trisha and I miss the quiet flow of the world several hundred miles south of here.

But there's an emptiness at the thought of returning. Olivia is dying. I'm in love with Oz. Eli is a man who taught me how to drive. He's also a man who has seventeen stars tattooed on his arm for me. I came here one person and I'm leaving here changed.

Changed.

It's extremely disorienting. I came here Emily Catherine and I'm leaving here Emily Star and I don't know how to reconcile the two worlds.

Me: I want to stay. For a little bit longer. There are pieces I still need to figure out.

My finger hovers over Send. Things that I need to figure out, like how Oz and I will maintain a long-distance relationship. Like if there's a chance that Olivia will live. Like why Eli gave me up. Like why my mother ran from a place that is so freaking weird and complicated and just as strangely fantastic.

I need to know why, but how do I explain that to Dad? How do I explain it without hurting his feelings?

"You look like someone ran over your puppy." Violet walks into my room and my heart jumps with the adrenaline rush.

"I thought no one was allowed in the house." Except Olivia, but she's somewhere in the massive crowd celebrating with Oz. From the silence of the crowd that surrounded the bonfire and then the rally of cheers, I assume that Oz patched in.

My foot kicks at the floor. I didn't see Oz patch in. Violet is right. It's a boys' club and the rules are not in my favor.

Violet regards the foot I toddler-reacted with then settles onto the window seat beside me. "I came in through the back."

"Eli said they locked it."

She shrugs and then with a twitch of her hand produces a key. I grab it from her. "That was supercool. You never told me you can do magic."

"I can't," she says. "But Chevy can. He taught me a few

NOWHERE BUT HERE   399

things, but that's the only trick I can get somewhat right. He has a knack for sleight of hand."

We had dinner together: me, Chevy, Oz, Violet, Razor and Stone. Oz and Razor carried the conversation by telling us stories of how they learned to ride a motorcycle. Both Violet and Chevy stared at their plates like someone had stolen a portion of their soul then set it on fire.

Chevy departed a while ago with a girl with bad blue hair. Violet left shortly afterward.

"Can I ask you something?" she says.

"You can ask me anything."

Violet plays with the ends of her hair as if she's searching for split ends. "Will you take me with you when you leave?"

I laugh and then it morphs into an awkward fading giggle as I realize she's serious.

"I have some money saved so I can buy a plane ticket for me and Brandon, and I guess I forgot to mention that we're taking Brandon with us, but I researched it online and I have enough to pay for the tickets. You said you have a spare bedroom and Brandon and I can totally take that. We already share a room now and I can guarantee the room in your house will be bigger. We don't eat much. Actually Brandon does, but I don't and I'll get a job so then I'll be able to cover the cost of food and…"

She's continuing in a ramble. In a way Violet has never done before. She's always so sure and so confident and she's never avoided eye contact in the entire time I've known her.

My mouth is hanging open and finally I discover my voice. "Why?"

Violet blinks. "Why what?"

"Why would you want to leave here?"

"Are you serious? Do you not see what's going on outside? How they're acting? How they're behaving? Those people are constantly inserting themselves into my business and I am over it. I can't get anyone at school or in town to take me seriously because my father was a part of the Reign of Terror. He's not even here anymore and I still can't get them out of my life!"

From my cracked-open window, the sound of men's laughter drifts in and so do the shouts, the occasional curse, the rumble of motorcycles coming and going and the loud, angry music.

Two months ago, all of this would have terrified me, but now I look out and see Pigpen laughing with a bunch of guys. I see Olivia with Cyrus near the bonfire. I know that Eli and Oz are somewhere inside the clubhouse.

"Is it that bad here?" I point then relax my toes. "I mean, yeah, they're sort of crazy, but they seem to care for one another."

"Oh my God!" Violet shrieks. "Are you for real? There's a reason why you're locked in here and the rest of them are out there. It's easy to love them if you can ignore the truth and you're doing exactly what they want. You're ignoring what's in front of you. Well, I refuse to live this way. I need to leave. I need to get out of here!"

"What about your mom?" I ask.

"What about your mom?" Violet spits. "Call her. Ask her if I can come."

She rolls her shoulders as if she's on the verge of bursting out of her skin and then grabs my hands. "Please. Please do this. Please call her and ask your mom to let me live with you. Tell her that I'm Christy's girl. Tell her that she owes us. My mother risked a lot for her once and your mom promised her she'd do anything to help her in the future because of it. Tell her that I'm taking her up on the offer. Your mom understands you can't go back on a promise. Just for the year. Then I'll get a job when I graduate and move out and I'll be able to take care of Brandon, but I have to get out of here."

Violet's eyes are wild, crazy, just as insane as she's acting right now. Her nails dig into my hands and I'm pulling to get free. "Listen, calm down. You're not making any sense. Why would my mom owe your mom? You need to calm down!"

I yank my hands away and Violet flies to her feet. "Call her!"

Freaking terrified, I also stand and attempt to figure out how I can maneuver past her for the door. "I don't know what your mom did for my mom, but I can't imagine that it's big enough for her to harbor you after you run away."

"Big enough?" Violet gathers her hair at the base of her neck. "It's huge. It's the secret they're keeping from you. It's the reason you believe that they are rays of merry fucking sunshine when they aren't."

"What?" I press. "What is it that's so huge that my mom would be okay with you running away?"

"My mom's the one that drove your mom out of Snowflake. The one who helped you two escape in the night. My mom kept the secret of where you went when Eli went to prison. That's right, everyone's precious Eli went to prison for eight years and it's your mom who turned him in!"

Violet's chest is moving rapidly and a strange sound leaves her throat as she goes white.

The blow slams straight into my stomach and I stumble back and land on the bed. There's a buzz in my head and my eyes flicker in front of me as I try to understand.

"Shit," Violet whispers as she shoves her hand through her hair. "Just shit. I didn't say that. Please, Emily, I didn't say that."

But she did. Violet said it and it's there and my gut twists in a way that feels like I'm snapping in half. "What did he go for prison for?"

"Emily..."

I push off the bed and get in Violet's face. "What did Eli go to prison for?"

Her lips thin out. "Attempted murder...aggravated assault."

The room spins. "Who? Why?"

"You're not going to like it."

"Because I'm liking what I've heard so far?" I shout. "Tell me, Violet! You cannot get this far and stop!"

She closes her eyes and whispers, "It was your mother's brother. Your uncle. Your mother's family didn't want her and Eli together and when her brother tried to break them up..."

A spark of anger propels me out the door of my room.

"Emily!" Violet is hot on my heels, but I'm faster. I jerk open the front door, my hand smacks the screen and the moment I'm on the front porch, there are two walls of leather vests in my way.

"I'm sorry, Ms. Emily," says one with a long drawl. "The McKinleys said that you aren't allowed to leave the house."

"What are you going to do?" I yell. "What the freak are you going to do to stop me?"

They look at each other. For too long. Long enough that

I have my answer. Nothing. There is nothing they can do to me. I slip past them and I'm down the stairs. Loud footsteps behind me. My name from their lips. From Violet's lips. But I don't care.

Eli served time in prison. He almost killed someone. My mother's brother. My uncle. An uncle I didn't even know existed. They've lied. They've all lied.

I'm halfway toward the crowd when a hand clamps down on my arm. I swing around and it's the prospect. "I'm sorry, Emily, but you're not allowed out here."

He's bigger than me. Taller than me. Weighs three times more than me. Anxiety shoots into my veins and I struggle to escape. "Get off."

"No," he says. "I've been given strict instructions that you stay in the house so I'm going to ask nicely for you to return to your room. If you don't, I'll pick you up and put you there myself."

It's there in his eyes. He means what he says. He wants me in that house and he'll force me to comply and what I'd finally begun to see as friendly isn't friendly anymore. It's big and it's scary and I wrench harder at his hold. "Let me go!"

His grip tightens and I'm pulling back with all my might and the words tear out of my throat. "Let me go! Let me go! Let me go!"

OZ

RAZOR EXTENDS HIS ARMS LIKE HE'S GRIPPING the handlebars of a motorcycle and he mimics being thrown to the ground. "And I said holy fuck, asshole, that wasn't a pothole, that was a damned canyon."

The guys around me burst into laughter and I join them then take another swig of beer. Pigpen walks by, fist bumps me and asks, "You out?"

I check the bottom of my beer then down the small amount remaining. "Yeah."

"I got it, brother." He's off for the bar and I'm buzzing hard. Tonight will be the only night I won't have to buy a thing. As Eli said, it's my night.

"You know what else is taken care of?" Razor smiles and a flood of sixth-sense concern swamps me.

"Do I want to know?"

More guys join our group and each of them have a shit-eating grin on their face. There's a whiff of strong perfume and my stomach twists. A month and a half ago, I would have been all over this, but there's a girl across the yard who won't understand and will end up hurt.

A delicate touch across my bicep and I look to my side. Early twenties, short pixie-cut brown hair and her tits are hanging in the breeze. "I hear it's your night."

Not anymore.

She waves a fifty in the air. "And your friends have bought you a lap dance."

Razor tips his chin at her. "We'll keep paying, too. Let us know when."

Her hand is on my chest, trying to guide me back into the chair behind me. Fuck me. Just fuck me because I don't know how the hell to get out of this. I gently attempt to remove her hands, but she's a damned octopus snaking her arms around mine.

"Get off!"

My head jerks in the direction of the faint voice.

"It's okay if you're shy," the girl says under her breath. "I promise I'll play nice."

Shy isn't my problem, but crushing Emily is. There's only one girl I crave to be with and she's alone inside Olivia's house.

Then I hear it again. "Let me go!"

The chick in front of me fades away as my heart stalls. That was Emily's voice.

Another hand on my chest and I shove it away. "Everyone shut the hell up!"

The guys surrounding us go quiet and peer at me like I've lost my mind. I strain to listen past the electric guitars.

"Let me go! Let me go! Let me go!"

Suddenly I'm pushing through the crowd. Grabbing guys and thrusting them out of my way.

"Oz!" Dad stands on a chair on the other side of the room. "What's the damage?"

"It's Emily!" I roar.

With my words the music rips off, guys snap their heads in the direction of the yard and I finally emerge from the clubhouse.

Red. I see red. Emily is in the yard, clawing to get away. Her arm locked in the grasp of a man. He's yelling at her. She's yelling at him.

"Emily!"

Her head whips to me and there's relief in her eyes. Pure relief and that causes a deadliness to unfurl within my bloodstream. She was scared. This man scared her.

"Oz!" she shouts.

My arm is yanked back by someone, but I'm a damned steamroller without brakes. At the sight of me coming, he releases her and Emily is pulling so hard that she falls to her ass. His hands are in the air and there's shouting all around me. My fist collides with his jaw and he lands on the ground.

A body slams into mine and I fight to go forward, fight to pick up the asshole and beat the hell out of him. Another guy rams into me and I don't go down, but they do stop my advance. A jostle of arms then Dad's in my face. "He's a brother! A Reign of Terror! It's a brother, Oz! We got this. Calm down! You hit a brother."

I breathe deeply to try to silence the pounding in my head. A brother. I attacked a brother, which can be an automatic out of the club. My eyes shoot to the asshole who laid hands on

Emily and I can't see him because he's surrounded by Terror cuts and there's lot of nasty words being tossed in his direction. The anger in the air is palpable.

I tear away from Dad and he shields me from heading to the group, but I'm going in the opposite direction. Emily's still on the ground, blinking, moving in slow motion. Her gaze snaps to mine and as she attempts to stand, I clutch her hand and draw her into me.

Emily's arms weave around my waist and she burrows her head into my chest. One of my hands presses her closer and the other fists her hair. I inhale her sweet scent to confirm that it's Emily. That she's safe.

She sniffs and I pull her back, framing her face with my hands. Another round of anger courses within me when I spot the moisture in her eyes. Dammit. "Are you hurt?"

She shakes her head and opens her mouth—

"Oz!" Eli stalks out of the crowd, his eyes narrowing in on my hands on Emily's face. "Let her go."

I shift then nudge my shoulder in front hers to protect her from Eli's wrath. Emily shocks me by surging forward. "You went to prison!"

Eli rears back like she slapped him and the blood drains from my head and out my toes. Someone told her. Someone told Emily the one secret we all knew and Emily was never supposed to find out.

"You went to prison!" she yells again.

There's not a sound in the yard except for shuffling on the porch. It's Violet and she holds her elbows to her chest. I briefly shut my eyes. *Violet.*

"Who told you?" Eli demands.

"It doesn't matter who told me. What matters is that you didn't and what matters is that the reason you went to prison was for attempted murder and the reason my mom left is because you tried to kill her brother!"

"Emily..." Eli drops his head and my soul is breaking for both of them.

"You lied," she spits out. She scans the yard as Olivia and Mom squeeze through the crowd. "You are all liars! You said you're legit. You said this isn't how you behave and you went to prison!"

Emily's shaking. She's shaking and she's wiping her eyes. This is killing her and that's when it hits me, I'm not the only one she fell in love with. She also learned to love her biological father. I touch her back, daring to offer her comfort, and her shoulders roll forward.

"Did you know?" she whispers to me. "Is this what *he* forbade you to tell me?"

A few hours ago, I told Emily that we needed to play our cards right to make this work. I could lie to her now to save my relationship with the club and Eli. I could act as if she doesn't matter to me, but I won't hurt Emily. "Yes."

She glances at me from over her shoulder and the pure pain there strikes me hard and fast. "Let me get you inside," I say so only she can hear.

"Emily," Eli tries again, but she raises her hand in the air.

"Just don't." I don't like how her body sways from one side to the next. "I want to go home, Oz."

"All right," I say softly, "I'll get you home."

Like I did the first night Emily arrived, I bend my knees and swing her up into my arms. And also like that night, Emily grabs on to me and rests her head in the crook of my neck.

Eli slides in front of me, anger marring his expression. It's vicious and full of death. For seven years, I've worshipped the ground he's walked on. Never giving a shit one way or another that he served time. But Emily was right. I should be concerned about integrity issues. I've betrayed him, but by hurting Emily, he's betrayed me.

"Let me get her down," I say. "And then you can deal with me."

The circle of men part. None of them will meet my eyes and I refuse to look anywhere other than straight ahead. Once I reach the porch, Violet opens the door then follows me in.

"Please don't tell Eli that I told her," she begs.

I say nothing as I enter Emily's room. Emily releases me when I lay her on the bed, but snags my hand as I start to straighten. "I messed everything up, didn't I?"

"No. It was messed up before we had a chance to do the damage ourselves." I remember Mom warning me off of Emily the night she arrived. The night I dragged Emily into that crevice at the motel and damned her to our world.

Mom said Emily was surrounded by land mines and Mom was scared of me becoming collateral damage. She said it like I had a choice in becoming involved, but I didn't. This fire was set eighteen years ago when Meg and Eli fell in love and had a baby. They tore each other apart then made decisions that continue to have a domino effect. Now Emily and I are left to battle the flames.

Emily sits up and backs into the corner of the wall with her knees drawn to her chest. There's a dip on the bed. Lars pads over then collapses at her side. Emily stares emptily into the room and lifts a hand on top of the dog's head. His droopy eyes flicker from Emily to me then he lets out a loud sigh.

I scratch behind his ear. "Stay with her, boy."

He whines and Emily slowly pets him. "Do you have to go?"

"Party's over and I have some explaining to do."

"I've cost you what you want. There're going to kick you out, aren't they?"

I punched a brother and from the show I put on with Emily, it's obvious she and I have been intimate. Yeah, I would say that the cut I'm wearing on my back will be gone by sunrise.

I put my fingers under Emily's chin, tilting her head up. "I love you."

Emily's dark eyes widen and if this moment wasn't so dire, I'd laugh at her expression. I swipe a finger across her smooth cheek. "I've never said that to anyone and I don't plan on it being the last time, either. I love you, Emily, and I'm telling you we'll work this out."

She goes to respond and I place a finger over her lips. "We'll work this out."

We study each other. She wants to say it back, I long to hear her utter the words, but not like this. Not tonight. We both deserve better than that.

"I'm going home tomorrow night," she admits.

I sit on the bed and press my forehead to hers. "I know."

"I didn't mean to cost you this." She barely touches the leather of my cut.

"Hey." I force a smile. "I like kids, remember? And as you pointed out, if I work with them I don't have to carry a gun."

A tiny spark of amusement shows in her eyes, but it doesn't quite diminish the sadness. "You really are good with kids. You joke, but you could do something excellent with them."

A wall inside me adjusts and it's physically painful. There's no choice but to think of a different future now. A future without the club. "I'll deal with that later. Right now, I'm worried about you."

"I don't know who I am anymore." She scratches her arm and I frown at the red welt forming on her skin. "Life used to be simple and now it's confusing and complex."

I settle a hand over hers, preventing her from making the hive bigger. "You're Emily. The girl who stormed into my world and changed it forever."

"In a bad way."

"In a great way."

"I don't know how to wrap my head around all this," she says.

I don't, either.

"Promise we'll be okay," she says.

"I promise."

The front screen door squeaks open and our time is slipping away. I lower my head as Emily tilts hers up. A movement of lips. A bittersweet taste. A simplicity that has morphed into something increasingly complicated. Her fingers entwine in my hair, yanking slightly, holding on with the understanding that we're on the verge of letting go.

"Oz," whispers Violet from the hall. "Wrap it up."

I take in Emily's lower lip and the small gasp that leaves her sends a shock wave throughout my body. I pull away and our chests move in unison. Another fast, chaste kiss to her lips and I'm off the bed. "You have my number?"

She nods then reaches out. "Hand me your phone. I'll give you my Florida numbers."

I produce it from the back pocket and Emily types quickly. Boots stomp down the hallway. This is it. This is going to be the last time I see Emily for a while. She offers the phone back to me. "Here. It's my cell and landline."

"I'm going to need time to work this out, okay? I'll call you when it's safe to chat. It may not be until you get home."

Because the first thing Eli's going to do is trash the burner phone he bought her.

"Okay," she says.

"Okay."

"Oz." Cyrus appears in the doorway and it takes every ounce of self-control to not kiss her again. Those big doe eyes are begging me to find a way to fix this now and stay, but unlike Chevy, I don't know magic.

"You need to head home," Cyrus states.

Home. His words are a kick to the gut. Once upon a time, he would say home and mean here. "Guess when it comes down to it, I'm not family, after all."

Emily extends her fingers to me and I quickly squeeze them. *I love you.*

I release her and stalk past Cyrus, shutting her door behind me. She needs space and they need to give it.

Cyrus mumbles something under his breath to me. Something to make his words sting less, but I don't listen. Olivia stands in the living room and she grabs my arm as I stride past.

"This is your home." Her fingers dig into my skin. "Don't you dare walk away from here and think differently."

I rub a hand over my face and point down the hallway. "Why did they lie to her? She's not in there bleeding because he went to prison. She's in there bleeding because he lied. Again and fucking again. Even now, he's not going to tell her, is he? He's not even going to try to explain his side of what happened. She's in there sympathizing with her mother when she doesn't even know the whole story. She doesn't know that her uncle tried to hurt them."

"You didn't tell her?" Eli emerges from the kitchen. The dull lamplight coming from the table next to the couch where Violet shrinks casts an odd shadow over him.

"I kept my word to you and didn't tell her, but I should. I should go in there and tell her everything I know."

"Then who did tell her?" Eli asks.

I keep eye contact with him and purposely ignore that Violet exists. For all her faults in the past few months, I still love her and I will never rat her out. I'll protect her because *that* is what family does. "You either tell Emily the truth before she goes home or I will."

I show Eli my phone containing her numbers and a muscle in his jaw ticks.

"That is not your decision to make," he says.

"Since I'm in love with her, it is my decision."

It's like the air is sucked out of the room as Eli and I glare each other down. I sense the million questions forming in everyone's mind, but Olivia sticks with what's currently important. "I've told you before, Oz, you don't know the whole truth."

"Does anyone? Emily's right. This entire family is messed up and dying. We all have cancer, problem is it's the lies that are making it fester."

I yank my keys out of my pocket. "Because I have always respected you, Eli, you have until she touches down in Florida to make it right with Emily or I'll tell her the version I do know. Then you and Meg can decide on whatever lie you're going to tell next."

I told Emily that I never said I love you before and I was serious. Not to some girl and not to anyone else in my life. I decided to tell her because, to be honest, I don't know if I'll ever see her again. Looking at Olivia as she watches her family implode, I finally understand that Emily isn't the only person I'm going to lose.

I wrap my arms around Olivia and it doesn't take long for her to hug me back. I kiss her cheek. "I love you."

She presses her lips to my cheek and whispers, "I love you more."

A lump forms in my throat and as fast as I let the moment happen, I abandon it and walk out the door.

Emily

MY BIOLOGICAL FATHER TRIED TO KILL MY mother's brother. My biological father tried to kill my mother's brother. I flip the cell in my hands over and over again as I complete the thought. It's one in the morning. Oz tore off on his motorcycle a long time ago and like he promised he hasn't contacted me. Yet I flip the phone over again.

My biological father tried to kill my mother's brother.

No wonder Mom ran and never looked back. No wonder she never told me about this and she refuses to discuss the past. How do you get over someone you loved trying to kill your family?

I've sat on the window seat watching the party aftermath. The clubhouse is still lit up like runway lights. The bonfire that had been raging before has now simmered down to where the logs glow red. A few stragglers hang out in the clubhouse and around the yard, but most everyone left shortly after my screaming fit with Eli.

Eli has stayed in the same spot since after Oz left and while I hate to admit it, it's the reason why I'm sitting here. He leans a shoulder against one of the massive Lincoln log poles and peers out into the yard. Occasionally, he smokes a cigarette and I'll watch as the red butt burns brightly in the dark night, but mostly he stands there and stares. All seventeen stars still on his arm. All the questions in my mind unanswered.

I know more now than I have before and yet the truth still eludes me.

My biological father, the man who treats me like a princess, the man who taught me how to drive his truck, tried to kill my mother's brother.

It doesn't make sense. None of it makes sense.

In less than twenty-four hours I'll be heading home and I don't trust anyone to tell me the truth…not my mother, not my father, not anyone. A few weeks ago, I believed everything my parents said, now I'll second-guess.

My biological father tried to kill my mother's brother.

I slip off the window seat and crack the door to my room. Once in the hall, I spot Cyrus asleep in his recliner with his hand extended over, touching the top of Violet's head. She's curled up in a ball on the couch also sound asleep.

My heart flashes with a quick ache. I never knew they were close, but as things go around here, I don't know much of anything.

I move down the hallway and pause in the doorway of Olivia's room. Her light is on and she's tracing a picture in a photo album.

"I lost a son once," Olivia says without looking up. "His name was James. He was restless living in Snowflake and died in an accident in Louisville. He never met his own son. Never knew that a woman was pregnant with his child. In a sad, pathetic tribute, we named your elephant after him."

She removes a photo from the album and holds up the one she had shown me when I first arrived. It's of me and her and pink, fuzzy James.

"You sent me on this bizarre scavenger hunt so I could find out that your surviving son is an attempted murderer."

"No. I did this so that you and Oz would end the vicious cycle and stop making the same damn mistakes of the generations that came before you, me included."

"My mom left. She broke the cycle. Me returning here, it's messed everything up."

She slams the album shut. "All your mother did was run and all she's taught you is to run. Running is still running. It doesn't matter if it's a physical move from one place to another or if it's to within yourself.

"Yes, her leaving Snowflake, marrying Jeff, placing you in a padded bubble of a world did give you opportunities you would have never had here, but it didn't get rid of the problem. You're still doomed to repeat the same mistakes your mother and your father made. You do it now. You ignore the truth, the world around you, in order to keep your illusions of safety. That's not living, Emily. The only way for you to break free is to understand the past so you don't continue to follow in their footsteps."

I cross my arms over my chest. "So Mom was in the wrong on this? She was wrong to run from a man who tried to kill her brother?"

Olivia closes her eyes and I'm reminded how sick she is

when she presses her fingers to her forehead. My stomach completely drops. "I still don't want you to die."

A bitter smile pulls at her lips. "I still don't want to die, either. There's more to the story and I'm praying that Eli will tell you before you leave."

Of course there is and of course she won't tell me and part of me understands why. I've lost respect for my parents—my mom and my dad—and they're going to have to work to get that trust and respect back. The three of us have time, but Olivia, she doesn't.

"Go to sleep." This time I'm the one flinging the orders.

I push away from the door and Olivia stops me. "Emily Star?"

"I love you, too." I glance over my shoulder to catch her placing a hand over her heart.

My throat tightens. Because I can't handle any of the emotions colliding inside me, I walk back into my room. The clock is ticking down until I return to Florida and I have no one in my corner who will tell me the truth.

I change out of my clothes and into a pair of jeans and new shirt. A brush of my hair and I tie it into a ponytail at the nape of my neck. A slide of my finger across the cell and I pray that the internet isn't having temper issues. It isn't and I do something it never crossed my mind to do before: I type my mother's maiden name, *Nader*, then *Kentucky* into a search engine. A ton of listings pop up.

If I want the truth, then what better place to get it than from the source, but to make that happen I need a first name and I need a ride.

I slink into the living room and crouch by Violet at the end of the couch. Her eyes snap open and I bring a finger to my lips. Olivia is more right than she can imagine. According to Violet, her mother once drove my mother out of Snowflake and my goal is to force history, in this case, to repeat itself.

"You once said you could get me out of here undetected." I raise my phone to her line of sight and she reads my internet search.

Violet peeks over at Cyrus as she slowly sits up. "We'll have to go through the woods."

I yank on the ends of my hair as the urge to vomit overwhelms me. Dad said this visit was about conquering fears. It appears he wasn't wrong.

OZ

I ROLL OVER AND INHALE THE SMELL OF THE BEACH. Emily's scent did transfer to the pillow. My eyes open and rays of morning light highlight the empty spot beside me. This bed never felt solitary before. Never felt like a deep, aching pit.

I've dozed, not slept, and a low murmur of conversation beyond my door causes me to slip out of bed. I snatch my shirt off the floor and rub a hand over my chest in an attempt to wake up.

Mom's on the couch with her feet tucked underneath her. Dad's beside her holding her hand. They've been a couple since they were sixteen and have loved each other through parents who smacked the hell out of them, an unplanned pregnancy, the years they could never make ends meet and then through the years where they blamed each other for life being tough.

They love each other and somewhere along the way, they learned to love me.

I shrug my shirt over my head and straddle the chair I had dragged into the living room over twenty-four hours ago when I had talked to Emily. I rest my forearms on the back of it and look at Dad. "Are they kicking me out?"

"You hit another brother." Dad scratches the back of his head and Mom presses her other hand over their joint fingers. "Even if he was a prospect, the club doesn't tolerate violence toward one another."

"But Oz was defending Emily," Mom says.

Dad and I glance at each other. Brothers have hit each other before and rarely are they kicked out the first time. There's a suspension from events and a fine. But none of those brothers had been intimate with the offspring of the two most important men in the club.

"They're holding Church tonight," he says. "And I'm going to fight to keep you in."

The seat creaks as I readjust. I fucked up, not him, and the thought of Dad placing his rep on the line for me doesn't sit right. "You said I have to be my own man in the club."

"That's the reason why I'm going to fight for you to stay in. If you want the truth I wasn't sure you were ready for the club. They had to talk me into letting you skip your prospect period."

My eyes flash to his and Mom's stroking Dad's arm in support.

"Standing up to Eli last night," he says. "That was the first time I've seen you be your own man."

What the hell? "Standing up to Eli last night is what's going to get me kicked out."

"No, son, the club is about standing up to things bigger

than yourself. If you get kicked out it's because you didn't show Eli respect and go to him when you developed feelings for his daughter. But as I said, I like the changes I see in you and I'm going to fight by your side."

I edge back in the chair—a retreat.

Mom shifts so that her feet are on the ground and she snags my hand. I try to pull back, because the touch catches me off guard, but she maintains a firm grip. "Did you know that your dad and I are here for you?"

"We were talking about club stuff," I say.

"You were and you weren't," Mom presses. "You do this. You've done this since you were little and I try to tell myself that it's understandable, but I need you to know—me and your father...we are here and we are on your side."

There's a warning siren in my mind. The threat of a familiar bleeding wound creeping forward from the recess of my memories. "I know that."

"I don't think you do, or maybe you know it in your head, but you don't *feel* it. You're a great son, but when we try to be there for you in the major moments, when we try to give you advice or stand by you, it's as if you don't trust us."

"I trust you." The automatic answer is easy, too easy, so easy that I understand that it might not be the truth, but what they prefer to hear.

"I'm sorry it took me so long to figure out how to be your mother." Mom's voice breaks at the end. "I'm sorry that I was young and selfish and that you learned to rely on and love Olivia before you could love and rely on me."

I push back all the way in the chair until I'm standing. "That's not how it is."

"It's exactly how it is. But you can rely on us now. It's killing me to see you go through losing Olivia alone. It's killing me to think that your father and I are sitting right here and you can't let us in."

The buzzing of phones. Dad releases Mom's hand and she inches to the end of the couch as she watches us check the message. Dizziness disorients me for a second then both Dad and I are moving. Digging keys out of our pockets. Grabbing our cuts off the table.

My phone rings and I answer it as I sprint out the door. "What's going on, Eli?"

The text was my worst nightmare.

Everyone come to the clubhouse. Emily is missing.

Emily

"DO YOU WANT ME TO ANSWER?" VIOLET'S IN THE driver's side of a nineteen-seventy-something-older-than-me Chevy Impala. Her cell rings and this time it's Oz's face that pops onto her screen. The first five times, it was Eli, followed by Olivia and now Oz is on the job.

He's worried about me and while I care for him and he cares for me, Oz doesn't understand this need to unravel my past, especially since he was instrumental in hiding it. "No, not yet."

It's eight in the morning and Violet's back to her kick-ass self. She assesses the house we've parked two properties down from. It's a nice neighborhood. The houses aren't stacked on top of each other. Instead, there's quite a bit of land between them. The buildings themselves aren't grand. Some are one story. Some resemble the house I'm interested in and are two stories. They're modest brick and vinyl with do-it-yourself colorful landscaping.

"So this is where your mom grew up?"

I squish my lips to the side. "My mom said she grew up in Snowflake."

"My mom said that your mom came to live with her grand-mother who lived in Snowflake during high school."

"Anything else I should know?" She's filled me in on what she does know—that my mother and Eli were an item, that they were tragically in love, that they got pregnant with me while they were still in high school, had me, got engaged and that my mother's brother got into a fight with my mom and in retaliation, Eli found my uncle and almost beat him to death.

Mom's family wasn't thrilled with her marrying a biker and Eli decided to shut my uncle up. My mind separates as I attempt to reconcile the man I've been around the past few weeks with the man who tried to kill his almost brother-in-law.

"Other than I'm sorry for losing my mind last night?" She's already apologized for that. A million times. "Will you tell me what's so horrible in Snowflake that you totally spazzed?"

"Let's handle one dramatic event at a time. So what exactly do you hope to accomplish by talking to these people?"

These people would be my grandparents. Violet didn't know my mother's brother's name, but I remembered her parents' names and this was the only listing in the Louisville phone directory that matched. "I'm hoping they'll tell me the truth."

Violet offers me a tilted head with a "whatever" gaze. "There's no such thing as the truth. There's what people wish would have happened."

True. "Maybe they'll give me enough of a picture that I can piece together the rest of the story."

"So we're clear, you're not visiting with grandma and gramps to get the truth. You're wandering over there in the hopes they'll say something that will make you like Eli again."

The skin on my arm itches and I sort of hate Violet for speaking so plainly. "Possibly."

"You know my opinion on the men in the club, right? That they aren't redeemable?"

"If you feel that way, then why are you helping me?" Then why did she fall asleep so close to Cyrus?

"Because you're the type who's determined to learn the hard way."

I'm not the only one. Her phone rings again and now Chevy's face appears on the screen. She glances out the window and I reject the call. "I think he cares for you."

"I think I'm two seconds away from leaving your ass on the curb."

Well played. "Wish me luck."

"Do you want me to go in with you?"

"No. This will be awkward enough without an audience. Mom gave me the impression that the reason they threw her out was because they weren't thrilled she was pregnant and that she'd decided to keep me. I've always pictured them being superconservative and from what you've told me, that guess is becoming solid. Could you imagine them having a daughter who fell in love with and had a baby with a biker? They had to go insane."

"Sounds like the makings of a true tragedy."

"Yeah." Yeah. I wonder what Oz and I will be. "If I don't

wave or text or something in two minutes, I'll need you to call in the cavalry."

I smile, she smiles and I'm out the door.

I chose the loose-fitting jeans and the purple top Eli bought me in Nashville in case Mom's parents really are conservative. The summer morning is warm enough that I'm starting to sweat, but that could also be the nerves.

The porch is nice. It's the plastic type that mimics wood. My footsteps sound strange against it and I lift my bangs away from my face as I stand in front of the door. Big deep breath in. Then another. A tickling flow of adrenaline leaks into my veins.

A push of the doorbell and I can hear the loud chimes from outside. One second. Two.

The door opens and across from me stands a much older version of my mother. She wears a pair of jeans and a blue button-down shirt. Nice and pressed. There are pearls in her ears and a gold cross hanging from her neck. Like Olivia, she owns older. Her hair is still blond and I can't help but wonder if it's dyed of if I'll have fantastic genetics. There are lines on her face. Particularly around her blue eyes and her mouth.

"Hello." She stares at me and I form the millions of responses to the hundreds of ways she'll ask why I'm here.

"Hi." It would be good to speak more, possibly explain that I'm not selling magazine subscriptions.

"I've waited a long time for this." A hesitant smile eases across her face and my lips turn down. Something isn't right.

A man walks up behind her. He's older, has gray hair, but what causes me to start backward in the same rhythm of my pounding heart is the black leather vest on his body.

There's a honk. A long one. A loud one. The heel of my foot dips off the back of the stairs and when I pivot to run, my hands smack into the chest of a man. He's Mom's age and he has the same eyes and nose as her, but there's a scar that slices along his cheek.

"Hi, Emily," he says. "Why don't you come in? I know Mom's been dying to meet you."

I swivel back to the woman, begging her with my eyes to let me go. The man behind her angles to respond to someone in the room and on the back of his vest are the words that cause me to tremble: *The Riot Motorcycle Club.*

"Come on." The guy Mom's age lays a foreboding arm around my shoulder. "Let's catch up."

OZ

WE'RE A FEW MILES OUT FROM EMILY AND I CAN'T sit still. Eli's pressed the truck to the max, but it's still not fast enough.

"We would have been faster on the bikes," I say.

I hate how calm Eli is. Since the moment Violet called and told me what had happened, he's been too calm. His entire expression smoothed out like marble. "Emily's not going to be in the condition to ride safely on the back of a bike."

A deadly snake slithers inside me, raising its head as it coils tighter in my gut. "If you think they're going to harm her, then why isn't anyone else with us? Why the hell aren't we calling the police?"

Eli slows at a stop sign, looks both ways as if we're on a Sunday stroll, and then turns right. Even though we told Violet to go, she hasn't. She's stayed right where she called me from—a spot a few houses down from where Emily went inside.

He parks behind Violet and it pisses me off how unhurried he acts. Emily's inside. Emily's inside with the Riot and what really makes me mad is that Eli won't tell me why. I informed him of the situation, he told me to get in the truck and we took off.

Eli didn't tell anyone else. He didn't call for backup. We drove for an hour and a half and until a few minutes ago, he stayed silent.

"Why aren't we racing in?" I bite.

"Because Emily isn't in danger. You and I might be. Even Violet isn't in the clear, but they won't harm Emily. Thirty bucks says she's in there with milk and cookies."

I don't know how he figures that, but there are more important issues here. "How are we going to handle this?" The gun's strapped to my back and I eye the one that's on Eli's hip. He's a felon and legally he can't carry, but that hasn't stopped him.

Eli waves to the two men in Riot cuts that exit the house and watch the two of us. "We're going to give them a few minutes to assess us and to let them figure out that we aren't coming in fast and hard. Then we'll walk up and knock on the front door."

"You're kidding me."

"Were you expecting to go in guns blazing? You and Emily watch too much TV."

There's no way this is real. "How did she end up on the Riot's doorstep?"

Eli circles the keys on his finger. "Meg's father is the head of the Riot."

It's like someone opened a trap door beneath me. "You're fucking with me."

"Wish I was. It's a long story. Long enough that I'm not sure I can remember all the working parts, but here's the short of it. The Riot deals with some nasty shit. Illegal is in their veins and Meg got hurt by them in the process. In high school, her parents sent Meg to live with a grandmother in Snowflake to finish out high school and to heal from some emotional wounds."

"And she met you."

There's an aching touch to the smile trying to form on his lips. "Motorcycle clubs were what she'd known. Grown up with. It was natural that she gravitated to us, but then she figured out that we were different. That we weren't like the Riot, and Meg's life began to change. Her parents were pissed when they found out about me and Meg and then they went radioactive when they found out she was pregnant."

With Emily.

"Olivia and Cyrus had already fallen in love with Meg and insisted she move in with us when we told them about the baby. With the club's backing, we promised to protect Meg and Emily from her parents and from her parents' club and that was the day battle lines were drawn."

"Did the Riot know that the Terror existed before then?"

"Maybe, who the fuck knows," answers Eli. "We were starting to branch out into other states, but we were still flying under the radar. When the club backed Meg, the Riot became very aware of us. The Riot was pissed we never asked their permission to form, never asked for their permission to ride, and we sure as hell didn't have their permission to keep their daughter and granddaughter."

"How did they react to that?" I ask.

"For two years it never stopped. Our guys would be hanging out at bars and the Riot would hunt them down and beat the hell out of them. It became a game to them to see how many of our cuts they could collect and hang on their walls. They'd try to run our guys off the road. Cause problems for us at every turn.

"It took a toll on me and a bigger one on Meg. Twice she told me she was going to leave. She packed her and Emily's stuff, but both times I talked her down. Then one night she got a phone call from her brother, asking if he could meet with her. Meet his niece. He told Meg it was a peace offering."

I lower my head. Even I know nothing good would have come out of that.

"Meg went, not telling me because your dad had been beaten up bad the night before and I was at the hospital watching his back. Meg thought she could fix everything."

Eli trails off and my hand tightens into a fist. I've never heard this. I've never heard that my father was taken down by the Riot so badly he was hospitalized. "What happened?"

"The bastard tried to take Emily. He hit Meg. Multiple times. Her own fucking brother hit her...in front of my daughter. Meg screamed and people heard her, so she and Emily got away, but then Meg came home and I saw the bruises on her body and I saw the terror on Emily's face."

I close my eyes. The rage I had felt the night before when I saw that guy grabbing Emily courses through me. "You went after him."

Pure anger flashes from Eli's dark eyes. "Fuck yeah, I did. That bastard hurt the woman I loved and my child. His club had sent my best friend to the hospital. Cyrus and the Terror wanted to wait a few days for me to calm down and then vote on how to handle this in Church. I wanted retaliation because every single time we called the police and the Riot faced a judge they got a slap on the hand because the police couldn't or wouldn't prove shit."

This is what I was raised to believe: that Emily's uncle had hit Meg and Eli had gone after him. They left out the part where this was linked to the Riot. They left out that Emily had always been a target. I was also raised to believe that... "Meg snitched. Dad said that Meg was the one that ratted you out."

"She did. She told me that if I went after her family in retaliation then I was no better than them. She told me up front that she'd call the police on me and that she'd leave with Emily. Meg knew me. She knew how mad I was and she knew her brother. She knew one of us was going to end up dead and she couldn't live with me dying. She also knew I couldn't live with being a killer so when I left to meet her brother, she called the police."

The police arrived to where Meg had pointed them, catching Eli in the act. Meg fled with Emily that night and Eli served eight years in prison. This is fucked up.

"Why not tell Emily the truth?"

Eli chuckles bitterly. "Where would you start? Somewhere between learning the ABCs and 123s you inform your kid that her dad's a felon and that her maternal grandparents would be, too, if the police got their shit together? Meg ran for her life. She ran to save Emily's life. Shit, Oz, what Meg did that night saved our club from annihilation because if she had stayed, every single one of us would have laid down his life for her and Emily and that's the game the Riot was playing. But by turning me into the police, Meg branded herself a villain. A snitch. She's no snitch. She's a hero."

I hear him, but… "You gave up custody of Emily."

"Meg begged me to give Emily up. Pointed out that the Riot wasn't above kidnapping. I told Olivia and Cyrus to back off and to give Meg room to feel safe, but what I didn't expect was her marrying Jeff and I sure as shit didn't expect him to show at my prison with papers to terminate my rights. He could offer my two girls the world and all I could offer was a whole lot of hurt.

"Maybe Meg and I didn't do it right. Maybe we made every wrong decision, but when I was released from prison and Jeff offered me the opportunity to see Emily at least once a year with the condition that I lie about the past, I jumped on it. Good, bad, ugly, call the decisions whatever you want, but it's worth any price to see my daughter and to see her happy."

Eli quickly glances away and I pretend that there wasn't wetness in his eyes. "Why are you telling me this now?"

He cracks open his door. "Because I'm trusting you'll keep your word and the moment Emily touches down in Florida you'll tell her the whole truth."

He's out of the truck and a roar fills my ears. Those words felt too final. I'm out after him. "What is that supposed to mean?"

Eli knocks on Violet's window and she rolls it down. Her eyes are red and puffy and she opens her mouth, but Eli holds up his hand. "Get out of here. Don't make me say it again."

Violet turns over the engine, and the two of us watch as she pulls a U-turn. As she passes us, I press three fingers to

my leg, and pray that Violet remembers the signal she created when we were kids. She meets my eyes then drives away.

When she's gone, Eli starts down the street again and I keep
stride. "That's your grand plan? Walk up the steps, ring the
doorbell and then they're going to hand over Emily?"

Eli steps in front of me and his entire tense demeanor tells
me to shut up and listen. "You are going to do exactly as I
say when I say it and you're going to do exactly what I ask
without questioning me. Do you got that?"

"Yes."

"I brought you with me because Emily trusts you and I
cannot have a repeat of last night. She'll follow you before
she'll follow me and I need her to follow you out. Can you
handle this?"

I can more than handle this. "Yes."

He wraps his hand around my neck and stares into my eyes.
"You're a good man, Oz."

Before I can respond, he's crossing the yard, up the steps
and ringing the doorbell. I follow, looking around for the
two guys that disappeared, searching for the threat that has
to be near. The door opens and my back twinges as if I have
a rifle trained on my heart.

The guy that answers is a massive man. Gray hair. Clean-
shaven and wears a Riot cut on his back. For the first time,
my own cut feels like a second skin. He runs his eyes over
me then studies Eli. "I thought we had this straightened out
last week."

I school my expression to hide the surprise that they've
talked. Eli shrugs. "We did, but Emily's headstrong like her
mother."

The large man releases a "Humph."

"Consider this a bonus to our negotiations. You spent time with Emily and now I need to collect my daughter. She has a flight to catch this afternoon and airport security is a bitch."

The man grunts out a laugh and extends his arm in a motion for us to enter. Eli glances at me from over his shoulder and then drops his gaze to the gun hanging on his hip. He then casually rests his hand near his piece. He's telling me to be prepared.

We enter and a heaviness surrounds me as I play out the number of ways I can grab my gun before somebody else has time to point one at me and pull the trigger. My mouth runs dry. This is real life. Real life. Not a game. Not a show that can be turned off or rewound.

We walk through a dining room as we follow the man who let us in, and it's not long before we gain two tails—men from the Riot bringing up the rear. The smell of bacon hovers in the air as we pass through the kitchen. Each step I take, I'm more aware of my skin, my blood, my bones.

A cold sweat breaks out along my neck. We enter a back living room and all the nerves quickly dissolve into a wave of protectiveness.

Emily raises her head and breathes out my name. "Oz."

Emily

MY MOTHER'S MOTHER, MY GRANDMOTHER, adores kittens. A curio cabinet to my left is filled with ceramic kittens in various poses and the wall contains several oil paintings of kittens in various stages of activities such as chasing butterflies or playing with yarn. The cherry on this kitty-cat sundae is the live cat. It's black with yellow eyes and it scowls at me from its perch on the end table. Its tail flicks left and then right with the beat of a second hand.

I've officially decided I like dogs. Specifically Lars.

Eli winks at me as he strolls into the room. Strolls. As if he, Oz and I are not in the nightmare they've described since Oz rammed into me outside the motel room.

Eli plops onto the couch across from the one my grandmother sits in. I'm in the chair in the middle experiencing a bad case of furniture tug-of-war.

I have an urge to hug Eli, to grab his hand and let him lead me away from this insanity, but I'm so terrified that I'm frozen. Literally. My hands are as cold as Olivia's.

My stomach growls loudly and the entire silent room glances at me.

"You could have fed her." Eli reclines on the couch and lays an arm along the back, reminding me of how Oz had done the same thing that night on the bench outside the room that became mine.

His thumbs hitched in his pockets, Oz watches me from the entryway between the kitchen and the living room. My uncle stands parallel to him a few feet away. Another guy hangs back toward the fridge. I swallow for the millionth time as my windpipe continually constricts.

"We offered," says my grandmother. "But she declined. Would you like something, Eli? Coffee, juice, arsenic?"

"Naw, poison's not my thing. Did Emily tell you that she has a flight to catch?"

"No. She hasn't been talkative to be honest," my grandmother says as my grandfather eases onto the couch next to her and rests his arms on his bent knees.

"She acts like she's terrified of us," he says in this mock lighthearted tone that gives me the chills.

A mock dismissive twitch of Eli's wrist. "Can't imagine why."

"You're the one with the felony record," interjects my uncle.

Eli points at him. "Emily, if you're going to watch TV to make an assumption on someone's life then think of any tragic TV show that involves drugs. Ten bucks the horrible ending is what happens to him in five years."

"You asshole." My uncle is on the move, Oz steps forward,

his hand reaching for his back and both Eli and my grandfather raise their hands while staring emotionlessly at each other.

Oz backs off and so does my uncle while I suck in air so I don't puke.

"You okay, Emily?" asks Eli.

I slowly angle my head toward him. Is he kidding? I'm not even close to okay.

"I don't want the deal," my grandmother whispers.

"What does that mean?" I ask.

My grandfather laces his fingers with his wife's. "Why did you come here, Emily?"

"It's okay to answer them," Eli says with a kindness that causes pain.

"I…" I clear my throat. "I wanted to know why Eli hurt…" I pathetically gesture to my uncle. "Him. I wanted to understand."

Eli peers over at Oz and I swear Oz nods just slightly. Eli nods back and then focuses on my grandparents. "The deal we reached stands as it is. Emily's going home to Florida and you're going to leave Emily and Meg alone."

The hair on the back of my neck sticks up. He told them we live in Florida.

"We weren't at the motel to hurt Emily," my uncle says. "We were there to protect her."

"From what?" Oz demands.

"From you. Meg turned Eli in for what he did to me. She's a snitch in your eyes and we sure as hell weren't going to let Meg and Emily walk into your territory and hope you guys were in a forgiving mood. We called Meg at the motel and told her we knew she was there and that we were watching her back."

The phone call Mom received that sparked her and Dad's late-night conversation in the bathroom. But still, I'm very confused. I wipe my hands on my jeans and will away the fuzzy sensation that suggests fainting.

Eli's shaking his head. "See, that's where you're fucked up in your thinking. The Terror doesn't operate by the same rules you do. It's not eye for an eye with us. We operate by our code while respecting the laws surrounding us."

"The Terror are wannabes," my uncle spits. "Men who can't hack the real way of life."

"No, they're men of integrity." Eli pats my knee. "You reminded me of that, Emily"

Eli stands. "Meg left you and she left me. Fifteen years ago we struck an agreement and I was under the impression we decided to uphold that agreement last week." He digs into his pocket and tosses his keys to Oz. "Remember what we talked about?"

Every head turns to Oz and my heart bottoms out when Oz's face hardens. No.

"Whatever this is," I say, "I don't want any part of it."

OZ

EMILY SLOWLY RISES FROM HER CHAIR. DO I remember what Eli and I talked about? Not sure I could forget and I'm catching on that I made a promise too fast.

"Meg was right about me, Oz," Eli says. "And I lost everything in my life that was important over it. Be more of a man than I was. You make the decisions that I didn't. Do you understand me?"

My heart is picking up speed and resolve turns into steel in my veins.

Eli lifts his chin as he addresses the head of the Riot. "You've wanted an eye for an eye, we made an agreement, and I broke the rules. You can take what's important to you now."

I pop my neck to the side to stop from throwing myself in front of him. I don't know what deal was reached fifteen years ago. I don't know what agreement was struck last week. But I know that the deal he's striking now involves his life in exchange for them staying away from Emily.

As sadness and anger pour through me, I begin walking across the room. One foot in front of another. I made a promise. I made a promise and I'm going to keep it. Tears are pooling at the bottom of Emily's eyes and she's already grabbed on to Eli. There's no way she understands what's going on, but it doesn't require a master's degree to figure out it's not good.

I clutch Emily's hand and she plants her feet firmly next to Eli. "What's going on? We're going to leave, right? All of us, right now. We're going to leave."

Eli kisses her forehead then lowers his head until he's eye level with Emily. "I love you. I have always loved you and your mother. Now, you need to go."

Emily's eyes go wide, too wide, and I shove away all the fear, all the pain at what I'm about to lose, and keep the promise I made. I wrap my arms around Emily's waist and I lift her off the floor. She's fighting. Shouting. Echoing the emotions tearing at me.

I'm dragging her out of the living room, out of the kitchen. On my heels is her uncle, yelling at me to move faster, but I tune him out and focus on Emily's screams because those are my screams. Her tears are my tears because I don't know how to save Emily and Eli. I don't know how to save them both.

Emily

THE DOOR SHUTS IN MY FACE. THE MAN WITH THE scar, my uncle, wore the look of death. He was wielding the judgment that should be reserved only for the Grim Reaper.

Oz's hold on me is strong and I keep pushing. My feet barely brush the ground as we go down the stairs. My throat is raw. The screaming won't stop. "Oz, please. We need to go back! We need to go back!"

My mind has fractured and is skipping between fast-forward and slow motion. My face is wet. My vision blurry. There's a chant in the back of my head that everything's okay. Everything's okay, but it's not. It's not. Eli didn't walk out with us. He didn't leave.

I'm kicking and Oz hesitates, enough that when I thrust back hard my feet land on the ground. Oz grabs my face and he is the only thing in my line of sight. "We have to go."

"I'll visit them." I choke on a sob. "I'll visit them. I'll live

with them. I'll write them letters every day. I'll video chat.
I'll do whatever!"

My heart beats so hard and so loud that breathing is causing pain. Living is causing me pain. "I'll give them whatever
they want!"

"That's the point!" Oz shouts, and I tremble with the vibration of his voice. He lowers his hands to my hips and I
know it's so he can carry me again. "That's the point. He's
trying to save you from this."

I grab on to his shirt and my head is shaking back and forth
or maybe I'm just shaking because none of this is happening.
"This is real life! This is real life and this does not happen!"

And there's a pop and my entire body flinches. I'm holding my breath and I realize Oz is, too. He briefly closes his
eyes as his fingers tighten on my hips.

"What was that?" I ask.

Oz begins to nudge me to the road, but I dig my feet into
the ground. "What was that?!"

A surge of adrenaline pours into my veins. I slip to the
right, and as Oz tries to capture me, I duck to the left and
run past. He's yelling my name. Telling me to wait. I don't.
I hit the door and shove through. Past the foyer, into the
kitchen and my entire world shatters when I see Eli on the
floor. Blood pooling on the white linoleum.

My knees collide to the ground and my hands hover over
his lifeless body. He's dead. Oh, God, he's dead. My stomach cramps and I bend over with the sharp sting. I never told
him that I love him. I never told him that I love him. Oh,
God. Oh my God.

"Emily!" the voice is echoed in my head and when I turn,

it's like Oz is sprinting toward me from a long hallway. My face is hot. My body is on fire.

He's dead. Eli's dead. My father is dead.

The man who claims to be my grandfather walks in our direction and I lean over Eli as if I can protect him, as if I can bring him back to life.

"Let him go," he says. "He's gone."

"Get away from us!" I touch Eli's face, angling him toward me. His cheek is still warm, but I hate how his head flops with no resistance. I'm not letting him go.

An arm around my waist and I'm off the floor. It's Oz and he's pushing me into his side, trying to force my head into his chest. "Don't look, Emily. Don't look."

My hand brushes against something hard. Something metal. And as Oz continues to drive my cheek into him, I catch sight of movement on the floor. A twitch of a finger. Eli's alive. He's not dead, he's alive.

My fingers wrap around the metal object, I pull it out and the world that was speeding up and slowing down ceases to move. All the shouts, all the chaos is silenced as I point a gun at my uncle.

OZ

IT'S LIKE A RUBBER BAND THAT'S BEEN STRETCHED and then it snaps with the contract. Emily owns everyone's undivided attention. She's shaking. Her body. Her head. More importantly her arms, her hands and the finger that is too close to the trigger.

The safety is off and I regret showing her where it was at.

"Give me the gun, Emily," I say.

"You don't understand," the woman with blond hair pleads. "Eli stole you and your mother from us. He almost killed my son. Eli *agreed* to this!"

A violent shiver racks Emily and fear snakes through me.

"Will you shut the fuck up?" I bite out and then maneuver so that I'm beside Emily. My hand hovers over the gun. "Give me the gun."

"He's alive!" She sobs then quickly swallows. "He's alive."

My gaze flickers to Eli and hope fights alongside the numb anger crawling within me.

"His finger twitched," she says.

Bodies do that. They twitch. Sometimes move, but I won't tell Emily that. "Then give me the gun and trust me to get us out of here."

She sucks in a breath. Another. And when I place my hands over hers, Emily releases her grip and I take possession of the gun. The moment I'm solely holding it, there's movement across the room.

I grab Emily and push her behind me and into a wall. With one arm keeping Emily safe, I aim the gun, pointing it at the one person who can call this entire showdown off: the president and Emily's grandfather.

There's guns trained on me. The sound of the safeties coming off reverberate in my head. But I don't look at that threat. I keep my focus.

The president steps into the kitchen and stands next to his son. Sure enough, a gun is in his hand, too. "How are we going to play this, son?"

I am not his son and Emily is not their granddaughter. There's a trembling inside me even though my outside is rock solid. Eli's unresponsive with a bullet in his chest. His blood spills onto the floor. The urge is to pull the trigger and to keep firing until we battle our way out.

There's a fluttering on my shoulder blade. A whisper of a touch that reminds me of what's important. "I'm going to pick up Eli, carry him out of here and Emily is going to walk out with me. And whatever debt Eli owed you will be considered paid in full."

The president tips his chin to the gun in my hand. "Don't

think so. We let you go and then you'll come back here and get your revenge later. I've seen it a hundred times."

"That's you." I click the safety into place and lower the gun in front of me. "That's how you play and I'm going to explain to you the rest of the game. I'm not going to raise my gun and get revenge and you're going to let us go and if you don't, I can guarantee there will be cops at your doorstep in the next few minutes."

He narrows his eyes on me. "You're going to snitch?"

Violet will if we don't contact her in fifteen minutes. I held up three fingers—five minutes for each one. "You have your code and we have ours and mine means taking care of my family. The choice is yours, but I'm telling you, I won't be the person going to prison."

The president studies Eli. "He's gone and, if he isn't, he won't make it to the hospital."

"That's my problem, but as I said, whatever blood has been shed between the two of you, it's equal now. Eye for an eye."

We continue to stare at each other and I break the silence. "Clock's ticking. I can start a countdown until we hear sirens if you'd like."

He tosses his hand toward the front door. "Get them out of here."

I'm in motion, yelling at Emily to leave while bending over and shouldering Eli. I grunt when I lift him. He's dead weight and I pray that Emily is right and that he's still alive. Emily's waiting for me at the front door and I shout at her, "Move!"

She does and the two of us are out the door. Eli's heavy and my knees start to buckle under the weight. "Get the keys!"

I'm still moving as Emily frees them from my pocket. I

jerk my head to the truck. "Get the truck. I can't carry him the entire way."

I see the flash of panic in her eyes, but she's running and I'm still going. Each step harder to take. There's a rev of an engine, a slam of brakes and she throws open the driver's-side door.

Emily slides over as I pour Eli into the cab. Emily's dragging Eli in as I shove. I jump in, flooring the gas, while turning the wheel to get the hell out. The front end of the truck cuts across the grass of a yard and then I even it out on the street.

I make a right, the wheels squealing, and I gun it for the expressway. I pass Violet going sixty and in the rearview mirror she starts off after us. When I hit the freeway, I dig out my cell and within one ring, Cyrus answers his phone.

"What the hell is going on?" he growls.

Eli's head is in Emily's lap and tears stream down her face. She presses a rag from the floorboard to his chest and she's whispering to him that she's sorry. So sorry.

"Is he breathing?" I ask her.

Emily presses her hand harder to the wound. "I don't want him to be dead."

Dammit. "I need a hospital, Cyrus. I'm a few miles south of the city, mile marker ten. Eli's been shot."

There's confusion on the other end then Cyrus spits directions at me. I cut over three lanes and take the exit, flooring it, pushing the truck to as fast as it can go.

Emily continues her mantra that she's sorry, so sorry, and it takes everything for me to not rest my head against the window and weep. Eli's not moving. He's not responding. He was dead weight.

"Oz…" Cyrus says. "What happened?"

I'm driving as fast as I can. I'm trying to save his son. I finally understand the land mines my mother had warned me about. "We need a lawyer. We need time before we talk to the cops. I don't know how we should handle this."

Eli spent years warping the truth to protect Emily and while there's a part of me that gets it, there's another part that wants to shake the hell out of him and tell him that these lies are what killed him.

"You got it. Anything else?"

"No." I hang up as the hospital comes into view. *Come on, Eli, you can't die on me now.*

Emily

THERE'S NO SOUND IN THE ROOM. IN MOVIES, there's a beep to confirm that people are alive. It's a track of their heartbeat. A reassurance that the person hasn't died. I detest the silence. There should be a beep.

The other problem I have? The ICU room is tiny. Too tiny. If something huge happens the doctors will need more room to save Eli's life. They told us that the next few hours are critical and if that's the case then critical means more room.

I'm curled tight into a ball in the chair. My finger traces the cold skin of Eli's finger that wears the heart monitor clip. Is it possible that the monitor is picking up my heart and that maybe his heart stopped beating again?

They've all been in and out. Olivia. Cyrus. Pigpen. Hook. Oz's mom and dad plus my own father. It's been busy as they flutter about and talk to me as if I'm on the verge of insanity. The only one who doesn't treat me like I'm cracking is Oz.

A sliding of the glass door and Oz enters the room. He

has two cups of coffee in his hand. He offers one to me, but I shake my head. I can't break this connection with Eli. If I keep touching him, then his heart will continue to beat and he'll stay alive. The monsters under my bed have returned and I'm convinced if I stare then I'll scare the evil away.

Oz props a shoulder on the wall next to me. Blood stains the sleeve of his T-shirt and he looks like he hasn't slept in days. "You saved his life."

"Are you kidding? If I had never visited Mom's parents then he would never have offered his life for me. I'm not sure how he can forgive me." I'm not sure how Oz can forgive me.

"Emily, if you had asked me to drive you into Louisville to meet your mother's parents, I would have. I didn't know your mom was Riot royalty and it turns out that only a few people did. Your mom being the child of the Riot was the most highly guarded secret in the club. You had no idea what you were walking into."

I suck in a deep breath. "But he was willing to give up his life for me and that never would have happened if I had stayed in Snowflake." If I had remained in Florida.

Oz crouches in front of me and sets a hand on my knee. "I've been talking to people over the past few hours. Lots of people. Olivia. Cyrus. Your dad. My parents. Eli even opened up before we went into the house. He made me promise I'd tell you the truth."

My throat burns. "I don't want to know it anymore."

He squeezes my leg and repeats, "You saved his life today."

"I didn't," I snap.

"You did," Oz pushes. "The reason the Riot hasn't bothered you for fifteen years is because Eli made a deal with them. His life for yours."

Oz is tired. He's mixed up. "That's the deal they made today."

"When your mom ran and he was awaiting trial, he went to the Riot and told them that they could kill him, get the revenge they wanted, as long as they left you and your mom alone."

"They obviously didn't accept it." Because maybe they had a shred of decency.

"They agreed to leave you and Meg alone as long as Eli stayed away from you. They wanted Eli to be as miserable as they were, living every year like they did, knowing that he had a daughter that hated him."

Hated him. My entire body flinches. I did worse than hate. I didn't like or dislike him enough to care.

"Turns out the Riot knew you were staying in Snowflake. Eli and the Riot have been in negotiations the entire time you were here and they made an agreement this week where the Riot, once again, agreed to leave you alone.

"It's why Eli was hot and heavy about you returning home this week. He knew they were going to be gunning for him and if you hadn't shown up on their doorstep and put Eli and the Riot in the same room, I guarantee they would have gone after Eli in a situation where no one would have been around to save him."

"This is too crazy."

"You don't break deals with people like them."

My forehead furrows. He's just trying to make me feel

better. "None of this makes sense. Eli came to see me once a year. That sounds like a violation of the deal."

Oz releases a ghost of that wicked smile I've come to love. "Eli's never been much of a stickler for details. He knew he was taking a risk and felt selfish for doing it, but he was careful and made sure no one found out."

"But he asked me to come and stay for two weeks this summer."

"He loves Olivia almost as much as he loves you. He wanted her to have a chance to know you and he convinced himself that he could make it work so that the Riot stayed in the dark."

My mind's a mess. "It still doesn't make sense. Normal people don't act like this. Normal people don't make deals to kill someone or not kill someone in exchange for staying away from their daughter. For real, who does that?"

"They're a gang. Think about the evening news. An eighteen-year-old stabs a sixteen-year-old. Someone shot their friend, so they shoot one of theirs. The violence continues, it escalates. It's not normal. It's not right, but it doesn't mean that it doesn't exist. What you witnessed today, all that I'm talking about, that's what Eli and your mom were trying to save you from—they weren't keeping you away from a motorcycle club, they were keeping you away from a gang."

"So if the Riot is a gang, then what is the Terror?"

Oz still wears his vest. The leather across the shoulder is also darkened with Eli's blood.

"The same thing I've been trying to tell you since we met—we're a brotherhood, a family. Our entire organization is built on respect and the only way you have respect is if it's built on love. We're not thugs jockeying for power. We're a group that supports and doesn't tear down.

"I won't paint pretty pictures for you. You've seen how we live. It's different, but different doesn't mean wrong. Society has their view of normal and we have ours. Being a part of the club means freedom to us. Freedom from what others dictate for our lives."

The muscles in my neck tighten. "If that's true, then why were you always doing what they told you to do?"

He lowers his head and a part of me hurts that I pushed him so hard on a day when he saved not only me, but Eli. "Because I thought doing what I was told was what being a part of the club meant…until last night. I get it now in a way I never understood it before. It's not about following, it's about respect. Me giving respect, earning it and then getting it back in kind."

I rake a hand through my hair. Life used to be easy. Life used to be simple. Now, it's complicated. There's a knock on the door and I turn. It's Chevy and he's carrying a flower. With a flick of his fingers, two more flowers appear.

Respect. Olivia had told me that if I allowed the club in, they would love me—that they would respect me—and Oz is saying that in order to gain the respect, I must give it.

I wave Chevy in and he edges the door open, leans in and offers the flowers to me. I accept them with a smile. He winks, and when he walks away, closing the door behind him, two Reign of Terror vests slide into view.

They're protecting Eli. Standing by him. They'll never leave his side. A little bit farther down at the nurses' station, Olivia harasses a nurse with Cyrus by her side. Beyond them is the waiting room and a sea of black vests. "They're watching over Eli, aren't they?"

Oz nods. "And if you let them, they'll watch over you, too."

Yes, life used to be simple, but I never had a family like this. "You said that Eli wanted you to tell me something."

Oz stands and extends his hand to me.

"I don't want to leave him," I say.

"You don't have to, but today seriously fucked me up. If you don't mind, I want to hold you and convince myself that this nightmare is over."

I lay my hand in his, and he pulls me up and then settles me onto his lap. He wraps his arms around my waist and I place my head on his shoulder as I reclaim Eli's hand.

Oz's heat sinks past my clothes, my skin, even my bones, and it's comforting my soul. I inhale his dark scent and it's the first time in hours I feel completely safe.

"Is it a long story?" I ask.

"Epic," he answers. "The craziest I've heard."

"I thought your job was to prevent me from learning the truth."

"No," Oz's lips whisper against my temple and there's a flurry of rose petals in my stomach. "My job is to love you."

Warmth floods my heart and I kiss his neck. I like how he presses me closer to him in response.

"After I tell you, though," Oz hedges, "I want you to promise me something."

"What?"

"That you'll leave here for a few minutes. Eat. Rest. Talk with your dad."

Panic cramps my stomach at the idea of leaving Eli. "I don't know."

Oz's arms create a protective shelter. "I want you to trust me to watch Eli while you take a break. Trust me to chase your monsters away."

His words cause my chest to ache while at the same time healing a few of the wounds inside me. "I trust you. I more than trust you. I love you."

I raise my head and Oz tilts his so that we're staring at each other. He caresses my cheek as his blue eyes soften. "You were supposed to wait to say that until we had a nice, peaceful calm moment."

"Well," I say with a sheepish grin, "if the Terror is my family, I'm not sure those moments exist."

Oz chuckles and lightly kisses my lips.

"All right," I say. "Explain it to me."

"Your mother is the daughter of the Riot Motorcycle Club..."

OZ

I SIT IN THE SMALL WINDOWLESS ROOM THAT HAS gray walls. Hook is on one side of me. Pigpen on the other. Razor's hanging tight near the wall. The room's so compact that our knees touch if we shift. It's the room the doctors used to inform the family of how Eli's surgery went. A few days ago, we learned Eli survived. Today, I'm learning my fate.

The door opens. Cyrus and Dad stride in and Dad motions toward Razor. "Give us a few minutes."

Razor offers me a fast pat-hug and leaves. This is the first time since the morning after my patch-in party that I've been this close to Dad. I extend my legs and cross my arms over my chest, feeling uncomfortable. The last words Mom said to me were an apology I never saw coming.

Cyrus drops into a chair and Dad leans against the closed door. "They're going to let Eli go home tomorrow."

Which means Emily will be returning to Florida. Her dad's been calm. Very patient. I see why Emily worships him, but that laissez-faire attitude he had in regards to the club, which we appreciated even as it boggled our minds, has disappeared.

Last night, Emily and I stole a few moments alone in this room and between kisses, she told me her dad has rescinded his belief that the club is a group of grown men playing dress-up. While I'm glad he understands the gravity of Emily's situation, it's made his interactions with any of us frigid at best. Not a great way to start a long-distance relationship with his daughter.

"How did the meeting go with the Riot?" I ask. Cyrus and a hand-picked contingency sat down for peace talks last night. Each man in the room was in the thick of it.

"Business negotiations with them have tanked," says Cyrus. "They want us to ask for permission to ride on their roads and they want a percentage of our profits for the businesses we run security for in their area."

Nothing new on that front. "How'd you guys respond?"

Pigpen flashes that supermodel grin. "We told them to shove it."

I offer him my fist. He bumps it. Pigpen is one of those men that we stand solid for. He fought in Afghanistan. Served several terms in the Army as a Ranger. He won't ask anyone for permission to exercise his God-given rights.

"What did they say about Emily?" I ask.

"They've agreed to leave Emily alone," Cyrus answers.

Bent forward, I rub my palms together. It's like there's a layer of razor blades between my skin and bones that won't allow Emily's safety to be treated so casually. "That's it? They shoot Eli, but don't kill him, and all of a sudden they decide to play fair? I'm not buying they suddenly grew a conscience."

Cyrus and Dad share a long look and Cyrus continues, "In the end, we don't know, but I reminded them that Emily lives in a different world. One that contains restraining orders and prison time for breaking those orders. Most of their guys have records and a gang task force watching their every move. Emily's a thorn in their side, but she's not a child anymore. She's an adult and they aren't going to force a relationship with someone who doesn't want it. It's not in their best interest."

"We'll keep a close eye on her," Dad says. "We've already contacted the head of the Florida chapter and they agreed to stay on the situation and let us know if the Riot run through."

"The best thing Emily can do," adds Hook, "is go home."

I let his words sink in. It's what's best for Emily and it's what's breaking my heart. "All right."

There's a long stretch of silence and when I glance up, they're staring at me like I've laid my head down on the guillotine. "What?"

"We can't push off the police anymore. They're coming to interview Eli."

"What about me and Emily?"

Cyrus inches to the edge of his seat. "Eli and I don't want Emily involved in this. You drove Eli in. You're the one who dragged him into the ER. Emily faded into the background. Technically the police got a statement from you when you brought him in."

Police arrived first. Lawyer later. I told the cops I found Eli bleeding on the floor. I wasn't lying. I wasn't keeping the truth from them, either. I was more concerned with whether or not Eli was going to die.

"They haven't asked to speak with you again," Cyrus says.

Eli and Cyrus want me and Emily to lie. Since I was young, Cyrus has been my guidepost. Olivia, the heart. I've always done everything he's said and when I have a problem, he's who I've sought advice from. "Do you guys mind if I talk to Dad for a few minutes?"

Without another word, Hook and Pigpen rise and leave the room. Cyrus stays seated. "Are you sure you don't want me to stick around?"

"You mind giving me a few with Dad?" I repeat.

Cyrus sizes me up like the question shocked him and I can't help the flash of guilt. It's like not discussing this with him is a betrayal. "I'll be right out there if you want to talk."

I nod and Cyrus leaves. Dad remains standing and I wonder if he's also replaying the last full conversation we had. "What's on your mind?"

"I thought this club was legit?"

He eyes me warily. "It is."

"Then why am I being asked to lie to the police?"

Dad eases into the seat beside me. "I don't think they consider it lying as much as they consider it not mentioning certain details."

A smile tugs on my lips as I remember Emily informing me with that impatient sway of her head that not mentioning something was the same as lying. She never has a problem calling me out on my integrity issues. "A few days ago, you said you'd fight for me."

"I did."

"What if I ask you not to fight for me, but at least stand with me? Because I'm about to piss a lot of people off."

★ ★ ★

My footsteps echo in the long hallway as I head toward the pinnacle of this running disaster. Razor's on guard outside Eli's door and he opens it the moment he spots me. The voice of a sportscaster drifts out and I hesitate.

What I'm about to do will change everything. Me. Emily. Eli. The club. My parents. Everything. But sometimes what we need the most is what we fight the hardest: change.

From the waiting room at the other end of the hallway, Pigpen's head snaps up. Soon the rest of the board appears as they stand. Dad walks ahead of me and holds up his hands in the nonverbal stop sign. I'm not sure if he agrees with my decision, but I straighten as I step inside, knowing Dad's on my side.

Except for Eli, the room's empty. Emily's dad took her out to lunch. Mom herded Olivia to an appointment. Razor closes the door and, with the click of a button, Eli turns off the TV.

He's lying on top of the covers in a pair of jeans. Because Eli's a tough son of a bitch, he was placed in a regular room a few days ago. He's shirtless and there's a bandage over his chest where the bullet went clean through. "You don't agree?"

Incapable of bullshitting. It's what I like about Eli. What I also like? He knows what's going on without anyone telling him.

"No. Emily doesn't lie and I'm not going to ask her to."

Eli rubs at the spot above his wound. "I don't want her involved in this, nor do I want her name on some police report, and I wouldn't think you'd want her to relive what happened. I especially don't want her to say anything that's going to cause problems for her. Think about it. There is nothing you or Emily can add. You didn't see what happened. You were outside."

He's right. It's the conversation Emily and I have had with the club's lawyer again and again. We never heard the Riot threaten Eli.

I assess the man in front of me. He's the person I've longed to be. He was always larger than life. The complete badass who I thought had it all. "You gave Emily up so she could have a better life, right? So she wouldn't be scared?"

Eli nods like I explained my concerns away. "Exactly."

"Do you know what Emily taught me?"

"What?"

That I don't want to be the man who people second-guess. I want to be known for my integrity. "That I'm good with kids, especially ones like Brian."

Good enough that maybe my future isn't as set as I thought it was. Good enough that I'm willing to do this for Emily and myself. It's time that I do what Dad has been waiting for me to do: become my own man.

Eli's cut hangs on the chair across the room. The skull with the fire blazing out of it stares at me. "Emily definitely had a different life than she would've had if she and Meg stayed in Snowflake. She has options now that she never would have if she had grown up here, but you and Meg were wrong."

Eli studies me from toe to head. "How's that?"

"You and Meg hurt a lot of people along the way in the name of protecting Emily. Told a ton of lies to cover your tracks and Emily still grew up scared. Whether she was raised in Florida or here in Snowflake, the result turned out to be the same. The lies—they were for nothing."

I slip the cut off my back and slide my thumb over my name: Oz. All I desired was to be part of the whole, to be part of the club. It's still important to me, but it's not important enough to ruin any more lives.

With a sensation close to being punched in the gut, I lay my cut on Eli's bed. "I'm not lying and I won't ask Emily to, either."

My footsteps fill the room as I head for the door and when I place my hand on the knob, Eli calls out to me, "Oz."

I glance over my shoulder. Eli gingerly swings his legs off the bed. A grimace mars his face as he pierces me with his black eyes. "Get your ass over here and help me get to the bathroom. I'm not going to fall and give them a reason to keep me here any longer and if my daughter is going to be in the room when I meet with the police, I'd prefer to do it with a shirt on."

"What did you say?"

Eli's slow as he gathers himself to his feet. "You fucking heard me, and get your cut back on. If you ever lay your cut at my feet again, I'm going to cut your balls off regardless of club rules, you got me?"

Even though he's asking for my help, Eli's moving fine toward the bathroom. "I said, do you got me?"

My brain whirls as I understand what's happening: Eli's changing his mind. "Yeah, I got you."

Emily

THE POLICE OFFICER SHUFFLES HIS FEET AND glances at the door again while I swat at the tears forming at the corners of my eye. We're in Eli's hospital room, but I'm the one cross-legged on his bed. He's fully dressed and sitting in the chair next to the desk. The club's lawyer is in the chair next to me. My father hovers off to the side and Oz leans against the wall.

I meet Oz's eyes again and he offers me a soft smile of encouragement. It's frustrating. So frustrating. I tear the tissue in my hand in half and sigh. I didn't see anything or hear anything and I don't understand how that's possible.

I scowl in Eli's direction. "An accident? What happened to you was an accident?"

Eli shrugs. "I don't remember. We have to take your grandparents' word for it."

My eyes slam shut. I told the truth, Oz told the truth and the doctor told the police officer that with trauma like Eli's it isn't unusual that he'd forget the moments leading up to the event.

The detective shuts his notebook and asks again, "Did they actually threaten Eli or you? Not how you felt, did they say specific words?"

I swallow the lump in my throat. "No."

"You left before the incident happened."

"Yes."

The officer addresses the lawyer. "We'll let you know if we need anything else."

And he leaves. Just like that. Goes. Another tear slips down my face.

"Jeff and I would appreciate a few minutes alone with Emily," Eli states.

The lawyer gathers his things and under Eli and my father's intense scrutiny, Oz saunters over to me in that sexy way of his and places a slow kiss on my cheek as his thumb wipes away a tear. "You did good."

I attempt to fake happy when he pulls away, but it falls short. I do squeeze his hand, though, then watch as he walks out the door. The tissue forms into a ball in my hand. "You lied."

Eli pulls on his earlobe. "Which time?"

My hand smacks the bed. "I'm being serious. You and I both know they shot you. That those people are mean and evil and that they shot you."

My dad and Eli look at each other, then Eli refocuses on me. "The truth is, I don't remember."

I brush at the wetness on my cheeks again with the back

of my hand. "Fine, but you know they shot you on purpose. The gun didn't freaking go off by accident. They. Shot. You!"

"Emily…" starts my dad and I round on him so fast I wonder if my head rotated.

"And you! You lied. Mom lied. You all lied! And for what? I mean, really, why? If these people were capable of shooting Eli—" I throw a pointed glare at him that causes him to shrink a centimeter "—then they are capable of breaking their promise and finding me. Don't you think that would have been valuable information for me to know? Like 'hey, Emily, look both ways before you cross the street, eat your freaking green beans because they're good for you, run like a rabid bear is chasing you if you see people from a gang called the Riot!'"

I'm shouting and when my throat grows scratchy, I close my mouth, but then try again. "Was it worth it? Were all these years of lying to me worth it?"

"Don't be mad at your dad," says Eli. "He's wanted to tell you the truth since the beginning, but it was me and your mom that wouldn't let him."

I tear the tissue into smaller pieces. "But he still could've told me."

"It was the terms of the adoption," Eli says. "I agreed to give up my parental rights as long as your dad kept it quiet. He gave me and your mom his word that he'd never tell you. That's how bad he wanted you in his life. That's how I knew you were in good hands."

My eyesight flickers between Eli and Dad. Pain wells up in me again. I care for them both. Otherwise I wouldn't be so mad, I wouldn't be so hurt.

Dad shoves his hands into the pockets of his khakis. "I didn't only fall in love with your mom. I fell in love with you, too. Your mom was willing to walk away if I didn't agree. I'm sorry you were hurt, but I'm not sorry for making the decision that kept both of you in my life."

"I'm not sorry, either," I whisper.

It's all messed up. It's all muddled, but if it hadn't happened, he would have never been my father. And as much as I'm heartbroken at what I've lost with Olivia and Eli, I'm not at all sad that the man standing beside me now is my dad.

The world is made of multiple pieces. All of them moving alongside each other, sometimes never touching. Coexisting, yet not. How many of us live our entire lives inside a single bubble? Maneuvering in what we believe is a forward direction when it's only in a circle among the same type of people.

My mother, my father and Eli lied. For whatever reason, they lied, and typically in my eyes, that's a cringeworthy offense. But maybe the world isn't so black-and-white. Maybe there's room for shades of gray.

Without what has happened, there's no doubt I would have stayed in the same bubble I was raised in and I'm not just talking about remaining in Florida. I never would have experienced anything new in life.

I take in the two men watching me, the two men waiting for my forgiveness. Eli and my father couldn't be more different. Blond hair to dark brown. Blue eyes to near black. Medical school to a GED. Shirt and tie to blue jeans and a black leather vest.

But there's so much they have in common. Both are hard-working, both intelligent in their own ways, both leaders within their communities and, more important, they both love me and I love them in return.

"What happens now?" I ask.

"You go home," Eli says. "You were here longer than either your dad or I expected."

I tangle the ends of my hair around my fingers. "And then what?"

"Life returns to normal," answers Dad. "Your mom and I are ready for that."

Per the club's request, Mom stayed in Florida. Everything between the Riot and the Terror is in flux and they didn't want another fireworks show if my mother made another appearance in Louisville.

And then I overheard a phone conversation between Dad and Mom. As much as she wanted to support me, she didn't want to come to Kentucky. As she told my father, she left Kentucky behind years ago and she preferred to keep the distance. I saw the relief on Dad's face—it was her way of saying she was still choosing him.

I peer over to Eli. "What happens to you and me?"

"You know how much I love shopping."

I laugh and his eyes flash with amusement.

I bite my bottom lip and inhale deeply. I long for more than once a year. "That's not good enough."

Courage in going against my mother and father has always eluded me, but that was before all of this. If my dad can love and choose me through this chaos then he can still love me if I disagree. "I want to see Eli more than that."

Dad and Eli do that thing where they look at each other again and I slice my hand in the air. "Nope, you guys don't get to make these decisions anymore. I'm not asking if you are okay with this. I'm telling you."

Eli scratches his jaw in that way that hides a smirk and my father folds his hands together and leans forward.

"What if I said you're safer with things going back to how they were?" Eli asks.

"I'd tell you that it's not your choice and that you aren't the center of the universe."

Dad laughs. Eli releases that grin that always makes me smile. "She really is her mother, isn't she?"

"One hundred percent," Dad answers with appreciation spelled out on his face.

Not true. "I'm also a little bit of both of you."

Their smiles fade and it's there in their eyes, the desperation that's aching within me. They want to belong to me as badly as I crave to belong to both of them.

Eli readjusts in his seat and clears his throat. "Does this have to do with Oz?"

My cheeks flare red-hot and I can barely peek at my father, who is currently not blinking. "It helps, but there's more to Snowflake than you or him. There's Olivia and Cyrus and Violet and I have a cousin…"

I meet Dad's gaze now. "Chevy's strange, but he's a cousin, and I think I'd like to get to know him. I think there's a lot of people here I'd like to get to know." My eyes drift over to Eli. "Some I'd like to get to know a lot better than I already do, plus my driving still needs some serious help."

"Ignition, gas, brake," teases Eli. "It's not that complicated."

"Says you."

"Hey, you were able to drive when it counted." Eli rubs

the area where he took a bullet…for me. A bullet that secured my future away from my mother's psychotic family.

"It's your call, Jeff. Yours and Meg's. I still want her to go home."

I open my mouth to protest, but Eli strikes me with a glare that informs me that speaking in this moment is not an option. "There's been too much chaos here, Emily. A lot of agreements have been made, but the dust needs to settle before I can be sure it's solid. I love that you want to be a part of this family, but your safety is still the priority."

Dad massages the back of his neck and I venture to continue with him. "If I need to go home now, that's fine, but I want to come back here, and if people from Snowflake happen to wander to Florida, I'd like the chance to see them. I'm not asking for your permission, but I am asking for your blessing."

"This is going to scare your mom," Dad says.

It will and I'm sure there will be times I'll be scared, too, but… "I can't let my fears or hers dictate my life anymore. It's time I explore the world."

Dad steps forward and kisses my forehead. His nonverbal gesture to let me know I've won. At least for now. Mom will battle this and Eli has a gleam in his eye saying that some old habits won't die easily, but I'm feeling more in control of my destiny.

"So, we'll work this out?" I say to Eli.

He nods. "We'll work this out."

OLIVIA DIED ON A TUESDAY. IT WAS SUNNY. A clear blue sky and a rare seventy-six-degree day in a late Kentucky July. All the windows were open in the house. Almost all the people she loved the most and who loved her in return gathered in her room.

Everyone but Emily.

The moment Olivia took her last breath, the shades of the window in her room billowed out with the breeze and the room filled with the scent of honeysuckle. Cyrus crouched beside her bed, placed their combined hands over his heart and then leaned down and laid his head on her chest. As he waited for another beat, another rise of her body for air, I counted.

One into two. Two into three. Three into she was officially gone.

She was fifty-eight years old and had lived a life so full that for a few weeks after her death everything surrounding me felt empty.

Empty until now.

My motorcycle rumbles beneath me and the wind blows on my face as I race around another curve. Riding is therapy for me. It helps me to forget. Helps me to not feel, but what's helping me heal are the two arms wrapped tight around my stomach and the delicate body pressed to mine. I let go of the handlebar and squeeze Emily's knee. She's home. Only for a week, but it's a week I'm going to cherish.

We've flown past the cabin, the pond, the house my parents have started construction on and the trailer that now serves as our temporary home. Emily and I are going farther and faster than we've been before and I love how she sits high on the back of my bike enjoying the sensation of freedom.

The end of the road is in sight and I drop gears then ease to a stop. I kick down the stand and Emily slips off along with me. She smooths back her hair from the ride and glances around the thick woods. "How far of a hike is it?"

"A half mile. Maybe three-quarters. I can do this alone if you want."

Emily's lips flatten to a fine line. "No, Olivia left this for me to do. I had no idea she'd enjoy torturing me from heaven."

I grin and Emily slightly smiles with me. We text. Talk on the phone. Video chat when we can. There's not a day that we aren't in contact, but having her here, being able to touch her body, seeing the emotion in her eyes, it's a million times better.

A breeze through the trees and a stray strand of her hair drifts across her dark eyes. I move it and permit my finger to trace her cheek as I tuck the loose piece behind her ear. A red path lights up her skin from where I caressed her. A blush that brushes against my heart.

I unstrap the backpack I had attached behind Emily, swing it onto my shoulder, then offer my hand, palm up to her. "Do you trust me?"

She scans the green forest and the small path that cuts through it as if the boogeyman lies in wait. "Do you mind if I go first?"

An eyebrow raises. Emily's terrified of the woods and that she's agreed to this hike is huge. "Are you sure?"

She wipes her hands along her jeans. "Yeah. I need to do this. If you can apply to college and Olivia can fight the cancer for as long as she did and Eli can take a bullet, I can hike in the woods. Besides, I took on the woods in the dark for a few seconds that night I left Olivia's. If I could do that then, I can do this now."

"All right."

She goes in and I'm not far behind. The path is narrow and the weeds high. We can only walk in tandem and, for a bit, we do so in silence. Each brief glimpse of her face shows strained panic, but my respect for her grows as she continues forward, confronting her fears.

A cloud blocks the sun and the forest darkens. Emily quickens her pace.

"I got in," I say.

Emily stops so quickly that I almost ram into her. She spins on her toes. "Got into what?"

By the excitement gleaming in her eyes, she knows, but I say it, anyway. "Don't go crazy on me. I'll be a part-time student. I'm going to be doing most of it online, and I'll have to drive into Bowling Green once a week for one class that has to be taken there."

Despite my warning, Emily's already hopping on her feet. "What are you majoring in? Just tell me what you're majoring in."

"Special education."

Emily squeals. Squeals. Then throws herself at me. Her arms around my neck. Her soft curves pressing into me. I tangle my fingers into her silky hair and keep her locked in the hug. "I've missed you."

She lifts her head and skims her fingers across my face. "I've missed you, too."

Our lips are a few inches apart and I've dreamed night after night of our mouths and bodies moving in time together. Emily shyly turns her head away. We haven't kissed properly since our night in my room. Kissing like that would require time alone.

We've been under Eli's watchful eye since she arrived two days ago. It doesn't help that I'm now sharing her with everyone in the club. Never realized what we experienced before will never happen again. Emily's not just my girl, she's now the club's daughter, sister and friend.

"So when you start school are you still going to work for the security company?" she asks casually, as if the answer doesn't matter to her, but it does. Working for the security company puts me in harm's way and it means I still carry a gun. I understand why Emily's gun-shy.

"College costs money," I respond. The gun's not currently on me as I only carry it when I'm on a run. Since Emily arrived, I've kept it in the safe in the clubhouse, but I've caught her searching for it when my back's to her.

"Humph."

I snag her hand and angle her to face me. "Even if I had the money for school, I'd still work for them. Not full-time, but when they needed me. This isn't just a job. It's a family business and even though I'm not blood-related, I'm family."

Emily sags. "I know. It worries me."

"Don't be. I can ride circles around most of those guys."

Emily rolls her eyes and the path widens enough that I can walk beside her and hold her hand. She's worried about the Riot. Things have been quiet with them. Maybe it will stay that way. Maybe it won't. Either way it won't change how we live our lives.

The forest gives way and we stumble upon the tiny campsite. It's not much of anything. A shack with four walls and a roof. Emily opens the door and recoils. "There're spiders in there."

I'd bet there's a few snakes, too. "It's used mainly for hunting. It's also where a member can lay low if he should need it. I can't say it's been used like that since Eli got in trouble."

Emily kicks at a board hanging off the outside of the shack. "I don't get it. Honeysuckle Ridge. Honeysuckle Ridge. That's all Olivia talked about. What was so amazing about this place that Olivia was dead set on me finding it?"

The bag on my shoulder grows heavier. I take her fingers again and lead her away from the shack. "Come on."

It's a short trip, but this time there is no path. I have to help Emily over a fallen tree and I walk in front so I can push down the overgrowth, but it springs up as soon as I lift my foot.

We step into a clearing and beams from the sun highlight the open stretch of grass. "This is Honeysuckle Ridge."

Emily sucks in a breath as her eyes drink in the world around her. "Wow."

Wow is right. Below us is the world. Thick trees. A view of the river. Far off in the distance I could point out my high school, the steeple to the church on Main Street. Even farther on the left I could show her the general area of Olivia's cabin and the long stretch that led us to Olivia's, then my place and that eventually brought us here: Thunder Road.

I don't do any of those things. Instead, I lay out a blanket, sit and motion for Emily to settle beside me. She does and my heart squeezes. The sunlight hits her hair just right and pieces of it shine. She's too good, too beautiful to be my girl. "What are you doing with me?"

She tilts her head. "Why would you ask that?"

"Daughter of a doctor, straight As, to be honest, completely out of my league. Special-education teachers don't make bank."

Emily rises to her knees and slowly inches toward me. The twinkle in her soft eyes pulls me in and the hypnotic sway of her hips engulfs me further into her spell. Her fingers whisper against my face. "I'm with you because you're strong and brave and you love people with a ferociousness that I have never encountered before."

Her hands drift to my shoulders and on impulse, my hands cup her waist. She's exactly like I remember—warm, sensual.

"Besides that, I love the way you look at me and I love the way you make me feel beautiful inside and out. Plus, you're missing a very important fact."

My eyebrows furrow together. "What's that?"

"Technically, by blood, I'm more gangster than you." The utter tease in her voice causes me to sweep an arm around her and roll her onto the blanket.

"More gangster than me?"

"Your parents are probably concerned I'm going to taint your pure soul."

We both laugh and the motion causes a vibration between our bodies. The day's warm, not hot, but my blood definitely increases in temperature.

"I mean," she continues, "it was me that kissed you first and then I blackmailed you into helping me and I'm pretty sure I seduced you that night we spent together."

"You're right," I whisper. "I'm completely unable to resist your evil charms."

"Well, if that's the case, why aren't you kissing me now?"

Not willing to miss this invitation, I lower my head to hers and lightly brush my lips over her mouth. Everything inside me tightens, heightens and becomes aware. She tastes so sweet. Her kiss like heaven.

We're alone on the ridge. Very alone except for the birds in flight and the trees surrounding us. It's a slow exploration. Hands recalling areas so glorious that every touch deserves the moment. There's no rush. Neither of us are hurried.

A shirt over my head. Her tank top used as a pillow. Bra straps lowered and us leaving lingering kisses on every spot within reach. Other pieces of clothing are eased down and slipped off. A breeze blows over the hill and goose bumps form along her exposed skin.

I cover my body with hers and we're moving. A rhythm

that builds in a steady progression. The urge is to beg for
more. Emily's bold but she's inexperienced. There are places I
want to take her. A million ways I long to worship her body,
but we have time and Emily is a forever type of girl.

Emily hooks a leg around mine and lets out a soft moan that
causes me to apply pressure to her hips. Our mouths move,
our touches grow more intense and instinct pushes us to the
brink. Emily encircles her arms around me, cries out and I
bury my head in her neck as the world shatters.

I slide off her while keeping her tucked close. We both
breathe hard as we share long kisses that say more than words
ever could.

"Do you mind that I want to wait?" she asks.

She's talking about sex. We've had several conversations on
the phone discussing what I've done and what she hasn't. She
grew up thinking she was the product of a one-night stand.
Though she knows now that she wasn't, she also knows, like
I do about myself, that she was unexpected.

Neither of us want that type of unexpected in our lives anytime soon.

I sweep the hair away from her face. "I can do what we're
doing forever, Emily."

"I like the sound of that," she says.

"Me, too."

She flashes me her beautiful smile, quickly kisses my lips
and rolls away from me.

"Hey." I reach for her and she giggles as she maneuvers out
of my grasp. "I wanted to lie with you for a while."

Emily's already slipping her bra back on. "We promised Eli

we'd make this a fast trip. If we don't return soon, he'll come looking for us, and I am not in the mood to be busted again."

I chuckle as I button my pants and toss my shirt on. "You're mine tonight and I'm not sharing. We're watching a movie and you're sitting with me. Eli can kiss my ass."

She tilts her head, waiting. "Deal."

I cup her face with my hands and draw in her lower lip as she takes in the top of mine. I'm trying to memorize every kiss. She'll be gone in a few days and even though I'll be making a run for the business through Florida in two weeks, each moment we spend together is crucial.

When we're presentable, Emily grabs the bag and holds it in her lap. The spark she had fades and she skims her hand over the material. "I wish I could have been there when she passed."

From behind, I enfold Emily into me and nuzzle the spot behind her ear. "You were there, in spirit."

"Is it pathetic that I didn't actually think that Olivia would die?"

"No." But she did. "We don't have to do this today."

"Yes," she answers. "I do."

Emily zips open the bag and pulls out the box containing Olivia's ashes. Olivia didn't choose the casket and she admitted it's because of the encounter that freaked out Emily. Olivia's last request was this: for Emily to release her ashes into the wind.

The box trembles in Emily's hand and I slide my fingers underneath hers to help support it. "Olivia told me that if this was too much for you, it was okay. She didn't want you to do anything that pushed you too far."

Emily sucks in a breath. "She told me that. But I want to do this. For her and for me."

She opens the box and inside is a plastic bag. Crude, I know, but Olivia asked that she be separated and left specific instructions of what was to be done with her remains. This box belongs to me and Emily. She asked me to be here with Emily when Emily released them.

Me and Emily alone.

A flash of white in the box catches my attention. "What's that?"

Emily retrieves an envelope and her eyes meet mine when we spot Olivia's handwriting. I take the box from Emily and nod for her to open it. She does and reads aloud:

"Emily and Oz,
Someday you'll tell your children a love story about yourselves. Maybe you'll be together, maybe you'll end up with someone else; regardless, what you've experienced is love. I know love when I see it. It's how I look at Cyrus. It's how Eli looks at Emily and Meg. It's what you two share whenever you look at each other.

Yes, Emily, Honeysuckle Ridge is a site used by the club and Eli did use it when he was trying to figure out how to handle his situation with the police, but that's not why I wanted you to find the place. I never wanted you to hurt with the truth. I wanted the truth to set both of you free.

You both have grown up feeling as if you weren't properly loved by those who should have loved you the most. People make mistakes. They make wrong choices at the worst moments. Never at any time were you not loved.

Know this. Cherish this. Love one another and be courageous enough to live your life and love more. Don't let fear trap you. You're both too young for that.

Honeysuckle Ridge is where Cyrus asked me to marry him. It's where Eli took Meg and told her that he was in love with her. This place has a rich history of love. That's the secret I wanted you to discover, Emily. This family is full of love and our love story contains you. Without it, we're missing a vital part of our soul.

Oz and Emily—love one another and if you need to part ways because you discover you belong with someone else, that's okay, too. Remember that you loved each other once and it's okay to just be friends.

Love the other people in your lives as if this was your last day because you never know if it is. I have loved you both. Your entire lives.

Forever,

Olivia"

We're silent. I read over the letter again, drinking in her every word. There's a mixture of sadness and joy coursing in my blood and it causes me to tug Emily closer. She leans her head against mine and it's like we're holding each other up.

Olivia loved us. We loved her. She's right. We never know how many days we have left.

Emily folds the letter with special care and offers it to me. I take it and watch as the girl I love carries out Olivia's final wish.

Unzipping the plastic bag, Emily stands at the edge of the

cliff and slowly releases Olivia's ashes into the air. "You said the truth sets you free and now you finally are."

Emily glances over at me and smiles softly. Olivia was right—the truth did set Emily and me free and through that, we found each other.

★ ★ ★ ★ ★

ACKNOWLEDGMENTS

To God: "Then you will know the truth, and the truth will set you free."

—John 8:32 NIV

FOR DAVE: FOR HELPING ME LEARN WHAT TRUTH in that statement above really means. I love you, always.

This book wouldn't be possible without the help of a motorcycle club that welcomed me into their clubhouse and lives, if only for a small window of time. I walked in with a head full of ideas of what to expect and I walked away envious of the relationships you share. You are an amazing group of people and I wish each of you love, success and happiness. A special thank-you to Mother, Fluffy, Rump, Loveshack, Bizkit and Cash. Your time and insights were extremely valuable and appreciated.

A special thank-you to my editor extraordinaire, Margo Lipschultz, and my agent, Kevan Lyon. I'm truly blessed to have the two of you in my life.

I've come to love and embrace the "it takes a village" concept over the past few years of my life. This is true not only in my personal life, but in my writing life, as well. Thank you and hugs to: Angela Annalaro-Murphy, Kristen Simmons, Colette Ballard, Kelly Creagh, Bethany Griffin, Kurt Hampe, Bill Wolf, my family and friends.

Look for WALK THE EDGE,
Razor's story, coming soon from
Katie McGarry and Harlequin TEEN!

Read on for an exclusive sneak peek...

RAZOR

HER FACE IS WHITE AGAINST HER RAVEN HAIR.
Ghost white. And I'd bet my left ball she hasn't breathed since
I spoke. Her hand is outstretched toward the busted cell on the
ground, but her wide hazel eyes are cemented on me. I turn
my head and I'm greeted by the amused faces of my brothers
from the Reign of Terror who stand next to their bikes in
the parking lot. They'll be harassing me about this for weeks.

Fuck me for trying to be chivalrous.

"You okay?" It's a variation of the question I asked a few
seconds ago, but this one she seems to understand as her body
slowly trembles to life.

"Um…" she mutters. We've been at the same schools since
elementary age, otherwise I'd wonder if she was a foreign
exchange student with limited English. "I only have twenty
dollars."

The muscles in the back of my neck tense. "I'm not going
to jack you for your money."

She quits breathing again.

"Nice to know your current bank account status," I say. "But I asked if you were okay."

Color returns to her cheeks as I pin her with my gaze. She accused me of trying to rob her. I know it, she knows it and she's now been informed that I'm not the asshole in this scenario.

"Yes," she finally answers. "I'm okay. I mean no... I mean...I broke my phone."

She did and that sucks for her.

Now her eyes flicker between me and the phone like she wants to pick it up, yet is too paralyzed to do it. Saving us both from this torture, I swipe up the pieces of the cell and lean against the wall opposite her.

The distance between us helps her breathe and that gulp of air was audible as she tucks herself tight in the corner farthest from me. This type of reaction isn't new. I've seen it since I was a child whenever my father or anyone from the Terror entered a room full of civilians. To everyone outside of the club, we're the big bad motorcycle gang bent on blowing the house down.

People and their hellish nightmare folklore involving us piss me off. I don't know why I told the guys to give me a minute. I'm late for plans I made with Chevy and some girls, plus I'm on call in case the board wants to meet sooner than later to discuss Detective Mike Barlow.

But something about how this chick looked alone and frightened messed me up. It reminded me... The thought stalls out in my brain and the trip-up causes a flash of pain in my chest. Fuck it, her expression reminded me of Mom the last time I saw her—the night she died.

My mom. I shake my head to expel her ghost from my mind. One visit from one bastard trying to use me and I'm being haunted by a past I can't change. That's what that detective wanted—to use me for info on the club. He's one of too many who believe the Terror are the devil's progeny.

"Is it yes or no," I say as I attempt to shove the battery into place. It's damn difficult now that the frame is bent.

"Yes or no what?" Her long hair sweeps past her shoulders. She has the type of hair that would have to be pulled up if she wanted a ride on the back of my bike. Gotta admit, I like her hair, especially how it has a shine under the lights of the school's overhang.

"If you're okay." I overtly glance around the mostly empty area to prove a point. "If we leave, you'll be alone and I don't care for that. There's some messed-up people out there. Fucked up enough that you shouldn't be alone."

Breanna swallows. I'd be number one on her list of fucked-up people. With a snap, the battery lodges into place. The casing takes me a few more seconds, but I wrestle that back into alignment, too.

She wears sandals with a heel and has pink painted toes. The girl fidgets, though. It's nerves. Her jean skirt displays some seriously mouthwatering thighs and her sleeveless blue button-down has flimsy enough fabric to hint at the outline of her bra strap. She's this mix between conservative and sexy and Breanna Miller is bringing it our senior year.

Under my scrutiny, she bends one knee then straightens

the other. Bet she hasn't realized how half the male population was staring at her tonight as she walked down the hall.

What she does know? That she's terrified of me. I stretch out my arm, inching her cell closer to her. If I were a great guy, I'd lay it down in the middle between us and let her scurry to it from there, but I'm not a great guy. I'm just good enough to stay behind to make sure she's not raped by some bastard with a coke addiction who could be wandering past the school.

"Not sure if it'll work," I say, "but it's back together."

Breanna nibbles on her lower lip, then releases it as she walks toward me. She accepts the cell, and this time, she rests her back against the middle column of the school entrance instead of rushing away. Still a nice distance in case she needs to bolt. "Thank you."

"You're welcome."

It's getting darker, faster, and, under her touch, the cell springs to life and brightens her face. There's no way I'm leaving her alone. Especially since we've had issues with a rival motorcycle club, the Riot. Over the past two weeks, the Riot have taken to joyriding near our town. They're testing boundaries and the club's on edge wondering if our unsteady peace agreement is floundering.

All of us are waiting for them to cross lines they shouldn't and ride into town. If the Riot does drive by tonight and they hear we've been at the school, they might check it out. Leaving this girl alone with the likes of them is like offering fresh meat to a starved wolf.

"Need a ride?" I ask.

She waves her phone. "No, thank you. My family is on their way."

Breanna peeks at me between swipes of her phone and I don't miss how her eyes linger on my biceps. Good girls like Breanna like to look, but they don't like to play.

A few more glances and a clearing of her throat. She's waiting for me to leave. Her life sucks because I'm not going anywhere.

"I'm Razor," I say, though I have no doubt she knows and, if not, I'm aware she can read the road name patch sewn to the front of my cut.

"I'm Breanna," she answers in this soft tone that dances across my skin. Damn, I could listen to that voice all night long, especially if she uses that sweet tone to sigh my name as I kiss the skin of her neck.

Yeah, I would definitely like to see this girl on the back of my bike. As I said, I'm not a great guy and earlier, I was just going for good, but Breanna's luck ran out. My bad side decided to take over. "I know."

The right side of my mouth tips up as her face falls.

I'm about to play Breanna like she's never been played before. I hitch my thumbs in my pockets and decide to enjoy the ride. "So, that twenty dollars? Why did you bring that up?"

"What?" She recoils.

"Do you have something you need me to protect?" I ask. She's lost and that's what I'm going for. "That's what I do— protect things. On the weekends I work for the club protecting semi-loads from being stolen. Can be dangerous stuff. Sometimes I've had to pull a gun. I'm assuming that's why you brought up the money. You need me to protect something for you."

She blinks. A lot. I have to fight to keep from smiling.

I press her again, knowing she'll feel so bad for calling me a crook that the next time I ask, she'll accept that ride. "Is that why you brought up the twenty dollars? Were you trying to hire me?"

And when she stares at me, unblinking, I know for a fact that Breanna Miller will be on the back of my bike tonight.

PLAYLIST

Theme:
"Hey Brother" by Avicii
"Counting Stars" by OneRepublic
"Umbrella (Travis Barker Remix)" by Rihanna
"Berzerk" by Eminem
"Ride the Wind" by Poison

Oz:
"Radioactive" by Imagine Dragons
"It's a Great Day to be Alive" by Travis Tritt
"It's Time" by Imagine Dragons

Emily:
"Summer Girls" by LFO
"Only the Good Die Young" by Billy Joel
"Standing Still" by Jewel

Songs that helped inspire specific scenes:
When Emily and Oz first kiss:
"Kiss Tomorrow Goodbye" by Luke Bryan

Eli toward Emily and Meg:
"Let Her Go" by Passenger and "Story of My Life" by
One Direction

Oz and Emily at the Pond:
"Crash My Party" by Luke Bryan

Oz and Emily's conversation the first time she's in the
clubhouse:
"One More Night" by Maroon 5

When Oz hits someone to protect Emily:
"My Songs Know What You Did in the Dark (Light Em
Up)" by Fall Out Boy

Eli and Meg's relationship:
"Springsteen" by Eric Church

Oz and Emily's future:
"Right Here Waiting" by Richard Marx